Praise for
The Queen of Palmyra

"Here it is, the most powerful and also the most lyrical novel about race, racism, and denial in the American South since *To Kill a Mockingbird*. Writing from deep within the belly of the beast, Minrose Gwin tells the story through the voice of Florence Irene Forrest, a girl growing up in a segregated Mississippi community where her father is a secret Klan leader while her main support comes from an African-American family. A story about knowing and not knowing, *The Queen of Palmyra* is finally a testament to the ultimate power of truth and knowledge, language and love."

—Lee Smith, author of *On Agate Hill*

"Minrose Gwin is an extremely gifted writer and *The Queen of Palmyra* is a brilliant and compelling novel. Set in Mississippi in the volatile civil rights era and then in New Orleans with the impending devastation of Hurricane Katrina, this novel powerfully reveals the effects of both human and natural destruction. The beauty of the prose, the strength of voice, and the sheer force of circumstance will hold the reader spellbound from beginning to end."

—Jill McCorkle, author of *Going Away Shoes*

"*The Queen of Palmyra* is an exquisitely beautiful novel. Through the eyes of a young girl, Minrose Gwin confronts the tragic face of racism and shows how it twists and destroys lives in a small southern town. Written with unflinching honesty, the novel grips the reader from its first page and relentlessly drives us to its conclusion."

—William Ferris, author of *Give My Poor Heart Ease:*
Voices of the Mississippi Blues

Also by Minrose Gwin

Wishing for Snow: A Memoir

The QUEEN of PALMYRA

Minrose Gwin

HARPER ● PERENNIAL

NEW YORK ● LONDON ● TORONTO ● SYDNEY ● NEW DELHI ● AUCKLAND

HARPER ● PERENNIAL

P.S.™ is a registered trademark of HarperCollins Publishers.

HarperCollins books may be purchased for educational, business, or sales promotional use. For information please write: Special Markets Department, HarperCollins Publishers, 10 East 53rd Street, New York, NY 10022.

FIRST HARPER PERENNIAL EDITION PUBLISHED 2010.

Library of Congress Cataloging-in-Publication Data

Gwin, Minrose.
    The Queen of Palmyra : a novel / Minrose Gwin.—1st Avon
paperback ed.
        p.   cm.
    ISBN 978-0-06-184032-6 (pbk.)
    1. Race relations—Fiction. 2. Mississippi—History—20th
century—Fiction. I. Title.
    PS3607.W56Q44   2010
    813'.6—dc22   2010003785

10 11 12 13 14   OV/RRD   10 9 8 7 6 5 4 3 2 1

In memory of Eva Lee Miller, 1910-1968

— *Part I* —

1

I need you to understand how ordinary it all was. At night the phone would ring after supper. My father would say a few quiet words into the receiver. Sometimes he spoke in numbers. A three, he would say. Or a four. When he put down the phone, he'd turn and look right at me. There would be a strange pleasure in his look, a gladness. He would ask me to perform this one small task; he'd tell me to go fetch him his box. The hair on the back of my neck would rise up and I'd run down the stairs to the basement where the furnace was. The stairs were just planks nailed to boards, no backs or sides to them, and when I was younger I used to be afraid that I'd slip and fall through to the dark underneath. But I lost that fear over the years and would count the steps and the one landing to the tune of "This Little Light of Mine." This little light of MINE. *One two three four TURN.* I'm going to let it SHINE. *One two three four DOWN. DOWN* being the bottom, the cellar floor, cornmeal scratchy but cool to my bare feet.

The box would be where it always was, on top of a stack of Daddy's old *Citizens' Council* magazines piled up on a table and so

covered in dust you couldn't even read the print. The table sat to
the left of the stairs under the one small high window. The window was at ground level outside and so shrouded in spider webs
inside and out that the incoming light seemed sifted through its
own loss, like flour after you add the cocoa. The webs were dense
and messy, the kind black widows make, though Mama had just
read in the Jackson *Clarion-Ledger* about a new spider in Mississippi, a brown one, discovered by a college girl writing a thesis
at Ole Miss. She was a pretty girl with a ponytail and a country
name. Peggy Rae Dorris. In the newspaper she's holding a dead
one between her fingers and she's eyeballing it close up. "The
Lady and the Spider," the caption reads. She says this brown one
is just as poisonous as the black widow but more dangerous because it's lighter in color and harder to spot. Nearly invisible on
some surfaces, like those banana boats from South America that
went up the Mississippi River to Memphis. When the men on the
boats found the strange brown spiders, they buried the bananas,
but the spiders surfaced and started their travels south to our fair
state, maybe trying to get back home. *Loxosceles reclusa* is the
spider's name. It lives under things, in hidden places. So watch
out in basements.

The box seemed glad to see me coming. It was tired of waiting. I blew the dust away and snatched it up. When I was little,
I had to struggle to lift it, but as I grew up, it became lighter, a
pleasure to hold in the palms of my hands, a crown. I'd get a good
grip on it and climb back up, my head stuck out to the side so that
I could watch every step to make sure I didn't lose my balance
and fall backward into the quiet darkness. No "This Little Light
of Mine" on the way up.

By the time I'd get back upstairs, Daddy would be standing
by the front door, ready. He looked like a bell waiting to be rung.
The commode would still be running from his having used it.

He'd have thrown cold water on his face, which brought up the roses in his cheeks. His hair was dark and waxed where he'd slicked it with sweet oil. Fresh khakis too, the creases ironed by my mother, who now stands at the kitchen sink, her back frozen in place against the darkening sky. The little front room with its crisp white curtains now in shadow except for one lamp, Mama always watching the light bill. Soon the two of us, my mother and I, will be alone in the growing dark.

Tonight, when Daddy takes the box from my hands, I can see how he loves the exchange, the way I know how to bring him exactly what he wants. It's the size of a lady's dress box, maybe even a small coat box, one you might open with a smile on your face, knowing something familiar yet surprising lies waiting under the tissue paper, like reaching under a setting hen and coming out with an Easter egg. A deep red wood, maybe cherry, and a brass plate on it with Daddy's granddaddy's initials, which are also my father's and his father's before him: WLF for Winburn Lafayette Forrest the First, who made the box with his own two hands in the early times, when the trees around here were so big half a dozen men could stand around their trunks and their fingertips still not meet. Later on, when I learn to work with wood, I will come to understand how much sanding with the finest of sandpaper and lacquering with the thinnest of lacquers would be required for that kind of smoothness. Sand and lacquer, then sand again. What a pleasure it must have been to finish it all and have just the right plate engraved with one's own initials, knowing it would be handed down to a son, then a grandson, who would polish the brass just to let it shine, let it shine, let it shine, and every year rub some boiled linseed oil on the wood to make sure it didn't dry out.

Of course the box had a lock. Not much of one, just a slit the size of a yellow jacket's hole. How Daddy kept up with that key I still don't know. I'd never seen it then, but knew from the size of the lock that the key to open it would have to be a tiny little thing. Doll sized, like the key to a girl's secret diary book. Small enough to hold under your tongue. I'd wanted to see what was inside that box since I was a crawling baby. The first thing I remember about myself is playing patty-cake over the box with Daddy. It between us on the floor, him kneeling like a big bull on one side and me on the other. When Daddy went, "Roll it and pat it and mark with a *B* and put it in the oven for Baby and me," I'd hit the box hard on the top, and Daddy'd laugh and say, "Lord, Sister, hit it one more time." And I would. *Whap.* I loved the sound it made.

I don't say a word, just hand Daddy the box. He takes it underhanded. He's the waiter and it's a tray with a nice piece of Mama's famous caramel cake and a full glass of tea, all ready for some lucky one. I cannot see his hands because they are under the box, but I know they are almost as broad as they are long, the fingers short and thick and flecked with tufts of little black hairs.

Now he will hold the box to one side, kiss me hard on the top of the head, and slip through the front door into the night. As he glides through the doorway, his Cloroxed shirt a flash of light against the shadows behind him, I touch the spot where he marked me with his kiss. "I'm going to give you a kiss that'll go straight down to your heart, Sister," he said once, and now I know it does because I can feel it begin its journey like a little burrowing creature. Down through the middle of my skull, sliding down the gullet, behind the collarbone, tunneling left through blood and bone and flesh till it finds its own dear home. Now he says, "Bye-bye, Sister," without turning around, and *click* goes the door behind him.

When the door shuts, Mama slams a pan into the sink. Then there is dead silence. I know she's not washing the dishes yet.

She's standing there in her apron with the faded clusters of sweet-heart roses, tied top and bottom nice and neat, looking out over the little backyard. Space enough for a clothesline, that's it, and weeds galore, really nothing more than an alleyway, but we call it the backyard. What else can we call it?

This much I can see without even looking in her direction. Mama in her apron still standing at the sink and looking out the kitchen window into the dusky light. Her arms turned in over the sweetheart rose clumps like she's about to gather them up from the front of her apron and make a pretty bouquet out of them to put on the kitchen table. But she's not thinking roses. She's thinking about Daddy's box.

"Get that thing out of my sight," she said to me one time. I had brought it up from the basement and left it on the table in the kitchen because Daddy was in the bathroom washing up. The table was little. When we ate, I'd have to sit at its corner so we'd have room enough for our plates. When Mama saw that box squatting dark and solid on her eating table like a big sassy roach, her mouth worked to one side and then the other the way it did when she tasted a bad egg in one of her batters. She reached down and gave the box a hard little shove so that it slid toward the edge of the table. Just as she did it and the box was sliding sliding and I was opening my mouth to say watch out, Daddy rounded the corner of the kitchen. You could tell he couldn't believe his eyes. His precious box. *Whap* went one hand on its top, stopping it in the middle of its skid. The other hand flew out at Mama, hawk to rabbit. He took her bony little wrist and held it between his thumb and first finger. How he wanted to snap it!

He steadied the box, then put his first hand under Mama's chin and clubbed her face up to his. "You better watch yourself. You better watch out." Each word chipped from a block of ice. That's all he said, but his hands did their work on her. The first squeezed tighter on the little wrist, the second pushed Mama's head back and up so high she couldn't move it. Her hazel yellow eyes flared down at me. She wanted me to go away, but I didn't. I watched.

Then she squinched her eyes tight shut and just stood there, still as stone. Neither one of them said a word after that, they just stood there locked together. Mama's neck pared back like a radish, so thinly white that you could almost see through it. Then after a while, he let her go and gathered his box into his arms like his own true child. She sagged, but stayed standing, her fingertips glued to the table's edge to steady herself while he turned and slammed out the screen door.

The next morning, taped up on the icebox, was a cut-out cartoon, a picture of two pretty blond ladies talking over a fence. One had on a lacy apron and carried a covered basket. The other had on a Sunday dress and a hat with daisies around the brim. The one with the apron was saying to the other one, "My husband and I have joined our Citizens' Council, have you all?" Hanging in the sky like a puffy white cloud over the two ladies' heads were the words A GOOD IDEA! The cloud hung up there like God himself had spit out the words. I saw the cartoon first thing when I went to get my orange juice. Then Mama came into the kitchen and went for the milk. She stopped short with her hand on the icebox door and stuck her face forward to read the words and made a little sound in her throat. That was all. She didn't say anything when Daddy came into the kitchen humming like he had a Christmas secret. She just cooked him some bacon and fried eggs on high heat so that the eggs were hard as plates and the bacon charred. She turned on the broiler in the stove and shoved in some buttered toast. She let it stay under the broiler so that the edges were black and the stove was starting to smoke. Then she slid the bacon and eggs and a river of grease onto his plate, dumped the burnt toast on top, shoved the plate down at him, and took one quick step back, as if she were feeding a mean dog. After that she went to washing up the skillet in the sink. He sat at the table and wolfed down his breakfast and read the paper. No paper chat. Nothing but chewing and swallowing. Once he looked up at her as she busied herself at the sink, his eyes flattened out, dark and dull as blacktop on the road. After he left for work, she pulled the two pretty ladies off the refrigerator and tore them into little bits and threw them in the garbage can.

My father had a way of vanishing into thin air when night fell. When he got all lit up for one of his meetings, he could walk out of the bathroom and take your breath away with his shine. Mama used to look at him like she was getting ready to lick his face before it melted into the night. Tonight I'm wishing he'd taken me along with his box out into the breathy dark, but in those early days of that long summer he never did. I always stayed with Mama.

After a while she turns on the water and I know she's wanting me to dry.

My mother washed dishes in a peculiar way. She washed each dish under running water hotter than I could have stood. She'd rinse off the grease and then soap up her fingers with a bar of Ivory and wash the plate or bowl or whatever with her soapy thumb and two front fingers. No washcloth, no sponge. It looked dainty and languid. Years later I would see an old woman on the Jemez Pueblo in New Mexico moving her thumb and forefingers in the same way to shape a pot out of clay the color of dried blood. The wrinkles in the woman's cheeks were so deep that their insides looked like new scars the same dark red as the pots.

After washing the dish or pot to her complete satisfaction, Mama would rinse it a final time and set it to the side, or, if I wasn't behind in the drying, hand it directly to me. There was no dish drainer. My mother didn't believe in leaving dishes out. She said they would draw roaches, which was a pretty safe bet given Mama's dishwashing methods. I wonder now whether her technique may have been partly adaptive, at least the running water part of it. She was always baking and having to wash the bowls and pans she made her cakes in so that she could use them over again to make some more. We had one shallow sink with porcelain stretching out in endless ridges on both sides so that the sink's monstrous shelf took up a whole wall with its hard white flesh, while the functional part, the basin, looked like a small puddle of suds in the whiteness. So there was no soaking, unless it was some pesky pot or pan with hardened drippings or icings after everything else was done. For those stubborn ones Mama used a rusty wad of steel wool she kept in an open jelly jar on the sink, if her fingernails didn't work.

It was my job to give back the dishes that Mama's finger method didn't get clean. Usually these were glasses, when her fingers didn't reach deep enough, or cake pans, at the point where the top of the layer and pan met in one hard brown line. If I rubbed hard with the blue-and-white dish towel and still there was a bit or smear or glob of something, I'd hold it up, look at it seriously, and then push it back toward her. She'd look up from her washing, glare at the item I held out as if it had insulted her.

"What?" she'd belt out, as if this were some mean trick I was pulling on her. Then she'd sigh like she had received some terrible bit of news, the kind that kicks you in the stomach. Wipe her brow with the back of her soapy right hand, sometimes leaving a trail of suds across her flat-cut bangs. Reach out and grab the dirty glass or pan or whatever like she was going to kill it sure enough. Then she'd turn up the volume of water and rinse it so hard that the boiling-hot water would splatter and I'd have to jump back from the sink. When she would thrust the hot dripping thing into my hand a second time, I knew to accept it, clean or dirty.

On this particular night it is 1963 and I am almost eleven years old, the first and last of my mother's children, just as she was her own mother's first and last, both of us remnants of a dreamed fabric. My name is Florence Irene Forrest, after the city in Italy, my grandmother Mimi, and my father in that order, my father always telling people that the Forrest has two r's, as in the great Confederate general Nathan Bedford Forrest. It's May, early May because the regular children are still in school. In the mornings I sit on our front-porch stoop, hidden behind the thatching of the clematis vine, and watch them go by. I am wearing a pair of old shorts with an elastic waist and a crop top that shows my belly button. My hair is cut short. The regular girls' shirts are tucked into their pleated skirts and they carry their books in neat stacks. Some of them tote little lunch boxes and satchels. Watching this parade of regular children on their way to school, I feel like a dead girl looking down from heaven on the trickles of the life she is missing out on. Only I don't feel like I'm in heaven. I tell myself that this too will pass. In September I will be a regular child again. I am not one at the moment because we've just moved back home after a year on the lam, and Mama says I need summer tutoring to make up for all the school I've missed. No need to enroll in May when you're Behind with a capital B. They will give tests at the end of the school year. I could get put back. Sometimes the things I would need to learn before going into the fifth grade stretched out before me like a rickety bridge over dark water, no land in sight. Vertebrates and clauses and phrases and quotation marks. The gross national product of Argentina. Where was Argentina anyhow? How many zeroes are in a million? It made me sweat to think of all I'd missed.

But here we are, returned like mail to its sender as if the past year had never happened. Stuck right back in this quicksand of a town called Millwood, smack in the dead center of the State of Mississippi. Swamps and piney woods all around us. Red-clay hills to the north. Tonight the mosquito trucks are out. They speed up and down the street so as to get to everybody and keep ahead of the poison they're putting out. Steam's rising from the spray. The honeysuckle is coming on strong, and it folds into the insecticide like sugar into vinegar. Daddy is long gone with his precious box, and the lightning bugs are commencing.

I'm ready to dry, but I can see that it's one of those nights when Mama's not in the mood for dishes because she has just put the plug into the drain and is filling up the sink with water and throwing in the dishes three and four at a time. They clatter, then float to the bottom. I'm standing right beside her at the sink so she can lean over and wipe her hands on the dish towel I'm holding out in front of me. She takes off her apron and runs her hands through her hair so that her bangs stand straight out like antennae on a bug. Then she turns her head the way a praying mantis will turn to look slow and serious at a tomato worm and gazes over my head out the window at the darkening sky. She doesn't put her hands on my shoulders the way she sometimes does, but I know to stand there beside her and be quiet. She is considering. The white sink crawls out longer and longer on the ledge of the shadows. Such a stillness settles over Mama as she looks out that I wonder whether she's breathing. Sometimes when she does this, I feel as though I'm going to float up off the floor and drift away like a cottonwood puff before she comes back to plant me in the good sweet earth, the here and now. Finally, she says, "Do you want to go for a ride?"

I don't bother to answer, just run into my room and pull my pajamas out of the drawer of my dresser. I tear off my clothes like they're full of fire ants and pull on my least raggedy pajamas, the daisy ones. All of my summer pajamas are raggedy. Mama says that's a good thing because it keeps me cooler to have some holes here and there. Aren't I lucky? When we take our night rides, Mama makes me get ready for bed before we leave so that I can go right to sleep when we get home, or if I fall asleep in the car, she can drag me in whining and limp and throw me down on the bed. When Daddy gets home, I'm supposed to play dead.

She's using the bathroom while I get ready, and now I have to use it too. Use it while you've got it, Mama always said before we'd head out for the night, and once when I didn't we had to stop for me to go in the bushes in pitch dark on the side of a dirt road in the middle of nowhere. The next morning I woke up on fire with poison ivy and Mama had to put calamine lotion all over Between The Legs, which is what Mama called private parts as if what was important about them was where they were placed instead of what they were for. She said that no matter how bad it itched, I should not scratch Between the Legs, it wasn't polite, so I'd sit down on a hard chair and rub myself back and forth like a dog, which I discovered felt surprisingly good though it made the itch worse.

On nights when Daddy got the call for a night meeting and Big Dan Chisholm next door gave him a ride, Mama and I went out in Daddy's old pea-green Ford. It was the first in a series of trash cars we would have in the coming months, since Mama ended up going through cars that summer like some people go through a bag of peanuts, casting the hulls far and wide or making them disappear into thin air. The radio didn't work when Daddy brought the Ford home from Big Dan's used-car place after we returned to Millwood that spring. When he told my mother about the radio not working—no, not a chance of it ever working—she flinched as if he had brought news of somebody dying. "Of all the cars in the entire world." She said each word separately, like it was a piece of unexpected gristle she was spitting out of her mouth. I was not surprised. Daddy didn't like radios or televisions. He said commie Jews ran all the stations, and he'd be damned if he'd pay good money to listen to their pinko propaganda. Mama had bought herself a little transistor radio for the kitchen with her cake money, but Daddy drew the line with TV. So I missed out on Dr. King and President Kennedy and the police dogs and hoses and children with little American flags being dragged into garbage trucks and the Cuban Missile Crisis, not to speak of Mr. Wizard and *Bonanza*. I might as well have lived on Mars.

After the radio fight, Mama went into her room and shut the door and stayed there for a whole day and night except to use the bathroom. She took two long baths. Daddy went around the house whistling loud. He made us corned-beef hash out of a can for supper, which didn't turn out at all like the way Mama made it, all nice and brown, baked in the oven in a Pyrex dish with Heinz ketchup for icing and sliced bell peppers in daisy chains on top. He mushed down globs of the hash in a pot to warm up on the top of the stove. Two plates of warm dog food we sat down to. "Eat up, Sister," he said, and picked up the spoon he'd put by my plate. I didn't say a word, just got up and went to the drawer and got out a fork, which was what I was used to. Then I sat back down, shut my eyes tight, and shoveled it in.

But in the end, it was this car or none, and the truth was the whole thing rattled so bad I doubt we could have heard the radio anyway. I liked riding alone with Mama because I could sit in the front seat. The woven upholstery on the backseat had rotted out and the springs were exposed. Over the years, all of our cars had had rotten backseats. Long ago, Daddy had gotten the bright idea to stuff them with Spanish moss, which gave me the feeling of being a little bird in a nest when I rode in back, which was comforting, but the moss got old and scratchy after a while and had chiggers in it that lived on my tender flesh and just waited for their next meal of Florence. In hot weather I would get out of the car with so many welts on the backs of my legs it looked like somebody had taken a switch to me. I'm not even talking about my butt, which was worse. Little Dan, the son of Big Dan who sold the cars and rented our house to us, passed a rumor up and down the street that I had leprosy, so that children I'd never seen in my life were trying to pull up my shorts to look at the backs of my legs. I had to wear long pants to go out and play, which made the chigger bites heat up and itch even worse than before.

The nights Mama took me for a ride, we told Daddy we went out for ice cream to explain the gas. This was technically true, but we actually went two places. The first was Joe's Drive-In, where we'd pull up and place our order through the little voice box next to each parking place and then a gum-chewing girl with a scruffy ducktail would bring me out a chocolate milk shake to go. No tray. On these nights Mama was always in a hurry, and she'd tap her forefinger on the steering wheel until I'd say, "Mama, stop doing that." Then she'd start up the old Ford and pull out of Joe's, popping hard on the clutch. We opened it up on old Highway 78, her arm on the top of the steering wheel thin and white, me sipping my milk shake just barely enough to get it started up the thick straw. I wanted to make it last all night.

We took a right by the lake, and then two more rights on dirt roads. I remember the rights because I'd slide across the slick seat into Mama's side three times and she'd nudge me back three times. When there wasn't much moon, like tonight, the deeper in we got on those dusty pitted roads, the more I felt our car was being taken into a giant mouth that first tasted us and then swallowed us whole.

Tonight, like always, we come around the last curve to find ourselves at the end of a line of stopped cars, engines humming backup to the swamp sounds, no radios, no lights, and so dark that you can't see the drivers. Mama cuts the lights, leans over, and opens the glove compartment. She pulls out an old green scarf and ties it around her head.

"Duck down," she orders, and I slide down a little in the seat. I'm short for my age, so it doesn't take much to put me out of view.

The dark woods have closed in around our car, and we sit with the car windows down listening to the bullfrogs tune up. Mama is fooling with her scarf, pulling it toward the front of her face so you can't tell who she is from the side. We don't speak, which, I later realize, was why Mama bought me the milkshake. To keep my mouth busy. She didn't want me getting chatty on her, which, believe me, I could do. Every so often the cars silently roll up a length or two like they're on an assembly line getting the next part put on. After a while we reach a circular driveway with a shed at the entrance.

There's always the same man behind the window of the shed. The first time I saw his face in the shadows, the flesh seemed to have been peeled back so that only the bones rose up to greet us. Bones and eyes, no flesh attached. Even in the dark of this night, I can see his eyes flash as he takes in the first sight of us, a white woman looking like she's in the worst rainstorm of her life and a white girl in raggedy pajamas with daisies. Is he scared of us?

I could be scared of him if I didn't know he was the bootlegger. Right under the lady and the spider picture in the newspaper was a story from Columbus about police looking for a Negro who ripped off a white lady's clothes and threatened her with an ice pick after she had shown him the kindness of giving him the glass of water he came knocking on her door asking for. She was just being nice and chipping some ice for him when he grabbed the pick away from her and had his way with her. "Don't believe everything you read," Mama said when she saw me trying to piece together the words in the article. "People make up stories."

We roll to the front of the line and the man steps toward the car. "Yes'm," he says. That is all he says. He looks at the ground.

"Two tall boys," Mama leans her head partway out the window.

"That be Schlitz, ma'am?"

"Whatever you've got that's cold."

"Yes'm." The man is waiting. He looks down at Mama's hands.

"Here." Mama pushes a half dollar through the window, then a little torn-off piece of paper with some writing on it.

The man reaches out his hand. It flutters a little, like a dark leaf disturbed by a slight breeze. He pockets the paper and the money fast.

"All right, it'll be all right now. Nothing ever happens until after midnight. Just don't go wasting any time, though. Get everybody inside, and the boys in the woods." Mama says all this in one long whispery breath. She doesn't look at the man.

The man lifts his head for the first time. His eyes are heat lightning in the heavy dark. Why is he so vexed? "Nobody round here wasting no time." His voice, which seemed to rise up out of the ground he stood on and shudder like a palsy through his whole body before coming out of his mouth, breaks off.

Mama doesn't say anything back, just pulls the car around the dirt circle to the other side of the shed where a woman nods to us and then pulls the beers from an ice chest and puts them dripping into two little paper sacks, one for each can, and hands them to her through the car window. The woman's eyes are heavy lidded. She looks downward, in the direction of Mama's door handle. A branch heavy with old sweet gum balls scrapes my side of the car and makes a star pattern against the little piece of rising moon. I reach out and pull one off and touch and touch again its sharp little points. The air smells like somebody's boiling collards.

Then the woman murmurs, "You watch out for yourself, Miss

Martha. Y'all watch out now." The words tumble out of her mouth soft and sweet, like a song you'd sing a baby to sleep with.

"Y'all too. Y'all too," Mama sings out and takes the cool damp sacks and hands them over to me. I put them on the floor between my feet, making sure not to turn the cans over so they won't spew up when I open them. She gives a little wave to the woman, and the woman nods and her lips move like she's saying a little prayer over us the way the preacher does right before we leave church. She and the man start walking up to the cars behind us. They're pointing to the way out and I can hear them say, "We sold out now. Drive on. Drive on now."

Then Mama and I turn out of the dirt in the opposite direction from the way we came in, though after a few miles the road will wind back around to where we made our turn and we'll hook up with old 78. The cars from the bootlegger are piling up behind us. Later, I will find out that bootleggers always have a way for you to get in and a way for you to get out. In case of a raid. When we make the turn onto the highway and the land opens out into long dark rows of cotton plants, Mama floors the Ford and takes it through its gears hard and long, stretching them out like she's pushing something big and heavy ahead of the car.

After a while she looks down at me in the dark and says, like always, "Pop me a top, honey."

I put my milk shake between my knees, squeezing it enough to keep it in place but not enough to squish the paper cup and make it overflow. I grope around on the floor for one of the soggy paper sacks that are starting to tear apart and bring out tall boy number one. "Ta da!" I hold it high.

"Put it down," Mama says. "Don't hold it up like that. Don't go acting the fool."

I reach into the glove compartment for the church key Mama keeps hidden in an envelope under the car papers. I puncture one side of the top of the can just a smidgen the way Mama taught me so that the beer would come out nice and easy on the other side. I punch the other side down good and hard to make a nice V-shaped hole. I take the one sip Mama allows, cough because it burns my throat the way ice sometimes does. A little beer and my own spit spray my arm. The air blowing on it cools me down. I'm thinking what a good life it is that we lead in our own secret ways.

Of course, all of this except the milk shake at Joe's is a secret. We are being girls together, and girls do things. And later on, when I got old enough to wonder why my mother would take her little girl to the bootlegger at all, and even later, when I found out that there was a white bootlegger for white people, I didn't have her to ask. She'd flown the coop by that time. Back then I reasoned that she took me because she needed the beer, and she took me to the black bootlegger so she wouldn't run into anybody she knew.

This was what I saw and nothing more than this. Us tooling down the highway, me sucking on the last of my milk shake now all melted, Mama's scarf now slipping off her head, her bobbed hair blowing straight out to the sides, like wings.

2

That spring we'd gotten lucky when Mimi managed to get our little white house with the pretty trellis back. The previous renters had packed up and vamoosed in the middle of the night, leaving some moldy mattresses on the floor, roaches galore, and two months' unpaid rent. Before we left for parts unknown, we'd lived in the house for three years, and it had been a step up for us. Then, out of the blue, Daddy had gotten it in his head he needed to find just the right job for someone of his talents. To this end, he dragged us all over the State of Mississippi and after that through parts of Texas that either flooded so bad he had to sweep the water moccasins off the front stoop of our apartment building or were so bone dry the earth had huge cracks, one of which Mama stepped into and broke her foot while she was hanging out clothes. We moved so much that there are places out there I lived whose names I don't know to this day.

During our year on the lam, I came down with mysterious ailments. Coughs, earaches, fevers, swollen glands, sore throats, what have you. Except for a few weeks in a little church school where each and every day began with singing, "The B-I-B-L-E, Yes, that's the Book for Me," etc., I missed the whole fourth grade. Mama worked for Kelly Girl here and there, but after a while they would drop her. In Houston, when they'd call at dawn on the pay phone right outside our apartment door on the concrete landing and say for her to go here or there, she usually had to say no, her little girl was sick again and she had to stay home and see about her. Sometimes, though, she shook me awake and whispered, "Honey, I'll be gone for just a little while. I've just got to go. Go back to sleep and don't mess with the stove," and I would turn my face to the wall on my cot in the living room, which was also the kitchen and dining room.

When Daddy finally got fired from his umpteenth job, which happened to be at Brown and Root in Houston, my mother didn't bat an eye. She blew her bangs up off her forehead. They had gotten longer and covered her eyes. Over the months she had seemed to be hiding behind them. The only way I could judge her mood was by the set of her mouth, which, at that moment, was even more pinched than usual. She marched out the front door, not even bothering to close it behind her. She called Mimi and Grandpops collect on the pay phone outside and told them to wire the money, we were coming home. She came back into the apartment, threw one baleful look at Daddy, who was sitting with his head in his hands on the couch, and then headed off for the bedroom. We heard her pulling the suitcases out from under the bed. There wouldn't be much packing. Nowadays she kept most of our things in the suitcases. There wasn't room in most of the places we lived, plus what's the point of unpacking just to have to pack again in a month or two?

"Win." Mama's voice sliced through the wall.

Daddy sat there a minute; his eyes darted around the room like he was looking for something he'd lost. Then he got up and went on into the bedroom like a dog ready to be whipped. He shut the door behind him. Mama started in on him the minute he walked in. She didn't even try to whisper. He could come back home or not, but she wasn't going to live like a gypsy anymore. They had managed before in Millwood, they could manage again. She had given him a year to sort himself out and now she had to get on home where there were decent doctors and people to take care of me so she could get back to baking cakes and making a living for this family if nobody else around here was going to put food on the table. We'd been dragged from pillar to post, and, like it or lump it, she was planting her feet back on solid ground. He could come if he wanted to, but she was going home and taking me and don't forget that her daddy is a lawyer.

When I heard her lay down the law like that, my sinuses all of a sudden popped wide open, and I felt like I just had poked my head out from under a smothering blanket. I took the first deep breath I'd breathed in a year.

After that night there were days of nobody talking and a flurry of boxes to mail our things to Mimi and Grandpops in Millwood (C.O.D.). About a week later I woke up before light. Daddy was kicking the leg of my cot. "Get up, Sister, hurry up." He spit the words out of his mouth one by one. They fell to the floor like stones. We took the Greyhound bus straight from Houston to Jackson, getting off only to eat nabs and drink Orange Crush and go to the bathroom in dusty depots with brown-stained spit-toons. Mama and Daddy made me ride in the seat between them for the whole day and night that the trip took. Daddy sat on the aisle and closed his eyes. Mama turned her head away from him to the window and looked out over the passing fields and swamp-lands and monster oil rigs until her eyelashes touched the dark circles underneath them and she fell into a deep sleep. I was the only one with my eyes open, and I wanted the window, for the air if nothing else, but knew better than to ask Mama. She and Daddy couldn't have stood to be any closer to each other than they were. I was the fly in the ointment that kept them together, and I needed to stay stuck.

The land whipped by. It was the last day of April when we left, and the trees were forcing out their new leaves. Everything looked hopeful, even the warthogs standing in clumps in the Louisiana swamps. They rubbed their snouts up and down expectantly on the old tree trunks and vines as if they were polishing themselves up for a party. There'd been a rain, and the restoration fern on the swooping oaks had perked up and turned from brown to green.

We sat way up in the front of the bus because Daddy said he didn't want to be close to Them. He said they stunk and their food stunk. When he said all that right out loud as Mama and I were climbing the steps onto the bus, Mama stopped short on the top step and turned around and looked down at him like she was going to kick him square in the face. I was on the middle step between them, and actually ducked. He shut up, but he shoved me into the second set of seats and then grabbed Mama, who was going on down the aisle, and told her to get in too. She jerked her arm away like his hand had burned her, but she turned around and, instead of making a fuss, climbed over me to the window seat. As the hours went by, I decided that the people in the back smelled fresher than I was beginning to and their little paper sacks with glistening grease spots made my mouth water. Their eyes flitted over us like lazy flies but never settled.

By the time we rolled into the Jackson depot on the second day, it was almost dark and the katydids were revving up. Sticky from the heat and leaden from the silent heavy journey, we tumbled off the bus into Mimi's talcumed arms, at least Mama and I did. Daddy hung back and shook hands with Grandpops and did a little bow in Mimi's direction. In honor of the occasion, Mimi had on one of her more subdued hats, a little black straw number with a cluster of drooping strawberries and a red wisp of a veil that stood straight up so that she looked like a Roman soldier. Mimi's hats were wild things. Grapes and feathers, cherries and ribbons and doodads. The top shelf of her closet was stacked with pretty-colored hat boxes, round and square, large and small, where all shapes and sizes and colors waited in their crisp tissue nests.

Grandpops squatted down in front of me, his bony knees popping, and asked, "Ready to read this old man some stories?" I answered, "Yes sir!" but when I tried to grin, my face split and then froze over again like a pond striving to come alive after a long hard winter. He reached over and took my hand and put it up against his cheek. "You're sure a sight for sore eyes, girl. Your grandmother and I been moping around like two old ornery bears," to which Mimi responded, "Don't you call *me* a bear, old man!" Then we all laughed, rinsing the ice from my heart, and Mama, Daddy, and I piled into the backseat of Mimi's Plymouth, me in the middle as usual, and headed for Millwood.

The little white house we'd lived in before was an unexpected surprise to us, at least the fact of it being there waiting for us with its lights glowing in welcome and beds freshly made, thanks to Zenie Johnson, who worked for my grandmother and helped her get it ready. Mama started crying when Mimi and Grandpops drove us up our old street. Daddy studied the other side of the street and looked bored. Mimi was thrilled with herself. About a week ago, right after Mama had called, Mimi had just been driving by when she saw the For Rent sign, which had just been put up that very morning. It was meant to be! She jumped out of the car and paid the first month's rent on the spot. She knew my mother would love coming back home to our old house. The moldy mattresses were gone, but Mimi had to get the bug man in to spray for roaches twice. Zenie's husband, Ray, had painted the inside and pulled the weeds in the back alley. I'd loved the little house the minute I'd laid eyes on it years back, but now it looked like a meringue, white outside and in, light and airy with starched white café curtains and pretty little throw rugs.

The house was oddly placed. It didn't sit on the street like other houses, but was tucked in behind another house, the Chisholm place, which was nicer and bigger with a long porch and rocking chairs that didn't pinch like the ones up at Mimi and Grandpops'. Our house was a little square box, high off the ground, the Chisholms' a lower extended *L* whose tail went almost up to our front door.

Perched up like that in the big house's backyard with a shaded path of small stepping-stones leading from the street to our doorstep, our place looked more like a little rich girl's playhouse, white-washed and clean and innocent. It was hidden and secret. You could barely see it from the street, and then only from an angle. When Mama would give directions to her new cake customers, she'd describe the Chisholm place, and then say we lived behind it. Ours came to be known as the house behind the house.

The house wasn't much on the inside, but we ended up paying $60 a month to live in it. Big Dan, who owned the Big Dan Ford place and who had gotten Daddy the radio-less car for next to nothing, rented to us. His wife called herself Miss Kay Linda, which she said meant "How pretty!" in Spanish if you pronounced the *Linda* as "Leeenda." Miss Kay Linda did not live up to her name. She was short and pudgy, and her hair was the color of the sky when there's a tornado coming, a sickly yellow. Her elbow fat crawled down her lower arms like melting lard. Mama and Daddy got funny little twitches around their mouths and looked straight down at the ground when she told us what her name meant and how to say it right.

When we'd lived in our little house those three years before our year on the lam, Miss Kay Linda had planted some clematis vines next to our front door and attached them with clothespins onto the lattice on either side of the front stoop. Soon after we moved back that May, Mama asked Miss Kay Linda if she could take down those clothespins, seeing as how the clematis was climbing just fine, and those old moldy pins looked like big brown warts up against the pretty whiteness of the flowers, but Miss Kay Linda said no, she wanted to keep the pins there, just in case. She had gone to a lot of trouble to get that clematis to climb and she didn't want to have it falling down all straggly with folks coming and going all the time. She was referring to Mama's cake business, which she didn't like being conducted in the house, and had raised the agreed-upon rent $10 a month to accommodate for the wear and tear that Mama's cake customers would cause with their comings and goings, plus adding a $50 deposit to the whole deal. "Which I'll never get back," Mama said.

Besides Little Dan, who started the rumor about me having leprosy, the Chisholms had a girl, May, and those two had a new swing set in what was their backyard and our front yard. There were two swings and a little ladder and slide. It was right in front of our living room window, and I would watch them swing on it. The spring we moved back, Little Dan was twelve and May my age. They might have been my playmates, but they'd always thought they were better than we were and treated me worse than dirt unless they wanted something, which was usually a piece of one of Mama's famous cakes since that was all we had of any value.

In the past Mama and a lady named Mrs. Polk had divided up Millwood's sweet tooth between the cake people and the pie people. The two of them had an agreement. Mrs. Polk would make the pies and Mama would make the cakes. When you wanted a pie for a Saturday Matinee Club meeting or a bridge party, you called Mrs. Polk and ordered chocolate, coconut, or caramel, the latter being my personal favorite. One of Mrs. Polk's five fulsome daughters would show up at your door several days later with a pie puffed up like a sail full of wind, meringue riding high on the breeze. And then whenever you wanted the best cake you could imagine, you called up my mother and put in your order: lemon, caramel, or devil's food cake with angel icing. Mama said the devil's food with angel icing should be a lesson to me about how both bad and good could look pretty and taste sweet. How they could get so mixed up, each with the other, that sometimes you couldn't tell which was which. What a danger those kinds were.

Mama said things like that while she was baking. Hard things that meant other things. Then she'd stare at me like she was a hundred-year-old oak tree and I was the ax that was going to bring her down. So I'd say yes ma'am, soft and easy, and when I spoke the words, they folded back the hardness in her eyes. Then she'd tell me to bring her a measuring spoon or the sugar or the shortening. I'd scurry for what it was that she wanted, and the commotion of my reaching and touching would unclasp us from the spell of her dark thoughts.

When we first got back to Millwood that May, people had turned to pies in Mama's absence. At first, Mrs. Polk was doing a better business than Mama. One problem was that Mama's cakes were so big. If Mrs. Polk's pies were sails, Mama's cakes were battleships. When you'd hand one over, the person you were handing it to would always go "Oh!" and have to lean back to adjust to the weight. In the past, ladies had ordered Mama's cakes more for birthdays or anniversaries or Easter when they were having a crowd of people, but right after we came back home, Mama got the bright idea of selling half cakes. When the word got out, the orders started coming in left and right.

After that, the house was burning up hot every Thursday, Friday, and Saturday night with the stove on from after supper until long past midnight. I slept with the windows pushed as high as they would go, a fan blowing right on me, no revolving, and my pajama top pulled up. Mama would be mixing and baking and icing and talking back to John R on WLAC. I knew all of Mama's cooking sounds. *Brush, brush* was the grater when she did the lemon rind, the loud scraping was the rack in the oven when she'd pull it out to adjust the height for the cake pans. The soft hen scratching was the wire whisk for egg whites.

The problem with half cakes was that you wanted to sell both halves, so the orders had to line up just so. Timing was important. When the phone rang with an order for a half, Mama might say, "Hi, Darlene. Well, let's see here. I have half orders for the lemon and the caramel for tomorrow, so I can give you one of those. Just not the devil's food." She would hang up, write *Darl* for Darlene, and beside the *Darl* put another mark the shape of half a cake in the spiral notebook she kept by the phone. A half cake looked like this: (. A whole like this: ( ).

The trick was to have the two halves make a whole on the same day or following day. Otherwise you were dealing with a stale half, which was no good to anybody, except me (within reason) and Little Dan and May. If you had a half order of, say, lemon for Friday pickup, then you could take another half lemon for Saturday, though not for Sunday, because by then it would be too far gone and Mama had her reputation to think about.

We divided the cakes at the last possible moment before a pickup. My job was to cut out waxed paper to fit the side of each cake to the exact inch. Mama had made me a cardboard model, and I kept a supply stacked up under a small plate on the kitchen counter. After Mama had sliced the cake in half, she pulled the halves apart, put the waxed paper up to the side of each half, and pressed with a gentle but firm hand, as if the cake had been a set of Siamese twins and she needed to stop the bleeding fast without damaging any cut vessels, so that both sides could bid adieu and go their separate ways.

The icings were the thing. They had to be timed to the split second, or else they would turn into wet sugar grit. When that happened, Mama would get mad as fire and start yelling her worst curse word, which was "Damn it the hell." She said icing was like some folks' lives: Timing is everything and when things go bad they go really bad. They settle into sludge. They cannot be undone.

Timing works only if you know your flame, which my mother did. She set her little white timer to four minutes for the caramel and five for the angel icing (two minutes with the top on the pot, three with it off) and the timer would go *tick tick tick BING!* throughout the night, though when the weather was stormy, timing would fall by the wayside and she had to use her thermometer instead. Even then, icing was finicky during thunderstorms. It could crystallize on a dime or just refuse to thicken up.

The icings required double boilers so that they wouldn't scorch, and there were mixing bowls and cake pans stacked up like skyscrapers all over the kitchen. Mama didn't believe in compromise when it came to her cakes. The devil's food had to have four layers. The caramel was a heavy white cake with three thick layers and between them a quarter inch of caramel fudge icing that tasted like velvet feels.

The lemon cake was the most challenging. It had six thin layers with clear lemon filling in between. It was iced on top with a divinity icing that can turn grainy on you in a split second if you're not careful. Don't even bother trying to make it if the weather's bad. Even if the divinity icing comes out perfect, your troubles aren't over. Sitting there on the table in front of you is a cake with six thin layers iced between and on top with the lemon jell. Your job is to spread the divinity icing right on top of the top layer of lemon jell *without blending into the jell* and making a globby mess! You have to have a feather hand and nerves of steel.

Mama did not deliver unless it was right down the street and then she'd send me. Daddy needed the Ford to collect policy money from his burial insurance clients, plus you can't have your week's income riding on a bed of chigger-infested Spanish moss. "Now be careful," she always said. "Watch where you step. Don't trip over the tree roots."

Some ladies, I won't mention names, snatched their cakes from me, patted their pockets, and said ever so sadly, "Oh dear, honey, I don't have the correct change, I'll have to bring it by later." And then they wouldn't. So Mama filled me up like a walking bank. I could easily whip out whatever change was needed. No excuses for you, Mrs. Have-Your-Cake-But-Not-Pay-For-It. Florence can change anything! I relished walking out our front door, pockets blooming and drooping with dollars and quarters and nickels and dimes, breasting one of Mama's masterpieces in full view, past Little Dan and May, past bony-hipped Mrs. Gardner on the corner, who looked like she'd never had anything good to eat in her whole life and told people the neighborhood was going down because of us. You knock on some nice lady's front door, like Miss Shirley Bishop, who has a sweet tooth and orders a half caramel almost every week. No need to say a word, just hold out Mama's cake and you'd make anybody happy to be on the receiving end. It was the best job I ever had. I never dropped a one.

When I finished up all my deliveries, Mama said her thank you by putting me out on the front stoop with a big slice of what she called her mistakes: cakes that didn't rise because of the weather or came out of the oven with a monster crack because someone, usually Daddy with his bad foot, stomped around on the floor. She put slices of her mistakes in the freezer, nicely wrapped in waxed paper. While I was out delivering cakes, she took out a slice, peeled off the paper, and put it on a little saucer up on the kitchen counter. By the time I got back, it had thawed out. If it was warm outside, she set me up on the front stoop with a glass of tea with ice and mint. No sugar because the cake was sweets enough. "Got to watch those teeth of yours with all this sugar," she said whenever I got a piece of cake. It was always Here's the cake and, for a little added treat, a lecture on tooth decay.

After we'd been back in Millwood about a week and Mama had started sending me out on deliveries, I was sitting on the front stoop with a piece of caramel cake and a glass of tea when Little Dan and May came sidling up to me like ants at a picnic. Little Dan's hair was wet-combed into a little mud-colored mound at the forehead like a dirt-dauber nest. Mama called him Mr. Smarty Pants Hairdo. She said he was going to lose his little mound one day and turn into one of those men who grow out the last straggly piece of hair left on their pitiful heads and plaster it down on top like a run-over baby snake. She said one day I'd go to buy myself a car at his daddy's place, and Little Dan would walk out onto the lot with a pot belly and a big old spit curl on his ugly bald dome, and I'd split my sides laughing.

"That one of your mama's good cakes?" Little Dan pulled out a comb from his back pocket, sucked on it like it was a popsicle, and then began to comb his little mound straight back like he was hot stuff.

"Um hum." I dug for a big hunk of caramel icing, held it on my fork and eyeballed it like I couldn't decide whether to eat it or throw it on the ground and stomp on it.

Little Dan stuck his comb back in his pocket and came closer. "You want to take a turn on my swing I'll hold your cake."

I snapped to. I'd been eyeing those swings since we'd been back, hoping to get an invitation. I passed over the cake plate and fork with the icing still on it, knowing it was the last I'd see of the cake, and headed for the swing set.

Little Dan and May grabbed at the cake, cramming big chunks into their greedy mouths and getting into such a fracas over the icing I'd left on the fork that it ended up in the dirt. What a waste, I thought, as I pushed myself off. I was barely getting going when Little Dan ran up behind me. He grabbed the swing, lifted it high in the air, ran behind it until it was over his head, and, last but not least, gave it a giant push that sent me to the moon. Then he settled in behind and started pushing me higher and higher. By the time I realized I'd been bamboozled, I was too high to jump and getting higher by the second.

"My mama says y'all are nothing but white trash," he hollered at my back. "Your daddy can't even hold a job he's so trashy."

I yelped for my mother, but she was hanging out clothes in the back. So I was riding air, screaming bloody murder, and Little Dan was running under the swing, making me fly. He seemed bound and determined to kill me, for what reason I don't know.

Then something happened I didn't expect. It started out good and ended up bad. You know when you're looking through the camera and you have the perfect picture and you're just getting ready to snap it? That split second when everything curls up like a cat? Just when I was ready to arc over the swing set and baby-bird it out, squash flop, none other than my own father rounded the back *L* of the Chisholms' place and took in the scene. Glory be, I thought. Daddy never comes home in the middle of the day, but here he is. Here he is! Galloping to the rescue like the brave men in the olden days Daddy was always telling stories about. Saving the day. In my mind's eye, I saw my-self as a damsel in distress, my golden locks fanning out behind me as I flew through the air. I was a beautiful sight to behold.

May took one look at Daddy and yelled at Little Dan to stop. Little Dan had already seen my father bearing down the stepping-stones Mama had put out for her customers, so he'd stopped his shoving and walked away real fast like he had nothing to do with me or the swing just happening to be up in the clouds, but not before Daddy saw what he'd been up to.

Before I could drag my feet to slow down the swing, Daddy was mincing toward Little Dan like a crab toward a dead gull. One of my father's legs was shorter than the other and the foot on his short side tended to flip under. Not only did he walk with a limp, he couldn't run or even walk at a good clip. His short leg and the brick-high shoe he wore on that foot kept him off balance at the speed he was traveling across the yard. He said this was why he never went off to fight the Koreans, because he couldn't chase them down. If Little Dan had had the good sense to light out, Daddy wouldn't have been able to catch him.

"What you think you're doing, boy?" My father snatched up Little Dan by the right arm and flopped him back and forth like he was using Little Dan to swat a fly. Daddy had on a short-sleeve shirt, and you could see the veins popping out of the muscles in his arms.

By that time Little Dan was screaming bloody murder, his dirt-dauber nest of hair unraveling all the way down to his nose. "You quit it!" he yelled. "Mama!" he yelled, but Miss Kay Linda was nowhere in sight. She'd gone grocery shopping. May sounded like she was singing, but it was really a moan, and then, all of a sudden, I was making a noise too because Daddy had gotten Little Dan down on the ground and looked like he was getting ready to stomp Little Dan flat like you'd do a roach.

Just then Mama rounded the back corner of our house, covered in clothes. Mama always took our clothes to a Laundromat
down the street to wash them, but she brought them home wet
and hung them out on the line. She had Daddy's shirts across
both shoulders and my pants under her arms. She was carrying a
laundry basket piled so high I couldn't see her mouth. Her eyes,
which are round anyway, were two big O's.

"Win! My God in heaven!" My mother dropped her basket
and ran for Daddy and Little Dan. Daddy's starched shirts flew
from her arms and stood up straight like little white soldiers in
the dust. Mama jumped in front of Daddy and pulled Little Dan
up out of the dirt.

I was still up in the swing dragging my toes in the dirt, tearing them up trying to get out of the clouds, but nobody was interested in my situation. They were playing tug of war over Little
Dan. Daddy wanted to kill him. Mama wanted to save him.

"He hurt me!" Little Dan grabbed the arm where Daddy had
him. "Broke my arm!" He scrambled to his feet and hid behind
Mama's back. Just as she turned around to look him over, he
jumped out from behind her and yelled at Daddy, "You, you, you
nigger!"

Mama spun around like Little Dan was a viper she'd just come
upon in the grass. "You! Dan. Shut your dirty mouth!" No such
talk was allowed in our house. I knew this because once when
Daddy said that word on the phone to Big Dan, Mama had gotten
cool as a cucumber and sat him down at the table after he hung
up and told him if he ever said it again in her presence—those
were the words she used, *in my presence*, and she struck the table
with her first fingernail three times, once for each word—she was
leaving to go back home to live with her mama and daddy. And
take me with her.

Now Daddy started to circle. He was half smiling as he crab-
dragged around behind Mama's back, where Little Dan was hid-

ing out. "Call me a nigger. I'll flat out snatch you bald headed, you little son-of-a-bitch." The words rolled out of his mouth like whipped cream.

"Win!" Mama's voice could have cracked a tree trunk. "Get in the house!"

Daddy was still circling and growling, so Mama leaned over and grabbed him by the belt. Little Dan scuttled up behind her so as not to get caught out in the open. Mama grabbed Daddy's belt and said his name over and over: "Win. Win, Win, Win. *Win!*" until he finally looked her in the face instead of trying to get around her to Little Dan. When his arms drooped at his sides, she spun him around, still holding on to his belt, and pushed him toward the front door. Then Mama turned to Little Dan, who was by this time brushing himself off and planting his nest back on top of his ugly head.

Little Dan looked hard at Mama. "He almost kilt me."

"No he didn't. Now listen to me, Little Dan." Mama put on her Kelly Girl voice. "Let's you tell me what I can do to make you feel better, and I'll tell you what'll make me feel better. What'll make me feel better is for you and May to let Florence swing on your swing every so often without half killing her. What'll make you feel better?"

Little Dan pulled his comb out of his pocket and stuck it in his mouth. He sucked on it a minute and then he pulled it out and said real fast and low, "A cake a week." His eyes were gnats, flitting here and there.

I'm thinking a cake a week! What a nerve. Even we don't get a cake a week! Even Miss Shirley Bishop doesn't get a whole cake a week.

Mama cocked one eyebrow. I could tell she'd settled into hating him as much as I did. "How about half a cake? I usually have a half left over." She smiled a thin, hard little smile.

"Every week?" He poufed his hair up with the slimy comb.

"Every week. Fifty-two weeks a year. No squawking about all this and no killing Florence. That's the deal. And that includes May too. We're all just going to forget this whole thing happened." May had perked up over the cake deal and was drawing close. Little Dan's nest had started to take shape and now my mother hated him so much she couldn't even look in his direction any more. She had her eye on me now. "Now Florence, you pick up these shirts and see if you can shake the dirt off them. Dan, go in and clean up before your mother sees you like that."

When Little Dan started for his back door, Mama's shoulders slumped. She picked up her clothes basket, straightened out the clothes on top, and went into the house. In about two seconds, Daddy came out. He stormed right by me, on down the stepping-stone path. He was carrying his precious box under his arm like a sack of potatoes. I yelled out, "Bye, Daddy." But he didn't even turn around, much less answer, and a minute later I heard the Ford start up and then the tires yelp when he scratched off.

When I opened the front door, Mama was rummaging around in a bottom cabinet under the kitchen sink. She pulled out a bottle marked "poison," with a skull and crossbones on it. It looked like it was half full of something clear like water and she was pouring some out into a glass.

"Mama! No!" I ran over and grabbed her hand. "That's bad stuff. That's poison! You could die!"

She looked down at me and laughed, and then she couldn't stop laughing. It sounded like the laughing that folks do on the Whirly Dervish at the fair when they're getting flipped and flopped every which way. It goes on and on like the person is going to die laughing before the ride's over. Like the hiccups.

"Unfortunately," she gulped a swallow between words, "it won't kill me anytime soon!" She sloshed her glass and some of the stuff spilled on my hands. I teared up, and not just because of the poison. First it was Daddy like to killing Little Dan. Then Little Dan calling Daddy a Negro, which I just didn't get because Daddy was geisha-girl white. Then here Mama was giving out her good cakes like they were popsicles. And last but not least: my mother drinking poison. All of it my fault.

Mama put the glass down on the counter. It didn't make a sound. "Oh honey, it's not poison, it's just a little moonshine. For when you have a bad day."

"Well *I'm* having a bad day too."

Her heart wasn't in my bad day. She took up her glass and chugalugged. She looked down at me over the now empty glass. Her round hazel eyes had withered into hard little raisins. "Well, I think you ought to go right out into the yard and have yourself *a good swing.*"

After she said the words, they became yellow jackets. You know how yellow jackets will land on you and just sit there and you know that if you swat at them, they're going to dig right in and sting the fire out of you? So you sit quiet and still until they take a notion to lift off. Then you shake yourself good and go on about your business. I stood there for a while waiting for Mama's words to lift. She had turned her back to me and was standing at the kitchen sink washing out her glass with her fingertips. When she was done, she didn't turn around.

So I just quietly quietly turned around and walked outside. I sat down on the front-porch stoop. No yellow jackets around, but real live bees in a frenzy of crawling and thrusting. The clematis was blooming to beat the band those little white flowers that make you feel swoony they're so sweet.

The bees buzzed around my face. I knew I could get stung if I made a sudden move, but it felt right to be in danger, so I just sat there. Still as death. I squinted my eyes and put my hands up to the sides of them like horse blinders. I was a tunnel. I could see straight ahead into what will be: there's the swing set, now empty, stiller than still. No children in this yard. Me, and Mama, and Daddy, now long gone, though this little house still holds crumbs of us, behind the stove a measuring spoon, under the refrigerator that cap I dropped but could never find from a bottle of vanilla. The roaches have nibbled up all the droppings of icing and cake and on the strength of the sugar have had millions of babies and grandbabies and great-great-grands that stare and scurry when a light is turned on at night. Now that we're gone, all they have to eat is somebody else's nastiness and each other. They've gotten scrawny and mean-spirited. They've grown larger wings.

Little Dan's grown, but he's not selling used cars for his father. He's sitting in a hard chair in a long room full of hard chairs, a stocky young man whose face is now more square than round. He's weary from a long bus ride. His mouth is a little open and he's about to fall asleep as he obediently tilts his head toward an Army barber with a buzzer in his hand, like a little boy whose mother waits with a comb. In a blink, the little nest is a pile of feathers on the floor. Then it's barely three months and Little Dan's being pushed out of a helicopter. Lost and hopping around a leafy jungle floor. Now he's fluttered into the bamboo. Now I can't see him anymore. He's nowhere in sight.

Through the screen I could hear Mama in the kitchen opening a cabinet door again. I hoped she was reaching for the pots and pans, not the poison bottle, but then there was only silence instead of the clatter of cake baking.

3

The second Saturday morning after we returned to Millwood, Mama came into my room with a carpet sweeper, which she propped up against my bed. "Okay, now, get on up and clean your floor. Make up your bed nice. Put on some decent shorts. It's pickup day." She sounded briskly cheerful and smelled like cough medicine. She'd trimmed her bangs short, drawn her eyebrows in perfect crescent moons. She was wearing a pressed blouse of white cotton so thin you could see the scallops of her slip under it and a little blue checkered skirt that had the look of a nice clean dish towel wrapped over the points of her sharp little hip bones. Her three-inch-wide black patent-leather belt was pulled in tight at the waist. She'd ratted her bob and sprayed it down so that it looked like a little spaceship had landed on top of her head.

Cake orders had been coming in hot and heavy all week since Mama put out the word that the first pickup would be Saturday. Over the past two nights she'd been up to all hours rattling around in the kitchen. Sunday pickups were nothing special with everyone in a hurry to get to church, but a Saturday pickup was something of an event. A flock of what Mama called her Cake Ladies came clucking in like pigeons. Usually they roosted awhile, and Mama had a big pot of coffee ready. They stood jammed up against one another in our tiny kitchen, holding their coffee cups and saucers high so as not to spill. They leaned over their cups into one another's faces and said things in half whispers.

This Saturday the cakes were lined up on the kitchen table. They rested on neatly cut pieces of cardboard with the edges of doilies peeking out from underneath like the wings of angels. The wholes on one side and the still breathing halves with their waxed-paper bandages on the other. From my bed, I could look across our little living room and see their iced tops hovering like puffy white clouds over the kitchen table.

In the kitchen Mama handed me a glass of orange juice and a piece of buttered toast and commanded me to eat over the sink. She didn't want crumbs on her nice clean floor, which she'd mopped at three o'clock that morning. In the past it had been my job to open the door when I saw a lady coming up the path of stones Mama had put down when Miss Kay Linda complained that the grass was getting tromped on. So I took my toast out on the front-porch stoop.

Directly I spotted the first lady questing up the path, and soon they all arrived and were carrying on in Mama's kitchen like she was hosting a family reunion. How much they had missed her! They were ever so happy that she was back in her rightful place as Millwood's cake lady. Nobody's cakes could get within a country mile of hers. Don't they look pretty all lined up like that? Martha, next week I think I'll have a lemon. It looks so nice and cool. This one's mother's gallbladder getting taken out or that one's baby's cough has turned into scarlet fever or now the outside agitators are trying to stir things up over in Clinton, which was only upsetting the colored, who desire only to be with their own kind just like we do. We've been blessed with good colored people in Millwood. Lord, down in Shake Rag, the *last* thing anybody wants is trouble.

When I heard them start on the colored, I opened the screen door and sidled on in, just in time to hear my mother say the word *Negroes*. She murmured it so lightly that at first I wasn't sure what she had said. She was leaning up against the kitchen sink, one hand on the long row of ridges. The first time she said the word it sounded like a little breeze sashaying through the two rooms. It wasn't "Negroes" really that she said, but "Nig-ras," with a kind of rasp to it. Once she'd said it, it did some business in the house, blowing out little chats here and there like candles on a cake. The ladies' eyes folded over their cups as if to keep the coffee warm. They seemed to be holding in one big breath. Then Mama said it again, this time spreading it thicker. "*Negroes*. What I mean is, they appreciate being called *Negroes*."

Then a skitter of ladies snatching their cakes and putting their money on the coffee table. I held the door as they bustled out, their mouths pursed. Out at the curb they clustered, hissing and quacking. Only my mother's friend Navis stayed behind. Navis typed the town's tax roll and knew what everybody in Millwood was worth. But in every other way she kept herself apart. She was shy with the other ladies. An oddball. She told Mama she hated to see the summer property tax season come around because her left shoulder ached unmercifully from throwing the oversized carriage on the manual typewriter down at city hall. In the summer she spent most of her spare time curled up on her Duncan Phyfe couch with a heating pad, her venetian blinds always tilted to the ceiling because of the glare on her eyes, which burned from all those little numbers. With no husband and children, which she said would have been horribly boring, she was different from Mama's other cake ladies. Mama had always said she liked Navis because she said anything that came into her head. They wrote letters back and forth the year we were away. Before we'd left Millwood, Navis had had a standing order for half a cake a week, just anything left over, darling, she'd say. After Saturday pickups she outstayed the other ladies and had a second cup of coffee with Mama. They would take their coffee out on the front stoop and sit shoulder to shoulder with the canopy of clematis hanging over them and bees and wasps buzzing all around.

Navis folded her arms over her chest as the ladies scuttled down the stone path with their cakes. She stood there looking out until they'd all driven off. Then she ran her hand through her short red hair. "What a bunch of nincompoops!" she said. She came up behind my mother, who was now standing with her back to us at the sink, put her arms around Mama's little waist, and pressed her head up against Mama's shoulder blades. "Martha girl, don't think twice about it. They haven't got a brain in their heads, not a one of them, and they'll be right back on your doorstep next week. They wouldn't miss coming over here for anything in the world. They'd miss the gossip, much less the cake! What else do they have in their miserable little lives in this hellhole?"

Mama laughed a little. The two of them stood there for a minute. Then my mother's body drooped and she leaned back and Navis held her weight. After awhile Navis patted her shoulder, pushed her forward a little, gathered a half devil's food off the kitchen table, and slipped out the front door.

After Navis left, Mama went into the living room and collected a handful of dollar bills and some change from the coffee table. A piece of her blouse had come out of her belt. She undid her belt by pulling it with one hand and then releasing it. She threw it on the couch. Mama loved that belt. It showed off her little waist, and she pulled it so tight that the hole had become a slit. Then she tossed the dollars and some coins on the couch. Some fell on the floor. She didn't pick them up but turned around and looked down at me. She had a fan blowing across the floor, first one side and then the other, the way she always did on pickup morning, so the dollars began to flutter here and there. I snatched them up.

She caught my arm and made me stop, so I just stood there until she said what she was so bound and determined to say. "Florence, listen to me, *we* say 'Negroes' in this house. I talked to Zenie *and* Uldine *and* Gertrude about this, and that's what they all said they like to be called. Negroes. Never 'colored.'" She grabbed at my head to make me look up at her. "Do you hear me, young lady?"

"Yes ma'am." I met her stare and we both froze solid for a minute. A heaviness landslid over me and I felt buried under it. Then some meanness rose up in me. From whence it came or why I do not know, but there it was, as full of itself as a peacock. "You going to make Daddy say it too?" I asked in a quiet little voice. I looked down at a knothole in the floor when I said it. I was expecting her to say in return don't sass me young lady, go get in your room. Which would have been fine with me. I was getting more and more nervous about making up the fourth grade. Mimi had given me a list of states and capitals and state birds and trees. I had plans to settle in and learn them all that very day.

What my mother did instead of fussing was slap me right across the face. Not too hard, but hard enough to make me miss a breath. Hard enough to make my eyes tear up, which made me hate her guts even more.

Then she said what I thought she'd say, but when she said it, her face looked like somebody had snuck up behind her and pinched her. "Don't sass me, Florence! Go get in your room. Right now."

I could see she'd added the slap into the deal because I'd added something else into my badness. An extra ingredient, like the broken pecans Mama mixed in with her caramel icing at Christmas. Except that they were good. What I'd added was gravel. A mouthful of it.

I wanted to say I was sorry, but something in my mother's eyes stopped me. She was trembling a little and looking down at me with both fear and surprise. I could see my reflection in her eyes, but it wasn't the same girl I saw in my father's eyes, the one with long blond hair that flowed like a river of gold. It wasn't a girl at all. It was the serpent crawled out from under the rock. The old poison come home.

On baking nights in the days to come, Mama would plop her poison bottle out on the counter like another one of her ingredients. As she mixed and sifted and clattered her way through the night, she'd commence to singing. She had a sleepy voice, or maybe I was just sleepy while I listened to it. Sometimes she turned on the radio and sang along. Other times she just spooned and crooned her own way through the soft May nights. Her favorite song was "The Wayward Wind," and she'd sing snatches of it over and over, how old Wayward was a restless wind that yearned to wander and how he'd left her alone with a broken heart. When she sang it, she belted out the "Now I'm alone with a broken heart" and then hum a few more bars before starting all over again. Every time she sang it, it sounded a little different and a little sadder. It brought tears to my eyes, but it made me happy too because when she sang it, I could tell she was shooing her sadness out of the house and into the night.

Not long after we returned to Millwood, Daddy started coming into my room and lying down with me while my mother baked. When he opened my door and stood a minute getting his eyes adjusted to the dark, he smelled like man sweat and cigarette smoke and sweet oil. The oil was in a hair balm he bought every other week from a door-to-door man named Mr. Fred Holcomb. It came in a clear jar with a piece of paper taped to it that said "Sweet Hair Oil." When Mr. Holcomb showed up in the early morning every other Saturday as May got under way, Mama kept him out on the front stoop because he couldn't be trusted around her cakes, which were lined up on the table and ready for pickup. If she didn't offer him a piece of something and she turned her back or went into the bedroom for some change, she'd return to find a poke here, a corner sideswiped there. The first week he came she didn't notice a finger hole in the side of the angel icing on a devil's food, and Mrs. Bell Leake called to ask what on earth had happened to her cake, it looked like somebody had poked it with a cigar.

I confess I didn't like the smell of that hair oil. Of course I didn't tell my father that. It was a sweet smell but not like Mama's burnt-sugar lightness from the baking, which came and went like a breeze when she moved. Or the sour bite of the cloves she chewed to cover over her poison breath. Mama had aromas that fluttered by your nose every now and then like pretty yellow butterflies. Daddy's hair oil smell reminded me of a swamp that was deep and muddy and got into everything. What I know now is that seeing and even hearing can confound you. Not smell. Smell is true. A body has to smell right. Of course, that was not my father's own true smell, but he took it as his own and the hair oil seemed to seep into his pores so that when he sweated, it came on stronger than ever.

Groping his way in the dark, Daddy would come sit on the side of my bed and take off his shoes and socks. Because of his short leg and turned-in foot, Daddy had to wear his shoes everywhere all the time. His brick shoe clumped when he walked and its weight made him tired. When he got his shoes off, he'd groan and stretch out next to me in the space I had left for him. Then he turned on his side and put one hand flat on my stomach right over my belly button. His hand was heavy yet light. Cool to my bare skin at first, then warming, then like fire. I was strung tight like him, he said, so I needed something to calm me down, like you'd put a gentle hand on a horse and say now whoa up. Just a pressure to pin me to earth so I wouldn't fly into pieces. That hand and my hidden parts all mashed up underneath. Liver, gut, bladder washed in the blood. It was like Daddy was the preacher and I was the offering and praise God from whom all blessings flow.

I would lie quiet under his hand for a long while, but then I would start to toss and turn.

"Sister," he'd say, "settle down now." I don't know why Daddy called me Sister. I was nobody's sister, nor would I ever be, since Mama had barely made it out alive from having me on Lou Ellen Chauncey's living-room floor.

This was before Mama came into her true calling of the cake business, and she was still the one and only Welcome Wagon lady for Millwood. Her water broke right there on Mrs. Chauncey's door stoop one dusty hot September afternoon, after she'd knocked on the door and Mrs. C had opened it wide. What a welcome! It was a precipitous birth, at least that's what the doctor called it. I was coming on strong when he and the ambulance men came bursting in the door, so they let me keep on, seeing as how I was so bound and determined to be born that I was tearing up my poor mother stretched out on Mrs. C's Oriental rug cursing my father—who was at that very moment getting fired for being surly to customers at Holcomb's Hardware—for having planted me with his Big You Know What. She rued all the stories she had read about girls and princes. She rued the night she'd seen him across the dance floor at the fall mixer. She rued that lock of hair that had fallen over his left eye and made her yearn to smooth it back. She rued the unaccountable way her feet took her across the room to him and the way her heart shifted in her chest when she saw his poor ruined foot. So this was why he wasn't dancing! She rued the way she'd followed my daddy right out the front door of the Millwood High School auditorium and into the sound of the cicadas. Now she rued it all, every last bit of it, right down to her toenails, which was the only part of her that wasn't hurting.

I came out a raggedy mess, trailing blood and slime. The doctor cut the cord and wrapped me tight in a clean red-and-white-checked dish towel so that I looked like a lively loaf of bread. He plopped me down on the sofa, which Mrs. Chauncey later told people she thought was a bit much, her nice living-room rug long gone from my mother's hemorrhaging and the sofa being almost brand-new. What kind of man was Winburn Forrest to let his wife work in that condition, anyway?

It was Mama who named me Florence. She'd come upon pictures of the city in *Look* magazine at the doctor's office and thought it was the most beautiful place she'd ever seen. All that art. Mama's name was Martha, and she believed in serious names. No Susies or Kathys or Judys or Peggy Sues. "You want a name that's worth all this trouble," she would say to me. She'd give her batter a thumping stir. "And don't let anybody call you Flo."

This was not the story my father told when he started coming into my room that May. Lying on his side, he peered at me through the shadows. I turned my head toward him because I loved to home in on his eyes. When the moon was bright, I could see my own face swimming in their soft darkness. I thought I looked beautiful, like a girl in a dream. The stories he told me were about brave Christian men who, yes siree bobtail, fought to the death like true soldiers for little girls like me and beautiful and pure women like my mother. In the early days they rode

horses. White horses. He would get excited in the telling and
start rubbing my belly hard. Round and round, like he was shaping a pot. One way for a while. Then the other way. Sometimes
he would flop over on his back and sing "Onward Christian Soldiers marching as to war, with the cross of Jesus going on before,"
sweet and low, like a lullaby.

Daddy's stories faded into the warning *no no no no* of the trains
that clattered through Millwood all night long, leaving only the
tracks of dreams. Valiant knights stamping out evil monsters in the
kingdom, saving the ladies in distress, riding off with them draped
like drooping Easter lilies across the fronts of their white steeds, the
ladies' long blond curls trawling the dust. My hair was short and no
color at all, but it was a different girl I saw in Daddy's melting eyes,
a girl in all white with that long blond hair flowing along behind
like a river of gold. Pure and innocent and beautiful beyond belief.
Sometimes, when I dreamed, Daddy's stories would get mixed together with my old storybook favorite, the gentleman rabbit Uncle
Wiggily, who limped along with his satchel and crutch seeking his
fortune, and who was always getting into scraps and having to be
rescued from getting eaten up by savage beasts and giants. They all
wanted a bite of him, old and tough as he was, but story after story,
book after book, he always got away in the nick of time. You have
to wonder how lucky one rabbit can be.

So I didn't really hear my father's stories so much as they
washed over me as if they were the sea and I was a lonesome
stretch of sandbar. I waited for them and they rescued me like
the brave men on the white horses. And when they came, they
flooded my heart and changed me into something unrecognizable and strange.

Finally, in the early morning hours when the oven had cooled
down, Mama would sift into my room to turn off my fan. She
would wake me up saying, "Win, come on to bed," and Daddy
would rise up like a dark mountain and stumble after her.

If my father could stumble through the long night and find his way back into this story, he'd say I wasn't telling it right. All this business about his box and Mama's icings and Mrs. Chauncey's ruined rug. He would say tell about the brave men of olden times, how they rode through the night on white horses, like heat lightning shooting across the sky. How they saved the precious ones from darkness. He'd say this story of mine has too much clutter.

But some stories are whiskery old men. You walk past them fast, but they snatch at you with their fingers of bone and make you stay. They hold you up to their faces and scratch you. But after going through all that, you still don't know them. You don't know the little boy who had one leg that was shorter than the other and a foot that turned in. The one who loved the smell of the sea in the old oyster shells on his mother's dresser. The one who wanted to grow figs.

That one, that dark-eyed boy, is the slippery fish. What's left is nothing but scum on the pond.

It's easier to look deep into what you know will stay put. What doesn't wander in and out and cry for mercy. The details. Our town of Millwood, a place on a map of the world as it was in 1963, stays calm in my mind in spite of the terrible thing that happened that summer.

It was called Millwood on account of there being a big cotton mill, which was the town's largest employer, followed by two plants that were always in danger of exploding and in third place a fish hatchery run by the government. The *Feds*, Daddy would say, and his lip would curl. The plants, the Millwood Fertilizer factory and the smaller sulphuric acid plant, roosted on the north-south railroad line like two buzzards eating roadkill. Their stacks pumped out twin clouds of black soot day and night, seven days a week.

A sign on the outskirts of town read: "Welcome to Millwood:

Transportation Hub of the South," and though that was an over-statement, it was true that the only reason Millwood had for ex-isting in the first place, with its bustle of factory and mill workers and county courthouse lawyers in their straw hats, was the fact that the Mobile & Ohio and the Frisco Railway lines crossed in a big X just west of downtown in the exact spot where Highways 78 and 45 crossed. We called the X Crosstown. There were pull-outs and railcar exchanges there, plus the Curb Market, where farmers brought in cantaloupe and watermelon and butter beans in summer and greens and turnips in the fall and spring. As May progressed and the produce began to come in, Mama took me nosing through the Curb Market for berries to garnish the angel icing on her devil's food cakes. "Hold up the baskets and look at the bottom for drips and stains," she'd command, "and watch out for trains, don't get near the track."

The trains went through Crosstown slow, but they made me jump and start when they'd lurch and bang together without warning, coupling and uncoupling like testy old lovers. The Ne-groes bought their tickets from the Colored Only window outside the Crosstown depot and stood out front to wait. When it rained, they huddled under the dripping eaves, being careful not to block the door.

The trains came through the other crossings all over town like noisy threads through a garment. You couldn't get them out of your head because once you did, here they'd come again. Mid-night, one thirty, three, four thirty. In the deep early-morning dark, they howled and blew and cried. When you first heard them, they seemed to call you to them. They wanted you because they were oh so lonesome, lonesome. But as they got closer and moved through the crossings dotted all over town they had to warn you against their loneliness, and then they screamed out no, no, no, no, their big cyclops eyes glowing, hunting you down.

If you grew up as I did listening to trains every single night, you could begin to hear the turning point where a train moves from its coming to its going. It is a slipping moment. The awful tormented thing that is coming does not come. In its place is something ordinary, just another clattery train to make you toss and turn in the heat of a summer night.

The people who worked at the mill and the fertilizer factory lived in Milltown, which was downwind from the factory just over the railroad tracks in Millwood. Milltown was actually part of Millwood, but it looked like a different place altogether. Up and down the streets you could see nothing but rented duplexes with peeling paint and a coat of gray powder rising from the red clay dirt like huge misshapen toadstools. The children who lived in them were so white they looked like puffs of cotton themselves, hanging on porch railings as if they had been dropped from a giant picker in the sky. No dusty crape myrtle blooming or pretty wisteria bells, just worn-out honeysuckle and weeds. The Health Department squatted in the dead center of Milltown, a monstrous brown toad of a building that made me want to whimper just looking at it when Mama would take me in for my free boosters and checkups.

Nobody in Milltown, where the poor white mill workers lived, ordered Mama's cakes. Neither did anybody in Shake Rag on the south side of the color line, which ran straight down Goodlett Street by the cemetery. White people called it Shake Rag. I never heard anyone who actually lived there call it that. Zenie, for example, would never in a million years say, "See you later. I'm going back to Shake Rag now." Instead she'd give Mimi's kitchen table a final swipe, tuck in the loose ends of her bun, and say, "All right. I wore out sure enough. Going home now. Done enough for one day's work. Way more than enough." When Eva Greene, who was Zenie's niece, came to live with Zenie and Ray that summer, she tossed her flipped hair and laughed out loud when she first heard somebody say Shake Rag. "Who's shaking that rag, I'd like to know," she said. "Only rags I've laid eyes on around here are dust rags. Nobody around here's *wearing* rags."

People lived in all sorts of places in what was called Shake Rag, ranging from two-story houses with rusted screens rolled up at the windows like curled eyelashes to a wisteria-wrapped school bus on a well-kept lot across the street from Zenie and Ray's. Mama told me four generations of folks lived in the old bus, no telling how many of each. They had to keep the windows pushed up in the heat and sometimes I saw a girl hanging out one window and playing one potato two potato three potato four with another girl hanging out the next one. An old man in the family kept bees in two white boxes behind the bus. There was a sign written on a board propped up against the side of the bus that said HONY," which Eva, who was studying to be a school-teacher and said there was never any excuse for misspelling with dictionaries in the world, snuck over to one night and put an E in the middle of.

Whatever kinds of houses they lived in, the ladies in Shake Rag had their zinnias and petunias planted out front and their to-mato and cucumber vines staked out in the back or the side alley if there wasn't a back. Down in Milltown the poor white people gathered up their sickly children and moved on. Who knows where. You hope for better days and better places, though places are sometimes not so easy to leave. Shake Rag people planted themselves on their front porches, babies blooming like dark red roses from the laps of great-grandmothers, who held them with swollen fingers in a death grip.

Mama took cakes up to Shake Rag all right, but they were of-fered in times of trouble, when Uldine Harris's grandson Earl Two jumped the M & O for Memphis after he sassed Mr. Wilkins in the drugstore and Mr. Wilkins cocked his head back and said, "Two, I know who you are and I know where you live." That was a caramel cake, icing still warm like fudge. When what happened to Zenie's niece Eva happened. That was a lemon, which Mama knew from Zenie to be Eva's favorite, but which Eva refused to touch.

That spring I returned home not just to our little white house behind the house but also to Zenie and Ray's in Shake Rag. Zenie had gotten stuck with me several years back when Mama became Millwood's Welcome Wagon lady, having not yet discovered her talent for cakes. Back then I was little; somebody had to keep me. Zenie had kept my mother while Mimi taught social studies at the high school. Why not me?

"I want Florence to love you like I do. I want her to *know* you. Really *know* you, the way I do." That was the way Mama put it to Zenie. They were smoking together in Mimi's kitchen, which was something they did when my grandmother wasn't around. Mama had gone in and pulled out her Winstons. Zenie had taken one and lit it off the stove and sat down in her white ladder-back chair. She left the eye on for Mama so she lit hers at the flame too, holding back her bangs. Then Mama pushed the kitchen swing door closed, right in my face.

I stood up next to the crack in the door and tried to keep up with the conversation. What I didn't hear was what Zenie said back to Mama's wanting me to know her. It was a lot softer and it had a little snort for a period.

Then Mama was talking again in a fast and happy little rush. "I don't think she'll be much trouble."

Zenie cleared her throat and said loud enough for me to hear, "They all trouble."

"Zenie, I don't want to make you do this if you don't want to. You know I'll pay you fair." Mama whispered this last sentence like it was a shameful secret.

The back of Zenie's ladder chair hit the wall. Once and then twice. The chair legs were worn down from years of her tilting. "We try it out. See how much trouble she get into. These legs don't go running after nothing no more." Zenie was over six feet and heavy. She had bad veins that looked like dark purple irises blooming up and down her legs, which she said felt like two tree trunks under her. Her legs were prone to sprout blisters and sores that ran and made scars the size of nickels. Her legs pained her all the time but especially when it was hot.

Now Mama's voice was a happy little brook bubbling along. "She's a good girl, Zenie. You won't have to be chasing after her. She's almost six now. Soon it will just be after school."

"Yes'm."

"Zenie. *Please* don't yes ma'am and no ma'am me. You know I don't want you to call me ma'am. I feel like I'm half yours."

The chair hit the wall once, but nothing from Zenie. Then Mama opened the door. She jumped back when she saw me behind it. "You listening in again, Miss Nosy?" she asked.

"No'm," I said, and she looked at me hard, narrowing her eyes.

Five years later, I still somehow ended up at Zenie's house in the late afternoons. It seems odd, I know, that a half-grown girl wouldn't be out running around town with the other children. The truth is, ever since we'd been back, people looked at me funny. I knew many of the children who were traipsing off to school so prim and proper, and for a short while I made it a point to hang around up at the sidewalk when they walked by on their way to and from school. I saw Helen Cooley, who used to play gypsies with me in the vacant lot down the street. I saw Elizabeth Lumpkin, who I'd spent the night with once and we'd made brownies from a mix. But their eyes slid off me, as if I were the ghost of a flesh-and-blood girl they had once known, the one who had left Millwood with her father and mother and had never been seen since. I knew it had something to do with Daddy, and maybe Mama too, after the colored-versus-Negro episode, but it wasn't anything I could pin down.

As I grew desperate, I even tried to catch the eye of that weasel May, who I wouldn't have given the time of day to a year before. She and Little Dan would hang around with their spoons at the ready on Sunday afternoons when Miss Kay Linda and Big Dan went down for their nap. Mama would bring out their half cake and set it on our front stoop without even looking in their direction. They would grab it and stand in the yard like pigs at the trough, gobble up their cake, and put the crumb-covered paper plate right back on our stoop. I snatched it up and put it in the garbage can. I knew that having to clean up after them would only make my mother more furious. When May finished her cake, I asked her nice polite questions like when school was going to be out or would she like to walk to the drugstore with me. But the only thing she ever said back to me was, "My mama says there must be something wrong with you. You'd be in school if you was right in the head," at which point I kicked her in the knee and that was the end of that.

Even my mother noticed my unpopularity and called some of her cake ladies to get their daughters over to play, but their girls were always busy with their tap-dancing or swimming lessons or what have you. Since Mama herself was busy bargain shopping with a handful of coupons for her cake ingredients and doing housework during the day to clear her nights for baking and poison drinking, I started hanging around in the mornings with Zenie, helping her with the chores up at my grandparents' while Mimi taught school and Grandpops went to his law office. Then in the afternoons, since I didn't have anything better to do, I followed Zenie on her dusty trek home like an overgrown stray pup.

When we got back to her and Ray's house in the afternoons, which were heating up now that May was progressing, Zenie would start up her window fan and then go into the kitchen and turn on the flame under the beat-up aluminum coffeepot. The kitchen would fill up with the smell of burnt coffee that had been sitting since morning. She pulled out a cup she kept over by the stove and poured it half full of the smoking black sludge. Then she got a pitcher of milk from the top shelf of the refrigerator, scalded it in a little pot until a film formed on the top, and poured it in, hot and steaming. While her coffee was cooling down, she dumped in sugar straight from the sugar bowl in the shape of a little house that sat on the table, filling her cup right to the edge. Then she seined her bag for pieces of yesterday's newspaper from Mimi and Grandpops'.

She spread out the newspaper on the table, groaned as she took a seat, and leaned over the print, sipping from her cup as she read. She'd talk back to the paper. "You *dog!*" she'd tell it, or "Oh, baby!" Sometimes she looked shocked. Once she burst out crying and shoved me away hard when I sidled up to see what was wrong. "Leave me alone, white folks," she said, and I could tell she'd read something that made her hate my guts. It's true that the pictures in the paper were enough to make a black person hate every white person on the planet. Dogs and hoses and billy clubs and gas. Snarling white men in uniforms dragging people with soaked clothes and bloodied faces into paddy wagons. Tearing their clothes half off. White faces so twisted they looked fiendish. I didn't blame Zenie for hating the sight of me.

When she was liking me all right, though, Zenie told me Zenobia the Queen of Palmyra stories that her mother, Miss Josephine called Aunt Josie by most white folks, used to tell to her when she was a girl. Zenie was Miss Josephine's firstborn, and Miss J took one look at her and said *Zenobia* right off the bat. She rolled the name off her tongue like silk, and nobody could talk her out of it. Miss Josephine worked for Miss Phyllis Milam until she, Miss J, got too old to maid. Miss Milam taught classics and she had books all over the place. So she and Miss J would get to reading about the heroes and ladies and lords and warriors and queens and such. Which is how Miss Josephine got attached to Zenobia, who was this Arab lady who rode at the head of her men into battle with her hair flying and one bosom bouncing out so they'd know who their leader was. Not to speak of the fact that Queen Zenobia told everybody her great auntie on her mother's side was Cleopatra and her great-grandmother on the other side was none other than the Queen of Sheba! When Zenobia wasn't fighting wars, she was riding around hunting lions and such. They say that she was the man in the family and she didn't lie down with her husband unless she got to wanting herself a little child. When she was captured and made to parade herself like a slave in the streets of Rome, those Romans put her in chains of solid gold!

Zenie liked her mother's stories about the Queen of Palmyra, and she liked to make up her own. You never knew how Zenie's Queen of Palmyra stories were going to end up. You only knew that, like Uncle Wiggily, the Queen was going to come out on top. One afternoon soon after I'd gotten back in town, my tonsils were acting up, and Zenie had me sitting on the chair beside her at her kitchen table. She'd chopped some ice for me to put down my throat. One sliver at a time on a cold spoon. My glands were hot rocks, and it hurt to open wide. I had a fever and it made everything seem far away. Zenie had her coffee cup. She was sipping hot, I was sipping cold. When she told the latest version of the Queen story, it was better than *Moses and the Ten Commandments* and *Ben Hur* all rolled into one.

So Zenobia the Queen of Palmyra is sitting right nicely up on her throne, and a poor captured lady slave comes into the palace and throws herself down in front of the throne and says, Your

Gracious Highness, the man he working me in the field from first light till dark and then he wearying me all night. When I get too worn out to work, he bring out the leather. Queen Zenobia sucks her teeth and say, can you cook, miss lady? And the lady answers, why yes ma'am I can. I'm a good cook and I can bake too. So the Queen smiles and says, how about whipping me up a peach cobbler? Yes ma'am, the slave says. She allows as to how she can bake the best cobbler the Queen had ever ate bar none, and she heads right on into the big kitchen and sends a boy out to pick some peaches. She kicks all the other cooks out of the kitchen and shuts the door tight. Two hours transpire and no lady slave and no cobbler. Folks hankering round the kitchen door and wondering why it's taking such a spell to throw together one little peach cobbler. Who this lady slave think she is to keep the Queen waiting and waiting? Now Queen Zenobia starts to get peckish, and when she gets peckish, she gets aggravated.

Then the kitchen doors open wide and out comes miss lady slave with the best-looking cobbler you ever did see. A gold color with peach juice just oozing out the top and sides. Queen Zenobia's itching to dig right in, but the lady slave says to her, wait up, ma'am. A lot of nerve, saying that to a queen. Then lo and behold she brings forth a dozen more cobblers, one right after the next, enough for everybody, and the Queen looks down from her throne at the lady like she's been sent from heaven and says you was thinking about everybody for your cobblers. You're a true teacher because you teach me to think about everybody in my kingdom. I want you for my helper, not my cook, except on Sundays when you can make us all cobblers! So the smart-as-a-whip Queen ruled her kingdom for many long years with the help of the lady slave. And the lady slave got her free papers and lived like a queen herself. The end.

Zenie set down her coffee cup. "You cold enough in the throat?"

I nodded. I was iced down to my toes.

We'd started on a game of gin rummy when someone knocked hard on the front door. I was about to win with three kings and a ten and some other card I don't remember. All I needed was another ten or another of the other card. This game was the most interesting thing that had happened to me all day, and I was on pins and needles when the knock came. I thought it might be my mother come to get me, but Zenie groaned and said, "Oh Lord, it's the policy man. You. Get the door."

I ran to open the door. The man on Zenie's stoop wasn't my father but it could have been. He had the same way about him that Daddy had when he'd started selling burial insurance a few weeks before, a kind of white-man strut that says you owe me. He was younger than my father and had a crew cut and a way of jutting out his chin when he talked, like a cock getting ready to crow. He was surprised to see me but not too surprised. He had seen stranger things.

He stuck his head in the door. "Hey there little lady, how you doing?" Then he changed his voice to a less friendly tone. "Zenie watching you? Where she at?"

Zenie didn't get up from the kitchen table. "She sitting right here in front of you, but she ain't got what you want."

The man sighed. He was halfway in the door by now. "When you want me to come on back by here?"

"Payday. Saturday."

"You getting behind on your payments, Zenie. You already shorted me one."

Zenie glared him down. "You can't get blood out of a turnip. Don't you go letting in the flies."

"Well, you better be figuring out how to get seventy-five cents a week to me, or you and Ray ain't going to be covered. Then you'll really have yourself some flies to deal with at a later date. I'm giving you a good deal for two as it is."

Even I knew that was a bald-faced lie, my father having just taken up the burial insurance trade. Zenie made a noise in her throat and picked up a doily in the middle of the table, turned it over, and put it back down. "Come on back Saturday afternoon, and I'll catch myself up."

The man breathed an exasperated sigh. His breath smelled bitter, like stale coffee. "All right, then, I'll be back, and I'll be expecting you to pay yourself up to date." He backed out the door, glaring at Zenie as he went.

When he was gone, Zenie gave a snort. "Bloodsuckers." She took a deep breath like she was getting ready to launch into a long list of bad names for the policy man, but looked at me and stopped short, for which I was grateful. I was mightily relieved that, shortly after we returned to Millwood, Daddy had found his niche in burial insurance after being in and out of this thing and that for so long. First the hardware store, next the drugstore delivery, then Sears & Roebuck's warehouse, after that used cars.

In those early days Daddy and Mama set out every day in a green Plymouth with a sagging burnt-out muffler. You could hear us coming a mile away. In the morning she packed him a bologna sandwich and dropped him off at his latest job. She dropped me by Mimi and Grandpops' or Zenie's, and then headed for the trailer on the outskirts of town where the Chamber of Commerce had its office. She'd put together her Welcome Wagon baskets and pick up her lists of newcomers to visit. Late afternoons she got me from Zenie's, then plucked Daddy from this or that street corner, his shirttail loose on one side or the other and his bow tie hanging on the lip of his collar like a tired moth. Watching for us on the corner (sometimes she was late) he had a puzzled look on his face, like some question had frozen there with no hope of an answer. When he worked on the car lot, my mother's eyebrows would be raised in expectation and a little smile would play on her lips. Did he sell a car, any car, even an old wreck? By then, she'd started up her cake business on the side, so at night she was up to all hours baking and ironing his shirts and putting a good crease in his khakis. She lost flesh, and the bones in her body looked like sticks that had floated to the surface of her skin.

He hasn't found his calling yet, Mama would tell Mimi and Grandpops. One day she dropped me off on her way to work and was half out the door before Grandpops said real quiet to her back, "How's Win doing down at the drugstore?" Up to a few days before, when he'd gotten let go for sassing old blind Miss Northcross (my mother and father never said *fired*; he either quit or got let go), Daddy's latest job had been delivery man for J & T Pharmacy.

Another minute and Mama would have escaped. She stood framed in the door, one nice polished high-heel shoe inside the house and the other out on the front stoop. The three of us—Mimi, Grandpops, and me—stood in the middle of the big velvet living room, waiting. I knew this conversation wasn't going anywhere good. Daddy was back home oiling his box. Mama had told me to stay out of his way. In the doorway, Mama seemed about to turn around to face Grandpops, but then she said, to the great outdoors, "It didn't work out. Seems like some men just can't work for somebody else. They got to find their own way. Free spirits." She took another step out the door.

Grandpops eyed the living room ceiling through his thick specs. "Free spirits. They any relation to free *loaders*?"

My mother stopped again in her tracks. Lately she'd taken on the shape of a drooping vine, but now the set of her back made it look as if a hard little tree had sprung up in the open door. She stayed there a minute more. Then she just walked on out the door and closed it with a click. Not a word out of her. She just went on.

When I helped my mother unpack boxes from our year on the

lam, I came across an old photo of me and her from back in her
Welcome Wagon days. Mama has the look of someone drifting
in the ocean waiting for a rescue. She has her arm around me,
but she's looking somewhere off in the distance, to my left, over
the long dark row of pecan trees in Mimi's backyard. The ones
that caterpillar worms build their webby nests in every summer,
requiring Ray to light torches with gasoline and get up on a high
wobbly ladder to burn them out. The webs curl up and vanish in
clouds of smoke. The busy worms sizzle and crackle like chitlins
in the pan.

But, now at long last, glory and hallelujah, Daddy had found
his true calling. A few days after we got back to Millwood that
spring, he went out to his first meeting since we'd returned and
met a man who sold burial insurance door to door in Shake Rag
and Milltown. This man was old and tired. He said he'd tell the
folks at Mississippi Assurance about Daddy. A big packet would
come in the mail and Daddy would get the old man's customers
and his route. No Boss Man looking over his shoulder; *he* is the
boss. What could be better?

Now that Daddy had a job he could live with, he was one of
three policy men in Millwood and out in the county too. Mississippi Assurance had burial insurance for poor folks so they
wouldn't get caught short. "Every*body's* got a *body*," he'd say to
folks in Shake Rag, and then flash his pearlies at them. They'd be
standing in their front doors, saying nice as spice, "Yes *sir*, that's
the Good Lord's truth." Then he'd say, "Now you don't want to
end up in a cardboard box, or worse, do you, Auntie?" and they'd
say back, like they were in the choir at church, "No, *sir*, don't put
us in no box!" And then he'd get them to sign the papers and
that'll be fifty cents a week from now on, seventy-five for couples,
twenty-five for each child. Mississippi Assurance had Shake Rag
and Milltown locked up. Daddy told people not to worry. He'd

take care of them when the time came, as it surely would. Some days, when he'd had a good day, we'd be driving home and he'd throw back his head, his curls loosening up from their heaviness, and belt out, "Blessed Assuuuuurance, Jesus is Mine. Oh what a foooooooretaste of Glory Divine. Wealth of Salvation, Purchase of Love. Wrapped in his Spirit, Washed in His Blooooood."

When the policy man left, Zenie threw her cards into the slush pile. "You win," she pronounced, and struggled to get up from the table.

"Wait!" I protested. "We didn't finish the game."

"Could tell you had it by the look on your face. Look like the cat that ate the canary. I ain't got time for fooling. Got to get some sewing done so I can pay that bloodsucker. Get on in the bathroom and wash up. Then go on out front and wait for your Mama. Tell her I need a raise."

4

To go into Zenie's bathroom I had to push aside a long curtain hanging ceiling to floor across where a door should have been. The bedrooms in her house had curtains for doors too. The curtains were light and airy, with green leaves all aflutter, as if they were floating down from invisible trees. Zenie and Ray's house was a Jim Walter Home. Her grandfather, Miss Josephine's father, had owned the lot but the house on it was falling in, so, after her grandfather died, Zenie and Ray moved into the two good rooms in the old down-fallen house and started their project of saving money for a Jim Walter Home. Zenie stopped taking her midday dinner at the kitchen table after Mimi and Grandpops were done and the table was cleared. Instead she carried her dinner and part of Mimi and Grandpops' supper home in a pie pan she brought back clean every morning; she and Ray made their night meal off of them. She put most of her money from working at Mimi and Grandpops' and taking in sewing into a savings account at the Millwood Bank and Trust. Grandpops was on the board of trustees of the bank, so he took her down and told them to set it up for her and they gave her a little navy blue book so she could bring it in every time she put her money in. She spent time looking at the book, working and reworking the figures until the edges got to looking like an old Bible.

It had all started when Zenie saw an advertisement for Jim Walter Homes in an old *Ladies' Home Journal* of Mimi's. She tore the page out, folded it up, and put in her purse. She took it out and looked at it again and again until the creases started to tear. PICTURE YOURSELF IN A LOVELY JIM WALTER HOME! ONLY PENNIES A DAY!

She still had the faded ad, which featured a picture of a pretty little family with a mother and father and three children all decked out like it was Easter Sunday. The girls had on shiny patent-leather shoes. They were standing in the front yard of a spick-and-span Jim Walter Home with trees and flowers and a white fence. They were the happiest family on the face of the earth to have such a Lovely Home, one of four floor plans available. When I was younger, it made me sick just to look at those white folks, which was what I'd taken to calling people of my color who had things I didn't have, such as a nice house they'd bought for themselves and pretty clothes. Back then, before Daddy found his calling as a policy man, even before we'd moved to our place behind Big Dan and Miss Kay Linda's, we were on the other side of town in a crummy duplex one street over from Milltown. I walked on my heels in my Sunday shoes because they pinched my toes.

Zenie said she couldn't care less what color the folks in the picture were. She thought the Jim Walter houses were the be-all end-all. I had to admit they did look pretty with their green sides and window boxes with red geraniums lapping over. What she liked most about them, she told me, is that they looked new. "Everything top to bottom brand spanking *new*," she'd say, and the pennies in her eyes would glow.

She and Ray needed a $300 down payment on the Cottage Style. Miss Josephine had given them half, and it had taken them two years to save the rest. Zenie had worked for Mimi six and a half days a week, coming in around 7:30 and leaving around 3 with a cold supper prepared in the refrigerator. A half day on Sunday, plus keeping me. Ray made good money. He worked from daylight to dark and sometimes, under a bare bulb in his shed, long into the night. He was a yardman in the warm weather and a handyman when it was cool, so some weeks were better than others. He could fix just about anything. People gave him their broken lamps, lawn mowers, radios, and all manner of stuff, and he bent over them like a genie in his little shed, making them good as new. Mimi paid Zenie $1.50 a day, or $10.00 a week (Mimi added in the extra quarter). Extra for holidays and canning. It was Grandpops' idea to pay Zenie's social security even though the law didn't require it for maids then, and Mimi sometimes said that they had nothing to blame themselves for when it came to treatment of the Negroes. Plus she gave Zenie all of her old hats (which Zenie told me she wouldn't be caught dead in).

When Zenie took the bus to the bank twice a month to put her and Ray's money into savings, she would take me with her. For insurance, she said. Once we got off the bus at Main and Goodlett, where the Millwood Bank and Trust Company was, she grabbed my hand just as we were walking up the steps to go into the door. I was seven years old then, but when we crossed Main Street, she treated me like a baby. The first time she did it, I jerked my hand out of hers, but she just snatched air until she got me again. She'd never held my hand like that before, like I didn't have good sense, and I didn't appreciate it. She clamped down. It made my palm sweat and itch and my fingers lose feeling.

She hauled me up to the teller's window and just stood there. First the teller dragged her pale eyes over Zenie like a net, holding her in view but not really looking at her. Then the teller looked down and saw me and her whole face melted and it was oh sweet little Florence this and isn't she growing that and what a head of hair I was getting and do tell my grandfather hello. Only then did Zenie let me go and take out her handkerchief with the wadded up bills inside and smooth them out on the counter. The teller picked them up the way you pick up something hot, handling the bills at the edges and dropping them quickly into the money drawer, not even smoothing them out. Zenie just stood there looking at the place on the counter where the money had been while the teller took her own sweet time writing something on a piece of paper and *bam!* stamping it hard. When she finally handed Zenie the piece of paper, Zenie pushed her little navy blue book with the frazzled edges over in the teller's direction, and the teller wrote something in it and stamped it. Zenie took her time looking first at the bankbook and then the piece of paper. Then she folded the paper up and put it in her little book and placed the little book back in her purse. We took the bus back to her house, where she unfolded the piece of paper and pored over the bankbook. When she was satisfied, she put a rubber band around the whole thing and put it in a drawer in a big dresser. Then she'd say, "Um, um, another slow day, another slow dollar," and shake her head.

When Zenie's bankbook said $275 (she'd already put Miss Josephine's money in to draw the extra interest), she wrote a letter to the Jim Walter folks and told them she and Ray were about ready for their house. The way she told it was here comes this white man with ducktail hair and a smile like sorghum molasses. He knocks and says, "Mrs. Zenobia Lee Johnson?" and she says, "You looking at her," not believing her ears. A white man calling her Mrs.! He comes on in and sits down and pulls out the house pictures and Zenie calls to Ray and he comes in and they point to the same picture at the very same time and say, "*That one.*" Two bedrooms. They were expecting Miss Josephine to move in when she got too old to do for herself. (What they didn't expect was that Eva would show up, though she ended up sleeping with Miss J, who by then was too old to care.)

Then Mr. Jim Walter says he'll go ahead and take Zenie and Ray's $275 now and they can send the $25 later and he'll take Zenie to the bank to close down her savings and hand it over. But Ray allows as how he thinks it'd be better to wait till they've got the whole thing and can send it all at once by Western Union and get a receipt. That's when Mr. Jim Walter knows he's not dealing with a bunch of fools. He whips out the contract, and they sign *Rayfield Eugene Johnson III and Zenobia Lee Johnson.*

When the house finally came, it came like gangbusters. Big old long truck with half a house on it bumping right up Goodlett Street, past Mimi and Grandpops', and on down to the other end of Goodlett into Shake Rag where Zenie and Ray's lot and the concrete-block foundation they'd had put down lay in wait. The truck drove up and the driver got out and said, "Where you want it?" Then Ray took one look and said he and Zenie didn't order half a house, they ordered the whole thing, and the man said, "Other half's up the road broke down. Be here later on." When Ray told him where to put the first half, the man drove the truck right up onto the ground and he and another man took it off in sections and fitted them together like a big puzzle on the foundation. Later that evening the other half came, and the next day when they got it up and put it together and sealed, everything looked just fine.

Then Ray went inside to look around. "Where the doors at?" he asked the man. There was a front door coming from outside into the living room and a back door opening from the kitchen to a drop-off into the backyard, but there weren't any inside doors to the bathroom, either of the two bedrooms, or the closets. Everything was wide open like one big room with nooks and crannies here, there, and everywhere.

"Inside doors ain't included," said the last driver, the first long gone.

Zenie told me she put on her best talking-to-white-trash voice and said, "Got to be a mistake, mister. I never did hear of a house that ain't got no doors in the deal."

"They is *extry*," the man hollered from the cab of his truck and revved up the engine.

"What they going to run us?" Ray yelled out as the driver shifted into first to pull out.

"Don't know. I just drive. Talk to the management." He threw the words out the window like pieces of gravel. The truck had started rolling, and the black cloud of exhaust covered up Zenie and Ray so that all the neighbors who'd been watching from across the street couldn't even see them.

By the time the smoke cleared, Zenie was inside at her sewing machine making her green-leaf-curtain doors from the material she'd gotten for window curtains, which would have to wait, and thinking where was she going to get some red geraniums for those window boxes, worry about doors later. Ray was rummaging in his shed for some curtain rods.

By the time Eva came to stay that spring of 1963, the green leaf curtains had been washed and ironed six times. I happen to know this because I helped Zenie hang them out on the line the sixth time. They were made of good material and were still nice and fresh looking, moving like ripples of water whenever there was a breeze coming through the house. Miss Josephine, who was so old now she'd bowed over like a live oak branch going back to the ground for support, had come to live in Zenie and Ray's little back bedroom.

The morning I first met Eva, Mama had dropped me off at Zenie's early and I was helping her make the George Washington Carver High School majorette outfits. They were a pretty gold with royal blue braid and wavy rickrack. Zenie had gotten up before dawn to start on the skirts, which were tricky because you had to cut them on the bias so they'd twirl when the majorettes did. She was provoked. She'd just cut one wrong and was trying to piece it in the back where it wouldn't show. She had just so much material, and she couldn't afford a mistake. She'd told me to go outside and play, which was her way of saying get out of my hair. I was laying low on her front steps feeling insulted—you don't tell a girl of almost eleven to go out and play. People were coming out on their porches in the cool of the morning. The lady next door was watering her petunias in their little round beds. She stood like a statue in her front yard. The water from her hose broke into a rainbow against the coming sun, drawing in birds to drink out of the puddles it made in the dirt.

Miss Josephine was inside trying to help Zenie, which I knew was aggravating Zenie even more. You had to leave her alone when she was figuring out the pattern of something. I was sitting on the front step thinking about nothing at all, just beginning to let go of being mad and enjoying the morning air and the rainbow the water made, when along came a taxicab. It stopped right in front of Zenie and Ray's house, which made me blink and blink again, since it was the first time I'd been at a house where a taxicab had stopped. Then out she popped like a party favor, all happy and smiling with two big suitcases and a little red hard box of a suitcase ladies used back then for their face and hair stuff. She was wearing a funeral outfit, navy blue suit with a white lace collar, high heels and stockings, and circle earrings with little pearls in them. My first thought when I saw her was that she must be hot in that getup.

Eva stopped short when she saw me. "Looking for my auntie, Mrs. Zenobia Lee Johnson," she said, and she said the *t* in *auntie* like an opera singer finishing up. She didn't say and who, pray tell, are you? but I could see she was thinking it.

I pointed to the front door. "She's in there."

She ran past me up the steps and burst in the front door, making a big commotion with "Auntie Zenobia!" then "Miss J!" then "Where's Ray?" There was yelling and scrambling around and everybody having a fit over this new one. I peeked through the screen. They were all hollering and jumping around like it was Christmas and she was snow.

I've got to say I was feeling out of things. Zenie and Ray didn't have any children, and here I was thinking I was the apple of Zenie's eye, no matter what she said about white folks. Then here comes this fancy one, turns out to be a niece I didn't even know Zenie had, calling her Aunt*ie* Zenobia this and Aunt*ie* Zenobia that, like Zenie was the Queen of Palmyra on her throne. I'd never heard anybody, not even Miss Josephine, call Zenie anything but Zenie, except for Ray who called her baby and honey and pretty little thing. I stayed put out on the step.

Then I heard Miss Wonderful say down low, "What's that scraggly white girl doing out there?"

I tried to smooth my hair down. Did I comb it this morning?

Zenie said, "That's Martha's one. I'm watching her."

"Ain't you got enough to do all day keeping that hat lady happy? Now you got to watch her big old grandchild too."

Zenie sputtered, then belted out a laugh loud enough to blow the roof off the Jim Walter Home. Then I heard her wheeze and gasp for breath. "Lord, Eva, don't get me tickled like that!" I knew that comment about my grandmother was sure to get Zenie going. One of her pet peeves was Mimi's hats. I hated being in the house when Mimi came waltzing in with a new hat. She'd call

me into her bedroom and I'd have to say the thing was pretty and
no, ma'am, I most definitely did not think it was too loud. Then
I'd go back to the kitchen and Zenie'd be banging pots around
and making eyes at me like the new hat was my doing. "Them
hats of hers cost more than some folks make in a month," she
would mutter while she pulled out the bottom broiler drawer of
the stove and slammed a beat-up cookie sheet down inside. Then,
bam, she'd kick the broiler drawer back. "All the hardworking
poor folks in the world, some right under her nose, and all she be
thinking about is piling up more hats on that dyed-blue head of
hers. Sinful."

Eva piped up again. "That girl out there's too large to need
watching. What she need watching for? Something wrong with
her? She mental?"

When she said that word *mental*, I felt as if an icy hand had
grabbed me. Mental. That would explain Mama not letting me
go to school. The way last year's girlfriends turned away when
they saw me. On the way to get my shots at the Health Department across the tracks in Milltown a few days before, Mama and
I had passed a house with a girl on the front porch. She was
a regular-looking girl in Milltown terms, blond and paper white
and skinny. She was older than I was, maybe thirteen. Her apple-
sized bosoms had popped a button on her shirt. All she did was
rock in a little rickety chair with no paint. Sometimes the girl
would be holding her arms out in front of her and whapping her
hands back and forth so hard that they looked like they'd go flying off and be lost in the yard's sky-high weeds. What was different about her, besides the rocking and whapping, was her mouth.
It looked like it had been propped open with an invisible stick,
and there was a line of spit running out of each corner of it.
Where the spit had dried, it made chalk marks that ran from her
mouth to her chin.

"Why's that girl always out there rocking and doing her hands that way?" I asked Mama as we drove by.

"She's mental, honey. Not right in the head." Mama looked out the car window at the girl. "She doesn't have good sense. That's all she knows to do. Personally, I don't think it's right to keep her out there like that. Just asking for trouble."

Then I saw it. When you see something you don't believe, something you know can't be true, then forgetting can shove re-membering out the door and if remembering ever does return home like that poor long-lost prodigal boy, forgetting wants to kill him. So what I first forgot to remember to see about the mental girl was that there was a chain wrapped right around her waist, like she was on a chain gang. It disappeared into her long pants and then came on out the end of one of her pants legs and curled itself around the porch railing. A secret that had slithered out for all to see, it glinted in the late-day sun.

Can a person be mental and not know it? If you're mental, how can you know it? Seems if you did know it, you wouldn't be mental. I touched the corner of my mouth to check for spit.

Everything in Zenie's house had gotten quiet. All you could hear was Zenie's fan squeak while it rotated. Then Zenie laughed like Eva's ugly remark was the biggest joke in the world and said something real low. The only word I could hear was "Extra." Something about me was "Extra." After a minute or two, Zenie said something about my mother. She started her sentence by saying "good woman" and ended it with "too much." There were a lot of words in between, but those were the only ones I heard. *Good woman* and *too much*. They were a relief because they didn't include *mental*.

After a while the front door burst open and here came Zenie and Eva and Miss J, laughing and carrying on. They stepped around me to get Eva's suitcases out of the front yard. Eva grabbed the heaviest bag and the small red case. The small one she handed off to me on her way in the door, which gave me permission to sidle on in behind her. Zenie took the next heaviest, and Miss Josephine held the door for her.

So there we were all sitting around in Zenie's living room and Eva was being nice as spice, telling me the *E* in her name sounded like "elephant" not "evil." Everybody was always putting a hard "ee" on it, which just drove her crazy.

That was just the start of it. Eva talked a mile a minute. She could give you her life story in no time. Born and raised in Raleigh, North Carolina, and a student at Tougaloo College right over in Jackson, which is a good school with teachers from big colleges up north. She even has a professor from Harvard University! She's going to be a schoolteacher. She loves grammar and diagramming. Lining words up just right so you can see how they make a path to somewhere. She'll teach me how it's done when she gets her stuff unpacked. This summer she's come over here to Millwood from Jackson to sell insurance to make enough to get her through her last year in school. Good policies for burying folks, plus insurance for hospitals and doctors. She's going to fix all Zenie and Ray's friends right up. She knows they're going to love to see her because this is her mama Marie's hometown. They're going to buy up policies left and right, and she'll give them a payment book and some already stamped envelopes. Then she's going back to Jackson to finish college in the fall, and the money will come pouring in. She's got it all figured out. Plus her company doesn't take advantage of Negroes. North Carolina Mutual of Durham, North Carolina, is the oldest (founded in 1898!), biggest, and best black-owned company in the United States of America. The Mutual gives Negroes their money's worth and more; it doesn't try to cheat them the way white companies do. Its mottos: The Company with a Soul and a Service, and Merciful to All.

When Eva told us all of this, Zenie and Miss Josephine got quiet. Miss Josephine's old bell of a head tolled back and forth, back and forth. "Um um, Lord have mercy," she said.

Eva looked around the place. "You-all got room for me to stay awhile?"

Zenie got up and went over to the front window. She put her hands on her hips. "We always got room for you, Eva, but this place's already got a policy man. *Some*body's daddy. Some others too. Told you that in the letter. How come you showing up here? You not agitating, are you, like some them people at that college? If you are, you better buy yourself some of that insurance because we going to be burying *you*."

Eva rolled her eyes at me. "This is 1963, you know. Times are changing. We'll talk about this later. Little pitchers have big ears." She turned to me. "What's your name, girl?"

"Florence," I said.

Eva smiled big and pretty. She had the prettiest set of white teeth I'd ever seen. Even and smooth, not like my snaggily mouth with this one that had come in big and crooked and another sideways. My mother was setting aside part of her cake money every week to get me braces.

"Hey, Flo," Eva said. "You want to see my stuff?"

I'd opened my mouth to say please don't call me Flo, though the O sound of it in Eva's mouth gave me a strange pleasure, when Eva popped the latch on her little red case and, bingo, out popped a top tray with lipsticks and tubes of this and that, with a shiny mirror above. My mouth dropped open even farther when she passed me the case. It was the first time I remember looking in the mirror and really studying what you'd call my features. Hair dusty looking and standing straight out. Round face the color of old sand that's been in the sandbox too long. Freckles sprinkled around like sand fleas. Yellowish eyes so light you could see straight through them. No eyebrows to speak of. Everything so light you could barely tell what was what. Ugly. I was amazed at how ugly.

I could see that Eva had what I needed. Her hair wasn't standing straight out. It had a nice round shape. It lifted on top, came down the sides of her face smooth and easy like water flowing down a little hill. Then it surprised you and flipped up on the ends. It shined from the oil on it, but it didn't smell heavy sweet like Daddy's. In fact, it didn't smell at all that I could tell, though Eva herself carried a whiff of rosewater and glycerin, which was just right. She had on glasses with little points on the ends sprinkled with rhinestones. They made her look nice and smart, like she meant business. Her skin without a mark on it. The color of Mama's devil's food batter after she adds the buttermilk, and smooth like that.

"You need fixing up, girl," Eva said, and pulled out a lipstick the color of a plum, the dark kind that shines. Everything she said to me had "girl" attached to it, and it made me feel like I was part of a club, the girl club, and she was the president and she'd picked me to come on in and join up.

"*Fix me.*" The words rolled out of me like I was in church and we'd started in on Glory Be to the Father and to the Son and to the Holy Ghost. I knew before the words came out that they should have been: no thank you, my mama won't want me painted up common. But I didn't want to hurt anybody's feelings. Plus Eva already had the tube rolled out and she painted my lips before they could say anything else. I looked again into the mirror and saw a blooming rose for a mouth.

"Needs blotting," I said, and all three of them got to laughing at that.

"Blotting ain't going to help when her mama catches sight of her," Zenie said with a frown.

Eva pulled out a brush and a jar of powder the color of cocoa.

"How'd you like some powder on that shiny little nose of yours, girl?"

"Oh Lord!" Zenie said and slapped her leg.

"Give me some!" I was getting into the spirit of fixing me up. I'd looked in the mirror. I knew what they were up against.

Eva looked at me and pursed her lips. "Maybe some foundation first."

"Won't match," Zenie grumbled, and then exploded with another one of her laughs.

Before I knew it, Eva was working on me with a bunch of pencils. Pencils on the eyebrows, pencils on the eyes. Then a dust of cocoa. When she was done, I looked in the mirror again. A definite improvement. I was starting to look really good. My eyes were big and round. I was brownish, like a piece of light toast. Not as dark as Eva or Zenie, but closer to them than to my mama or daddy.

"I'm colored!" I hollered out. "I look colored!"

The words came out of my mouth like splashes from a pretty waterfall, happy and playful, but they froze when they hit the air. Everything in the room froze with them. Everybody had been laughing and talking and playing, even Miss Josephine. Now nobody said a word. It was as if a giant vacuum cleaner had come through and sucked all the words out of the room so that there was only air and dreamy dust. Then Miss Josephine let out a long sigh, and quicker than a flash Eva tossed her cute little powder and brush set into the red suitcase and slammed it shut. *Bam.*

Zenie pushed herself off from the couch and headed for the bathroom, batting the green leaf curtain aside, the way you'd cut cane in the field, and rummaging around. When she came whipping back into the living room with some toilet paper and cold cream, she headed straight for me, her mouth a thin straight line. She was going to wipe me down before I could do a thing to stop her.

"No! I want to show Mama!" I loved this dark me. I wanted eye shadow and mascara. I wanted Eva to curl my eyelashes if she could find them. I wanted to look like Eva.

Zenie took hold of my face and rubbed in the cold cream. Then she raked her scratchy toilet paper over my cheeks. She was being rough with me. She was mad as fire. There was something I'd gone and spoiled. Hard wipe across the mouth. Was she going to wash my mouth out with soap? My eyes were filling up just as I thought it. I'd managed to sneak into the secret club; then somebody noticed and I was kicked out.

I looked over at Eva. She had turned her back. No more hey girl this or hey girl that, I'm going to teach you how to look passable and diagram sentences. She was looking out the front window.

"When's she getting picked up?" She said it without turning around.

Zenie was still working on me. She'd gone back in the bathroom and now she had a washing cloth, wet and hot. "Directly," she said without moving her mouth and started washing me down. The washcloth smelled like buttermilk. It had gone sour, and it made my face burn.

When she finished with me, I looked around at them. Miss Josephine was staring off into space as if nobody but her was in the room; Eva was still planted at the window looking out. Zenie took the dirty washcloth and threw it into the tub and then walked slowly back through the living room and into the kitchen. I stared for a minute at a bright dot of sun on the gray linoleum floor, but nobody said a mumbling word. All of a sudden I remembered what Mama had told me about not saying *colored*.

So, I thought, that's it, that's why Zenie and Eva and Miss Josephine were acting this way. But it was too late to say *Negro*; I beg your pardon, I know better, I meant to say *Negro*. When words splash out, they are gone forever. You can't catch pieces of water in your hands and hold onto them. They run through your fingers and splatter where they will.

Eva broke the silence. "Ride's here." She said it without turning around.

"Nice to meet you," I said real quiet, as if I thought Eva might be asleep in her pose at the window. She nodded her head but still didn't turn around, so I headed out the door and down to the street where Mama waited, flicking ashes from her cigarette out the car window. My face still stung.

When I went around and opened the car door, there was a cake sitting on the front seat beside my mother.

"Be careful with that," Mama said as I picked it up and sat down with it on my lap.

The cake was white and looked naked. It had no icing and only one layer. "Who's it for?" I couldn't imagine who would have ordered it.

"Gertrude. She's diabetic, so I made it with a little juice." Mama stuck her cig in her mouth and put the car in gear. Gertrude lived a couple of blocks over from Zenie. As usual, Mama was intent on breaking Daddy's rule about Shake Rag. He said there was a difference between picking up somebody or something in Shake Rag and visiting up there. The first thing was Conducting Business, the second Socializing, which Daddy had forbidden Mama to do. He himself was up in Shake Rag all the time collecting his policy money door to door, and I was up there almost every day with Zenie, but all of that was Business. Over the years Mama had visited this one and that one with her cakes. She didn't tell Daddy, and neither did I.

Gertrude worked for Mimi as an extra server when she had the Saturday Matinee Club. Mimi was civic minded, and all of her clubs had civic duties except for the Saturday Matinee Club,

where the ladies ate chicken-salad sandwiches and tomato aspic
at card tables covered in white linen tablecloths and then played
bridge all afternoon. Gertrude got dressed up and wore a lace
apron when she came to work for Mimi's special occasions. Zenie
didn't care for Gertrude's fancy ways. "What that woman think
we running here, a plantation?" she'd say. When Gertrude would
show up in her nice black dress and tie up her apron with a flourish, Zenie's already long thin lips would get longer and thinner so
that they looked like they were reaching for her ears.

The real problem was that Zenie didn't like Gertrude from
church. Zenie and Gertrude were both Heroines of Jericho at
Saint John the Baptist, but they'd had a falling out over the communion glasses. Who was supposed to wash them. Zenie said Gertrude had agreed to do it for Sunday the fifth of March but hadn't
done it and had blamed it all on Zenie, telling everybody that
she, Zenie, was supposed to have done it for that Sunday, which
was most definitely not true. It was Gertrude's turn to wash, not
hers. The worst part of it was that nobody discovered the glasses
were still dirty until the deacons were passing the trays and then
the preacher held one up to the light in front of God and everybody and said *Humph*. Then people started really looking at
them and saw they had purple streaks on the rims from the last
month's grape juice and red and pink from the ladies' lipstick. Of
course they drank from them. What could they do? Turn down
Jesus's blood because of germs?

"Prissy," Zenie would hiss behind Gertrude's back. I'd be helping the two of them, Zenie filling the plates in the kitchen and
Gertrude going back and forth taking them into the living room.
Gertrude had a nice shape and her waistline showed to advantage in the apron. She'd sashay in and out to get the plates and
serve them to the ladies at the four card tables in the living room.
Every time Gertrude would go out of the kitchen with her plates,

Zenie would make a noise in her throat like she was getting ready to upchuck, then mince her six-foot self around the kitchen like a poodle carrying an imaginary plate, and I would fall out laughing.

But Gertrude's sashaying days were over. A week ago the doctors had to cut off her left foot on account of the sugar sickness and trying to work when her toes were crusting over with sores. It was a surprising case in someone so young. Mama was bringing a special plain white cake to Gertrude that had been sweetened with fruit juice and had no icing, which was the only kind of cake Gertrude could eat and only a little bit at a time. She'd also brought Gertrude some old magazines, some clematis from our front porch wrapped in a wet napkin, and a Sears and Roebuck catalog. Gertrude loved glamour magazines. Her little living room was stacked all around with old magazines that leaned here and there with ladies on the covers doing this or that in frisky dresses, their hairdos gleaming like golden halos.

First off Gertrude launched into telling us how her foot had looked like a burnt-out stump before it got taken off. Right then I started seeing flecks of cotton before my eyes and Mama took one look at me and shoved my head between my legs so I wouldn't pass out or upchuck. My usually pinkish Mama looked very white herself especially sitting next to Gertrude, who was on the darker side and looked even more so in her white nightgown and the white gauze dressing wrapped around her ankle where her foot had been. The gauze had yellow spots sprinkled across it like the lemon zest Mama put on the tops of her white iced lemon cakes. Mama reached quickly into her purse and pulled out her Japanese folding fan and started fanning herself hard while she pushed up her bangs to wipe the sweat. They stood straight up and out, like those crab pinchers you see on big greenish beetles who are aggravated and ready to fight. Then she remembered me and started fanning me too. Gertrude had a round fan made out of palmetto grass, and she was working it hard.

It was horribly hot. Gertrude had two windows in her front room, but they were both closed and you could tell they were sealed shut forever with paint globbed around the cracks. The air was so still in the room you felt that the words coming out of your mouth were making a breeze. Zenie had been over there that morning cleaning and the place smelled like Pine Sol. I was betting that Zenie was feeling pretty bad about her ugliness to poor Gertrude and was trying to make amends.

"It's close in here," Gertrude said. "Going to be a hot summer." She was stretched out on the couch, her foot on a pillow. Her crutches were propped up beside her. This Gertrude was a different person from the woman in the lace apron.

"It's awfully hot in here. If it's like this in May, you're going to roast the rest of the summer." Mama started fanning Gertrude too. "Do you have an electric fan, Gertrude? Anything to cool you off?"

"Can't say as I do. Till this happened, I was working this time of the day, so I didn't need one. That's all right. Heat don't bother me too bad."

"Well, I'm going to try to find you one. A fan. I'll call the church and see if anybody has one they're not using." Mama sounded determined.

"Don't worry yourself about it." Gertrude looked over at her bottle collection on the windowsill. The little bottles were all shades of blue glass and whistle clean so the late afternoon sun sliced through them, spattering blue over the bare floor like little pieces of sky had fallen into the room. "Look how pretty my bottles look there in the sun. Well now. You tell your mama I'm sure sorry I can't come back to work for her."

Mama rose. This was her cue and she was grateful for it, plus

I could tell she felt bad that Mimi wasn't there visiting with Gertrude too. Mimi had a good heart but a weak stomach; she didn't visit Uncle Nash, her own brother, in the VA hospital until his war wounds healed. "I'll tell her, and I'll be back with that fan." Mama looked hard at me. I scrambled up, dim-witted from the heat.

Gertrude shifted her leg on the couch and smiled politely. "No, don't bother nobody about that fan. Johnny down the street is coming up tomorrow to put me in a screen door. If that doesn't cool me off, I'll order a fan from Sears."

When we got into the car, Mama sat behind the wheel breathing hard. "Lord, that place is an oven," she said. I could tell she was scheming. When Mama was trying to figure out a scheme, she would rub the tip of her nose and run her finger down over her mouth to her chin. Then it would go right back up to the nose. After a bit of rubbing, she started the car, the tip of her nose now flaming up against her still pale face. She didn't say anything else, just drove straight over to Mimi's and parked in front under the big oak tree that had uprooted the curb and the sidewalk it grew between.

"Stay." She said it to me like I was a dog. In less than two minutes she was marching back down the walk with one of Mimi's electric fans and a big glass of ice water. Before she could stop me, I stuck my hand in the glass and grabbed an ice cube out of it and shoved it down the front of my shirt.

I eyed the fan. "She said don't worry about a fan."

Mama looked at me in exasperation. "Well, she couldn't have possibly meant *that*."

In another few minutes we were back up in front of Gertrude's place. I didn't have to be told to sit tight. In another minute, though, Mama came dragging back to the car with the fan. She threw it onto the Spanish moss backseat and got back into the car. She turned to me with a stunned look. "She doesn't want it. I tried to talk her into it. I told her Mimi had sent it. She said she was *fine*. Can you believe that? *Fine*. I told her it was hot as Hades in there, and she said no it wasn't. It was *fine*. Don't trouble myself or my mother."

"Maybe she didn't want charity."

Mama looked at me, shocked. "This wasn't charity. It was just a *fan*, for God's sake."

"Maybe it felt like more than a fan."

Mama looked down at the steering wheel. "Well, maybe so. Maybe I came on too strong. I guess I should have introduced it more casually."

"Like, hey Gertrude, I got an extra fan in the basement. You want to use it? Or something like that." I stuck my head out of the window to get some air.

Mama nodded and gazed over at Gertrude's house. "I bet I hurt her feelings. Damn it the hell, I could kick myself." Her voice sounded like it had gotten caught on something ragged.

We tooled around awhile after that. Mama pulled out a half-pint bottle of Old Crow in a paper sack from under my side of the front seat. She took a sip and starting driving around and singing in her cracked off-key voice about how in the sweet bye and bye we shall meet on that beautiful shore. Up and down the highway, then out into the country, raising clouds of dust on some back roads that kept turning into dead ends. I could tell Mama was down and out. She didn't want to go home. After a while, though, she perked up and started in on "Mack the Knife" and I gave her some much-needed backup to try to keep her in tune.

It was still hot as fire but getting toward suppertime when we high-stepped it into the house. We were both singing at the top of our lungs about scarlet billows starting to spread. Mama stopped short in the doorway, and I bumped into her. Directly in front of us Daddy was sitting on the sofa looking peeved. His brick foot was up on the rickety coffee table, which came from Mama's grandmother on Grandpops' side and which Mama said was the only decent piece of furniture in the house. He was smoking a Lucky Strike and had the newspaper wadded up and was hitting it over his knee.

"Where you girls been?" His voice was light and heavy at the same time.

Mama hesitated. I could see she was weighing her options. Tell the truth and get Daddy mad. If he'd told her once, he'd told her a million times, he didn't want her going to take people things up in Shake Rag. Let them alone up there, folks don't want to mix. Or tell a bald-faced lie and run the risk of getting caught and making him madder.

Mama was eyeing Daddy. Lately he'd been especially ornery and jumpy; something was gnawing at him, like those chiggers that dig into your tender flesh and stay alive for weeks by taking bites out of you every so often. The night calls had been coming hard and fast, and I'd been burning up the basement stairs bringing the box up to him night after night. One of his eyes was twitching as he looked up at us; a lock of hair, heavy with Mr. Holcomb's oil, fell in his eyes.

"Messing with a fan up at Mother's," Mama finally answered, looking hard at me.

I smelled trouble and took off for my room. Shut the door like a whisper. Sat down on my bed, crossed my legs Indian style and started picking at the nubs on my spread. There were only four rooms in our house, and mine opened onto the living room. So I heard Daddy when he said, "Yes ma'am, I know that much. Just now called over there and your mama told me you took a fan of hers up to some woman in Shake Rag. Didn't I know that?" His voice went high. "I said, no ma'am, I did *not* know that, but

I found it very interesting since I told Martha not to go visiting around up there. Messing with a fan my ass."

Mama answered hard and quick. "If you know so much, what you asking for?"

Daddy came back hissing low. "Asking because I'm the husband and you my wife. That's what I'm asking for."

"Don't go bothering with me, Win. I need to get supper on."

All of a sudden there was a scramble, then a dead silence. In that silence something shifted like a sigh. Mama started honeying her voice up. I could hear only snatches because she'd started talking real low and fast. "The poor woman . . . so I thought . . . don't worry, honey . . . sorry to worry you . . . all right . . . I won't, I promise."

Then I heard the *clump clump* of Daddy's shoe. Then the front door slammed and I knew he was gone and I could come out. Mama was sitting on the couch. Tears rolled down her cheeks though she didn't make a sound. She was rubbing her wrist, which had a thick red line around it like when you give someone an Indian burn. When she saw me standing in the door, she put her arm behind her back. "All right now." She cleared her throat. "Let's get supper on so it'll be ready when he gets back from his errands." The *he* sounded like a stone on her tongue.

She snatched me up with her good hand and dragged me into the kitchen and grabbed a paper sack full of speckled butter beans she'd gotten down at the Curb Market at Crosstown. Then she shoved the sack at me and pushed me down in her chair at the kitchen table. "You shell," she said, and I said, "Yes ma'am," and picked out the first bean.

5

The next day was just another ordinary Friday at Mimi and Grandpops'. Wash day. Though it was still not yet June, the greedy heat had already snatched any pleasure from the day. Grandpops read his almanac and said it was one of the hottest Mays on record, now getting to 90 by noon. Even the mimosas were blooming early. Zenie complained that her legs, wrapped in the elastic hose she wore, felt like they were going to catch fire and burn. "What June going to bring if this what we got on our plate for May?" she muttered balefully. "Guess we just be going up in flames."

"Don't forget to put the sheets out for Uldine," Mimi calls out to Zenie on Mimi's way out the door. She's headed over to the Curb Market to get some strawberries. Uldine, the grandmother of Earl Two, who left town on the run from Mr. Wilkins, washed white folks' clothes for a living. She had long limber arms and a way of tying the wash tight and putting it up on her shoulder in one easy swing. She picked up the dirty wash on Friday morning and brought it back clean, starched, and pressed on Saturday afternoon. She came in a beat-up old car that she kept running while she collected the wash.

One time, just one time, in all the years Zenie worked for Mimi, Zenie just flat forgot to put out the sheets and laundry. When Uldine came by for her pickup, Zenie had already walked on home to the Shake Rag end of Goodlett Street, and Mimi was at the beauty shop getting a permanent. Uldine I bet sighed a big sigh when she opened the front door and there was no nest of dirty sheets right inside on the floor. She sure wasn't going to go traipsing through some white lady's house, so she went back out onto the porch and looked around. Sometimes Zenie left the sheets out there. Still she found nothing. That's when she decided to ring the doorbell but nobody was home so nobody came. What a humbug! And the car out there barely running! Against her better judgment she peeked inside the front door again, but then some busybody white woman came driving down the street and gave her The Look that said What you doing peeking into white folks' houses.

Uldine was so aggravated that she charged Mimi for the extra trip to show she didn't have the time to come by white folks' houses for the fun of it. Meanwhile Mimi and Grandpops needed their clean sheets and clothes. Mimi said it was only fair, since the whole thing was Zenie's fault, that she do them herself. So when Mimi says don't forget the sheets, Zenie curls her lip and says under her breath she wishes she *could* forget the damn sheets but she knows she'd end up having to wash them herself for free. She says this while Mimi is backing her gray Plymouth out of the garage without bothering to look behind her though it's doubtful she would've seen anything anyway had she bothered to turn around and look; she was so short she could barely even see what was coming straight at her, much less what was behind. When Mimi got behind the wheel, her head resembled a party favor hanging between the top of the steering wheel and the dash.

The minute the Plymouth bumps out of the driveway, Zenie takes off her apron—she always took it off when Mimi left. She goes down deep in her chest and raises up a big sigh, which sounds more like a cough, and says, "All right, come on." We head for the hall and the stairs. She drags herself up, step by step, stopping at the landing to get her breath. I help her with the beds. It's a friendly thing to jerk and pull on the sheets and huff and puff and growl along with her, though I know I should be studying the social-studies lesson Mimi has left for me about the legislative, executive, and judicial branches of the state of Mississippi and how they balance each other so nicely. Social studies is boring; how Mimi could teach it day after day, year after year, I do not know. Though truthfully, I hadn't made any progress to speak of with any of my studies. Mama seemed to have lost all interest in my education, as well as everything else except her cake baking and poison drinking; Daddy thought public schools were run by communists and worried about integration coming to Millwood. Though Grandpops meant well, he was still buying me little children's books. Mimi was struggling to finish up school herself that May. Though it was hard to imagine that this summer would come to an end, I knew in my heart of hearts that the earth would turn and September would show up as bright eyed and bushy tailed as Uncle Wiggily himself. The thought that the day will come when I'll have to face the music gives my stomach a big hard kick.

There were three beds, one for Mimi, one for Grandpops in his smaller room off Mimi's bedroom (his for sleeping only, hers for sleeping and sitting), one for overnight company, which was usually me. Zenie and I pile up the sheets and pillowcases. They make a big puddle of white in the upstairs hall. Then the two of us together hoist the pile up and carry it over to the banister, trying not to lose any pillowcases on the way, and drop it over the railing to the hall below. When the sheets hit the air, they puff out like parachutes. Then Zenie and I both push our breath out and say, "Whoo!" Zenie because she's huffing and puffing, relieved to get that part of it over, and me because I like to see the shapes the sheets make when they land. When I was little, I'd get on the banister and ride it down as fast as I could to see if I could beat some of those flying sheets to the bottom. I had to turn two fast corners, and it all depended on how fast I could whip around them, coupled with how fast the sheets were falling. Some days they fell like rocks; others they took their own sweet time, just making a slow sweet slide off the banister and then floating for the time it requires to take one long breath of air before landing *whop whop* on the dark oak floor below, like cooked divinity icing plopped down on the top of one of Mama's cooled lemon cakes.

Back then, when I'd zip on down the banister, Zenie would lean over and holler at me. "What you doing now? Trying to kill yourself like a wild Indian, then I be blamed and Lord knows what happen when you-know-who come home and find out I gone and let you kill your sorry self. You too old to be playing the fool. Don't get paid enough for this kind of monkey business."

Today I turn back to help Zenie put the clean sheets on the bed. My job is to change out the pillowcases. This is better than me helping her with the creases and tucks, because I'm sloppy and Grandpops and Mimi in their next-door bedrooms both like a tight corner. Then we carry the dirty pillowcases downstairs, pick up the sheets off the hall floor, lay one of them out on the living-room rug, a dirty one for sure but still white as anything from Uldine's laundry bleach, and pile the rest of the sheets and laundry on top. We bring the corners together and tie them up like a napkin lunch for a giant.

After we finish with the sheets, Zenie goes back into the kitchen and takes her apron off the door hook. She puts it back over her head like you'd harness an ox to the plow. The apron isn't part of her; she hates it. It covers most of her bosoms and lap in white, though the white is stained with grease and juice and smears of something that looks like blood. She brings in a paper bag of corn from the back porch, and sets me to shucking it, and when I'm done, starts to cut the corn off the cob. When she has her pile of cut corn in a bowl, she heats up bacon grease in the black iron skillet so dinner will be ready at twelve sharp, when Grandpops will come walking home from his law office down the street and Mimi will get back from the market. Meanwhile, my mother has called and said she's going to the store for some sugar and will run in for a bite if Zenie has enough. Do we need anything? In this heat she's going to be dying of thirst for some ice water when she gets there. Could I please get a pitcher ready?

When we are all assembled around the table, Zenie brings the food in. Her breathing is heavier than usual, and there are big wet half circles under her arms. A small glass of buttermilk for my grandfather, who puts his corn bread in it and mushes it up. While the corn bread gets soft, he bows his head and says all in one breath Lord thank you for these and all our many blessings in Jesus Christ we pray amen.

While we eat, Zenie sits at the kitchen table in the ladder chair fanning herself with the bottom of her apron because the kitchen is as hot as blazes. She isn't leaning back or starting in on her own meal because in a minute she'll have to pass out some more corn bread, then collect the plates, then serve the strawberries Mimi got and angel food cake. When I was little, she'd come out to sweep under my chair. "Need to tie a chicken to your chair to eat up this mess," she'd say under her breath, and I'd giggle at the sourpuss look on her face, then reach out and pat her shoulder while she bent over the broom. Her shoulder would twitch my hand away like a fly that was bothering her.

At the round oak table I have the best view, straight out a row of windows with old-time nandina bushes. In the winter there are red berries and in the summer the little white syrupy blossoms pressed up so tight to the screens you can see all kinds of things.

Wasps with drapey legs, tasting and thrusting. A brown spider munching on a fly that trembles for its head, which is pretty much gone.

We don't talk much at the table. My mother carries a grudge against Grandpops she doesn't bother to hide, the reason being that he did everything but tie her up to keep her from marrying my Daddy. Zenie's lips are sealed. All she knows is that my mother was her Grandpops' baby who left the nest too soon. She was a smart girl. He wanted her to grow up slow and steady. Go to college. Learn how to make a living for herself. Find a man who could hold his head up in the world. Plus something about the whole thing didn't sit right with Grandpops. The way my father didn't ask; he just took. The way Mama let herself be snatched up like a chicken for the pot without anybody talking to anybody. Nobody saying I'd like to marry Martha, sir, I love your daughter and I'd like to ask for her hand in marriage. It was just up and go to the JP, and like it or lump it, we're man and wife. All this from a high-school dance!

My mother is telling Mimi about a lady she met at the grocery this morning. A new wife who, when she found out Mama used to work for the Welcome Wagon, just burst out crying that she's lonesome lonesome, nothing in this town looks right. Even the angle of the sun is wrong.

Mama looks through Grandpops like he's not there. He's mashing down his corn bread into the curdled milk and taking up his spoon. He curls his long straight face down around the glass of buttermilk as he listens to her story. I see how his hair is parted straight down the middle in one thin line.

My grandfather never meant harm, and word of his good deeds fell on our ears like manna from heaven. It made me proud to hear the stories people told. He had a knack for knowing what people needed. A suit of clothes for a funeral. A loan for college.

A job. Zenie told me that back during the Depression when no-body had a pot to piss in, he lent Mr. Lafitte Sr. the money to set up his grocery down the street from her. The store is still going strong, and Mr. L has paid back every cent. Today Grandpops wears a blue-striped seersucker suit, and his stick elbows make parentheses that keep him from toppling over into a pile of bones. He's all bone, just as Mimi, with her drapey arms and sausage-roll bosoms, is all flesh. He wears glasses with lenses so thick they make his eyes look like a big catfish's, and he can't be without them. He has a lazy eye too. It goes toward his nose and makes him see double. The left side of his specs has little lines across the glass, so you can barely see his eye behind it. Mimi says if there's a fire and he can't find his glasses, they'll burn up for sure.

I smile at Grandpops to try to make him feel better, but he's used to Mama's cold ways and is preoccupied with getting the last of the corn bread out of the bottom of his glass. In a minute he'll put down his napkin and ask us to excuse him and pop his head into the kitchen and say, "Real good, Zenie," and she'll say, "Thank you, Mr. T," the T being for Taylor. A nice first name. If I'd ever had a child, boy or girl, I would've named it Taylor. Then he comes around behind my chair and puts his pointy fingers on my shoulders, and asks me if I'm ready for a story. I know this is coming so I'm thinking ahead while I polish off my strawberries. I am reviewing my options. Grandpops needs perking up, so I'm trying to decide between two of his favorites: *Uncle Wiggily's Airship*, where the old gentleman rabbit flies all over the place having just one big adventure after another with giants and lions and what all, and Grandpops' Uncle Remus book, which is also about one smart rabbit who's always getting into scrapes but wiggling out of them somehow or other by fooling everybody who wants a piece of his flesh.

I follow Grandpops into the cool dark living room. I'm expecting him to say all right, what'll it be, when he reaches into his briefcase and pulls out a new Uncle Wiggily book. *Uncle Wiggily's Travels.* "Christmas gift!" he says, though it's not Christmas or my birthday either. I try to act enthused. Uncle Wiggily is my old favorite too, but I'm worried that I should be reading books with smaller print about people in the real world instead of animals who talk in words that nobody would say in a million years. At least this is a new story; maybe there are some regular words I can learn from it. I get up next to Grandpops on the slippery satin couch and feel his hip bone clamp into my side so that I feel like a little boat that's been anchored fast. There is a picture of the gentleman rabbit on the book cover. He is a big old jackrabbit who limps along on long, lean back legs. He has rheumatism so he uses a crutch. He wears round specs and a bow tie like Grandpops.

Grandpops opens the book to the first clean page, the color of sand. I tuck my head against his skinny old arm and draw close to the smell of new paste. I start in. Grandpops and I have a way of reading books. I read what I can, which isn't as much as it should be, and he reads the rest. Over the past few weeks, I've read more and more of everything he throws at me—*The Saturday Evening Post, The Christian Observer*, Mimi's book of myths and legends—and he's read less and less. *Uncle Wiggily's Travels* I breeze through, stumbling only a couple of times when the letters don't line up and I have to sound them out.

Uncle Wiggily has been feeling quite sad. He's been hopping along a dusty road seeking his fortune as usual when he looks in his trusty valise for lunch, and lo and behold, he's forgotten to pack one. He's the most miserable rabbit in the world because he's hungry as all get out and getter hungrier by the minute, but then he runs into a pretty black cricket with the jolliest laugh he's ever heard. Ha, ha, ho, ho, he, he!

Mr. Cricket can't help laughing all the time because the world is so lovely, with sun shining and birds singing and brooks babbling and all. Happiness abounds in the lovely, lovely world.

Oh dear, though. A skillery-scalery-tailery alligator has just jumped out and is all set to eat, first Mr. Cricket, then Uncle Wiggily. But ha, ha, ho, ho, he, he, the black cricket starts to laugh harder and harder, then it's Uncle Wiggily laughing too, and then, glory be, Mr. Skillery-Scalery-Tailery is laughing so hard, big old alligator tears are rolling down his scaly cheeks. He can't help himself. Of course, Mr. Cricket and Uncle Wiggily are long gone before the alligator can stop giggling. Hop, hop, and they're nowhere in sight.

"You've got Uncle Wiggily down pat," says Grandpops at the end of the chapter. "All right, got to get on back to the office." He shuts the book and hands it to me. "More tomorrow. After that we can graduate you to something harder. We need to get down to the county library and ask what a big old fifth grader ought to be reading." He pats me on the head and gets up, sidesteps the pile of sheets, and goes over to the mirror by the door. He fixes his bow tie in the mirror and takes his hat from the table by the front door. He gives himself a big smile in the mirror and squints at his teeth to see if they're good to go. He puts his hat on his head and then tips it to me as he opens the door and calls out to the house, "All right, I'm gone."

Zenie hollers from the kitchen, "All right." Mimi doesn't answer. She's upstairs taking her nap. Mama's long gone. She must have slipped out the back door while we were reading.

Grandpops walks out and the door clicks shut behind him.

Zenie is still working in the kitchen making a cold supper for Mimi and Grandpops. I sidle in and ask her if she's got any new Queen of Palmyra stories up her sleeve.

She hands me four pieces of bread and some butter. "Spread

that." She starts to peel and slice a cucumber. "No, but did I tell you that the Queen gave her slave girl an elephant for her very own? They used to ride on it together, one in back of the other."

"The slave girl who baked the cobblers?" I want more story than that.

"Yep, that one who was her favorite in all the kingdom." She hands me pieces of cucumber. "Put these on the bread."

When I finish making the sandwiches, she wraps them in a damp dish towel and puts them in the icebox.

"Get on out of here so I can mop the floor," she says.

I feel sleepy hot, and when I swallow, the hurtful lump in the back of my throat returns. In the living room I eye the pile of sheets, which looks like a cool white nest. I go over and untie the wrap sheet that's holding the nest together and crawl right in. When I pull the sheet back over me, the nest turns into a cocoon and I'm the ugly brown worm who's going to come out a pearly white butterfly. All I can see is light because I have folded myself up in the whiteness of the sheets, which have such old tender edges and folds. I rub an edge between my thumb and forefinger.

But today Uldine comes early. She opens the door and grabs the pile by its ends, and tries to pick it up. Then she commences to hollering and carrying on when I wake up and start wiggling around under her hand. She throws the ends down. What now? she must think. What bed of vipers is this?

But before I tumbled out, I was dreaming of Palmyra and roiling to and fro on the back of an elephant draped in satin and gold fringe. There was a parade and a jivey band with cymbals and rows of dark little children and a nice lady slave fanning me with giant palms as I passed on my elephant. Peach cobblers stretched out before me as far as the eye could see.

I was the Queen of Palmyra.

When I told Zenie my Queen of Palmyra dream that afternoon at her house, she had finished the Carver High majorette outfits and was starting on the uniforms for the band. The Carver band was the jivingest band you ever saw and that's what made me think of my dream. My job was to feed the gold braid in a long even line through the top of the sewing machine so she could keep on sewing straight and fast on the blue serge material she was making the uniforms out of. This way she could finish up faster and have some time to make me some doll clothes out of the band uniform scraps. I was standing behind the machine facing her as she sat on her bench, foot to the pedal.

"What do you think, Zenie?" This was my favorite way to start a conversation with her.

"Beats me." She didn't raise her eyes from the material sliding evenly through the machine.

"Guess what I dreamed." I scratched a mosquito bite on the back of my leg with my toe.

"What." She kept on sewing. "Watch out now. Keep it feeding in straight. Don't let up on it. I'm too tired to tear these out and do it over."

"Dreamed I was riding an elephant. Dreamed I was the Queen of Palmyra. Zenobia the Queen of everything. I was on an elephant in a parade!" I grinned big. "I went to sleep in the sheets and dreamed it all in flash right before Uldine came in and almost picked me up with the sheets!"

Zenie pulled her foot off the pedal like it was a biting dog she'd kicked. She looked up at me across the top of the sewing machine. I saw for the first time how light her eyes were. The color of pennies. Thick like copper with something behind them, the way a coin isn't just a coin but stands for something else that's more than itself.

"Queen of Palmyra my foot. You ain't no Queen of Palmyra."
She said it with such scorn it made me mad.

"Well, why not? I can be anything I can think up. You ain't
going to stop me."

"Pretending it so don't make it so." She looked hard at me.
"Can't make yourself any old thing you want to be. Don't work
like that."

"Yes ma'am, the Queen of Palmyra on an elephant! Can if I
want to." I stomped my foot.

She glared at me. The penny copper in her eyes was usually
melty. Now it looked cold and solid and thick. She leaned over
the sewing machine so that we were nose to nose. "You can't have
everything you want. Some things just *belong* to folks. You got no
truck with them. They none of your doing."

I threw my end of the braid on the floor. "How come you being so ugly? I'm not helping you anymore because you're so ugly
to me."

"Well, I got news for you. You ain't much help no how. And
I'm getting sick and tired of white folks messing with my stuff."
Zenie stood up and put her hands on her hips. She looked down
at me the way I'd seen her look at roaches running across the floor
before she took off her shoe.

When she did that, the lump in my throat throbbed a big
throb, and I started to blubber. I was a chicken at heart and I
didn't want to be the Queen of Palmyra bad enough to get Zenie
so mad at me she'd make me go home and I wouldn't get to help
her sew.

"Oh hush, crybaby!" Her eyes cut across me like heat lightning. But then she sat back down and started straightening up
the material around the sewing machine needle. So I wiped my
snotty nose on the back of my hand and started to pick up the
braid. "Go wipe that nasty nose and wash them hands before

you take hold of my braid," she commanded and I fled for the bathroom.

Zenie had every reason to be sick and tired of me. May had come to a close. As June came on hotter than ever and settled in, Mama started dropping me off at Zenie's early almost every day, before Zenie'd go to work at Mimi's. Mama said she had things to do, though I didn't see any evidence of them when I got home. The cake ingredients for the nighttime bakings were still laid out, but there was no supper on the stove or the food to make it with in the refrigerator. Mama and Daddy's bed wasn't made and dust balls piled up in the corners throughout the house. Mama would set me out in front of Zenie's house right around the time Eva, all perky and fresh in her navy blue suit, would be leaving to go sell her policies. As far as I could tell, my remark about looking colored had gotten to be water under the bridge. Eva would flash me one of her knock-your-socks-off smiles, give me a little wave and say, "Bye, Flo." Then off she'd go in her high-heel pumps carrying a little black satchel looking for all the world like she was heading off to work in an office in New York City. I'd watch her from Zenie's front step, walking straight and tall but with a nice sway, getting smaller and smaller as she went on down the dusty street.

If I got to Zenie and Ray's before Eva left for work, the bathroom would be steamed up, and the smell of rosewater would have sweetened up the house like sugar in tea. The screen door would bang and Zenie would watch Eva go down the front steps. Zenie stood in the door, her arms folded. Sometimes she buzzed deep in her throat like a hummingbird who's zooming through the air to start a fight. Sometimes she just shook her head. Then Zenie would walk on down to Mimi's to start the day's work, and I'd trail along.

In the afternoon we'd walk back and here would come Eva

at suppertime, hot and fretful as a colicky baby. She'd have spent the whole long ugly day knocking on folks' doors thinking she was going to get a big fancy welcome. Thank you, baby, you're so sweet and pretty, but we already got our assurance, they all said, though they were real polite about it. They asked her in, of course, and told her the story of how her mama had run off from Millwood after her roguish father, Jake, had visited some cousins. He had spent the summer of 1939. They'd just had the tornado to top all tornados that spring. It had blown away just about everything in the town, including a few people, and Jake had come down from Carolina to help his cousins the Harrises rebuild their place. They told her stories about her little mother, who was just a slip of a girl, taking one look at Jake hammering away out in the hot sun (what a pretty long neck he had!) and losing her heart on the spot. What a sweet girl her mama was. How pretty. How she favored her pretty mama. How that summer Jake would go out in the late afternoon and catch crappie the size of your thumb and give them away. He was a city boy, from Raleigh, and he didn't know a thing about fishing. He thought he was giving people something real fine, so folks would smile and say thank you. Then they'd throw them out for the cats or use them for bait.

So the people in Shake Rag gave Eva everything else she could possibly want in the way of refreshment and friendliness and stories partly because of her little mama who had flown the coop, but mostly for Zenie and Ray, who had stayed. But when she came by that first time, they all said they wouldn't buy any insurance from her on account of how attached they were to their policy man, my daddy or one of the two other white men who worked for Mississippi Assurance.

"Why buy white when you can buy black? Why pay more when you can pay less?" she would ask them, and they'd just look at her and shake their heads. She was just plain ignorant, and crazy to boot, they said, if she didn't know the answer to that question. That Tougaloo girl was going to get herself in hot water around here. Don't they teach them *anything* in college? At first clumps of ladies from the St. John's Heroines of Jericho would come by Zenie's and whisper to her in the kitchen. Zenie would hum and worry. Then the ladies stopped coming.

Zenie and Ray talked about Marie and Jake too, but it was in whispers, about how he had turned mean and nasty and her weak and watery, putting up with his shit. And they did mean shit. At home and abroad. Eva was smart as a whip and they weren't a bit surprised that she'd left home a long time ago given the situation, but they wished she'd found somewhere else to run to. Millwood wasn't where she ought to be, though they guessed she came to them because they were her only family except for Jake's kin, who they didn't know but speculated were probably as evil as him.

When I think back, I always wonder what might have changed the way things turned out. Maybe if I hadn't been so worn out all the time. The heat curled around everything, twisting and bending us to the shapes it had in mind. We trembled before it; it made us helpless and tired. Most of the time I felt like a climber without a rope scaling up the side of each day. I could slide off the edge into the dark valley any old time. The summer lay ahead, a burning desert that seemed in June's heat to stretch out endlessly before us.

If Mama let me stay home, which was rare, one minute it would be noon and I'd be sitting up at the table with a spoonful of cold beans from the can going into my mouth. The next I'd wake up with my head on the table, dirty dishes and Mama snoring away at her afternoon nap. Her face looked as if it'd been sprinkled with cayenne. Her breath smelled like burnt cabbage. Daddy was out collecting his policy money, mad because the you-know-who can't scratch it up. When they said you can't get blood out of a turnip, he would give them a warning. "*I* can," he would say. And when he said that, they'd move one long slow step back into their front doors all the time nodding like he was making a good point and saying, "Yes sir, next week we'll have it for sure." And they would.

I knew all this because my father had started taking an interest in me. I was just one of Daddy's interests. Daddy was a joiner, despite having grown up out in the country. He was voted most outgoing boy in his class at Mill County High the same year his own dad hanged himself with a calf rope in the barn early one frosty December morning so that his oldest son, my father, would find him when he went out to help with the milking. Why his dad planned it that way nobody knew, except Daddy thought he didn't do it in the house on account of there not being any rafters strong enough to hold his weight. He was a big man with meaty hands grown thick and rough from milking the herd and whipping his five boys into shape. Two years before, Daddy's mother had just fallen away from life, like it was a rope she couldn't hold to anymore. Her hair turned white and she lay down in her hospital bed like it was a port in a storm and died sweet and quiet and determined. This is what I gathered up from the pieces of talk I heard here and there, though not from Daddy himself, who never spoke about his father's dying, or his mother's either.

My father loved his meetings. The hall closet was stuffed with different hats and tassels and pins and outfits. Breakfast with some old men once a week at the drugstore. Dinners at noon at the King Plaza Hotel. He was a member of the First Baptist Church Southern Branch, the Moose Lodge of Millwood, the Knights of Pythias, the Masons, the Sons of Confederate Veterans, the Shriners, the Mill County White Citizens' Council, and I'm leaving some out. He was against Integration and Communist Fronts and Outside Agitators and Mongrelization and Jews Sucking up the World's Juices. Later on it would be Fluoride in the Water. He was for Things as God Meant Them to Be. All neat and divided up. This one here. That one there. The blessed purity of things was what he called it.

Daddy had a map that he pulled out on the coffee table on nights he didn't go out. It said United States of America at the top but it didn't have the states outlined, much less the capitals, which was aggravating, since I was still trying to memorize them both and it would have helped to see the shapes of the states and their placement on the map. Mimi was sitting down with me on Saturdays and teaching me social studies from her high-school students' books: agricultural products and material goods in Poland and other far-off places, economic opportunity and the melting pot of America, the amendments to Constitution. But the things I'd needed to have learned in the fourth grade but did not, like the states and capitals, I had to get on my own. There were lines all over Daddy's map, but they were marked in pencil for when he changed his mind and erased them and drew them all over again. One line was wrapped around where, I know now, California and Arizona and New Mexico are supposed to be. He had this idea about how folks would be happier if they were cohabitating with their own kind, so he was working on a plan to move people around. He said it'd be like the Japs during the war. Off somewhere. Nobody bothers them and they don't bother nobody. Live and let live. It's all a matter of boundaries and categories, he said, and when he said the words *boundaries* and *categories*, his eyes shone like he'd made them up out of his own head.

As June wore on, Daddy started taking me on his policy rounds at least once a week. At night he told me his stories about brave brotherhoods who saved the women and children from terrible harm. He said I was finally getting old enough to be inter-

esting, plus he said I wasn't as dumb as I looked; he could teach
me more than those damn schoolteachers ever could. At night
his stories and hot hand pushed back sleep. The forlorn whistle
of the midnight Frisco would come and go, and sometimes the
one-thirty, when Mama baked late. On the nights Daddy went
out, Mama made her night runs to the bootlegger with me riding
shotgun. She kept on carrying the little notes from time to time,
but most nights she just made a liquor run, no fooling around
with milk shakes or beer or little pieces of paper. She stayed with
clear stuff—moonshine, gin, vodka—and poured it into her poison bottle when we got home. On Sunday, which was supposed
to be a day of rest, I had to get dolled up to go to church with
Mimi and Grandpops. I sat between them in the church pew, and
they'd take turns pushing me from side to side when I slumped
into sleep. My eyes were always grainy and my hair thinned out.
My brush filled up with it. I felt like those walking-dead people
you see at the picture show who can't stop moving. Zombies.

Zenie was the only one who would let me take my rest. That
summer I felt better on her couch than any other place in the
world. It had a handy washable slipcover Zenie had made out of
some velvet-feeling material the color of dark plums and a little
folded cloth out of the same material to put over you in case of
chills. Plus it had pillows on both ends to put my head on and
prop up my feet. The more I slept the better she liked it. Zenie was always busy, either with her sewing or cooking for Ray,
Eva, and Miss Josephine, not to speak of her regular job with my
grandmother.

Ray never said much to me, but he didn't seem to mind me
around when Zenie was keeping me. His shed, which he'd built
out in the backyard, was a ramshackle-looking thing because
it was made from left-over pieces of wood he'd gotten from his
handyman work. Sometimes when Zenie would tell me to go out

and play, I'd go out back and stand in the door of Ray's shed and watch him sharpen things with a big file he had. He was careful. He never took his eyes off the blade when he'd say, "How you doing, lady girl?" I'd say, "All right, how you doing today?" He'd say, "Can't complain too much." We'd have us a good chuckle and that would be all we'd say. But he let me stay and watch as long as I stood back. Zenie told me he'd rather work at home in his shed than at people's houses, though he did some of both when things that needed fixing were too heavy to carry home. He wore overalls and blue shirts buttoned all the way up to his chin and heavy black shoes. He usually had on a hat that looked like the ones that Grandpops wore except it was all beat up and the band had a sweat line around it. He wore it at a cocky angle and always put it in the same spot, on a little table in the kitchen, when he came home. Whenever Mimi came out to tell him what to do in the yard, he took it off and held it in his hands. Then he looked like a newborn chick with his hair all pressed down flat. When Mimi was telling him to weed that bed or water that one, he cocked his head a little like he had a crick in his neck. Ray had an artistic streak in the yard. He planted a good bed, making pretty scallops and circles with the daylilies and iris he'd dig up and divide in the fall. I liked to watch his hands working the clay, his knuckles gray with calluses and raw skin, the palms a pearly pink like the inside of a seashell. For a while I thought Ray was shy. Then I realized the Ray I saw wasn't really Ray, unless he didn't know I was watching.

When he was doing something for Mimi, like weeding her big beds of peonies, he'd come to the kitchen door pouring sweat out from under his hat and wiping his face with a handkerchief. He never set foot into the kitchen, much less the rest of the house. Zenie would fix him a tall glass of ice water in a jelly jar and he would take it on the back steps. She'd wipe her hands on her apron and go stand out there with him in the hot sun. They'd put their heads together and talk and talk like they hadn't seen each other in a hundred years. He'd say something, and Zenie'd throw her head back and laugh out loud. Once, when he hauled off and puppy-bit her shoulder, she laughed and petted his head like he was a pup sure enough. Then she threw back her shoulders in a way I'd never seen, as if she was starting up a dance.

There was a little room in the back of Mimi and Pops' garage that was usually kept locked. I always thought it was for sharp tools, but once, when the door was ajar, I looked in. There was nothing at all in it except the nastiest-looking commode you ever saw. It didn't have a place to sit on, much less a lid, and it was pitchy with grime. No toilet paper. No lavatory to wash in. When I asked Zenie what it was for, she said it was for folks who worked in the yard and had to use the bathroom. She was frying corn in a skillet on the stove when I ran into the house after my discovery.

"You mean like Ray?" I asked.

She didn't turn around. "Um hum."

The thought of Ray, who was the neatest man alive, who even cleaned off his tools and lined them up just so, having to use that nasty bathroom made me feel sick and ashamed of Mimi and Grandpops for even having it in the first place.

"Why can't he come inside and use the bathroom?"

She kept stirring the corn, her back to me. "Dirt on his feet. Might track it in."

"You could clean up that bathroom out there." I wanted to be helpful.

"You think I'm messing with that nasty thing out there, you crazy, girl. If he got to go, he can go in back of the garage. Good clean ground." She turned around and looked down at me. "Ray don't mind dirt, but he do hate nasty. He wouldn't have me clean that thing out there even if I wanted to."

When I'd wake up from my naps on Zenie's couch and hear

Ray and Zenie talking, I liked to keep my eyes shut and just listen. When my Mama and Daddy talked, it was like little hummingbirds fighting over a piece of the yard. Fast and hungry. Where's supper and how long and are you going out tonight and who called and what kind of cake did they want.

The way Zenie and Ray talked when they thought I was asleep made me see butterflies in my head. It wasn't the words, it was the way they had of flitting back and forth and finally lining up just so. Touch and then touch again. Melting the lines Zenie's and Ray's sentences made.

The back door would creak and creak again. Then there'd be a click.

"Where you at, baby?"

"Right here, right in front of you. You blind?" Zenie would come around the corner from somewhere else in the house.

A chuckle. "Glad I ain't. How'd I be able to see your pretty little face?

"Little? What you talking about little? Nothing on me little."

Another soft chuckle. "Well, now, I wouldn't say *nothing's* little."

"Hush that mouth, you going to wake up the girl. Ain't you got nothing better to do than come in here bothering me when I'm busy working? What you so full of yourself for all of a sudden?"

"Man can't all the time be studying work. Got to get some pleasure in this world."

"Whoa horse. Got a peeping-tom girl on the couch and a restless old one in the back. What you think going to happen here, mister? You and your pleasure just going to have to hold up."

"Me and my pleasure willing to hold up a good long time for a pretty lady. But is the lady willing to wait for her pleasure? That's what I'm wondering. Sometimes ladies don't want to wait."

"This here lady can wait till doomsday if she has to, mister. Want some tea?"

"I sure will take some *sugar* with that tea."

My mother didn't talk sugar; she poured sugar into bowls and mixed it with shortening until you couldn't tell which was which. When Daddy came home, he gave her a peck on the cheek and then hollered out, "Give me some sugar, sister," and started up nibbling on me like I was a bowl full of left-over icing, which made Mama turn away and start rattling the pans.

A week or so after Eva had come, my mother was baking her cakes and my father and I were tucked in. He was telling me his favorite book in the whole world, *Bomba the Jungle Boy and the Swamp of Death*. Daddy loved Bomba, and he knew the stories by heart. Though I was getting sick of Uncle Wiggily, I was sicker still of Bomba, despite the fact that he was an actual boy instead of an animal. Even though Uncle Wiggily had the rheumatism, the old gentleman rabbit still managed to fly around in his airship with his crutch and valise. Grandpops, who walked with a cane when his own rheumatism acted up, said Uncle Wiggily overcame adversity. Despite the fact that he was so crippled he could hardly walk, he had adventures galore. Plus he was lucky as he could be. He got stuck in mud holes and trees but there was always somebody to pull him out. Everybody loved him and loved his catnip tea, which could cure the epizootic. His ant friends fed baked beans to a hungry giant so the giant didn't eat up Uncle Wiggily. He laughed along with the black cricket when they got loose from the skillery-scalery-tailery alligator, who was laughing too.

But Daddy was dead set on Bomba. What I'd found out the hard way by that time was that people will get their own story like people get a dog and no other dog will do, no other dog is sweet and good like *their* dog. Zenie had her Queen of Palmyra stories, Grandpops favored Uncle Wiggily and Uncle Remus, Daddy thought Bomba hung the moon. Grandpops read a few pages of Daddy's book and said to forget Bomba, it was nothing but poisonous trash. I knew Zenie wouldn't take to Bomba in a million years, so I never bothered to tell her about him. When I told Daddy the Zenobia story, he said Queenie should go back to Egypt where she'd come from. He thought Uncle Wiggily was an old fool.

Daddy told me I'd come to appreciate Bomba when I knew more. Knew more about what, I asked. The world, he said, the world. World or no world, that night I was feeling too tired to listen to Daddy talk about Mr. Smarty Pants Bomba. Besides, I knew the story.

Bomba is a white boy who got left in the Amazon jungle. He's smart and strong and brave beyond compare when he's in deadly danger, which is nearly always. The man who wrote *Bomba the Jungle Boy and the Swamp of Death* says Bomba has the simple dignity that is the end and aim of good breeding. One minute he's saving folks from the slimy, evil-smelling dismal swamp of death. Or the hideous painted-up cannibal savages. Or stinky anacondas and monster boa constrictors. All of which are hungry as all get out. Everything bad in the Bomba story is colored black. There are black streams of sluggish water, black mud that catches your feet and drags you down to death. The boa is a huge black rope whose red blood gushes out when Bomba skillfully kills it with an arrow. Not to speak of the savages who are so black you can only see their paint.

Bomba talks about himself like he was somebody else. Plus he's long-winded. When his native sidekick Gibo, who's dumb as a stump, yelps like a sick puppy, "Oh help me, Master, this black swamp's demon slime is sucking me down," Bomba hollers back, "Let Gibo be of good heart. Bomba will help Gibo." When Daddy would read this part, I couldn't help but think that by the time you got all those words out, Gibo would have been long gone.

So great is Bomba that Gibo plumb worships him. "Great is

Bomba," Gibo says, but what Gibo doesn't know is that Bomba just used his white brain to get out of this mess. He found some vines, and pulled himself and Gibo out. Gibo thinks it's a miracle, but that's because he's a stupid native. In Daddy's Bomba book there are natives, who are like Gibo, nice but witless, and there are savages, who are cannibals with war paint and big appetites for white-boy flesh.

Bomba's problem is that he wants to come home to his whiteness, but he can't find it. His blond-haired parents are long gone, and he doesn't know how in the world he got dropped like a hot potato down in the jungle with all the savages. When he accidentally rescues a bunch of smart scientists, he's so happy to see their white faces he can hardly stand it. They tell him he's the whitest boy they ever met, by which they mean he's the smartest and nicest. Then they shake his hand, which is the biggest thrill of all since only equal white men shake hands. Natives don't, and certainly cannibal savages don't. They eat hands, plus every other part. So now he's being admitted to the white brotherhood. His whiteness is complete. Glory be and Hallelujah!

The white scientists tell Bomba about the world of white people. Great cities with real houses, human voices coming from boxes, real fathers and mothers who love their children and take care of them, men who slap each other on the back and laugh together. No wild beasts or black mud holes or monster snakes. No black savages.

When I opened Daddy's Bomba book, it had the smell of an old house that had collected dust for a hundred years. It made my chest seize up and sometimes set off an asthma attack so that Mama would have to take me into the bathroom and run the water in the tub to get some steam. There was a single sheet of notebook paper inside. I'd folded and unfolded it so much that the creases had torn. This was Daddy's book report from when he was in the fourth grade, which was the grade I'd just missed this past year. It read:

> Winburn L. Forrest September 12, 1936
> My favorite book is Bomba the Jungel Boy and the Swamp of Death. It is real good. Poor Bomba! Hes a nice white boy, but here he is in a jungle with all these black stinky cannibal sauvages who want to eat him up. Then he gets suck up in that black swamp. But he will escape the black swamp of death because he is white and smart.

That Friday night, when he told me the Bomba story, Daddy was lying on his back and rubbing my stomach. I was about to melt from the heat of his hand. We were both sweating. He moved restlessly in the bed, like he was about to get up.

When he took a breath in his Bomba story, I snuggled in closer, wanting to keep him interested. "Daddy, guess what."

"What." He sounded preoccupied. He kept on moving around and rubbing my stomach.

"Zenie has a niece who's trying to sell policies in Shake Rag."

His hand paused in mid-rub, and he stopped moving. "What you say, girl? What niece? Selling insurance? A *nigger* selling insurance? For crying out loud. Whoever heard of a nigger girl selling policies? What kind of policies she selling?"

I lay very still. His hand, still heavy on me, had clinched up so that his fingernails raked my skin. "I don't know. The kind to bury people, I guess. Maybe some other kinds. For doctors and medicines and stuff like that."

"I'll be goddamned."

"She's a nice girl," I said quickly. "She's just working her way through that college in Jackson."

"What college in Jackson? That Tougaloo place?"

"I think that's what she said. Started with a T. Sounded Indian."

He sat straight up in the bed. "I'll be goddamned. That girl's an outside agitator! All them people down at that Tougaloo. Conspiring. Nothing but troublemakers and agitators. N-double-A-C-P and them Evers brothers. They're over in Harmony now. Guess they've made their way to us. Got to vote and eat at Woolworths and taking over the library and taking over the schools. Taking over everything. Goddamn."

I sat up fast. "No, no, she's just a regular girl, Daddy. She's not agitating anything. She's just trying to make money for her last year so she can go teach grammar and stuff. She's not trying to cause any trouble. Daddy, she's *nice*."

He stayed a while longer but didn't go on with the Bomba story. He just lay there quietly, stroking my leg. Then he patted my stomach nice and easy. One, two quick businesslike pats. Then kissed the top of my head like always and got up. He put his shoes and socks back on and his shirt too, which he'd hung on the doorknob.

After a while I heard him talking on the phone and clumping down to the basement to get his box. Then I heard Mama say in a slurred voice, "Win, where you going to at this hour?" and the front door shut without him saying a word back.

I lay there for a long time. First I was burning up and threw off the sheet. Then I shivered like I had a fever and pulled the sheet up around my neck. When the midnight Frisco came through and let out its *no no no no*, it seemed to be saying something urgent. Then whatever its message was fell away and dissolved like a web, or the fragile beginnings of one, leaving me uneasy and restless, as if there were something I'd forgotten to do.

I thought about getting up to talk to Mama for the company,

but I knew from the way she called out to Daddy that she'd been into the poison, which now seemed to follow her around the house. Empty but still strong smelling glasses turned up in odd places, like on the back of the commode after she'd cleaned the bathroom or the top of my dresser along with bottles of Windex and the furniture polish. Plus I was too tired to get out of bed. Daddy and his stories and his hand never rested me; they gathered me into a knot. I just wanted to lie there and untie myself. Let myself go.

It had started to rain outside. First it was a soft wistful sound, then it began to pour. I heard thunder in the distance. When I'd interrupted Daddy, he was just coming to his favorite part, where Bomba's about to be eaten by bloodthirsty cannibals. They've got him cornered up a tree. Now I'm just minding my own business trying to get a little rest and it's me getting chased up the tree. Now it's my white flesh they want, my blood they want to drink. Naturally, Bomba's long gone.

They're circling the tree I'm parroted away in. They're wearing paint and headdresses of wild feathers and they're carrying spears and bows and arrows and knives. I'm about to wet my pants I'm so scared. Then here comes one of them with a torch and I can smell the gas and he pours some on a rag and puts the rag on a broom and starts firing up the leaves and branches like Ray does the pecan trees to get rid of the caterpillars.

In fact, he looks like Ray.

"Ray, is that you down there?" In my dream I'm choking and coughing up here in this burning-up tree. I'm counting on Ray to save me, carry me off on his white steed.

"Sure enough," the cannibal yells up, "and I'm going to roast you like a partridge in a pear tree." Then he throws back his head and his hat—Ray's hat—goes flying. He waves his spear and lets out a war whoop.

"Ray, it's me, Florence, Martha Forrest's girl," I holler again from the top of the tree. "Zenie keeps me. You know me! How you doing today?"

But the tree is burning and the smoke is making it hard to breathe and all I can hear is whooping and hollering. Ray and his friends down below having a birthday party and I'm the cake. Now I'm thinking about an old postcard of Daddy's that I found pressed up in the Bible that had belonged to his dad. The card was a picture of a burnt-up man lying on the ground on a pile of blackened logs. The man was so burnt he looked like a tree trunk felled by lightning. There were a whole lot of people standing around him, white people: mothers and daddies and little children and babes in arms. The strange thing was that they didn't look sad or worried. They looked like they were having a church picnic on the grounds. A party. One little boy with a big smile on his face was holding up a chicken leg. My idea of a postcard was the one Mimi's sister Nell sent to her from her trip to Florida. Pretty blue sky, white sand, and sky-high waves a blue-green color. Who would send a postcard with a picture of a burnt-up man on it? Who would they send it to?

Now in my dream, everybody changes places. Now it's Ray perching in the burning tree. He's a big dark bird and folks are trampling his hat in the dust below. And me, I'm down here on the ground having the party with all the white folks in the picture. I don't know what's worse: being up there or down here, though I guess anything's better than getting burned to a crisp.

Then I see Ray has grown wings. He can fly. Now he's opening his wings (they're huge) and laughing, like Mr. Cricket in my Uncle Wiggily story. Ha! Ha! Ho! Ho! He! He! Finally he answers my question about how he's doing. "Can't complain too much!" he calls out as he flies away. Now he's up in the clouds and far far above me. Now he's a speck in the night sky, red with flames.

6

I woke up the next morning feeling jittery.

"Where's Daddy?" I asked, as Mama came swooping through my room with a cloth stirring up dust right and left. On the kitchen table her Saturday cakes were laid out in all their splendor. Her cake ladies had placed their usual orders that week just as Navis predicted.

"He's gone to a meeting," Mama said. "Get on up and make your bed right for once." She looked skinnier than usual, her black patent belt pulled tight. I wondered if Daddy'd come home last night.

I got out of the bed and headed for the basement. My father's box was gone. There was a rectangle of dust around the clean spot on the stacks of *Citizens' Council* magazines that were its resting place. The headline on a magazine on top read "BOYCOTT THE BOYCOTT! JACKSON MAYOR THOMPSON DEFIES OUTSIDE AGITATORS." I looked at the clean spot on the magazines. My stomach felt like I'd swallowed a bucket of nails.

The phone rang as I was climbing back up the stairs. It was

Mimi, who asked Mama if I'd like to go to the beauty parlor and get a haircut. Mimi said I looked shaggy, and she'd made an appointment for me. I jumped at a chance to (a) get out of the house, (b) improve myself, and last but not least, quiet the churning in my stomach.

"Going to the beauty shop gives me a new lease on life," Mimi said on the way home, patting her fresh do. She'd had her usual blue rinse and her rolls of curls had a frisky bounce, like hydrangea blossoms quaking in a little breeze. Her fingers were still pink from having been soaked in a kidney-shaped bowl while she sat under the hair dryer and read the *Ladies' Home Journal*. Jansie the manicure girl, whose daddy worked at the mill, had taken Mimi's pudgy fingers in her peeling hands (Jansie had developed allergies to the soap she used) and patted them dry, creamed them up, and pushed back the cuticles with a little wooden stick. Mimi shuddered a bit when Jansie rubbed her fingers and hands with the cream. Now that Mimi got a manicure every week, she said she would feel a rush of pleasure just looking at Jansie coming to get her from under the dryer, Jansie's dyed red hair slipping from its bun, her uniform stained with shades of pink and red polish like poppies. When the cream had soaked in, Jansie painted Mimi's sweet baby nails in "Dusky Rose," which Mimi said was a ladylike color, dark enough to notice, but not garish. The color of pink crape myrtle, not the hot pink but the grayish pink that looked like dusty cotton in the field with the old red sun swinging low in the sky. Not too loud.

I was feeling fresh too, my hair cut in a neat bob and puffed out from the rollers, which made me look like I had three times as much hair as I really did. Since Mimi was so full of vim and vigor, she'd decided it was time to give me my weekly social-studies lesson to catch me up in school. I was sitting in Grandpops' mean old chair, which kept me alert. That chair can stab you out of the blue. It's always hungry and it wants a piece of you. There are two such chairs in the family. The evil twins. They used to sit side by side in my grandparents' bedroom like Venus flytraps, golden wood shining to invite the unsuspecting victim. Nobody in the family but my Grandpops would get near them. For some reason, maybe because he didn't have any extra flesh to grab onto, they didn't bite him. He made a big to-do about sitting in his favorite one next to the fireplace. "I don't know what you think is wrong with this chair," he'd say, and rub the curved arm of it. "This is a *good* chair." Mimi got furious one day when she sat down in hers and got nipped in the back so bad the thing made a hole in her brunch coat. "Piffle," she said, "he can keep his chair, but that's the last bite this one's taking out of me." She hauled it over to Mama in the trunk of her Plymouth with the lid flapping and banging and said, "Here. Put a pad in it." Mama was glad to get it but she never got around to the pad. You can be rocking along feeling safe and good, and then, oh! it takes its slice out of you.

I leaned forward to avoid Grandpops' chair's pinch, rocking just a little, my head in my hands, but I was having a hard time holding up my end of the lesson; I was plain worn out. Sitting under the hair dryer had made me sleepy. I'd studied the branches of the government and their functions, but I was more interested in a magazine piece I'd read at the beauty shop about Jackie Kennedy and her pretty clothes and pretty children. Everything about her was pretty. I loved the way she held her head at a tilt. I loved her pillboxes in the magazine pictures and the way they sat like crowns on her perfectly smooth hair.

Mimi had a way of bribing me with chocolate-ripple ice cream and vanilla wafers, which I was busy mushing together in a clear green sherbet dish. Depression glass. As usual, she was making the most of my social-studies lesson to display one of her too-loud hats. She'd plopped a silky brown number with one enormous velvet rose on the right side of the brim on top of her fresh hairdo. A red rose, but a swarthy red that looked like it'd been oil-painted right onto the rose, which flopped up and down while Mimi talked and rocked. Even given the rose, the hat might have just barely squeezed under the wire of too loud except for the fact that sprouting out of the side of the rose were two bright green leaves as big as Mimi's hands. To make matters worse, the leaves were also velvet, so they flopped, making Mimi look like some-body's round-faced stuffed bunny with curly blue hair and ears, a rabbit that had seen better days.

"I think it's sweet. The way your daddy takes such an interest in you," Mimi said out of the blue. Her chair did a little bounce. She nodded at me over her social-studies book. The rose bobbed along with her, but the leaves waggled back and forth helter-skelter, like someone was shaking the rabbit's poor head.

Then her eyebrows shot up and disappeared into the leaves. "Florence Irene," she said.

I snapped to. Looking back at myself, I can see the crevasses of chocolate ripple in the sides of my mouth. A smudge here. A smudge there. Vanilla wafer goo on my chin. (It's easy for the woman I am now to see the girl I was then. Not so easy to know who rides the space between us, the in-between one this story is coming from.)

Nobody called me Florence Irene unless I'd done something. I thought of all the sins I had committed in the past month. Too many to name.

"Florence Irene." Mimi said my name a second time, her rab-bit ears quivering. I'm the cabbage and she's ready to take a bite.

"Yes ma'am." I stopped rocking. I tried to look into her eyes, which were a cloudy blue, almost gray.

"How's your mother doing? Is she behaving herself?" She tossed the last question into the air between our chairs. It hung there, a dead man swinging in a noose.

"My *mother?*" Surely she meant me.

Mimi bobbled her rabbit ears. Yes, she meant Mama, not me.

I opened my mouth, then closed it. Actually my mama was not behaving herself. She was riding wild and free through the nights that Daddy went out with his club friends, taking me with her, though I begged her to leave me at home so I could get a decent night's sleep. Joe's for the milk shake, which I was starting to get sick of; I'd gone through chocolate, vanilla, strawberry, and banana. Bootlegger the next stop. Sometimes she'd pass those little bits of papers to the dark man she now called Eugene, sometimes not. Then up and down county roads with a fifth of Old Crow or a pint of moonshine depending on what she had a taste for, zero to sixty in as fast as it took to open your mouth and tell somebody you wish they'd take it easy. One time a bunch of boys in a souped-up car pulled up beside us to drag race, and then peeled off in a panic when they saw a grown woman and a girl in the car. I bounced along, sometimes clutching the door handle in case I might need to make a quick jump for it.

Once, when I was in the third grade, some serious mothers volunteered to drive us children to the state park in the next county. I rode with Mary Frances McDougal's mother, a tall buck-toothed lady who drove so slow it felt like we were crawling on all fours. I got to sit in the front seat with Mary Frances and Miss Mac, as she liked to be called. This was before seat belts, and when we'd make a turn or stop, Miss Mac's skinny tree-limb arm would come looping out in front of us. *Whap* on the chest. "Don't want you two flying through the windshield," she'd say cheerily. "Children are precious cargo!"

To think of myself as a child, and precious cargo to boot, made me glow inside. Folks in my family were always acting like I was grown up or the wallpaper, one of the two and sometimes both at once. When Mama was behind the wheel and I was riding shotgun, she acted like she didn't even know I was there.

Everything was between her and the green Ford, which one of them would get the biggest kick out of the ride.

"She's behaving," I said, and the minute I said it the crack in Grandpops' chair gave me a big pinch. I startled up, slopping some ice cream out of my dish and onto Mimi's rag rug. "Oh, damn it the hell!" It just popped right out, as if the ice cream had had a big red cherry on top and I'd just spit it out.

Mimi stopped rocking and lowered her head so that I was eye to eye with the rose. "My sakes alive. Where'd you learn to talk like that?" The question zipped toward me as quick and determined as a mockingbird whose nest has been disturbed.

I didn't say anything. We both knew who said damn it the hell.

"I don't want you to talk like that, Florence Irene. You were raised better than to talk like that," she said, and her leaf ears took a hop. "And your mother shouldn't be saying it either! It's a good thing your daddy is taking an interest."

I was getting tired of the way Mimi was ragging on my mother, her only child. Wandering around Mimi and Grandpops' house, playing with Mama's old-timey dolls with china faces and lips painted red on eggshell faces, I used to get myself mixed up with my girl mother. When Mama would tell me a story, like how she used to line her dolls up on the swing on the front porch and push them real easy to get them to sleep, I'd do it too, and when I did it, I'd stir myself up like soup and all the ingredients of me would melt together and change. I'd become my girl mother. I'd drink in her thoughts and my mouth would say the things I thought she would have said. My name would be Martha Irene, not Florence Irene. I always thought Martha went better with Irene than Florence did anyhow.

All of this is to explain why I said what I did to Mimi, which was: "You look like Honey Bunny in that hat." Honey Bunny is a big old stuffed rabbit I got for Easter when I was three and have kept ever since. I still have him up in my closet. I myself love Honey Bunny, but Honey Bunny has a big round face with hanging down cheeks and an expression that makes everyone laugh when they look at him. One ear up, one ear down. So what I said to Mimi was an ugly and treacherous thing to say and I was the first one to know it. I feel bad about it to this day, especially after all my grandmother ended up doing for me. It reminds me of the time Little Dan told me I looked like a frog and he and May started calling me Florence the Frog. After that, whenever I looked into a mirror, all I could see was Frog with a capital F. No matter how too loud her hats were, Mimi thought she looked *pretty* in them. In fact, I noticed that the wilder they were, the prettier she thought she looked. She even put her hats on in front of the mirror so that she could see herself in the act, her soft arms with their drapey flesh swinging in love with her hatted self, like a caged bird doing a mating dance with its own image. Honey Bunny, my rabbit, was definitely not pretty, and we both knew it.

So what happened was this. Mimi snatched the hat off her head and smacked me with it. In the scuffle, the rose, which I guess had been hanging by a thread, fell off kerplop into my dish of nicely melted ice cream so that it had chocolate splotches all over it. Mimi took one look at the ruined rose and screeched at the top of her lungs, "You, you! Get on out of here! Just get on out!" So I ran on out, down the stairs, through the kitchen.

"What you gone and done now?" Zenie was leaning back in the ladder chair waiting till Mimi got through with me so she, Zenie, could take me on down to her house for the rest of the afternoon. She looked as if I'd just woken her up from a sitting-up nap. She was already provoked at having to wait to go home.

"Told Mimi she looks like Honey Bunny in that stupid rose-leaf hat of hers."

Zenie looked up at me in disgust. "Well Miss Smarty Pants, getting her all put out with you. Said she going to drive us home when the lesson's over. Expect we got to walk now."

"She was talking ugly about Mama."

Zenie rolled her eyes. "Listen here, girl. You can be mad inside and nice as spice outside. Won't hurt you none. Just zip it up. Zip it up and stay out of the doghouse. Me, I get mad as fire at that woman every day of the week, but she don't know the first thing about it."

"How come you don't say so?"

"Cause the good Lord didn't make no fool. Got to keep on working, Miss Know-It-All. It don't grow on trees, and she ain't the worst."

"Well, I ain't working for her."

"Maybe you is, maybe you ain't. Sitting around having conversation with her in those getups of hers is pretty hard work to my mind."

I grinned. "I get ice cream."

"More than I get waiting for you." Zenie didn't crack a smile.

So here we went dragging on back to Zenie and Ray's. Zenie was slow as Christmas on account of the phlebitis in her legs. She had on her heavy stockings, which, though hot as blue blazes, made her legs feel better. By afternoon the stockings always had pus spots on them where the sores came through. When we got to her house, I would put hot packs on her legs so she could get the stockings off without tearing into the sores.

Zenie lived on the same street as Mimi, just on the Shake Rag end. I was carrying yesterday's newspaper, which Zenie brought home every day. She had her satchel with her purse and handkerchiefs in it and some biscuits wrapped up in waxed paper and a jar of last year's sweet pickled peaches Mimi told her she could have when she cleared out the shelves before the new crop came in down at the Curb Market at Crosstown. We were trudging along by the cemetery. The headstones looked hazy in the heat. Trees bent low as if their branches were trying to get back to earth for a drink of water. Zenie was moving slower and slower. I was beginning to think we were never going to get there. She told me to quit rushing her; it was my fault we were having to walk. Her legs pained her.

Then just as we got up by the cemetery, we saw somebody sitting on a headstone. A Negro lady. We got close enough to see who. It was Eva. She was sitting on a marker that said Daddy Gone Home. She had on her nice navy outfit. Her shoulders were moving up and down fast. She had the shakes.

Zenie didn't say anything. She just started walking faster and faster and saying under all the huffing and puffing she was doing, "Oh sweet Jesus, oh sweet Jesus." I was running to keep up.

When we got to Eva, we could see that she was all messed up. Her hair wasn't sliding down smooth and flipping up nice, but sticking out every which way, like somebody had stuck their fingers in it and ran it straight up and left it there. Her little white suit collar was hanging half off and there was a little burnt circle that looked like ringworm on her left cheek. In one swoop, Zenie pulled her up off the headstone. In Millwood people didn't sit on other people's headstones. Plus this was the white part of the cemetery.

"What? What?" Zenie's voice was different than I'd ever heard it. Hard and low. Troubling the air. She'd grabbed Eva's arms to get her off the headstone and now she was shaking her.

Eva started flapping her arms like a chicken. "Get off me. Get *off* me!" She flapped here and there and Zenie let go. Then Eva just stood there jerking around and whining low in her throat.

Then she just folded up like a box. Zenie was fighting her fall here and there trying to hold her up, but she was scrabbling at Zenie like Zenie was a tree she was trying to climb. Then Eva folded for sure and started sliding down the front of Zenie's dress.

Zenie hollered at me to grab on and we brought Eva down easy onto the Daddy Gone Home grave. She lay there flat on her back with her arms splayed out looking like Jesus cut down from the cross. Zenie made a groan and came down on her knees beside Eva. I knew the kneeling down must have about killed Zenie. She'd just been talking about her legs and how much they hurt. Zenie's penny eyes filled up with something, not tears, but worse, a wideness that had no beginning or end.

"Have mercy," Zenie whispered. It wasn't a cry when she said it but a low, long drawn out disturbance of the air that didn't stop when the words did. There on her knees beside Eva she froze and looked all around us in a full circle. No one was around.

Eva was still stretched out with her eyes closed. The lids on her eyes were twitching and her lips were mumbling to themselves something I couldn't hear.

Then Zenie looked up at me like she was seeing me for the first time in her life.

"Get Ray." She said it like it was a cold spring of water running from her lips. "*Get* him."

So I ran for Zenie's place and burst in the front room yelling for Ray. Miss Josephine was sitting in her big chair with the doilies on the arms. From the depth of the chair she looked out at me like she'd just been waiting years for me to come in and say that very thing. She didn't say why or what, just pointed to the back door with one long trembling finger.

I ran straight out the back door, jumped from the bottom step to the hard-packed red dirt below and headed for the shed.

I was trying my dead-level best to yell, but seeing Miss Josephine's look had changed me into a little bird that could only chirp. So "Ray" came out like that. Chirp, chirp. Light and sweet-sounding. The kind of sound you'd expect to wake you up on a bright and sunny day. Not the kind of sound that will make a man put down his file, cock his head, and look up. So when I burst into the shed, Ray didn't look up, he was squatting down to sharpen a lawn mower, but when he did look, it all started to happen. Ray taking that one look and jumping to his feet. Both of us running back to the cemetery. He ran out so far ahead of me that he disappeared over the little hill that separated Shake Rag from the cemetery. He had held onto his file, which had a sharp point. I was left thinking, as I ran by myself with no one in sight, this isn't happening, nothing has happened. But when I saw Ray's hat lying in the dust, I knew I was wrong. Ray was careful with his hat. I stopped and picked it up.

I came over the hill and there was Ray carrying Eva, with her arms wilted at his sides. Zenie was limping along behind, carrying Ray's file and crying out something, not words but something else. A sound that signified, but not anything in particular. Then she started saying, "In broad daylight." She said it over and over as if it were the chorus to a song.

Ray's hair was plastered to his head where his hat had been and sweat was beading up all over his face. He looked down at me like I was a snake under his feet and said, "Get on back to your mamaw's. Get on back. Get out of here." He spit the words out like they were a bad taste in his mouth.

I didn't want to go back. Maybe Ray hadn't thought about how much help I could be. I wanted to run ahead and tell Miss Josephine to get the bed ready for poor Eva and make up a cold pitcher of tea. I looked to Zenie to let me, but she flicked her hand at me *no* and I knew that meant I had to go. I was worried about Eva too, and wondered who in the world would have hurt her like that. A crazy man whose door she knocked on by mistake? A hobo passing through town? A criminal who'd escaped from Parchment Penitentiary over in Jackson? Did she have a fit and fall on a cigarette lighter someone had offered? My mind was a busy dragonfly, lighting on one possibility after the other.

Heading back to Mimi's I passed the cemetery again and something caught my eye. A piece of white beside the Daddy Gone Home grave. It looked like something Eva had dropped, maybe one of her pretty handkerchiefs with the "E" stitched out with little flowers, but when I drew close I could see it was a dirty wadded-up piece of paper with wide lines on it like my school notebook. There was writing printed in big letters on it. Three words. *Go Home Bitch.* When I said them out loud, they came out of my mouth like a hissy snake.

So here was this note about going home bitch, lying right there on the grave of somebody called Daddy who had already Gone Home. It hit my funny bone in a peculiar way, like the electric shock you get when you hit your elbow wrong. It went straight through me and burrowed down into my stomach, where it shook and trembled and tried to find a way out. I'm sorry to say I started laughing. Once I started, I couldn't stop. I can make excuses. I can say I was tired. I was aggravated too. Here poor Eva was all sick and hurt, I'd done all the running back and forth, and I thought I deserved to get to find out how things turned out, how the story finally ended. But instead here I was having to walk by myself all the way back to Mimi's from whence I'd just come, when she was likely still mad as fire at me for what I'd said about her looking like Honey Bunny.

So I laughed. And the more I laughed the funnier it got. Old Daddy Gone Home and the note about going home and me without a home to go back to, stuck in the cemetery between Shake Rag and Mimi's. I sat down in the grass on Daddy Gone Home's grave and held the piece of paper and bent over laughing. The grass over the grave seemed soft as a bed, the ground beneath giving and loving. I laughed so hard I thought my jawbones were going to crack wide open. I thought my heart was going to pop out of my chest. So I lay back on the spongy mound and laughed some more until I got the hiccups.

Then a strange thing happened. I guess I went dead asleep because before long I saw Eva and my mama dancing the cha-cha around in the sky, Eva in her nice dark suit with her hair flipped just so and Mama in her old loose baking dress and sweetheart rose apron, her bangs standing out like electricity was racing through her body. They were dancing up toward heaven. Left, two, cha, cha, cha. Right, two, cha, cha, cha. Then they did a couple of shuffle ball changes, and Eva grabbed hold of Mama's apron strings and they turned their backs on me and cha, cha, chaed right up amongst the clouds and through the vault of heaven. Mama leading the way and Eva holding on for dear life to those apron strings. Neither one of them looking back. Then they were gone and I knew it was for forever and eternity.

When I woke up, the sun was almost down and I felt a weight pressing on my neck. Was I getting strangled? I opened my eyes and there was my flesh-and-blood mother bending over me breathing hard, holding her fingers to the side of my neck and calling out my name.

"Damn it the hell, Florence, what's wrong with you, honey? Are you sick? Did you faint?" She rained questions down on me like she was a thunderstorm and I was the helpless earth. "What you doing in the cemetery lying here like this? *On a grave!* Where's Zenie, for God's sake?"

There was something about the sound of her voice that made me want to bawl my eyes out. I just held out my arms and tried to pull her down to me. I wanted her to lie down in the grass on the giving ground and for us to lie there together forever and forever amen. I had lost my mother, and now she was found. Blessed Assurance, Jesus is Mine.

But she didn't get down. She scrambled to her feet and grabbed my arms. She jerked me up and pulled me along toward the Ford, which was parked right in the middle of the street, I guess at the place where she first saw me lying there on her way up to Zenie's to pick me up. I was glad to be rescued and tried to come along, but I felt like my bones had melted into a puddle. I could barely walk I was so dog tired from running for help and laughing and sleeping, so she put her right arm around my waist and pulled my left arm around hers and half walked half dragged me to the car.

"Where's Zenie? Where *is* she?" she hissed the questions this time. She cranked up the car and we shot off. She expected answers and fast. She was mad as fire at Zenie for not seeing about me, for leaving me in the *cemetery* of all places, so I told her what happened with Eva, the way her hair was messed up, the ringworm-looking circle on her face, me running to get Ray, and Ray having to carry her home. At first Mama was asking me things, like what Eva looked like, were her clothes torn, was she bleeding. Then she stopped asking and got real quiet. She leaned over me and opened the glove compartment and pulled out a pack of Daddy's Luckies. "Open it," she said, and I pulled the red string and took off the clear paper, then the silver paper, and then she snatched the pack out of my hand and pulled out a cigarette and put it in her mouth. "Light me up," she said. I pushed in the cigarette lighter and, when it popped out, I put it up to her cigarette. She looked hard at it for a minute before drawing in. Her hand was shaking on the wheel as she drove us toward home, and she was sucking in and blowing out like her life depended on it. The only sounds I heard the rest of the way home were her sucking and blowing and underneath it all the old muffler in the Ford whining like a dog that wants to be let out.

When we pulled up in front of Big Dan and Miss Kay Linda's and started down the stepping-stones to the back, where our house was, Mama commenced running. I just trudged along behind. What's the hurry? We're just going home.

But Mama ran down the path and busted in the front door of our house like the place was on fire and she was going to rescue somebody. "Win!" I heard her hollering for Daddy before I got in the door. "Win! Win!" Daddy's name cannonballed out of her throat and bounced off the walls.

But there was no answer because Daddy was not home. The house seemed to call back "Win! Win!" as if it'd lost my daddy too and couldn't find him either.

Mama got her poison bottle out from under the sink and pulled out a clean jelly jar from the cabinet and poured it to the top. Then she looked around like she didn't know what to do next. Her hair was wet around her face. She ran her fingers through it and the bangs stood straight up like little soldiers. She paced the kitchen for a minute. Then she let out a sigh and started to rummage around in the refrigerator for her shortening and eggs and buttermilk and slammed them down on the counter. Saturday was a big baking night and I knew she had seven whole cakes and four halves to make because I had taken most of the orders. She didn't say a mumbling word to me, so I figured supper was a lost cause. I went and got on my bed and before I knew it, off I went again, just like at the cemetery. Seemed like every time I stopped moving, I went straight to sleep.

When I woke up it was deep dark and the place had cooled down. I knew it was real late. Wee morning hours, past baking time. I heard the *no no no no* of the train and guessed it was the one-thirty M & O. I lay there for a while trying to get back to sleep, but my stomach was growling and carrying on. Then the phone rang, and I heard Daddy say "yeah" into it after the first

ring. Then he said "number three" and "all right." Then he hung
up. No good-bye. I'd already put my feet on the floor to go down
to the basement for Daddy's box. When the phone rang late and
Daddy talked numbers, that was a sure sign he was going to want
me to get it. But then I heard Mama come out of her room and
say, "Win." They went back into the bedroom and shut the door.
They stayed there for a long time. Then Daddy came out and
made a call. I couldn't hear exactly what he said, but it sounded
like "sick" and "be careful," and by the time he hung up I knew
he'd be staying home this one night and we could get some rest.

After a while I heard Daddy's snore, which sounded like a
little motor trying to start. I was hungry but there was nothing in
the kitchen but Mama's pretty cakes lined up and shining in the
moonlight. I opened the refrigerator. It was bare except for some
milk. I drank a glass and then got myself a sharp knife and ran
it up under each cake where the icing had lapped over onto the
cardboard. I turned the knife a little so the sharp edge scrapes
off just a little icing and cake from underneath. If I was careful,
it wouldn't show. I licked the knife, careful not to cut my tongue.
I went around to each cake and took a little from underneath on
each one. When I was done, you couldn't see a thing. The cakes
looked pure and new. In the moon glow they looked like those
flowers that bloom only at night when no one's watching.

I tiptoed back to my room and put on my pajamas and got
back into bed. I was not a bit sleepy, having slept all over town,
including bedding down with the dead ones. My heart beat hard
to the sugar. After a while I heard another lonesome train come
through town, calling out something that sounded like *lost,
lost*. And under the train whistle, I could hear my jittery heart
going *clickety clack*, like wheels flapping the rails.

Then I heard another sound: my mother crying. Soft, but
settled in for the long haul.

The next morning Mama's cakes were lined up on the table like little girls with lacy doily collars ready for Sunday School. Daddy was still asleep when here came the cake ladies tiptoeing in single file down the path from the street (my mother still well enough to have Sunday pickups, though that time would soon be over). Some of the ladies had rollers and pin curls in their hair, but they all were dressed and powdered up for church. Mama's eyes were puffy from crying but she made her lips into pretty curls. She handed the cakes out at the door since the ladies were in a rush and Daddy was still dead to the world. Hello to this one, how're you doing to that one, she whispered, and pocketed their money in her apron. When the last cake lady walked up the path to her car, Mrs. Winifred Long with the second of two cakes for her twin girls' birthday party (to which I was not invited), Mama's eyes filled up again.

There was one cake left on the table, a six-layer lemon with the divinity icing. My mother looked at me and looked at the cake and said, "All right." I didn't know what *all right* meant. Was she telling me to get ready for church? It wasn't like Daddy's "all right" when he hung up the phone. Daddy's "all right" closed things down; this "all right" coming out of Mama's mouth opened something up. So I just stood there waiting for a clue as to what was going to happen next, and I was thinking that's what I've been doing all summer, just waiting for the next thing and never ever knowing what it's going to be. Then Mama went into the bathroom for a while and came out smelling like toothpaste and lilacs. She looked at me hard, spit on her hand, and wiped it across my hair. Her spit smelled like apples that had been on the ground too long. A sweetness that had given way to something else.

"All right. Can you get the cake?" she whispered, and I whispered back, "Yes ma'am."

"Let's go." The words were so soft they seemed to curl out of her mouth like smoke. She wanted them to rise and blow away before Daddy woke up.

My heart started skipping rope. Where were we going? I slid my hands under the cake. Lemon cakes were Mama's heaviest on account of there being so many layers. Plus the jell is heavy. I hadn't had a thing but icing and a glass of milk since noon the day before, and the way my heart skipped and hopped over and under the cake made me nervous. Mama held the front door open, and I passed through with the cake held close to my chest for balance like she'd taught me but not so close that it would press up against my front. She came along behind, missing every other stepping-stone up the walk to the street where the green Ford was parked. Against my better judgment, I gave her the cake to hold while I got in the front seat. When I got settled and she bent over to give me back the cake, she almost fell headfirst into my lap. I pushed her back and took the cake from her like it was my own little baby. Nothing had happened to it. It was still perfect.

I was expecting a wild ride to some cake lady's house, but instead Mama drove in a slow crawl down Goodlett Street to Shake Rag and Zenie and Ray's place, as if the Ford were a broken vase whose pieces she was trying to hold together.

First thing we saw when we drove up was Miss Josephine sitting in a straight-back kitchen chair under the good-sized mimosa tree in Zenie and Ray's front yard. The mimosa was blooming to beat the band those whiskery pink puff balls. The tree made a tent of lace and fluff over Miss Josephine's head, like she was sitting under a giant pink and green petticoat. She was bent over like always, but this morning her white hair was a mess, flying all over the place instead of tucked into its neat little bun. She had a big pile of mimosa leaves in her lap and was just counting away, throwing the counted ones in a pile on her right, pulling the uncounted ones from the branches on her left. The bottom third of the tree was bare of leaves. There were piles everywhere, wilted and tucked-in looking, like mimosa leaves get when they're touched, much less ripped off the tree. The yard was getting to be a mess.

Ray was sitting on a pallet he'd set up for himself outside under the tree. Was he sleeping outside? He had his head in his hands. No hat. When he looked up, his eyes seemed darker, all black, even in the bright morning sun. The light, the busy flecks of gold, all long gone. In their place, a swamp of still water.

All in one breath Mama said, "Morning, Miss Josephine. Morning, Ray." Miss Josephine didn't even look up.

Ray nodded but didn't get up or look my mother's way. Mama didn't notice. I did. Ray had nice manners. He always took off his hat when talking to a lady, black or white, but today he didn't have it on. Did Zenie drop it on the way back from the cemetery? I would have taken good care of it if they'd let me come along back to the house.

Mama didn't stop walking. "Zenie and Eva inside?"

Ray nodded and looked hard at a spot on the ground.

Mama told me to go sit down by Miss Josephine while she visited with Zenie and Eva.

The last thing I wanted to do was stay outside. Ray was eyeing me like I was poison, and Miss Josephine put me in mind of the mental girl on the porch in Milltown. Plus I wanted to see Zenie and Eva too. Eva ought to be feeling better, even if she was still scuffed up some. But Mama grabbed the cake from me and started shimmying up the path to Zenie's front steps. On the pallet Ray put his head back in his hands and watched the street.

While Mama was inside, people came and went in the yard patting on Ray and Miss Josephine. Two old men in suits came to stand in the middle of the yard and pray. Good Lord Jesus, give us strength to carry our burdens and strength to cast them away.

Make us instruments of Thy peace and strong in every battle. Turn our enemies away and make us victorious over the Satan in our midst and his followers. Bring us peace, oh Lord Jesus, the peace that passeth understanding. Now and forever and ever. Amen.

Zenie's Heroines of Jericho ladies from St. John the Baptist brought dishes with checkered cloths over them. They stepped around me like you'd step around poison ivy. Ray talked to some men who came up and watched the street with him. Miss Josephine was still counting leaves out in the yard and folks were trying to get her to go in out of the heat but she told them she couldn't leave, she was afraid she'd lose count. Ray looked through everybody like they weren't there. "Go on in," he'd say, but he wouldn't look at them when he said it. He just kept looking right and left, right and left, like he was expecting Hitler's Army to come marching down the street. Morning sun was rising and it was getting hotter. Trees lapped over the still streets; everything was already tired and steamed up.

So I hunkered down next to Miss Josephine. Mimosa leaves are hard to count. When you pull them from the tree the way she was doing, it pains them and they turn in on themselves. Do you count the one frond with all its feather parts? Do you notice that each feather has dozens of its own little leaves that need counting? It's multiples of multiples, one set of leaves growing out of another set, no end to it. Work of a lifetime to count out one tree if you do it right and Miss Josephine was doing it right. She'd finished high school before she had to start maiding, and was just as good at numbers as she was at reading books. Every time she reached one hundred she heaved a big sigh and pulled out a piece of paper she kept wadded up in the pocket of her dress over her bosom roll and made a single mark on it. The paper was filled with marks on one side, and she'd turned it over and started in on the other.

I should have been worrying about how sad everyone was, but this was before I knew how sadness can ride the wind, planting and reaping itself over and over, and not always in the same plot of ground, before it leafs out and flowers. Even now, as I remember sitting and watching Miss Josephine, sadness is lighting here and there, like mimosa fluff on the thick air. But, then, sadness had yet to fold itself around my heart and tuck me in at night.

What I was thinking as I watched Miss Josephine go through each and every leaf frond—singles, multiples, multiples of multiples—was how hard it must be to move through those leaves again and again and not lose count. How it must be the only thing you can hold in your mind if you're going to do it right. No what's for supper or doesn't the feathery leaf feel soft or isn't it hot today thoughts. No thoughts at all. For to get off track just one instant will make the whole job of counting come folding in on itself, like a deck of cards you pile up just right. A breath, a touch, some trouble in the air. Then, what a waste!

7

The hot sun had browsed halfway across the sky, but no sign of my mother. I was still folded up like an old dog by Miss Josephine's feet. She was wearing some satiny slippers, torn in some places and thin in others. Parts of her feet and toes bumped out here and there so that they looked like little bags of new potatoes. Ray's eyes were slits; just to look at him you'd have thought he was dozing in the sun, but he still watched everything that came up the street, his head cocked sideways in his hand. Miss Josephine hadn't missed a beat counting right along on her leaves and the leaves of leaves, forever and ever amen. Did she even know I was down here next to these worn-out feet of hers?

There were mimosa fluffs all over the ground, trodden down like runny globs of pink cotton candy somebody had dropped out of one of those cardboard cones. It made me sad to see them ruined. Nobody was around. Preachers and Heroines of Jericho long gone. All of Ray and Zenie's neighbors who'd been sitting and fanning on their porches or front stoops or watering their petunias and zinnias had up and done a vanishing act since Mama drove up. Not even little children playing in the street. It felt like the whole place was holding its breath. The Ford was starting to look bedimmed in the heat, a green place you could see in the desert that turned into nothing but sand when you drew near. The sun was in my eyes now. I knew that if Mama didn't come out soon, I was going to lay my heavy head down on my hand like Ray had his and then I'd be out like he was pretending to be.

"Ray?" I let the name come out of my mouth soft and easy like a spit bubble that's sure to break with heavy breath. When I said it, I could feel something settle in him. Something that said No. He didn't move an inch. His eyes were still almost closed but I spied them cutting in my direction, waiting for something else, his name in another register he couldn't say no to, and hoping it wouldn't come.

I could make my eyes into slits too, a trick I did when something popped up I didn't want to see, like Mama reaching for the poison bottle. I squinted my eyes up so that everything turned to fuzz and cast-iron gray and I could see the feathers of my eyelashes fold over the furry little nest of gray inside my head where my eyes used to be. The oasis in reverse because it was not the thing that went away, it was the seeing. When I did it the other day, Mama looked over the glass she was pouring the poison into and said I looked ridiculous all squinched up like I'd just swallowed a lemon. She asked me whether my eyes were bothering me. Could I see all right? I said I could, that was the problem. I didn't want to see my one and only mother drinking poison. She looked hard at me and said, "Well get out of the kitchen then. Get out of the house then." The words came out of her mouth like batter, soft and sweet and thick. So I walked out the front door and went to swinging on little Dan and May's swing, which Mama's half a cake a week had bought me. Something came over me and I began to swing higher. It was as if something huge and invisible was behind me, pushing me harder and harder. A wind. A hurricane. If I fell and broke something, Mama would have to put down the eternal glass and come running. She would have to stay by my side in the hospital every minute of the day and night. She would have to forget about the poison.

I pretended I was up in the trees Bomba-style. I let go of one chain with one hand, then one with the other, but I couldn't make myself let go of both at once, though I wanted to. After a while Mama came out on the front stoop and stood under the clematis vine. She folded her arms over her chest and watched me. Her head tilted to the side. Lips tucked up inside her mouth. After a while she said, "Oh honey, come on back in the house, it's too hot out here." Then she turned around and went on back inside. The screen door slammed behind her. I acted like I didn't hear her, but I stopped kicking the dirt to get higher and, after a while, the swing came on down and finally it just floated in the air like a paper boat on a still pond. The bushes and little Dan's house looked blurry because of the sweat running in my eyes.

When I went back in, Mama was nowhere in sight, which is hard to accomplish in our house because there's so little place to go. She'd made me a sandwich, egg and olive with lots of mustard, which is my favorite. It was sitting there on the kitchen table with a glass of milk and a slice of devil's food with angel icing and a nicely folded napkin and fork. I took one look and went into my room and pulled Grandpops' gift, *Uncle Wiggily's Travels*, out of my stack of books I kept under the bed. If I'd wanted to edify myself the way Mimi said I should, I would have picked out one of the work sheets Mimi had given me from her class, but they were, to my mind, dull as dishwater, plus I had to look up every other word. I came back into the kitchen—still no Mama—and sat down, propping the book up against one of the heavy pots she'd put on the table to dry.

Uncle Wiggily's going along the road with this jolly black cricket that made the skillery-scalery–tailery alligator laugh like a fool and soon they come upon a little boy with an awful toothache. His mama takes good care of him and she's done everything she can possibly think of to make her little boy's tooth stop aching, including putting mustard on it. So the old gentleman rabbit and his cricket sidekick tell the little boy a funny story about a dumb monkey who made faces at himself in the mirror because he thought he was looking at another monkey. Well, the little boy's just laughing and laughing at the monkey story, and while his mouth is hanging as wide open as a barn door, his mama sneaks right in and puts a string on his aching tooth. Then she jerks hard on the string and pulls out the bad tooth, and that is that and the little boy is healed in a minute. Glory be! His pain is forever gone.

I wished it was that easy and Eva's hurt was like a rotten tooth. Pull it and that's the end of that. But a burn, that must take a while to heal. Even then, burns leave scars. A boy in my first-grade class had burned his hand on a stove when he was little, and it looked like a spider's web. Fragile and delicate, as if it might tear apart if he threw a ball or gripped a pencil.

When Zenie's screen door at long last slammed, it made me jump. I'd been gone. Dead asleep. The chiggers had been having a field day on my legs. My throat felt like I'd swallowed a mouthful of warm clay, which wasn't altogether a bad taste, a little sweetness to it, considering the fact that I hadn't had a bite of anything the whole miserable day and no supper the night before. Dying mimosa leaves everywhere and Miss Josephine still counting away, though slower than before, and Ray on his pallet now staring straight ahead, the whites of his eyes red through and through. The sky had a purple cast. Where'd the day gone? The mimosa leaves left on the tree were folding back the way they always do at the end of the day. They were tired, time to rest. Soon Miss Josephine would have to quit for the night. You can't count what you can't see.

Who was it coming on out Zenie's front door? For a minute I thought I saw Eva, pretty and perky like always, running out down those steps all ready to say what you-all doing out here in this heat, Miss J? Let's get on in the house now, baby, and I'll make us a pitcher of tea for supper.

But it was my mother coming down the front steps like each and every one would be her last. Down one, then stop. Down another, then stop again. She looked like the Holy Ghost had eaten her up and spit her out. Pinched. Cold sober. One side of her face a splotchy red. Had she been slapped? Or sleeping hard like me?

When Mama finally got herself down Zenie's front steps, she didn't look over at me on the grass, just headed across the yard for the car. I scrambled up and ran around to my side of the car. Jumped in quick. She'd have left me otherwise. I know it now, and I knew it then.

When I got into the car, huffing and puffing, she didn't start it up right away. She just sat looking straight ahead. "She wouldn't have my cake," she said. "She wouldn't even look at it."

After a while, Mama started up the Ford and drove slow like before, down Church Street, left on Main, right on Jefferson, to a tombstone granite building on the corner, right across from the courthouse square. Chiseled into the granite by the front door was a sign that said MILL COUNTY SHERIFF. COLORED ENTRANCE ROUND BACK.

She grabbed her purse off the floor of the car and took out her silvery tube of lipstick. She pulled out her little round mirror and put on one thick coat. It looked like red candle wax. She rummaged through her purse for some Kleenex and couldn't find any so she blotted her lips on the palm of her hand, looked hard at the red heart that was left, and then rubbed it away with her thumb. She reached into a side pocket of her bag and popped a clove in her mouth.

Outside the car there were two clumps of white men watching us like we were a covey of wild game. Sitting ducks. I eyed them back. There were five or six of them in the courthouse square across the street squatting on some steps leading up to a big statue of Nathan Bedford Forrest on a prancing horse. They were leaning against the horse's back legs. Their shirttails were out and they were sipping something out of little brown bags, real little, so I was thinking paregoric, like my great uncle Nash who was wounded used to drink. He carried a little bag like that around and took pulls from it like it was the most natural thing in the world. The horse men's heads were nodding. No soldiers of the cross old Nathan Bedford would want. When we got closer, I could see that their eyes were red.

Right outside Mama's car door was the other bunch. They were parked hard on some old beat-up benches. Red-eyed too, but in a different way, a meanness coming up through the whites of their eyes, popping out like the little drops of blood on your finger when they pricked it at the Health Department and squeezed. At first sight they looked like they had on uniforms, but if you looked closer you could see they were just matching khaki pants and shirts and holsters with guns snuggling friendly-like, up close to their hips. One real light skinned man with eyes the color of gravel had his hand resting nice and easy on the handle of his gun. He rubbed it back and forth; it was a comfort to him.

I was scared Mama was set on me staying in the car, or worse, sitting me down on one of those benches. I'd already decided I'd take my chances with the paregoric clan if push came to shove. When she opened her door and got out, I jumped out fast and ran around to the curb. I offered my hand to her, which I never did.

I wished she'd taken it, but she didn't. She just marched through the gun-toters and I scrambled along behind.

The room we walked into smelled like men. A sharp bite in the air like hard-boiled coffee. Stale smoke and ashtrays piled high with butts. There was a lady at a desk who looked at us like we'd lost our minds coming in here. Her whole face pointed forward until it reached the tip of her nose, like it was wanting to crawl right off her shoulders and go someplace else. Her desk was a mess of folders in high stacks that leaned this way and that, with papers easing out like sneaky prisoners about to make their getaway.

"I need to talk to the sheriff," Mama said right off. I was thinking I would have led into it better, maybe saying good evening and allow me to introduce myself and my little daughter Florence and would you mind calling the sheriff in so we can have just a moment of his time?

"He's busy right now." The lady bird-dogged the air.

"I don't mind waiting. This *is* an emergency, though." Mama stood there with her arms folded, not budging an inch.

"Just a minute, ma'am." The lady was disgusted; that I could tell by the way she had her nose up in the air like we'd just broken wind. Did we smell bad? I looked down at my outfit. My shorts were beige and they had grass stains all over them. I'd had them on yesterday when I'd been rolling around on the grave. Some little mimosa tips were sticking to them, though that was from today and Miss Josephine. The shirt looked even worse. It was yesterday's, maybe even the day before's. Pink knit with what was left of a teddy bear on the front. It was kind of tight, I noticed, now that I was paying attention, and had chocolate smears from the last baking. Plus more grass stains and mimosa tips and something else hard and dark that didn't look like chocolate.

Mama looked better and worse at the same time. Better because her clothes didn't look like she'd been rolling around in the dirt the way mine did, worse because she was the mother and supposed to look all right. She didn't. Her lipstick was too loud and had settled into the corners of her mouth, her hair was stuck to her head in little greasy bunches, her sleeveless blouse wrinkled down the front and coming out of her black patent belt, which I noticed had been pulled two holes tighter than its usual pulled-out slit. Her arms were sticks.

The lady got up and went through a door marked by a torn sign that said NO. No *what* was what I was thinking, when a skinny little man came through the door like he was on his way to a fire, the nosy lady right behind. He had a white napkin floating down his collar and two shiny wet worms for a mustache. The mustache had yellow corn-bread crumbs sprinkled across both halves.

Mr. Sheriff marched up to Mama like he was going to walk right through her on out the front door. He said, "What can I do for you, ma'am?"

I could tell he was mad; here he was, working on a Sunday and now his supper's getting cold because of this crazy woman he's got to deal with. I felt about the same way, except I hadn't seen my supper yet, dinner or breakfast either. One of the Heroines of Jericho ladies had brought a pitcher of ice water out into the yard and that was all that had gone down this old gullet the whole long day.

"I want to talk to you about Eva Greene, Sheriff," Mama said. "She's been bothered and nobody's done anything to try to find the men that did it."

He raised his eyebrows. "Bothered? How bothered?"

Mama took a deep breath. Red splotches were crawling up the sides of her neck, like an army of invisible ants were eating her alive. They were almost to her ears. She lowered her eyes, looking down at the sheriff's napkin, sighed a deep sigh, and leaned into the side of his face and whispered so that I could barely catch the words. "They *fooled* with her."

Now Mr. Skinny seemed nice and worried too. "Don't know nothing about no lady getting bothered. Greene with an e? Don't know no Greenes. Who her people? Where she at now?"

He whipped a little spiral notebook and pencil out of his shirt pocket and started writing something down. But when Mama got to the kin question and said Zenobia and Rayfield Johnson, the man stopped dead and looked at her like she'd just upchucked all over the floor. "Hold your horses, ma'am. You talking about some little colored gal?"

Mama looked daggers at him. "She's hurt too. They burnt her. With a car lighter."

"Who you say you is, ma'am?" He took out his notebook again.

"Martha Forrest, Mrs. Winburn Forrest." Mama chomped down on her clove with her front teeth. She was puffing hard through her bottom lip so that her breath was blowing her bangs straight up. Her lipstick had whiskered the corners of her mouth.

The sheriff looked up from his notebook. "*Win* Forrest?" When Mama nodded, his eyes turned sly and skittery. "I expect that *husband* of yours is worried some too. Maybe he can help y'all find out who-all bothered that little colored gal." The words came out of his mouth all in an excited little rush.

Now everything turned quiet, quiet. Suddenly Mama's face looked like it had been melted down and pressed with strange hands into a shape I'd never seen. Something that had been holding it in place all these years had finally been let go. *Husband* just hung in the air like a rotten fig oozing juice.

Mr. Skinny stood there staring her down, not a word out of him either. Even the nosy lady, who'd been breathing hard behind me, seemed sealed up, shut up. The words that any of us might have said were flushed quail, forever gone.

Sometimes a space in time feels like a slap in the face. First you don't breathe, then you touch the spot, then you can breathe again. Anybody who's been slapped knows this. That's why you can live with getting slapped once every now and then, just not over and over all the time. You need the quiet spaces between.

My heart jumped once, then twice. The sound of it cut through my ears from the inside out. All at once I felt as though I were carrying my head like a punch bowl full to the brim and about to slosh over.

So I said, "Mama." I made it whiney, which wasn't hard, and quiet, which was. I put my hot sweaty hand on her cold limp one and pulled gently so that she slowly turned toward me like a sleepwalker. Then I took her out of there.

When we got back in the car, I knew just one thing. I was sorry about Eva getting bothered, and I knew it was worse than ugly talk—the burn told me that—but I was getting to be hard-nosed; right then I had one thing on my mind and one thing only: I knew I had to get me something to eat.

The last thing on Mama's mind was feeding me. She was sitting behind the wheel looking straight ahead like she didn't even know where she was. The paregoric men and the mean-eyed gun-toting men were having a contest to see who could stare us down the hardest and the guns were winning, but she didn't care who was running their nasty eyes over us. She was cogitating something, but whatever it was was hers alone. Nobody else's. She didn't even see them or me or anybody or anything. In fact, lately I'd been feeling like Mama couldn't see what was right in front of her face. I'd been feeling like I was my mama's eyes. She was blind as a bat at high noon.

So I pushed on her arm. Hard with my knuckle. Turning it. I wanted to hurt her. Make a bruise the size of my fist on her bony little arm.

"I want to go on by Mimi and Grandpops'. Drop me off up there." I spit it out like a mouthful of nails.

Mama didn't answer, but I could tell she'd heard me because she moved her arm a little when I pushed on it. I laid my head back and closed my eyes and waited. In a minute she started up the car. I didn't open my eyes. I didn't know where she'd take me. Home, Mimi's, Zenie's, the bootlegger's. With Mama behind the wheel ripping up and down the county, you never could tell where you were going to end up. I was getting sick and tired of being so here and there all the time. I wanted to be like other children. Precious Cargo. I wanted to have a set bedtime I could whine about and glasses of milk and dentists and somebody telling me to eat my collards for the iron. I wanted to grow up dense and thick with blood and flesh and bone, and I was beginning to think something else was going to happen instead. That I was going to get myself lost somewhere between places. Look at what happened to Eva.

Riding with my eyes closed not knowing where Mama was taking me and thinking about all the bad things that had already happened to Eva and seemed ready to happen to me, I started to cry. Not like a crybaby, but quiet. No carrying on. Just eyes overflowing the far corners like a pot boiling over on the stove so quietly you don't hear it. When you smell smoke and finally find out it's boiled over, it's hot and burnt and dry as a bone in the desert, bleached white in the sun.

Mama took me to Mimi and Grandpops'. I didn't open my eyes until she stopped the car at the curb. By then my face was wet and so was my shirt. She didn't wipe me up, but she handed me her handkerchief with Martha written across it in blue script and hyacinths reaching over either side of her name like heavenly guardians. Then she leaned over and kissed me on the lips, which is something she'd never done before in her life, something nobody had ever done. She kissed me so hard it broke the skin on the undersides of my lips.

"The lights are on. Go on in," she said and when she said it, she looked deep inside my eyes like she was searching for a lost fleck of color. Then she reached over me so that the tips of her pointy bra pierced my side and opened the car door. She gave me a little shove so that I slid across the slick plastic seat and out of the car. Once she got me going I couldn't stop until my feet hit the curb. Then she leaned over again, pulled the door shut, waved a little wave, and drove off.

I stood there on the curb. The green Ford with Mama in it was bumping down Goodlett Street getting smaller and smaller. Then it became nothing but a piece of smoke and curled up and vanished into thin air. The night was steaming around me, the way it gets right after the still darkness gathers up the heat of the day like a mother taking up her baby out of a warm bath. When I looked up at Mimi and Grandpops' square brick house on its little hillock, I could see the two of them through the front window. They were sitting down at the table for supper. Grandpops was facing out so I could see his long grave face straight on. He was bringing a fork up to his mouth. Mimi was sitting by his side, her hydrangea curls all plumed out on her head, which was cocked in Grandpops' direction like she was listening to him say something important. There was a ceiling light that dangled over their heads and made them look like speckled trout, pretty and silvery and slick. My mouth watered.

I couldn't take my eyes off them, so when I took two steps through the hot breathing dark I tripped over the black roots from the oak tree that snaked up from the deep between the curb and the sidewalk. Went down hard on my knees, *wham bam*, like a sinner before an angry God. Crawling through fire and brimstone to get to the Promised Land.

Kneeling there, I knew I was between one thing and the other thing. I knew I could just walk on down the street and vanish into thin air like my mother had just done. Just flat not go on to the next thing. Anybody can do that anytime, that much I knew. I prayed for God to send me Uncle Wiggily with his trusty valise and walking stick and, last but not least, some supper in a red plaid bandana. I wanted Uncle Wiggily to tell me a funny story and make me laugh so hard my mother would hear me and come on back and pull me up off the ground and clean up my knees and take me on home. Then the old gentleman rabbit and I wouldn't have to jump the midnight Frisco and be hobos in a world without end.

Then Mimi slowly turned her head away from Grandpops and toward the window and the dark beyond where I was kneeling. She looked like a bird dog on the point. She smelled me.

All at once I was up and scrambling up the steps, sparks firing up and down my legs. I pushed down the front-door handle with my thumb and went right on in. Mimi was halfway through the living room on her way to the door to see what was out there in the dark. There was a stir, but no what are you doing here girl, or where's your mama and daddy, honey. Nobody breathed a word about my mother or father. The Honey Bunny hat was long gone and Mimi wasn't mad at me anymore. She washed off my knees and put Mercurochrome on them. She was telling me about the tuna salad and tomato aspic she'd made on account of it being such a hot night. I wasn't surprised. Tuna salad, tomato aspic, and hamburgers were the only things Mimi knew how to fix. Even her coffee was bad.

"You want a hamburger honey?" she said all at once like she wasn't able to breathe quite right, and I said, "Yes ma'am, please," in the nicest way possible. To help out, I went to the kitchen drawer and pulled out a knife, spoon, and fork. I got them in my fist and put them down where I usually sat at the table, facing the window, fork on the left, knife and spoon at the right, like Zenie'd taught me. I sat down at the table cool and calm like I'd been invited to supper and arrived a little late.

Grandpops handed me a tuna-salad sandwich, no crust, and said he was glad I was there to take this aspic off his hands, he'd had it two nights in a row and it gave him heartburn. He handed me his little green glass sherbet dish and his own spoon, which was clean.

"I got a spoon," I said and gave him back his in case there was ice cream for later. Mimi liked to pour each aspic into its own separate dish unless she was making it for the Saturday Matinee Club and then she used her big star mold for show. The aspic shook when he passed the dish. It had half a green olive on top. I popped the olive in my mouth and dug into the aspic. I knew what it was: V–8 (two cans of the small but tall ones), two packs of Knox's sparkling gelatin, onion juice (not much), cayenne to taste. Boiled up and cooled down, which is what I was feeling like right now. Molten.

Grandpops said it was awful late for me to be coming by but he was glad to see me. He got up and poured me some milk. I drank it down, and got myself some more.

He sat back down at the table. His eyes narrowed watching me drink the second glassful. "What you had to eat today, girl?"

"I don't know, can't remember." Just when I was answering him back, I could feel my eyes cutting away the way they do when I'm lying. I can't help it; they start cutting away from the person I'm lying to. I try to corral them like they're the sheep out of the pen and I'm the collie dog, but they get away from me.

Grandpops leaned his bony elbows out over his plate. "Try to remember."

"I can't," I said again, which was in the strictest sense true. If you don't eat anything, you don't remember anything. Then he stopped asking, and his mouth marched in a line across his face.

He got back up and went digging around in the refrigerator and pulled out a pot of something. He took it over to the stove where Mimi was flopping her hamburger, which was smoking up and making my mouth water. She poured a good shake of Worcestershire on top of it and peppered it up, which made it sizzle and smoke even more.

"Got a hungry girl here. Let's heat up some of Zenie's peas for her to go along with that hamburger." Grandpops carried the pot over to the stove eye. Mimi didn't even look up, just reached over and turned it on. I knew I was doomed to eat those peas, though I was so hungry I didn't care, just hoped they were field peas, which I tolerated, instead of English peas, which I didn't much care for unless they were real little and came with potatoes. They were standing close to each other at the stove with their backs to me. They were eyeing each other sideways. Their mouths trailed down the sides of their faces like matching parentheses.

I was eating the last tuna sandwich, relishing the crunch of the celery, and watching them eye each other at the stove when they thought I couldn't see. When they both turned around at the exact same time like two halves of the same person and looked back at me nested at the table, I knew that look. When I was still going to school in Millwood before Daddy's escapades, it was the way the teachers looked at The Children's Home Children, who were not regular children but orphan children. Holy Roller children. The Pentecostal Children's Home, which looked like a bigger version of Mimi and Grandpops' house, was a redbrick two-story building out from town. About a dozen or so orphan children lived there. I remembered them from when I was in the first grade here. Their clothes bloomed large around their stalk bodies. They came to school in a bus that said Children's Home. They trooped off the bus looking neither left nor right, just trudged on into the schoolhouse. They sat in a row in the cafeteria and bowed their heads to pray while everybody else was laughing and talking. Then they opened little packages of waxed paper like Christmas presents and brought out corn bread, sometimes hard flat biscuits.

At night sometimes you could hear the Holy Rollers moaning and hollering across town. They sounded like something coming up from deep under the swampy ground. On Holy Roller nights I tossed and turned. In my mind's eye I saw the orphan children dancing around, their drapey clothes billowing out like the clouds of heaven. I wondered, if they were orphans, why were they so happy? Did they feel light and free, having no parents?

I was still sitting at the table, but suddenly I couldn't get the food to my mouth anymore. The air around my face felt gauzy. In my mind I was back to being little and wrapped in Uldine's sheets.

"Come on upstairs, honey," Mimi said and pulled on the back of my shirt. Grandpops was gathering up the dishes to put in the sink. Upstairs Mimi pulled me into the bathroom by the shirt and before I could say thank you ma'am I can take it from here, she yanked the shirt over my head like she was whipping a pony and threw it on the floor.

"Got to get you some decent clothes," she said low under her breath, like I was not even in the room, much less pressed up to her middle. "Get your pants off." Her voice sounded worn out. She went over the tub, put in the plug, and started the water. Then she walked out and shut the bathroom door and I thought I was home free. I got myself a washcloth and towel out of the bathroom closet and got into the tub. Then, lo and behold, here she came back, opening the door without even knocking. I was used to taking a bath by myself, and I pulled the washcloth up in front of Between the Legs. No "excuse me" either when she put a towel down beside the tub and knelt down, letting out a little groan while she settled her knees, which had arthritis, and the front of her left leg, which had sciatica running down it, she was always saying, like a little stream of boiling-hot water. Then I saw she had the purple glass she always kept full of water on the table beside her bed, the table that she put in front of the door between her room and Grandpops'. Plus a bottle of Breck shampoo with a pretty lady on the front.

"Mimi, I'm too tired to get my hair washed," I said, and I heard myself sounding like a whiney baby, but she was already pouring the soapy water over my head.

"*Dirty*. This head is *dirty*." It came out grit between her teeth as she started pouring water out of the glass over my head. Once she got my head soaking wet, she poured cold shampoo on it, which woke me up big-time. When she started digging her fingernails into my scalp, I could tell she meant serious business so I squinched my eyes tight.

"I can do it!" I yelped, but she didn't even answer, just dug deeper and deeper into my nasty head. How dirty did she think I was? Then she took the washcloth I was holding over my privates and slapped it over my eyes, tilted my head back and poured bathwater over it. After the pouring business was over, she belted out, "Hang on," like she was worried I was going to hop up out of the tub and run around the block. I couldn't open my eyes because of the water in my face so I just sunk down into the water, which was by now barely warm, with the washcloth still over my face. I felt myself wanting to turn over on my side, like you do in bed when you've been in one position too long and part of you has gone to sleep.

After a while she was back and pulling on my arm to stand up and putting a towel around me. She brought in a satin slip of hers for me to sleep in. It was slick and didn't cover anything to the north of my waist and was so long I had to hold it up to walk, like a lady going to the ball. She got the slip on me and as I was standing there holding it up, she started rubbing my head dry with another towel. When that was done, she combed my hair, which was still wet, pulling my head this way and that. I felt like a doll that a crazy baby girl had gotten hold of.

My hair's nothing to jump up and down about, plus it's hard to comb wet because it's kinky and clumps together. My mama'd taught me to always use creme rinse, which Mimi didn't seem to know about, and to comb it out slow and easy starting at the ends. I was too tired for this business, and my eyes were starting to tear up again and I was thinking damn it the hell, this woman is killing me.

When Mimi started digging around in the bathroom closet, I wondered what was next. Then she came out with a new pink toothbrush in a little plastic case. I was afraid she thought I was such a baby she was going to have to brush my teeth, but she handed it to me, case and all, and pulled some toothpaste out of the medicine cabinet. "I saved this just for you." She said it like she'd just brought me an Easter dress from Montgomery Ward when all it was was a dumb toothbrush. I knew she was wanting me to say thank you ma'am. I didn't. I just pulled the toothbrush out of the case. "Rinse it off. It might be germy," she said, and unscrewed the toothpaste and turned on the water. I put the toothbrush under the water and then held it out to her. "*Voila!*" she said and squirted a big wad of toothpaste onto the brush.

After I brushed my teeth, Mimi put me into my mama's old bed in her old room like it was all planned. Sometime later Grandpops came shuffling up the steps in his bedroom slippers and sat down on the bed. I was long gone by then, but I knew he was there by the heft. Then he patted my damp head and walked out of the bedroom humming "This Is My Father's World," which is my favorite hymn, because it brings out the prettiness of the world, all that's fair. The birds their carols raise, the morning light, the lily white declare their Maker's praise.

Sometime during the night I heard the phone ringing. There were windows on both sides of the bed. They were open and there was a cross breeze making the curtains curl at the edges like dark tulips. The straps on Mimi's slip had slipped down over my shoulders so the slip was only covering me from the hips down. I tried to pull it up, but it was stuck under me. I was cold. So I grabbed at the sheet, but it wasn't enough.

I could hear Grandpops talking into the phone downstairs. I couldn't hear what he was saying, but I could see his words. Bits of gravel he was throwing up against a wall. Then I heard Mimi get out of bed. "Shush," I heard her say. Then he quieted down and I sank back into the cold.

The next morning I opened my eyes to Zenie looking down at me. Her face looked darker than it was really. It blocked out the bright sun coming through the window. It was hot already. Late morning, I was thinking. I kicked off the sheet. I'd slept a good long time. I opened my eyes wider. Her mouth opened like a long dark tunnel. What is she getting ready to say?

Actually, I don't remember anybody in particular telling me about how my mother had gone and run the green Ford smack-dab into the right side of the Memphis-bound M & O passenger train. Maybe it was Zenie blocking the sun who said it, but likely not. Maybe when she saw my eyes open in the morning light, she called in Grandpops. For me it became a fact that seemed to have risen up out of the earth and made itself visible, just like the fact that she did it at Crosstown, where everybody in Millwood had to pass over to get where they were going. There were parts of the Ford all over the place. A boy found the car papers up in a tree a block away. By doing it there, at Crosstown, she kept herself in front of our eyes for always, for whose heart was so closed they could not think of her as they bumped over the tracks on their errands and visitations? After she did it, they installed crossbars there, but it did not matter in people's minds. Who did not taste hot metal when they heard the Frisco shriek through our dark town on its ten-thirty run north?

The surprising thing was that she lived. The fact that the train was creeping along as it always did coming through Crosstown must have saved her. Also, there were skid marks right before she hit. Had she changed her mind? I like to think that maybe my face rose up before her eyes at that moment. That she saw a picture of me in her mind. Maybe I was sleeping, maybe I was looking at her head-on. I like to think that I looked dear to her, dear enough to produce some sort of jitter, the foot moving from accelerator to brake on its own, the way your stomach will grip up at the smile of the beloved one, even if you don't want it to. Even if all that is in your heart is the next mimosa leaf.

Especially now, I can stand on the tracks and watch her face behind the wheel in the red glow of the Crosstown crossing lights looking toward the cyclops eye that is coming for to carry her home. But I can see her on the inside too, looking at me looking at her, my own true eyes shining through the night, saying *no no no no.*

Some stories are uneasy sleepers. They roam a dark house, gliding like silk from room to room. Touching a sleeping form here, tucking in a cover there. Maybe they will wake up on their feet and be confused as to their whereabouts. Or maybe they will unlock the front door without a sound and walk on down the street and out into the night, never to be heard from again. Because some stories can just up and leave. You don't know where they went, or whether they'll ever come back. Their leaving throws up its arms and leans forward into such an emptiness that the words rise up and say no.

— *Part II* —

8

It's hard to say what happened next. There's always the story wanting to live its life, whether you want it to or not. So it may wander off, leaving you to say all right then, I give up, let's go ahead and just shut this book. Uncle Wiggily finally got himself eaten up and this story is plumb over. But just when you settle into thinking that, the story comes back from its wanderings and says why hello there, here I am again. Was I gone long? Did you miss me?

What I remember is that I was under the bed. I wasn't thinking that I was under it. I was thinking how cool the wood floor was. How dark. Then I started looking at dust balls, how soft and colorless they were, like old ladies' hairdos. I saw a dead roach. A big one, on its back with its little claw feet curled upward. I was still wearing Mimi's slip. I could see it trailing below my feet. My top was bare, but I didn't care. I felt good and cool.

I kept seeing feet. Not feet exactly, but shoes and ankles. At the time I didn't attach them to anyone in particular, but they came and went with voices attached to them saying this thing or that. But of course I knew them. The black wingtips topped off with seersucker cuffs were Grandpops'. And the silver brocade slippers with little jelly rolls of stockings on roller garters around the ankles belonged to Mimi. One set of shoes stood for a long time right in front of my face. They were huge white nurse-type shoes. The right had a good-sized hole cut for the side of the big toe. The left had a hole cut on the outside for the little toe. The shoes were scuffed up and the heels were wore down on the outsides. Upward from the shoes, thick white stockings covered elephant ankles.

"Will somebody please tell me right now what it doing under the bed when its mama going to be all right? What it think it *doing* under there? Its mama going to be *all right*. Hey. You hear me? You gone deaf and dumb, girl? Come on out of there and quit playing the fool."

Zenie called me *it* when she was being extra nice or she wanted to talk me into something like helping her with the garbage. I wasn't biting.

"Got one at home won't get out the bed. Now this one won't get out from under it. Got better things to do than pull folks out from under beds. Got enough trouble of my own to contend with." Zenie sounded disgusted enough to spit.

I turned my face to the wall and went on off to sleep again.

When I woke up again, the first thing I noticed was that it had gotten to be late afternoon. There were long points of light on the floor. Pretty and peaceful on the dark wood. There were no thoughts in my head about anything except those points of light, how they seemed to lie still over the floor but really were inching along from the dresser to the door. You had to keep watch over them to see that motion.

I was lying there watching the points inch along across the floor when it began to dawn on me that someone besides myself was breathing in the room. I didn't see any shoes so I thought I was making it up in my head. But when I listened hard, there it was. In and out. A little *whoosh*, then a pause, then another little *whoosh*.

All of a sudden the monster in the bed above me shivered and shook itself. Then the breathing started up again. *Whoosh*, pause, *whoosh* again.

Then a giant sigh. Long and drawn out.

I wiggle-wormed myself over to the edge of the bed. I held up the spread and pushed my head out a little. Hanging off the side of the bed directly above me was my daddy's own hand. I'd know it anywhere, with its little bunches of black spider hairs. Looking up at it, I could see the palms with lines crisscrossing back and forth like tiny little roads you'd take a trip up and down. I knew the little lines meant something because when I went to the State Fair on school day I had seen the gypsy reading palms. I didn't have the fifty cents to get her to read mine, but I hung around and listened to her tell people about their lifelines, how long or short they were. Some of them had the true love line, some didn't. I wished I knew how to read the story of my father's hand lines. The truth was that his lines were all about the same, not long or short, just crossing and crisscrossing. Always coming back to one or the other. Not going anywhere in particular.

When Daddy's hand came down and touched my face it felt so feathery and nice I shut my eyes and enjoyed it even when the place where it touched me started getting wetter and wetter. We lay like that for a while, me on the floor under the bed with only my face out, him on the bed with his hand hanging down touching my face, which just got wetter and wetter. Then I got to crying so hard that my back was thumping the hard floor making a racket. That's when he rose up, making the bed heave and quake, and clumped his feet on the floor, shoes and all. He'd been lying there with them on. In one long gathering motion he leaned down and got me up under the arms and pulled me out, the drowning one, naked on the top with Mimi's wedding train slip trailing behind me. He picked me up off the floor, and I buried my face deep in his neck. I didn't look at him, just went to him like he was the last one on earth. One of those brave and true men on the white horses who rescue you from harm and drape you over their steeds like a lily and ride off with you into the night because you are Precious Cargo.

"Come on, Sister," he said into my hair. "Let's us go on home."

He went clumping on down the stairs with me, slow and loud. There was a bustle below, but I didn't move my face out of his neck to see who was there. I heard voices talking about a car. Daddy needed one.

Then I heard Grandpops say, "Win, leave her here with me and Irene and Zenie. You got Martha to worry about in the hospital. How you going to take care of them both?" And Daddy saying back between his teeth, "I been at the hospital all night. Then come up here and find my baby girl under the bed. What kind of taking care is that? Best thing you can do for everybody right now is let me have the damn car so I can take my girl home." I had my ear right next to Daddy's throat. I could hear a growl behind the words, coming up deep. He was the dog and I was his bone. Nobody was going to take me away from him without a killing fight.

Next thing I knew he was carrying me out through the kitchen. I looked over his shoulder. There Zenie sat in the ladder chair. It was tilted back against the wall like always. But something was different. She looked at me dead-on, but with a bored look that didn't know me anymore. I was a ragamuffin she had nothing to do with, getting taken through her kitchen, an orphan girl Daddy had found on the street and was just carrying through, the way the salt man carries the bags over his shoulder to the basement to clean the running water. Daddy's head didn't turn in her direction. She didn't speak to him or he to her. After we passed, I heard Grandpops come into the kitchen and tell Zenie to go on home, take the rest of the day off. Then he said he was going to go down to the sheriff's office and talk to him about the hooligans who hurt Eva, to which Zenie said, "Maybe you do better than Ray."

Daddy carried me out the kitchen door and onto the screened-in back porch and out the back screened door, then down the steps to the driveway, his shoe scratching gravel, and on into the open garage. He opened the back door of Mimi's Plymouth and hoisted me headfirst onto the backseat, facing rear. I pressed my face into the cloth upholstery and settled into the smell of the backseat. Mimi's White Shoulders and Grandpops' pipe rolled into one smell that was sweet but also sharp and bitter. Then Daddy took Mimi's slip, which probably was dragging ground right outside the car door, shook it off, and laid it over me like a sheet. I felt tucked in good and comfortable. Precious Cargo.

He got into the front seat and backed out the car and drove us the ten blocks home. After he parked the car and got out, he opened the back door and said, "Sister honey, come on now and get on out of the car. You about to break my back." He didn't say it mean or anything. Just old-man tired.

So I crawled out backwards, hoisted the slip up over my chest, and picked up my train. I put it over one arm and started walking down the path of stones Mama had made. I looked up and saw Big Dan and Miss Kay Linda standing like statues behind their screen door. "Y'all need anything, Win?" Miss Kay Linda called out. "No, we're just going to bed," Daddy called back. "All right then," she said, "but just let us know." They kept standing there and watching us through the screen.

I stopped on the path, but Daddy came up behind me and pushed me on. We went on into the house. When we got inside, I couldn't look at anything. Just kept my head down so I wouldn't trip. It was almost dark. For a minute both of us stood there in the living room with the shadows starting to play on the walls. We stopped right inside the front door. What were we waiting for? The voice that would call us out of this nightmare? "Y'all home? Wash up for supper"? The clatter of a beater in the kitchen? A sigh from the bedroom and ice cubes in the glass?

Then Daddy pushed me on through to the kitchen. When he turned on the light, we both jumped. There was food piled up everywhere, plus a big mess of day lilies on the kitchen table in a vase I'd never seen. I was used to seeing all of Mama's cakes lined up, so at first I thought that was what I was seeing. But it wasn't. Instead, it was food of all shapes, sizes, and colors. My eyes popped. I'd never seen so much food all there together at once, especially in our house, where it was usually slim pickings except for cakes and moonshine. Mrs. Polk had been there with one of her caramel pies. There were loaves of bread long and round, some of Miss Kay Linda's famous iced cinnamon rolls, a ham cut in little diamonds and covered with brown sugar and mustard with pineapple circles with cherries in their middle all over it. A casserole with French-fried onion rings on the top.

Each piece of food had a card or a note attached to it. Daddy picked the cards up like they were breakable. I could read enough to see that they all had the same word in them. *You.* They said, "Thinking of *you*" or "Praying for *you*" or "God Bless *you*" or "We're here for *you*." I never thought *you* could be on so many people's minds at once.

When I opened the icebox to get a drink of cold water, we got another shock. It was packed full. Bowls of potato salad, one with bacon, one without. A plate of stuffed eggs with a half a little green olive on top of each and every one. Chicken salad with grapes, of all things. Casseroles with aluminum foil on top with little notes that said, "Heat for 30 minutes at 350. May be frozen. Keep your strength up. We're praying for you each and every day."

I held the door and we stood there looking at it all. All of a sudden my mouth started watering the same way my eyes had done when Daddy's hand had come down from on high and touched my face. There was no stopping it. I was drowning in it.

"Whooee," Daddy said, and rubbed his eyes like you'd do when you saw something you didn't believe. "You hungry?"

"Don't know" was what I said, not because it was the truth but because it didn't seem right to be hungry as a horse when your own mother was lying up in the hospital with a broken this and a broken that, and *under observation*, whatever that meant, for having just run herself into the side of a train accidentally on purpose. But I just stood there beside Daddy holding the tail of Mimi's slip over my arm because I couldn't bring myself to close the icebox door. If Mama had been there, she would have said, "Close the door, Florence, you're just running up the electric."

Daddy looked down at me. "Go get that thing off and put on your pajamas. Wash your face. Then see how you feel. Your mama would want us to eat." Which I knew was an out-and-out lie, but I went and did what he told me and put on my pajamas with the daisies and washed my face, which made me feel more like myself, except I started tearing up again when I spied Mama's little plastic comb-and-brush set with some of her hair still in it on the back of the commode. I didn't brush my teeth.

When I came back into the kitchen, Daddy had pulled the stuffed eggs and one of the potato salads out onto the kitchen table. He was standing over the table taking hunks out of the ham with a little paring knife. When I came into the kitchen, he reached over and waved a hunk of it with a cherry in front of my face and I opened my mouth and baby-birded it. It leapt up in my mouth, alive and excited to be there. All I wanted in the whole wide world was another bite of that ham. Then he opened a drawer and got out another little knife and spoon. He handed them across the table to me so that I could dig into whatever I wanted. Mama would have said, "This is no way to eat. Fix yourself a plate and sit down," but of course, Mama wasn't there, and if she had been, there would have been next to nothing to eat anyway. I started sawing on my side of the ham, then I ate six stuffed eggs, one right after another, in what seemed like two seconds. Then I started scooping up the fried onion rings off the top of a casserole, which turned out to be French-cut green beans and mushroom soup. Given my options, I passed on the potato salad.

We stood there for a long time under the one bright overhead light in the kitchen. Daddy's head and shoulders cast a deep shadow over the table. The more I ate, the more I wanted to eat. The kitchen was the only lighted place in the house. The other part was getting darker and darker, which made me feel like I was being watched by the darkness in the rest of the house the way a cat watches a baby rabbit just out of the nest. If Mama had been there, she would have gone around pulling the curtains closed and turned on the lamp in the living room. Fussing about how, no matter how much she dusted, the bangles on it were always a mess.

All at once, thinking about Mama dusting made a piece of ham get bigger on its way down my throat. Plus something was tickling the back of my throat. A praying-for-you stranger's hair in the stuffed egg? The thought made my chest seize up and my stomach take a jump. Then my mother's long-goneness filled up my whole throat and it was Katy bar the door because what had gone down had just taken a U-turn and was coming right back up. I ran for the bathroom and barely made it in time. The ham came out of my mouth whole, then the rest all sour and mixed up. I knelt down and leaned over the commode for a long time. I'd take a break and just lie on the cold tile, then set to it again. Daddy came to the bathroom door, which was open, but he didn't come in and hold my head and put a cold washcloth on my head, the way Mama would have done. He just stood back from the door, turning his head in the other direction, and chatting me up while I was busy upchucking.

"Sister, I can't come in, honey. You don't want Daddy to get sick too, do you? You all right? You all right now?"

I couldn't see him at all now because he'd moved back to one side of the door so he wouldn't have to be looking in. But I heard him still talking to me. "Flush it, honey. Smells bad. You all right?"

I kept on till it all came back up. Then I flushed the commode for the last time, I hoped. Mama had showed me how to wet some toilet paper and wipe up the lid when I made a big mess, so I did that and then sloshed some water around in my mouth and brushed my teeth real good, all the time getting encouragement from Daddy. "Okay, good, you must feel better. You just ate too much too fast. Get on to bed now. Just go on to bed."

I didn't answer, just did what I needed to do to get the taste out of my mouth. My pajamas needed changing, so I opened a drawer in the dark and got out my last pair and put it on. (Mama would've made me take a bath right then before I put on my last pair of clean pajamas.) I put my arm through a raggedy hole in the top, making it tear more, and got confused about where my arm should go but then figured it out. I was sweaty, both from getting sick and the heat, so I turned on the fan and got on top of the bed. I could hear Daddy banging around in the kitchen. He was having a time getting all that food crammed into the icebox.

I could hear him pulling some things out and putting others in, muttering to himself. What did people expect him to do with all this food?

That's when I started thinking about how strange it was that things can go along so nice for a long long time. The cakes all laid out, and the beer spraying your face on summer night rides and people playing with each other so sweet and nice like Zenie and Ray, and Mimi's tomato aspic, and Eva's little red suitcase of makeup, which would cover up that bad place on her face if she'd just get out of the bed, and Daddy's pretty box that his great-granddaddy made with his own hands to be passed on from son to son. It was all so wrapped up together that I couldn't see for anything why Mama had to go and do what she did. Tear the web. What was the purpose to it? You tell me.

The night air outside had turned to syrup. Mimosas, I thought, which made me think of Miss Josephine. Had she finally counted all the leaves she could reach? Was she satisfied? I was more interested in the blossoms, sweet beyond anything, but mixed with something else. Dust? I remember my mother twirling them under my nose to wake me up when I was little. They made me sneeze and laugh. Maybe they would work on Eva and make her forget about the hooligans, I thought; maybe Miss Josephine was concentrating on the wrong part of the tree.

After a while, Daddy came in and took off his shoes and heaved himself down on the bed. Under the hair oil, he smelled deep-down dirty, the way you smell when you sweat over old sweat and don't bathe or change your clothes for a long time. Nasty. If he'd come into the house smelling like that, Mama would have said, "Win, what you been into? You're going to run us all out of the house. Go get yourself a bath before you do another thing!"

When he fell down on the bed, he rubbed my stomach for a minute like he always did. Then he started humming a hymn. I could put the words to it. "Just as I am without one plea but that thy blood was shed for me and that thou biddest me come to thee, oh Lamb of God, I come. I come." It wasn't one of my favorites. When I heard it, I always saw someone having to reach out and hug a bloody Jesus. I'd never heard Daddy sing it before. He usually favored fighting songs. "Onward Christian Soldiers" was his favorite. His humming was long and drawn out. Mournful. He was lying flat on his back and so was I. When I turned to look at him, he didn't look back but I could see his eyes were wide open. After we lay there awhile, the ten thirty came through. *No no no no.* That got me going again. Then he got going too, and not quiet like me, but sobs that shook the bed. He rubbed on me while he was crying and I patted his hand. Then right in the middle of a sob he fell dead asleep. I turned my face away from him and crawled farther to my side of the bed to get closer to the window and the night air. His dead hand fell on my back when I turned. It was so heavy that it seemed to be dragging me back to him, but then, as I moved farther away, it fell like a log onto the space I'd made between us. I looked out the screen at the shapes moving in the little breeze outside. The limb of an old cedar bush touched the screen again and again as if it were reaching for something inside.

I lay there for a long time. Daddy seemed to be trying to gallop full speed through his sleep so that by the time he had to get up he would have gotten as much of it as possible. He was breathing hard and fast and he twitched and snorted every now and then. His weight made it hard to stay away from him. It made a little hill out of my side of the bed, and I kept sliding down. Finally I gave up trying and let myself fall back toward him. I burrowed deep into his side. By then I'd gotten used to the smell. It didn't bother me anymore. I was the bat and he was the cave.

I'd just about settled when I had a thought that woke me right back up. Everything was dead quiet. No pans sliding in and out, no radio, no spoons stirring or whisks whisking. If Mama had been there, she would have been in the hot kitchen baking right this very minute. The thought made me gasp. Mama's cakes! Three wholes and two halves, all due for pickup tomorrow! I had seen the list.

In a flash I rolled out from Daddy's backbone and sat straight up. I needed to get up and make the cakes or Mama's whole business would go down the drain. Hadn't Mama just told Daddy last week, when he was ragging on her for working too hard, that if it weren't for her cakes, we'd have gone to the poorhouse a long time ago? I could see the word spreading like wildfire through Millwood. Martha isn't making her cakes anymore. Who's going to make them now? Then some lady we never even heard of popping up out of nowhere and saying, don't worry, I will!

So I got up real quiet. I knew that if Daddy heard me, he'd say, Sister, get on back in this bed, so I shut the door to my room real quiet—just a *click* was all—and stole into the kitchen. The next thing I did was preheat the oven. Then I got Mama's little tin recipe holder with the fleur-de-lis on it where she kept her index cards with the cake recipes. I knew most of them by heart, but I wanted to be sure of all the measurements. Then I went to the telephone and found this week's list. I was relieved to see there weren't any orders for the lemon, just the devil's food and caramel, both of which I could make with one hand tied behind my back. I just hoped Mama had gotten in everything I needed before running herself into the train.

Which she had. I looked in the back of the icebox. It was all there. Which gave me pause. Why, if she was planning on running herself into the train, did she get together all the ingredients for the cakes she had to make? There were two possible answers. The first was that it was all an accident, she didn't mean to do it.

Too much moonshine, which was likely in any case. The second was that she expected me to have the sense to carry on the cake business. Now all the hours she had me in the kitchen helping her made sense. She was training me to take over, to carry on when she fell by the wayside. Whatever the case, Mama was alive! She was going to come home after she got out of the hospital and went over to Jackson for a while. I heard them say so. My job was to make sure she had her cake business to come home to. Lucky it was summer and I hadn't started back to school.

I went over to the kitchen calendar to see how much of June was left. Not much, as it turned out. Lately my mother had been crossing out each passing day with a big X, as though she were a convict biding time in Parchment Penitentiary until she could tunnel out to the world of her real life. About a week's worth of days in June were now X-ed out, including this Saturday. July was right around the corner. My main thought was how long I could take care of Mama's cake business. I saw I had less than three months before school commenced. I was still worried about Eva and her burns and Miss Josephine and her leaves. I was worried that my mother would be sprung only to run herself into another train. I was worried I'd get kicked out of the fifth grade. So it was a blessed relief to worry about holding down the cake fort. This was something I could do something about, and, when my mother got home, she would love me for saving the day. She would take one look at the pile of money I'd have made and know that she couldn't do without me.

So I started. Mama always made me get everything out first, which was no easy job since Mama kept all her ingredients in the icebox, even sugar and flour so they wouldn't get bugs, and Daddy had pushed them all to the back to make room for the ham and other stuff. I had to pull all that out, which made me feel a little sickish since it was all the stuff I'd just thrown up. But I sat it all back on the table, trying not to look at it, then got the sugar and flour and eggs and milk and shortening out from the back of the icebox. Then I put all the other stuff back in. Nice and tidy. Next I pulled out pans, bowls, the whisk, spoons, measuring cups, two little sharp knives for cutting the shortening into the flour, and so on. Finally I had it all ready. I started in, greasing the pans, cutting waxed paper to fit them, and greasing the waxed paper, so they'd be all ready for the batter. The stove could take eight pans at a time. Mama would double and triple recipes, but I was afraid I'd mess it up if I tried that. So I just made the cake batter over and over, the same thing. I had two whole devil's foods and two halves, so that made three total, I figured. Then I had one whole caramel and two halves, so that made two of them. I decided to do the devil's food cakes first. I'd have to turn them out, ice them up, and wash pans before starting on the white batter for the caramel cakes.

I was going along just fine. It was hot as Hades, but I had Mama's fan set up on her stool. I set it to rotate so it'd cool the cakes when I got them out. For once I was glad my pajamas were holey because Mama was right, it is cooler. I was about two hours into it. Outside the night was buzzing. The sheep frogs were *baaa-ing* outside the window. I could see why Mama liked this time. It was her and the night outside, nobody else. The devil's foods were out of the oven and cooling on little racks. I'd mixed up the angel icing and started cooking it up in a double boiler, which I was watching like a hawk and stirring every few seconds. I was timing it, plus I planned to use the candy thermometer on it too. I wasn't going to take any chances with a grainy mess. So I was doing right well, considering. The angel icing started bubbling along, so I beat in the cream of tartar, and in about a minute everything was just right for it to come off the eye.

Which is where I made my mistake.

Two mistakes, actually. The first was that I got flustered and forgot to turn off the eye, so the flame was still going right along. If I had just turned that off, none of the rest of it would have happened. Then I couldn't find any pot holders. I'd used them to take the cakes out of the oven. What had I done with them? I looked around and they were nowhere in sight. I touched the pot handle of the top double boiler. It was too hot to hold. So then I made mistake number two. I snatched up a dish towel. I had to move fast. The icing was boiling up a storm, and meanwhile, the pot under it had suddenly boiled dry and was starting to smoke (again, the mistake of not turning the eye off), so I couldn't see any way around it. I grabbed the pot of icing with the dish towel. When I did that, part of the dish towel dragged down and touched the eye and took the flame. I held on to it because I wasn't about to let that pot of icing go and fall. I'd put too much work into it. All I had to do was get the bubbling pot over to the sideboard part of the sink, where it could cool off. Then I could throw the dish towel into the sink and turn on the water, which I'd seen Mama do a million times to put out a little fire. She used dish towels for pot holders all the time.

I got the icing to the sink. What I didn't count on was that when I put the pot down, carefully I might add, the dish towel touched Mama's apron that was hanging up on a nail by the sink, which of course wouldn't have been there if Mama had been doing the baking, so it took the flame, which flared up because just that very minute the fan moved in its direction. It was no fault of mine that the apron was there, or that the apron was right next to the yellow-and-white-checked curtains Mama had gotten at Kress's and hung over the sink. Cheery, she'd called them, nice and cheery. So of course they caught on fire too, the fan still moving in that direction. I was hitting the apron and curtains with the dishtowel, but that just made things worse and my fingers were getting burnt. I dropped the dish towel and started running water in the sink. I had in mind getting a glass to throw some water on things. I could have put it all out if the little cloth tab on Mama's apron hadn't just then burned through. When it did, the fiery apron, with both its ties burning and standing straight out so that it looked like the cross of Jesus on fire, kind of floated down onto a pile of newspapers in the corner between the sink and stove. Soft and easy it went, and then curled up on the pile.

When the newspapers started up and the curtains had set in good and I saw the fan making its lazy turn to come back, I started hollering for Daddy. He burst out of the bedroom door shaking his head from side to side looking like Bomba just woken up from a nap in the trees. He didn't have his shoe, so he rocked from side to side coming across the living room. He came much slower that you'd expect anybody to do under the circumstances, but who am I to point fingers?

"What you gone and done?" he roared. "What in hell's name you gone and done?"

I started toward him. The kitchen was so smoked up I could hardly see him. I was screaming Daddy Daddy by this time. I was being the biggest baby in town. He got to me and snatched me up by the arm, and dragged me over to the front door. He opened the door, kicked the screen out and threw me out on the front stoop.

"Stay back and shut up!" he hissed. Then he disappeared inside. I heard things banging around and water running. Smoke was curling out of the kitchen window like it was a chimney. I couldn't believe it. First my mother runs herself into a train, then I burn down the house and kill my father. All in one day.

I was jumping from one foot to the other. I wasn't sure what I should be doing. Should I run out into the street and holler Fire? Should I keep quiet so Big Dan and Miss Kay Linda wouldn't find out that the house they'd rented to us was about to go up in smoke?

One thing I knew I had to do was go to the bathroom before I wet my pajama bottoms. So I went over into the shrubs and squatted and pulled down my bottoms and let loose. Just as I did, I saw that the smoke had stopped coming out of the window. I heard some more *whapping* noises from the kitchen along with the running water from the sink. I pulled up my pajamas and went back onto the porch stoop. I didn't sit down. I wanted to be able to take off fast if the fire came roaring out the front door. But it didn't, and soon everything got quiet. I waited. Then I had a thought. Last year at Christmas a whole family of five had died in their beds just from smelling smoke! Maybe Daddy was inside lying on the floor breathing his last breath of smoke while I was standing there on the front porch like a fool. Maybe he needed artificial respiration.

So I went back into the house. I opened the front door and there was Daddy, not breathing his last, but sitting on the couch staring into space. Every second or two, he'd cough and rub his eyes. When I opened the door and he looked up at me out of the smoky darkness, I felt like that baby rabbit out in the open. His eyes shone hot and wild. I looked into the lighted kitchen and saw puddles and burnt things in the sink and on the floor. Soggy pieces of my cakes splattered all over everything.

Daddy leaned forward and picked up his cigarette lighter that had been lying on the coffee table. "Come here you," he said, so I walked over and stood in front of him. Then he said, "I ought to snatch you bald-headed. You know what fire feels like?" I said, all whiney and quiet, "Yes sir," and he said, "Hell no you don't, because if you did, you wouldn't have done such a damn fool thing as setting the kitchen on fire. You just a chip off the old block. You your mama all over again, taking us all down."

I started up blubbering again. "I didn't mean to. I was just trying to get Mama's cakes ready for tomorrow so she wouldn't lose her business. It was the cup towel. I didn't mean to start a fire . . ."

He grabbed my arm and jerked me down on the couch next to him. The stink coming from him had gathered itself; his mouth smelled like garbage.

He pulled my arm straight out and turned it so the soft underside was up. His hand over my wrist was so tight it burned. All the time he was rasping hard, deep down in his throat. Was he still winded from fighting the fire? He used the thumb on his other hand to open the top of the lighter, then to flick the flame on. "Yes siree," he said, "what I'm thinking is you need a good lesson. Teach you a thing or two about fire. You holler out loud and I'm going to beat the living hell out of you." Then he jerked my arm around again so that the underside was down. Then he passed the flame under it real slow.

He must have done it to the other arm too—it was burnt like the first one when I woke up—but I don't remember the second one.

Which was the beginning of something new. Up until then, I could remember anything. When Mama or Mimi or Zenie would forget something that happened, they'd ask me, and I'd remind them. I was Miss Smarty Pants about it too. "Don't you remember," I'd start off, "it was Miss Lucy who said she'd pick up her cake late." Or: "No, it wasn't milk Zenie said we needed. It was coffee, don't you remember?" And so on. If I knew about it, I could remember it better than anyone else could.

So not remembering the other arm was the commencement of something new. To this very day I still can't see it. And it's the seeing, isn't it, that lets us catch slippery things and hold them forever in the mind's eye? Of course, even if you can't see something, you can remember it. I'd gotten good at squinching up my eyes so I couldn't see Mama go for the poison bottle or take a sharp curve on a dime, but that doesn't mean I don't remember her doing it. So maybe this was just a natural thing, to go a step further. I was squinching up something bigger than my eyes. Only this time it worked. You can't see what you don't remember.

9

When I woke up it was bright day. I was flat on my back on the couch, the kitchen was cleaned up, burnt-up curtains taken down, dishes washed, everything neat and tidy. By looking, you'd never know anything had happened, unless you looked at the kitchen ceiling, which had sooty circles on it right over the sink. I felt loggy, and when I looked down at my sides, I saw white pieces of gauze taped on the underside of both arms. When I lifted my arms to look, the smell of Ungentine and stale smoke rose with them.

The house was dead quiet. Had Daddy left for good? I wouldn't have blamed him. Here he was sad and all worn out, trying to see about me after what Mama had wrought, me playing dead under the bed. Now look what I'd gone and done. I wanted to go into my room and crawl under my own bed, but I was scared to move myself from where he had planted me. I just lay there on the couch and opened my eyes and let the water roll out and soak the couch.

After a while, I heard him. He was coming up the stairs from the basement. *Thunk, thunk* went his shoe on each step. I sat up on the couch. I had to rest my arms on my lap with the top sides turned down. I was sweating through my pajamas. The door to the basement opened and he came toward me and turned. It was a blessed relief to see his face. He was grinning and had the box under his arm. He walked right up to me and looked down at me. My neck hurt from looking up at him. My eyes were burning hot, but my arms felt like they'd been packed in ice from the coolness of the Ungentine.

"Honey. Look a here. I got *things* to show you." He stuck out the box.

"I got to go to the bathroom." I got up off the couch and backed up. I wanted to keep some distance. What things? My arms felt heavy in their bandages, stiff cold wings hanging at my sides.

Daddy waved his arm in the direction of the bathroom. He seemed in a hurry. "Well giddy up and go then, and get on back. Going to show you what's in the box. You a big girl now."

I ran for the bathroom. I couldn't believe I was finally going to get to see what was in the box. I sat on the commode and looked down at the wing bandages on my arms. My arms didn't hurt a bit, thanks to the Ungentine. When I was done I pulled up my bottoms and headed back into the living room. The box was on the coffee table. Daddy was on the couch, one leg folded over the other. The little key had sat itself down nice and comfortable right beside the box. I sat back down on my end of the couch and looked down at the box. It squatted there, waiting.

"Open it," Daddy said, and winked like it was Christmas. "But first you got to promise you can keep a secret."

I almost laughed out loud. Seemed like everything I knew in life was a deep dark secret. Bootleggers, hats, Daddy and Little Dan, Eva getting messed up, what the sheriff said, burns. Right down to that nasty commode in Mimi's garage. Seemed like I didn't know a single thing that wasn't a secret.

"Yes sir," I said.

Then Daddy made a strange move with his hand. He stretched out his pointer finger and put it over his top lip, right under his nose, like Mama showed me to do when you're trying not to sneeze in church except that he didn't press, he just held it there while he talked. "Because everything in this here box is a secret, handed down from my granddad to my dad to me, generation to generation, so you can't ever tell a soul what's in here or you'll break the chain."

The way he said it made me feel proud and righteous, like I was a link in a golden chain that could stretch on and on through all eternity. "I won't. I swear. Ever and ever, amen." I put my finger up the way he had his, right over my top lip. We sat there and looked at each other, our fingers in exactly the same pose. Two statues trying not to sneeze. Mirror images.

When he picked up the key and handed it to me, my chest seized up. The key felt warm like it had just gotten solid after being hot and molten for a good long time. It went into the hole like it had found its one true home. The lock opened up smooth and easy. When I started to lift the lid up, Daddy said, "Keep the key in the lock so you don't lose it."

I froze. I wasn't sure whether Daddy wanted to open the box himself. He was breathing as if he'd just run a race, which of course was impossible because of his foot. He got up and went over and pulled Mama's living-room curtains together. Then he said, "Go on, open it. It won't bite." He slapped his knee and he-hawed. "What you thinking's in there? A big old slimy snake?" And he reached over and tickled me in the ribs.

So I jumped and hollered and in a scramble I opened it. I don't know what I was expecting to see, maybe some gold and silver for a rainy day, pirate's treasure like Uncle Wiggily finds sometimes. Or jewels. Rubies and sapphires, like the Queen of Palmyra would wear around her bare neck when she was riding wild and naked and free. So I got to say I was disappointed. All I saw at first was an outfit. Folded nice and neat like it just got delivered from Sears and Roebuck. A cloth outfit like a bathrobe. Black and shiny. It was kind of pretty, I'll give it that, the shininess made it look like an oily starling looks in the bright sun. Black with other colors underneath. Plus it had a nice crest on the left side over the chest, the kind you see on a man's nice suit coat. A white cross with tips that fluted out at the ends. A box inside the cross and a red upside-down comma inside that. It was pretty. The shiny black with the white-and-red design.

Daddy reached in and pulled it out. "Look," he said, and he stood up, put his arms through the sleeves, and wrapped it around himself and tied it with a little black rope with tassels. Then he reached back in and got something else. At first I thought it was a matching hat like Mimi had for a few of her good dresses, but no, it was a hood, or maybe a big shiny sock. When he popped it on his head, I could see that wasn't right either. It wasn't a hat and it wasn't a sock. It was a mask. Soft and loose so that it flowed nicely into the neck of the robe. No skin showing between. It had a pointed top that stuck up and cut-out holes for eyes. Nothing like Daddy's other club outfits with silly little hats topped in tassels and what-all that Mama always laughed at and said, "Win, you look ridiculous in those getups."

For a minute Daddy stood in the living room not saying a word, just standing there in the black outfit, mask and all. His eyes peeking through the holes didn't look like anything like his or any person's. They looked like a pair of eyes floating in darkness all by themselves, seeing everything and everyone. He looked good and scary. Ready to go trick-or-treating. I was hoping he'd let me wear the thing on Halloween. When people asked me what I was, I'd tell them I was the biggest cockroach they ever would see. No, I'd carry a can of bug spray so they'd get the idea and not even have to ask.

"Well, what do you think?" he said from inside the thing. I could barely hear him.

"What do you *do* in it?" I asked, not having a good answer to his question.

He pulled off the top part. Sweat was rolling down the front of his face, getting in his eyes so that he was having to blink hard. A lock of his hair fell over his returned eyes. He grinned at me the way a boy grins, joyful and eager. "I'm the Nighthawk. We all were. Granddad, Dad, and me."

The Nighthawk. Daddy made it sound proud and brave, maybe even royal. A knight, or at least a sheriff, so I tried to erase the picture in my mind. I saw a fierce bird with a razor beak swooping down in the dead of night to tear a bit of soft fur that scuttled across the forest floor. A cry and then only silence.

When I looked at the box again, I saw some more stuff in the bottom. A Bible with a pretty marker in it. A big knife—no, a little sword in a metal holder. A Zippo lighter. Two flags rolled up. I unrolled them a little and knew right off what they were. One was the flag of Dixie and the other the flag of the United States of America. Old Glory, Grandpops called it. A little cross of Jesus made of two pieces of board. Some cards. A vase. Not a pretty one, just an old glass one the florist will send you if you have to go to the hospital. Mama had a whole long row of those under the sink from when she had me and almost died on Mrs. C's floor. It was a good stash of stuff, but not jewels or precious metals. More like what you'd find in the back of the hall closet.

The cards interested me because they looked like the place cards that Mimi used when she had the Saturday Matinee Bridge

Club at her house. They bent in the middle and stood up. Mimi's favorite chore was to figure out where to put the place cards around at the four bridge tables. "It's no fun to get your pants beaten off," she'd say. "You want an even contest." She'd let me help her put the little cards around. She saved them and used them over and over. She always put a strong player across from a weak player. "Bridge should be a *stimulating* experience," she'd say. "Let's put Joyce across from Jane Stuart so she can teach her how to bid. Joyce is an atrocious bidder. You never know what she's going to come out with." Mimi's cards had little fleur-de-lis on them. The ones in Daddy's box had two red eyes on the top, the kind that follow you wherever you go. Under the eyes were the words, "The eyes of the Klan are upon you. You have been identified by the White Knights of the Ku Klux Klan."

"Sister," Daddy barked my name and jolted me out of my bridge-club thoughts. "Don't you want to know what the Nighthawk does?"

"Yes sir," I lied. It was more interesting looking through the box. Maybe there were some jewels hidden in secret compartments.

Daddy came over to the couch and stood over me. He still had on the robe. The mask hung from his hand like an Easter basket. "Well, he's bound to guard everybody else, make sure nobody gets into meetings who ain't supposed to. Who don't love God and his country and his race and the great state of Mississippi. He gets to wear this special robe. It's black, when everybody else's is white, and shorter than everybody else's in case he's got to move fast. When some folks, I won't say who, is being bad, we got our ways to make them behave. First we give them a fair warning. But sometimes they don't listen. Sometimes we got to whip them good. Like the police do with the criminal element. Like Bomba with the cannibals."

Daddy seemed unaccountably excited. His eyes glowed the way they did when he'd go out at night with the box under his arm. I could tell he had in mind he was telling me the best news I'd heard in a long time.

I didn't know what to say. What are you going to do when your one and only father wants to run around in a Halloween getup and whip people? Say you're proud? I just hoped he wasn't going to wear it out in public.

"The Nighthawk takes care of the important things too. For when we get together. He sets everything up for the meetings." Daddy pointed at the stuff in the box. "See, everything's all here. Nice and neat."

While he was going on and on about being the Nighthawk and his precious box, I was thinking three thoughts at the same time. Both my arms had started up burning and stinging under the gauze, and I was wondering whether the second arm was burnt bad. Mama was always worrying about scrapes getting infected and had a heavy hand with the iodine until she discovered Mercurochrome, which kept infection at bay just as well and didn't sting. That thought led me back to Mama. I wanted to get into the hospital to see her. I wanted to say, Why did you do it, Mama, why did you run yourself into a train when you were supposed to be coming back to pick me up? Somebody had said children under twelve weren't allowed in the Millwood Hospital, but I had in mind putting on some of her high heels and lipstick and surprising her. She'd get a lift out of it, I bet she would. Everybody said I was the spitting image of her when she was little. Maybe when I pranced in, she'd think she was getting visited by herself and take herself back.

Thought number three was that my stomach was clawing up my insides, trying to get out and go live in some other girl's body, and Miss Kay Linda's sweet rolls might make it stay. The third thought was getting more pressing by the minute. I was eyeing the kitchen counter, trying to catch sight of those rolls, hoping they were still there. That Daddy hadn't eaten them up this morning while he was cleaning up my try at burning down the house.

By now, he could tell I wasn't paying attention. Here he was explaining things to me, grown-up things, he said, and I wasn't even listening. I wasn't even interested. "Well, missy, see if I tell you anything no more, it's like talking to a brick wall," he said. He clawed at his Nighthawk outfit and pulled it off and shoved it back in the box and slammed down the lid and clicked the little lock shut. The key he dropped into his shirt pocket.

"That's it, Sister, show's over." He looked down at me like I was a piece of something he'd dropped on a nice clean floor. "Go get something to eat. I'm going to call your grandma to come get you so I can get over to the hospital." I was a bitter pill for him to swallow. Lord knows he was trying.

He locked up the box with a hard little click of the hinge between his fingers and headed for the basement.

"I'll take it back down, Daddy." I was thinking we could get back into the swing of things, me carrying the box up and down, him doing the taking and giving of it. When I stood up this time, I felt dizzy.

"No." That was all he said, but it hung in the air, not wanting to leave the way normal words do. It wanted to stay and eye me and not let me get away. Ungrateful child that I was.

So when the phone rang, I wanted to run over and hug it. But I answered nice and polite, expecting a lady wanting to put in a cake order. Mama had taught me to answer the phone saying, "Forrest Residence, Florence speaking," so it would sound like a business, both for her cakes and Daddy's policies, though his customers didn't call on the phone like hers did. When I asked her why not, she said his customers didn't have phones. Sometimes the Mississippi Assurance district manager would call to speak to Daddy and Daddy would tell him he was busting his butt; he didn't know how much more he could do.

So I answered just that way, but it was only Mimi.

"Florence, honey, are y'all doing all right over there? When did you get up? Did you get some breakfast? Are you feeling better?" Her voice sounded far away.

"I'm just getting ready to get some." I heard Daddy clumping down the basement steps.

"Have you got anything to eat over there?"

"Enough to sink a ship," I said. "How's Mama?"

"About the same. She's going to be all right, don't you worry, honey. She is just having a bad time right now. Now you go eat something. We need to keep up our strength. Let me speak to your daddy, honey."

I turned around and saw that Daddy was back upstairs from the basement and standing behind me. "It's Mimi," I mouthed. Mama always liked to know who it was before I handed over the phone.

"Good," he said, louder than he needed to, and took the phone. "Miss Irene, listen, you right about Florence. Can y'all watch her for me? I got to get to the hospital and then I got to talk to Big Dan about another car and get back to work." He paused. "I don't know what to do with her. I mean you got to watch her every dadgum minute. She almost burned the house down last night." He was eyeballing me while he was talking. Then his eyes froze solid on my face. Not a blink. My arms started to burn like the lighter was at them again. I held them straight down. "Burned her arms pretty bad too. No, I just put Ungentine on them. They'll be all right. Yeah, I'll bring her on in a little while."

He stopped talking and listened for a minute. "I don't know.

Silly fool thing to do." Now his eyes were little mice running over my face and arms. "Something about baking cakes for Martha. Lord knows nobody's thinking cakes today."

That's when I got it. You can make up what happens and it can *be* that. Smooth as eating a piece of lemon meringue pie. Whatever story you want is yours as long as you can think up the picture you want to see and make somebody else want to see it too. Then the story you make up can take up a long and happy life that you and everybody else can watch happening over and over in your head, forever and ever, amen. Uncle Wiggily taking up his trusty valise and his crutch and setting out to seek his fortune through thick and thin. Bomba swinging through the trees. Queenie and the lady slave. It's yours, and you can say, Here it is, ain't it a sight to see? And somebody else can say yes siree bobtail, it sure enough is.

Now Mimi had this picture of me in her head. Dumb silly little Florence pretending to cook, starting a fire some fool way. Maybe catching the sleeve of her shirt on the flame, before she even got started good. No greasing the pans, measuring just right, using a broom straw to check doneness. No pretty cakes lined up just right on the table, all ready for the icings. No double boiler. No careful stirring. Now, right this minute, Mimi was telling it to Grandpops, the poor child so silly on top of all this that she caught the other sleeve on fire too, instead of turning on the water in the sink. "Lord help us all. What next?" she was saying to him and heaving a big sigh. "We sure enough got our work cut out for us." Stupid little Florence was the story they all hatched up.

They worked it out so Zenie had me daylight hours part of the time at Mimi's and part of the time at her house; Grandpops picked me up at Zenie's on his way home from work in the afternoon, on Friday reaching into his pocket and passing her some folded bills. They watched over me like hawks watch a field full of rabbits. Daddy came and got me from Mimi and Grandpops' right after they'd fed me supper. I'd sit on the swing outside on their front porch waiting for him. He'd told me to be out there. He and Grandpops weren't speaking. They had had a falling out about Mama. Grandpops wanted her to come stay with him and Mimi for a while. Daddy wanted to send Mama to Whitfield, which was where Zenie used to say she was going to send me if I didn't behave.

Daddy had gotten himself an old Chevy with tail wings. It made popping noises. When you heard it the first time you thought somebody had tied firecrackers to its underside. When I was sitting waiting on the swing and I heard it pop-popping up the street, I'd think, "Swing low sweet chariot, coming for to carry me home," and go on down to the curb where Mama had dropped me off that night she ran herself into the train.

While I went from this one to that one around town, Mama was supposed to be getting rested. It wasn't long at all before she was out of the hospital, insurance run dry, Daddy said, and he'd taken her down to Whitfield in Jackson, broken bones and all. He told me she was going to visit the people there for a while, nobody knew how long. She was going to get electric shock treatments. It reminded me of stories Zenie told about the Chickasaws getting removed. They just drifted away from home because everybody said that was what they had to do. I wanted to see my mother before she left. I was thinking Daddy could've let me ride with them to Jackson in Mimi's Plymouth, which he took Mama in because Grandpops said Daddy's piece of trash wouldn't make it to the county line. But Daddy said no, Mama was sicker than sick and she needed peace and quiet, that's all, for a good long time. She was not good company.

When Daddy left me off at Mimi's that first morning after the fire, Zenie was already there. She was in her chair leaning back and fanning herself with one section of the paper while reading another. Mimi had gone back to the hospital to visit my mother. Zenie's face looked like it had gotten longer since I'd seen her. She wasn't just reading the paper at her leisure. She was combing through the pages like she was looking for something in particular. Daddy had dropped me at the front, so I slipped in the front door. The living room was dark and still as a pond, so I hightailed it to the back of the house. Zenie stopped reading when I came into the kitchen. She looked hard at my arms.

"Come here, you." She flicked the paper. I came on over and stood in front of her. She took up my left arm and turned it from side to side. She looked at the top and then she looked at the underside. Then she took up the right one and did the same, like she was looking for ticks on a dog.

"Ow," I said. The turning back and forth was like getting an Indian burn.

She raised one eyebrow. "What you gone and done to yourself? How come you trying to bake cakes in the dead of the night? Don't you know how to light a stove, girl? I made sure and showed you a hundred times. How come you to go get yourself in a fix like this?"

She took a deep breath and started back in. "And what you doing cooking in long sleeves for anyways, with it hot as fire? Don't you know no better than that? What you wearing get you all burned up like this?" She reached out and grabbed my hand and started pulling at the tape on my arm to undo the gauze. "Where them burns at? Top or bottom?"

"Don't go hurting it!" I jerked my arm away. "It's all right the way it is. Don't go undoing it all."

"Might need changing out," she said, grabbing at me again. She was on her feet and coming at me. "I'm going to get the scissors. Take a look at it."

"No! Let me alone!" I'd never hollered at Zenie before, but I did now. "Don't touch it. Don't touch me!" My voice sounded odd to me. I was mad as fire and giving orders to Zenie like she was being the bad baby and I was the grown-up. I was expecting her to stop short and whap me good for giving her sass the way Mama would have done.

But she didn't. She just stopped short with the scissors in her hand, and gave me a look that was a river long and deep. A look that said she had been waiting for this very moment, for me to be bad like that. Just like Miss Josephine's look three days back had said she'd been waiting for me to bust through the front door yelling for Ray. Zenie knew it would come someday, and here it was, a vileness in me that she knew was there before I did. She'd been waiting for it to pop out, an evil just waiting for the right time and place to be born, and here it was at last, rearing its ugly horned head.

When I saw that look, all I could do was stop talking. I could not say Zenie, I beg your pardon, Zenie, I'm sorry to have hollered at you, disrespected you. Because I saw in her face that I had set something loose. It could not be taken back, or even slowed down. Not for even a minute. It wasn't a story that had a beginning and an ending, it was a fire that licked its way out into a bigger and bigger circle. No, no, stop, I didn't mean it that way, you could say, but it always moved beyond your watery voice. It did not hear you.

She looked but she didn't say a mumbling word. Then she just turned heel and walked over to the drawer and put the scissors back and then moved to the sink slow and tired, and started up washing the breakfast dishes.

At first I thought she'd get over it, that it was just another humbug, but she didn't, at least not for a while. Oh, she'd be nice enough, but it wasn't the kind of nice that meant I like you. It was the kind that called attention to its niceness, the way Mimi called attention to her too-loud hats. Do you want some more strawberries? Eggs or waffles this morning? Are you ready to go home now? A niceness like the decorated cakes at the grocery store. It had nothing to do with whether the ingredients were pure and right, whether it was butter not Oleo or real vanilla not imitation; it was just on the outside.

That afternoon I sidled along home behind Zenie for the first time since Eva had gotten hurt. I was hoping I could help Zenie with some sewing or cleaning to get back in her good graces. She didn't say a word to me while we were walking from Mimi's house to hers, she was so busy nursing her grudge. Every now and then she'd mutter something under her breath about people being ungrateful.

When we got up to the house and went in, Miss Josephine was back in her chair. She wasn't talking to anybody either. She was through with her counting. The mimosa tree was stripped bare up as high as she could reach. She'd tried to get Ray to bring her a ladder, but he said he wouldn't because she'd fall sure enough and then he'd have her on the bed too.

There were only two beds to go around for the four of them, and Eva had been spread-eagled on Miss Josephine's bed for a week. Miss J was having to sleep with Zenie, and Ray had ended up on the couch. I knew all this by hearing Zenie talk to her friends on Mimi's telephone when Mimi wasn't in the house. The day before, I'd come out of the bathroom and caught her crying into the phone, not saying a word to whoever was on the other end, just holding it up to her cheek and crying.

The minute we got inside the front door, Zenie pushed me in the direction of the green leaf curtain hanging in front of Miss Josephine's bedroom door. "Get on in there and tell Eva a story. Tell her about how you almost burned down the place, she'll get a kick out of that."

I went over and peeked around the curtain. Eva didn't look like she was about to get a kick out of anything. She was propped up in Miss Josephine's bed like a stuffed toy you see in rich white girls' houses. Sometimes they prop a bunch of them up on the prissy little pillows on their beds. She looked a sight. Her hair had lost its puff and was slicked straight back. If it'd been long enough, she would have had it in a bun in back but it wasn't, so the ends stuck out behind, like an ugly ducktail. Her face was ashy. The burnt circle on her cheek had made a big light brown scab. Around the scab was a perfect pink circle, the beginnings of a scar. She looked like she had in mind that she was somewhere else, that she wasn't propped up in Miss Josephine's nice soft bed in Zenie and Ray's Jim Walter Home in Shake Rag in Millwood, Mississippi, but somewhere much worse. She was just staring into space. She had on a blue nightgown with lace at the neck and was covered up to the waist with a white sheet. Her hands were on top of the sheet. She looked down at them like they were a puzzle she hadn't put together yet.

Zenie was standing right behind me on the other side of the curtain. I could tell she was ready to give me a big push right through it, so I piped up and said, "Hey, girl! How you doing?" kind of peppy and frisky, like I was talking to a sick dog. I almost clapped my hands the way you'd do to get a dog's attention. I was trying to perk her up some, hoping that if I could get her talking and being happy again, Zenie would stop being mad at me. I was prepared to make a fool out of myself.

I started off with some advice. "You ought to put some Ungentine on that place on your face. Daddy put Ungentine on my arms and it cuts down on the sting."

Eva twitched her head a little. I took the twitching for a good sign. She might have been struck dumb, but at least she wasn't deaf to boot. Then the twitching turned into something else. A snicker, then a giggle. "*Daddy* says put Ungentine on it!" The words came out of her mouth like the dry heaves. Then she started cackling like a witch, mean and nasty.

I decided to ignore her. I held onto the edge of the curtain and started in on The Story. "Hey, Eva, you won't believe what I gone and done. Set the whole dadgum kitchen on fire. Almost set the whole house on fire. Almost burnt Daddy to a crisp." I said it all in a rush. I almost believed it myself.

By the time I got to the end of the story, her lost eyes had come running back home to her ashy face. She still didn't say a word, but I could tell I had gotten her attention because she turned and looked over at me. So I kept on, trying to get her interested in the details. "Yes siree, I'd just got my three devil's foods out of the pans just fine and they were out there on the table cooling and then there was the icing all cooked and ready and I couldn't find a pot holder so I got a cup towel to get it off the fire . . ."

"*You* burnt your arms?" The question came as a thief in the night. Her lips moved so fast and she said it so soft I almost missed hearing it. After she said it, she turned her found eyes toward me. She had the look of a statue that had decided to say a word or two. No more.

I opened my mouth then shut it. My tongue felt thick and muddy, a creature in a swamp that was trying to rise up through the muck and roots and bog. It couldn't, it wouldn't. I just sat there thinking I needed Bomba right then to grab ahold of a vine and swing over and rescue me in this story. No Bomba, and my mouth was full of the jungle.

So I changed into the statue, but not a speaking one. Eva looked hard at me, and something fierce leapt up between us. "I know how Flo got burnt, I know how Flo got burnt." She made it into a soft singsong that one little child would sing to another. It didn't sound a bit like Eva, but it was a blessed relief to me when she sang it. She didn't have to say anything ever again as far as I was concerned. I loved her for singing it. I loved her for knowing The Story wasn't true.

It seemed like a blessed relief to her too because right after she said it, she reached down and lifted the sheet off herself. It slipped over to one side as she rose up and put her feet on the floor. Her feet looked strong, even if the rest of her didn't. She had wiry toes, which seemed longer against the light linoleum floor. They were brown right down to the tips, which were pinkish. Her feet were long and flat to the ground. No arch to speak of. She sat for a while on the side of the bed looking down at those feet stretched out in front of her on the floor. She seemed to be thinking about them. Where they could go. What they could do.

"Dizzy," she said, with a little shake of the head.

Behind me Zenie said, real quiet and easy, "Take it slow. Just sit for a little bit and let it pass on." I don't know how long she'd been standing there.

Eva kept on sitting on the edge of the bed and looking at her feet stretched out. She touched the scab on her face, then started picking it.

Zenie came over and took her hand. "Don't fool with that thing," she said, "you'll make it worser. You'll raise the scar."

All of a sudden Eva bent her head over and started laughing. "I'll be scary-fied, sure enough," she said. "Yes siree. I got myself good and scary-fied!" Then she stomped one foot, then the other. "*Peckerwoods.*" She said the word like she was upchucking something nasty.

Then all of a sudden, her eyes caught mine and lit a fire between us. "You out there walking around," she said. "Guess if you can do it, so can I. You got to *live* with him."

Then she rose up in her blue nightgown, and the ripe bed

smells rose with her. "Whooee, got to clean this self up," she whispered to herself, and she swept past us in a cloud of blue.

I got a good whiff of her as she went by. "Eva, you need some Mum." That's what Mama always said to me when I was dirty and smelly. "A little Mum never hurt anybody," she would say, handing me the jar of cream to dab under my arms. Not too much or it would glob up, particularly if you used baby powder on top of it.

"Need more than Mum," Zenie said. "Need a good scrubbing."

Zenie and I stepped back and watched Eva pass. She whipped back the green leaf curtain to the bathroom and disappeared. Then under the curtain we saw the blue gown drop to the floor. We looked at each other for a minute. The water in the bathtub had started up. Then Zenie put her hand on my head. "All right," she said, and I knew she meant the sheets. They smelled to high heaven. I reached for the top one. "Don't hurt its arms," Zenie sang out to me, and walked over to the other side of the bed. The words sounded like music sure enough when they came out of her mouth. I was grateful for them beyond measure.

"I won't." I sung it back to her across the bed. A mockingbird song, changed but the same. When I sang it, I all at once saw my mother's face from the midpoint of a long dark burrow, the kind rabbits make. Turn one way and I see her young with round eyes that ate up the rest of her face. Turn the other, she's old as dust with puckers and whiskers. That's when I knew my own mother would live; she'd tunnel out. Eva had risen from the dead and come back to us. Mama would too.

What I didn't know was how many ways there are to be dead. People say dead's dead, but that isn't exactly it. There's the buried dead, but there's also the walking talking dead. Later on, I'd come to think that what Mama really wanted was the first thing. Walking talking was what she had to settle for.

10

While Eva was fixing herself up, Zenie poured a glass of tea out of the pitcher in the icebox and eased herself down on the couch with a groan. I came and sat down beside her. She had the sheets soaking in Clorox in the sink. Miss Josephine had nodded off in the easy chair.

"Want some tea? There's more where this come from." Zenie held up her glass.

"That's all right."

"Some cold biscuit on the stove."

I patted my stomach. "Still full."

"Want to lie down?" She patted the couch, so I laid myself down, thanking my lucky stars that I was back in Zenie's good graces. I had to lie flat on my back on account of my arms. It hurt to bend them. I couldn't lie on my sides at all. I curled my legs up so I wouldn't be putting my dirty feet up next to her. But that wasn't good enough.

Zenie pushed on my leg. "What's all that sticking to the bottom of those feet of yours? When was the last time *you* had a bath?"

I did a U-turn of myself. All the better to see Eva's bare feet under the curtain. First she stood on one foot then the other. *Clatter slam bang* was all we could hear. She was busy. First I smelled Alba lotion, then rosewater and glycerin, then something sweet like jasmine, something new I'd never smelled on Eva or anybody. She was piling it on, I could tell. Maybe she'd been saving it to rescue herself.

A few minutes before, Eva had whipped out the curtain and sailed out of the bathroom wrapped in a towel. Her hair was dripping, making little dabs on the linoleum. She glistened all over. I looked at her and thought, shine little glowworm, glitter, glitter. Then she disappeared behind the curtain to Miss Josephine's room.

She made such a ruckus behind the bedroom curtain, opening and slamming drawers, talking to herself about where this or that was, that she sounded a little mental. In a minute or two, here she came sailing out again in a pair of shorts and a hot pink halter top that bordered on being too loud. She had her little red makeup case in her hand and right back behind the bathroom curtain she went.

Used to be Zenie and Eva would call out to each other back and forth through the curtain while Eva was getting herself beautified, but Zenie didn't say anything. She just sat with her tea glass wrapped in a little cloth. Eva was the picture show she was waiting to see. The smells were the previews. Every now and then Zenie took a sip and let out a long hopeful breath.

After a while, Eva stepped out from behind the curtain. She turned herself in a determined circle that ended in a little flourish. "Do I look all right?" The question was schoolteacherish: there was only one right answer.

"*Sure* you do, honey," Zenie broke into the question before it was over.

"You do," I piped in. "You look real nice, Eva."

Eva did look just fine. In fact she looked fine from every angle. Her hair was still slicked back, but now it looked shiny and clean. She'd put a couple of pink bow barrettes in it, which neatened up the loose ends. She had on lipstick and rouge and powder. She'd covered the place on her face with makeup so the circle from the cigarette lighter was barely noticeable. She looked brand-new.

"I'm going down to Lafitte's to get us some ice cream. What kind y'all want?" Now she was digging through her billfold.

"Chocolate ripple! Let me go too." I loved going to Lafitte's Grocery in Shake Rag. It was more a dark cool alleyway than a store, with cigars and pickles and salt pork and candy all stuffed in behind glass counters you could make a breath on. The ice-cream freezer was at the back of the store, where it was so dim you could barely make out the flavors. It was the coolest place in town this time of day. Plus I was hungry for the sight of other people going about their business in an everyday sort of way, and there was always somebody hanging around Lafitte's.

Zenie pushed herself up off the couch and smoothed back her hair. "We all go."

"No ma'am. You sit yourself right back down. You been working your fingers to the bone. I'll bring you back whatever you want." Eva had her hands on her hips looking up at Zenie. "Just tell me what it is."

"You doing no such thing. You go, we all going. Everybody in the house going, and that includes yours truly." Zenie drew herself up. Her lips got tight over her teeth. She was keeping her voice low, but there was a don't-mess-with-me look in her eye. I knew that look from way back.

Eva put her hands on her hips. Zenie towered over her, but she stood her ground. "I'm going on my own, Auntie." There was something in the quietness of her voice that outmatched Zenie's will and her bigness. Plus you could tell Zenie was dog tired and would a whole lot rather be sitting in her cool dark living room than trudging through the heat of the afternoon on some fool errand.

"Take this one then," Zenie said, and pointed to me.

Eva looked down at me smushed down on the couch with my head in the hole Zenie left. She threw back her head and laughed out loud. "What good *she* going to do me?"

I raised my head. "Take me," I whined. I could act the baby. I goldfished my lips into a pout and stretched out my arms. Then I got into the spirit of it and threw back my head and pretended to cry like a baby. "Whaaa. Ice-cream cone, ice-cream cone, I got to have ice-cream cone." Which was true, I wanted it bad. Lafitte's had some open cartons and a scoop and some cones. You could get yourself the biggest scoop you could make stick on a cone. Mr. L always let me do it myself. I must have been special in his eyes because he scooped everybody else regular dips. What I wanted even more was going to Lafitte's with Eva. I was proud of her rising from the dead like that, and I wanted to see her walk in the world, queen that she was, and have people say how lucky I was to get to trail behind her.

"Hush," Zenie said. "You're going to wake her up." Meaning Miss Josephine in her chair, though there was a fat chance of that, I thought. Her mouth was open, and her fingers were twitching like they had more leaves to count.

Eva looked down at me and I could tell she saw something more than just me, but something I might become. Not a stray dog the way I thought of myself most of the time, but something valuable and secret, the way Daddy thought of his box and the stuff in it. Something that gave her that Queen of Palmyra feeling. When I had that thought, about the Queen of Palmyra, suddenly it came to me who I could be to her. I could be her own lady slave. I couldn't make cobblers, but I could bake cakes. I could be her girl sidekick. And I wasn't a dumb native like Bomba's friend Gibo. I had good sense. I could be a succor in time of trouble. If she needed to go bouncing into battle, I would rip my shirt off too and get on my horse and follow to the death. It would be better than having long flowing locks and being rescued like a drooping lily.

I hopped up off the couch. "Take me," I said, "and I'll be your lady slave."

When the words popped out, everything stopped short. I looked up at both of them. Their mouths had dropped open, the way they did when I said the thing about being colored. There was dead quiet for a minute; then Eva started giggling little-girl giggles. On the couch Zenie bent over double, slapped her thigh and started sputtering.

"What in the world is she talking about?" Eva's question sounded like a horse whinny.

"Remember that old story I used to tell you about Queenie and the lady slave?"

"The one with the cobblers? That's what she's talking about?"

"Um hum." Zenie sounded on the verge of being disgusted with me again. I looked down at the floor. I was still worried I'd gone and spoiled the whole thing, the way I'd done before when Eva made me so brown and pretty. I had a picture in my mind like a picture in a storybook. Me and Eva making a beautiful parade to Lafitte's. I would get a palm branch to wave next to her face to keep her nice and cool.

Zenie pointed a finger at me. "You. Go brush your hair and wash your face." Zenie never told me to use the bathroom like Mama did, but I knew that's what she meant.

I ran for the bathroom. I made it fast. They could change their minds on a dime. Then a thought hit me. I didn't have a red cent, and ice-cream cones were a nickel.

I came back through the curtain. "I don't have money for an ice-cream cone."

Eva was already at the door. "I got money. Not much respect, but enough money for ice cream. That's one thing I got. Come on, girl, if you're coming."

Zenie walked over to the door just as Eva's hand was on the knob. "Tell me you not going in *that*." She pointed at Eva's front. The hot pink halter top brought out the copper in Eva's face and arms. It tied around the neck and at the back. It didn't show any navel because of a little skirt that hung off it, but the skirt didn't go all the way around the back. Plus there was a plunge in front that showed a softness where Eva's bosoms gathered strength. I had on a crop top that Zenie had made me last summer. It showed more flesh than Eva's halter, but my flesh was paltry.

Eva looked down at herself. Her face puckered for a minute. Was she going to disrespect Zenie? Tell her it was hot as fire and she was wearing the pink top? She was thinking about it, I could tell, because she had squinched up her mouth and was chewing hard on one side of it. Then she looked up at Zenie. She opened her mouth to say something, then looked down at me, then shut it. "Hold up," she said to me, and went back into Miss Josephine's room. In another second she whipped back the curtain. She was wearing a regular button-up shirt with little cap sleeves. It had little blue and green flowers on it and a little round collar. It was buttoned up to the next to last button to the neck.

"This good enough? It's sure hot enough."

Zenie nodded. "Bring me back some vanilla to put my peaches on, and make haste with it or it'll melt. If you not back in half an hour, I be sending Ray after you."

Eva made a mock bow and opened the door. "Let's go, lady slave," she said, and I hopped to.

So here we go down Moses Street, which was the main drag

of Shake Rag, like Main Street was the main one for Millwood. Eva had her parasol to keep the sun off the tops of our heads so we wouldn't get sunstroke in the heat of the afternoon. It was the parasol that made it seem like a parade. I gave up staying under it. The sun didn't bother me as much as it did Eva, though the heat from it made my arms itch under the bandages, which weren't covered by the umbrella anyway. So it's Eva with her parasol and me bringing up the rear, thinking I wished I had one of those big palm leaves to fan her with or at least a long stem of mimosa. Both of us barefooted. Her putting one strong flat foot in front of the other like that was the most important move in the whole parade. Not looking down, though, but holding her head high, not looking right or left either, just moving through the world like a queen going to do battle with a terrible foe. And I didn't feel like her pet dog either or even her lady slave. I felt like her own brave-hearted sidekick. All I needed was a sword and a white horse.

The sun beat down. I tried to walk in Eva's foot path, but her stride was too long. I could hit every other one, but not keep the pace. People were watching. I couldn't see their faces in the windows, but I saw their outlines behind screen doors and at windows. I could almost feel their breath blowing us along, they were watching so hard. Then, as we got on down the street, they started coming out from behind. They came onto their porches and their stoops, even though it was the heat of the day. They brought out their peas to shell or their watering cans to water or the newspaper.

Some just nodded and smiled. Some said, "How y'all doing?" Some just gave a little wave. Eva replied in kind but she didn't stop or even slow down. We kept on moving like we were being unraveled from a tight knot of thread. There was no giant hand to stop us. We had to go our limit before we could stop unwinding. Then all we'd be was a thin line of thread stretched across a long distance. Easy to break.

When we got to Lafitte's, there was a bunch of old men sitting outside on rickety benches that backed up to the front wall of the store. Their arms poking out of their shirtsleeves looked wasted away, the way old people's get if they live long enough. Some of them were smoking pretty little wood-carved pipes and some were chawing. On trips to the store with Zenie, I'd seen them get up and spit brown juice out to the side of the store. It made a puddle line in the dust. They were always in front of Lafitte's. They weren't pink-eyed with meanness like the gun toters outside the sheriff's office, or dozy like the ones under Nathan Bedford Forrest's horse's butt. They looked satisfied with themselves. They had done their life's work. Now they were taking a good long rest. One man liked to whittle little pieces of wood and once he gave me a little dog with a bobtail. It had had a pretty yellow tone, and he said it was cut from pecan.

Sometimes Mr. Lafitte, a little man with marcels, would be sitting out with them, and sometimes his grown son L Junior would be standing in front of them, one foot up on the bench talking loud and making grand moves with his hands. They'd all be laughing and beating their legs. People said L Junior could tell a good story, but I never got to hear one because Zenie always made me come on inside the store with her and not listen to the men's goings-on. She'd push me through them and their guffawing. L Junior would nod and tip his straw hat and stop his telling till we got through. I always felt like I had come upon a picnic. A whole lot of people eating potato salad and sweet pickle and me not even getting a single bite.

When we rounded the curve in Moses Street, the store and the sitting men were square ahead. They eyeballed us like we were ghosts risen up from the grave. I'd seen men old, young, and in between cast their eyes on Eva. They all looked the same, bees on a flower, wanting to burrow in deeper and deeper. But this wasn't that kind of look. It was a look that said they couldn't believe their eyes. Even L Junior in the middle of his story looked taken aback. Eva just raised her head up higher and cut her eyes back to me. "Come on, don't drag behind," she said, and I came up and walked beside her. I tried to bring my head up tall too. I wanted my neck to be long like hers. Everything felt momentous.

The men tipped their hats to her when we went by the benches and one of them got up and opened the door to the store. "How y'all doing?" she asked and smiled a little.

There was a long moment of quiet. Then they all sighed and nodded carefully as if just a little "All right, how you doing, baby?" would be just too too heavy to drop into the soupy air.

Eva nodded back to them and we swept on through the open door. Usually while Zenie was shutting the door on the men outside, we could hear them starting right back up again, but today there was not even a whisper.

Mr. L was polishing his glass cases with vinegar and newspaper. The place was cool and dark and empty of people except for him and us. It smelled like pickles and tobacco. He was trying to scrape a spot on the glass with his fingernail so that at first he didn't look up. When he did, he made a noise in his throat and look a step back.

When Eva said "How you doing, Mr. L?" he remembered his manners and said he was fine and how was she? Everybody fit to be tied about her and here she is right in front of his very eyes looking mighty fine. Mighty fine indeed. Mrs. L was going to be greatly relieved, she'd been praying for Eva. All the Heroines of Jericho had. Eva said to tell Mrs. L it worked and she was feeling better and wanted to get her and me and her auntie some ice cream. Could we fix our own cones?

Mr. L threw down his sour wad of newspaper. Not only could we fix our own, but we could have doubles on the house. "Get what you want. All you want." He made a grand sweep of his hand to the back where the cooler lay. Then he peered over the shining glass at Eva. The store was dark except for a few dusty pieces of light. The thrown light caught the bottom parts of their faces in the glass below them. It made their mouths seem to tremble. Then Mr. L cocked his head, leaned over the glass case he'd just finished polishing, and said real quiet: "When you leaving?"

Eva frowned. "Leaving? Who says I'm studying leaving? I'm staying right here."

Mr. L shook his head. "Girl, what you studying if you ain't studying leaving? You got to get out of this here place. What, you low on cash, baby?" He patted his pocket.

Eva wanted to get on with the ice cream, I could tell. She was moving a step or two back, but she couldn't just walk away from Mr. L. He was being fatherly. Mr. L's hair wasn't gray, but it should have been. You could tell he just wanted to give her the benefit of his experience.

"Just not leaving is all I'm studying." She said it quietly and pleasantly, but it was as if she were Moses and had carved the words in stone.

He leaned farther out over the glass case and tapped his finger on it, which left more smudges. "Listen up, missy. Nobody want to see you laid out on a board. Getting shipped back home in a box looking like that Till boy. That's if they ever find what's left of you."

That got her goat. She glanced over at me, then leaned over the glass case to meet him head to head, eye to eye. "I'm not letting a bunch of peckerwoods in sheets run me off." She sounded like a snake hissing. Mr. L pulled himself back.

"You crazy?" He swatted the air with his hand. "Get on out of here while you can do it on two feet. A pretty little lady like you. You can go anywhere. Do anything. You can have a *life*, girl. You can go to Paris France. Zenobia and Rayfield ain't told you that? What your mama and daddy say about this?"

"They can all tell me to go home till they're blue in the face, but I'm twenty-three years old. I make my own decisions, and I got other plans."

I was rooting for Eva in this fight. I didn't know what a peckerwood was, much less in sheets—I pictured him as a mean Holy Ghost running amuck—but Eva was fast becoming my Queen; she had gumption and I knew she wouldn't run, I knew she had that thing in her that said No. Nobody was going to push her around without a fight. What she said set me to thinking about my mother and wondering whether she had it too, whatever it was the Queen of Palmyra and Eva had. Seemed to me Mama hopped back and forth like a baby bird on the ground between saying no with a little n and saying come on, world, stomp on me.

Of course, it takes gumption to throw your whole self at a train. To think of yourself as a burst of light. Splayed limb from limb like a chicken getting cut up all at once. I know what happens to people who get run over by trains. An arm in the tall grass, a leg a half mile down. Where's the head? Nobody can find it. Then it turns up in a feedlot in another county.

Where was Mama now? Was she glad to find herself still attached to herself or did she feel like she'd lost some part just by thinking it? Was she sitting up in the hospital studying coming home to her sweet good daughter? Did they clean her up? Was she wearing the pretty nightgown with the puckered top? Did her bangs rest straight and smooth, or was she a bloody mess? Did Daddy tell her I almost burned down the place? The one who tells the story gets to say who's bad and who's good. Then the story rises up and puts on its clothes and goes out into the world. He'd made me out the bad one and him the good one. Saving the day. Keeping me from burning down the house.

Eva tossed her head and leaned back from the glass. Her eyes caught a torch of light. "That ice cream still on the house?"

Mr. L narrowed his eyes. "Yeah, but you better enjoy it, it may be your last."

"Maybe not," Eva said. "A change going to come. Maybe not today, maybe not tomorrow, but a change going to come. Look at Harmony, over in Leake County. They brought in Medgar Evers and the NAACP and the Justice Department people, and they're finally starting to get registered. Look at Winson and Cleo Hudson down there. Things are changing."

"Blood be shed first. You plumb foolish, you don't know that."

Eva looked hard at him. "I may be foolish, but at least I don't run scared. That's more than I can say for some people in this podunk town. Present company excepted."

"Better scared than dead."

"Maybe. Maybe not. Some say scared *is* dead."

"Dead's dead. There ain't *nothing* worse than dead."

Eva made herself taller. "Yes there is."

The two of them locked eyes. In the glass case their faces had iced over. They looked like people felled dead in battle. Killed, but still standing with eyes wide open.

Mr. L started up again. "You one hardheaded girl. Where'd you get such a hard head?"

"Maybe from beating it up against a wall all my life."

"There such a thing as too far too fast."

"There such a thing as going nowhere no time."

I touched Eva's hand. "Come on, let's get the ice cream." I tried to say it the way it was bound to taste. Sweet, cold, kind to the tongue. I wanted her to want it too. Want it more than she wanted to tell Mr. L a thing or two. She was stepping out of line. I could see it in the way Mr. L had tucked in his mouth and the way he talked to her like she was the one about to burn down the house. Here he'd been thinking his good fatherly advice would be respected. That Eva'd nod her pretty head with the little-girl barrettes and say yes sir, meek and mild, but here she was giving lip to a man old enough to be her grandfather. When she wasn't even from around here. It was disrespectful, she'd be sorry when word got back to Zenie and Ray. He was only giving her the best advice possible. The benefit of his experience. I could see he was thinking all that and more.

The minute I said ice cream, Eva unfroze herself, only too glad to break away from Mr. L. She reined in her stubbornness and put on a fake smile. Armor. "Thank you, sir, I appreciate it," she said in a molasses voice, and squeezed my hand tight. What "it" meant she didn't say. She looked down at me and pulled another fake smile out of her boundless supply. "Come on, Flo. Let's take Mr. L up on his kind offer." We walked hand in hand till we got to the ice cream at the back of the store.

We escaped into the dark cave of the back. She seemed to forget she was holding my hand so it just butter-slid out of hers. Her voice changed back to normal. "What kind you want?" When she took the scoop out, her hand was agitating like she was ready to swat a fly.

"Chocolate ripple."

"A double? Dumb question, right?"

"I guess. No, wait, one dip chocolate ripple and one dip banana." Which took some thought.

She gave me a real smile. "Girl, you know how to live. Think I'll have that too. Now, here, take these two cones and hold them. I'll put in the banana first for the chocolate to run on." She leaned over the freezer to scoop out of the cartons of ice cream open in the bottom. She reached her arm down. In the light from the cooler I could see the chill bumps rise up on her arm when she put it down in the freezer. I wanted to rub her arm, warm her up. I decided then and there I had to love her whether she loved me back or not. I especially loved the way she bent over the freezer, herself so warm and it so cold. She took my breath away.

Then the front door of the store opened. It had a little bell on the doorknob, which is what I heard. Then I heard talking. A white man's voice. Mr. L answering. More talking between them. I heard the white man say what's she doing down here and Mr. L say back I done already told her. Then I realized who the white man was. It was Grandpops. When I turned around, I was holding one cone and Eva had the other one. She had gotten us the two banana scoops and was digging in the chocolate ripple, which was frozen harder. She was having trouble getting it out.

Grandpops took his time getting to the back of the store. He didn't say boo to me, he just looked hard at Eva's back and said to it, "What you doing bringing her out on the street with you for? I come to pick her up at Zenie's and Zenie says she's off gallivanting with you." He didn't even say afternoon, how you doing, Eva? which he normally would have done.

Eva jumped and spun around. She looked scared and lost for a minute, then she got cocky again. "She wanted an ice cream so I took her. Don't see harm in that." She held up the scoop. Evidence.

Grandpops gave me a quick look. "Florence, get on up to the front of the store and wait for me there."

I backed up five steps. The one banana scoop was running down the side of the cone, so I started in on it, listening hard. My arm pained me and the tape on my bandage pinched when I bent my elbow to eat, but I suffered gladly. Mr. L was back to his polishing. He poured his vinegar onto the newspaper and squeaked across the glass. There were several shelves between me and Grandpops and Eva, so I couldn't see them anymore. All I could do was listen.

Grandpops was fussing at Eva. "Everybody knows why you brought her out, we're not fools, and I'm sympathetic, but what you doing using her for cover against those hoods? I'm surprised at you, Eva. I thought you had better sense."

"Nobody's going to hurt her down here." Eva had the same tone with Grandpops that she'd gotten with Mr. L. "What's so bad about taking her for an ice cream?"

"Who you think you fooling with that talk?" Grandpops was a quiet talker. But now his way of speaking took on something I'd never heard from him. It wasn't loud, but there was a warning behind it. Behave yourself, don't go burning down the house. The story he was making up in his head was that Eva was the dumbbell native and he was Bomba saving me from the fire the cannibals had set. If she wanted to stay in that tree and get herself burnt up, that was her own business.

I'd forgotten to lick and my ice cream cone was turning into sludge. It had dripped down my hand. I didn't want to be saved from ice cream or Eva, but she was melting too. I heard it.

"Yessir." She put the squeeze on the word, clamped it shut at both ends.

Mr. L had stopped with his squeaking. He had his back turned and was messing with his shelves, but I could tell he was all ears. I was still trying to get control of my ice cream. I was sucking on the bottom of the cone. No napkin. Time passed without anybody saying anything. Then Grandpops sighed. It was a long sigh that said listen to me, listen hard.

"All right, look, I told Zenie and now I'll tell you. I don't want her going out on the street with you anymore while you're still in town. You hear me? It's too dangerous."

"Yessir."

" When you going back?"

"I haven't decided." I knew the way Eva sounded, and the voice that came from the back of the store didn't sound like it belonged to her. Her voice had hills and valleys, pretty little streams flowing through. This voice was flat; it went straight on out to where the sky met the land. This voice was a desert.

"What you mean you haven't decided? It's time, Eva, past time. Have you thought what kind of briar patch you're getting Zenie and Ray and Aunt Josie into? You're putting your own people in danger persisting here."

"Born and bred in the briar patch," Eva said, dragging out each word. "We're all born and bred in the briar patch."

Grandpops glared at her. "Have you lost your mind? Shake Rag's got one policy company, and we all know who works for it . . . and what he is. You got to stop all this foolishness. Can't nobody buy from you. Don't you know that? You think those Carolina people in their big fancy offices going to care one flip when you come back in a box? For heaven's sake, think about somebody besides yourself. Think about your own mama and daddy. Don't be such a dadgum fool."

There was a long silence; then Eva said in her desert voice, "Yessir," and there was something in it that was spiked and sharp. A cactus with needle points.

There was another silence. Then Grandpops sighed a big sigh. "All right, then."

He walked over to Mr. L's gleaming glass case, nodded at Mr. L, reached into his pocket and pulled out a nickel. He put it down on the counter. *Clank.* Mr. L just looked down at it. He didn't pick it up.

Grandpops headed toward me and then stopped. He looked back at Mr. L, who was a statue. "Is that enough?"

Mr. L didn't answer. He pushed the nickel back across the counter and looked at Grandpops.

"All right, then. Thank you kindly." Grandpops picked up the nickel and pointed me to the door. When we got outside, the benches were dead empty.

He'd been on foot like always when he came by Zenie's to get me and had to track me down at Lafitte's. So we set off for home walking right past the cemetery and the Daddy Gone Home grave, where Eva had been stretched out on the ground. We tried to make our path under the overhung shade of the big oaks and pecan trees, keeping out of the drilling line of the late sun as much as we could. The resurrection fern on the big oaks was dead brown. The nandinas bent over. Even the bees were quiet. Still everywhere, except for a little round wren that seemed to be following us through the tree limbs singing. A singing fool, he was, with his little brush of a tail. Singing his beating heart out in the dust. Nary a care in the world.

My grandfather's wingtips were brown from the dust. Usually he could put up a fast pace, but this afternoon he was dragging. There was a catch in his breath as he walked along. His skinniness made him look old. His neck hung between his chin and his chest like a turkey wattle. I was mad at him for taking me away from Eva and for getting ugly with her just when she had made it to rise and shine and let me go with her down to Lafitte's for an ice cream. (What a crime!) I wanted to take up for her. So I started in on how sick she'd been and how she'd finally risen up out from her sickbed. When we passed the Daddy Gone Home tombstone, I showed him where she had been stretched out when Zenie and I found her all hurt and burnt. I gave myself some credit for getting her out of her sickbed. In my private mind I had the notion that she was Lazarus and I was Jesus, but of course didn't say so. If I just had a chance at Mama, I bet I could chat her up out of bed too.

Grandpops petted me on the head and pushed his hat back on his head a little. He pulled out his handkerchief and wiped his face off. "Don't get too attached. Eva'll be going on home soon I expect." He said it quiet and sad, like he would personally miss her, which I didn't much believe since he seemed to want her to leave so bad.

Then I had an idea. I got the notion that there couldn't be more policy *men* but Eva was a girl. So there could be policy *men*, my daddy and the others at Mississippi Assurance, and a policy *lady*, Eva. Why not?

I told it to Grandpops. He stopped in the dust all of a sudden, like he just couldn't take another step. What he said, he said carefully. "Honey," he said, "man or woman, it doesn't matter. There's only just so much business. It's a simple case of economics. Plus, Eva's ruint herself in this town. She's always going to have trouble. Some places can turn into a briar patch. That's what Eva said about herself."

I stopped in my tracks. "Br'er Rabbit was born and bred in the briar patch. He *loved* the briar patch. That's what Eva said about herself."

Grandpops sighed. "Unfortunately Eva isn't Br'er Rabbit." He started walking again, this time picking up the pace with his long legs, he breezed by the rest of the cemetery like a bent-over crane eyeing the tombstones like fish he wasn't hungry for. We were at the last of the graves. I could see my grandparents' house up the block on the corner. "Let's just get on home, honey. It's been a long day. Don't worry about Eva. She'll be all right. She'll go on back up to Carolina and get herself another job and have a fine time. She'll have a fine life up there. Raleigh's a city where she can make her own way."

The way he told it, Raleigh sounded like heaven. I remembered the dream I had of Mama and Eva cha-cha-ing their way up to the pearly gates. I wanted to go up to Raleigh too. We could get on the northbound M & O, take the Frisco east. Mama, Eva, and me. We could get a Pullman sleeping car, though I knew we couldn't all sleep together. Eva would have to go in the colored diner car to eat and she'd have to sit up to sleep, but it was only one day and one night, and then we'd all be together when we got there. People lived in apartments in Raleigh. We could get a high-up one so we could see the whole dadgum town light up at night. Eva could sell her policies like gangbusters, and Mama could be the cake lady of Raleigh. Days I'd go along with Eva knocking on doors and offering protection. I could show her a thing or two. I knew how to smile and be sweet when the door opened a crack and somebody said, "Yeah?" I'd done it with Daddy. Nights we'd have a nice cool supper of potato salad and cake. After supper, Eva would go dancing at the juke joint down the street and I'd help Mama in a big shiny kitchen with a new stove and two sinks and dozens of pots and pans. We'd bake hundreds of cakes, and the word would spread. We'd have to turn orders down because Mama wouldn't want any helpers except me. I would be careful to use a pot holder and the three of us would live happily ever after.

11

My arms scabbed up after a week of burning and stinging. Then the scabs fell off, and each arm had a little wavy line going down the inside, following the long blue veins up and down as if it was one of them too, though not with the true red blood running through, but with white from the scars. When I bent my elbows, the insides of my arms felt scratchy, as if someone was trying to strike a match on them.

Eva watched the progress of my arms, and I watched the progress of her face. Our burns closed up about the same time, but both left their scars. We shared a jar of Alba lotion, which she'd lightly touch to the scar on her face, which was still tender, and I'd dab up and down the lines on my arms.

"When's your school starting up?" she asked one morning. I was doctoring my scars on Zenie and Ray's front stoop when she came outside.

"Not till September."

Eva sat down next to me. "You ready?"

When I told Eva how unready I was, she shook her head and pointed to the Alba. "Your hands clean?"

I nodded.

"Put some of that on my place too. Don't rub it."

As I put a bit of the lotion on her circle, she cut her eyes at me. "Do you know how to diagram?"

"Diagram what?"

"Sentences, stupid. Boy, you're in big trouble if you never heard of diagramming sentences. What grade you say you going into?"

My heart sank. "Fifth."

Eva's mouth dropped open. "Lord, girl, what they teaching you in that white fourth grade? If they aren't teaching you to diagram, I'm going to have to rethink this integration thing. You white folks do better coming to our schools."

When I explained about Daddy going on the lam and taking us with him, she touched the circle on her face and looked thoughtful. "And now your mama's gone and flown the coop too. And no wonder about why."

I glared at her. "Mama'll be back."

Eva leaned over and touched her shoulder to mine. "Sure she will."

Time passed. A week? A month? Three days? Time was a wheel spinning in the open air. It didn't move anything forward. It got hotter than ever and Mama wasn't home yet, but soon, Daddy said, soon she'd be coming home. She was getting her brain shocked, and it was supposed to make her feel better, which I guess meant she'd be less inclined to run herself into trains. I thought of the shocks as little tickles. I pictured her laughing, saying aw, quit it now, no fair.

She wrote me little hen-scratched notes, but they didn't say what she meant. "Dear Martha," one said, though I knew she meant to write "Dear Florence." (Why would a person write to herself?) "I miss you so much. See you soon. Love, Mama." Once she sent just an envelope that said on the back: "Florence girl, how could you put me in this place. Your own mother. Come get me now. Martha Irene Riley." Daddy had crumpled that one up and put it into the wastebasket, but I found it. I told Daddy we had to go over to Jackson and get her out of that place, but he said not yet. In a little while. Soon. He'd thrown out her big poison bottle, the one under the kitchen sink, and had torn up the house looking for other bottles, which he found stashed mostly in her shoeboxes on the top of her closet. Half pints of Old Crow tucked in under tissue paper like sleepy babes put down for a nap between high-heel pumps size 5 ½. Wickeder by far than Mimi's too-loud hats.

Every morning I climbed on time's wheel. My father would drag me out. Rise and shine, Sister. Up and at 'em. Make hay while the sun shines. In the night I became the dough he was pushing into shape. You have to love the dough you work, and I knew he loved me. Why else would he tell me about the dangers that could befall good decent white girls? Why else would he want to protect what was deep inside me, true and pure and beautiful, soon to be born? I woke up with the smell of his hair oil on my skin. I soaked it up and it became my smell too, so that I couldn't even smell him coming into my room anymore.

The heat never left me in the cool early morning hours the way it had before, when Mama had come in and taken him back. Now if I turned over and woke him up just a little, he wouldn't know me. He would jump out at me like a hungry cannibal and grab me by the shoulders and hold me down until I screamed, "Daddy!" to wake him up all the way. So I lay still as death. If I had to go to the bathroom, I slid out so careful careful that nobody would know. It seemed that, even when I got up, a part of me stayed behind with him. Only the inside left, the shell of me stayed.

So I was glad if the phone rang and he had to go be the

Nighthawk. He still let me get his box, though I could tell he was not over being mad about the way I had disrespected his things. I would bring it to him like before, but my heart wasn't in it. I was older and wiser. You could tell by the way I carried it, with one hand, balancing it on my hip. Now I knew that all he had in it was a Halloween outfit and not much else. Common everyday things, not jewels of the crown, like I'd once thought. Somewhere he'd gotten a bat that he kept in a corner of the basement next to the box. One night when he got the call and I went down to the basement for his box, there it was, propped up. At first I didn't know to get it too, but then he sent me back down for it. After that, it was part of the deal. The box and the bat. When I brought it up, I asked him if there was a ball and he could teach me to hit. He said it wasn't that kind of bat.

"It's a stick, not a bat, Sister," he said. "See, it's thinner than a bat."

He was right. It was as long as a bat and curved round like a bat, but not as wide.

"What's it for, then?"

"It's for being the Nighthawk. It's a headache stick." Daddy picked it up and took a one-armed swing with it. He grinned and rubbed his chin. "You don't want to get in its way, or it'll give you one bad-assed headache. You think twice about sassing somebody coming at you with a headache stick. This thing'll teach you a lesson you'll never forget."

Before he left at night, he tucked me in. He made me get into the bed and pulled the sheet up over me. Then he turned out the light. He thought that would make me stay put.

After he got washed up to go out, he stood in the doorway to my room. "All right now, I'll be back after a while. Don't get up for nothing or nobody. I'll tan your hide if you get near that kitchen, you hear me?"

I said what I was supposed to say, which was "yes sir." Then he went clunking out the door. I waited until I heard the Chevy roar off. It was a trash car from Big Dan like the green Ford, but I appreciated the firecracker noises it made. On foot or on wheels, Daddy made noise coming and going. He could no more sneak up on you than a train barreling down the tracks. When the sound of the car finally died out, I turned the light back on to read. Somehow, in the month of May, Grandpops reading to me had turned into me reading to him, even parts of the *Saturday Evening Post*. If I didn't know a word, I'd sound it out, and if that didn't work, I'd just be a playful kitten and scamper right on over it. No one word is that important. Semicolons stopped me dead, but I learned to hop over them like Uncle Wiggily hopped over the railroad tracks on his way to big adventures.

But I'd gotten to be a reading fool. When Mimi took me to the county library one afternoon and I saw all those books just sitting up on the shelves waiting for someone to read them, I felt like I'd just walked through the pearly gates.

If I got tired of reading at night, I'd get up and go sit in Mama's closet and smell her clothes. When I first opened the closet, they looked forlorn in the shadows of moon glow. Her sugar smell had faded, but if I grabbed a bunch of her everyday dresses and pressed my face up to them hard, I could still get a whiff of it. Sometimes, most times, I'd cry into them, leaving them wet and bedraggled and worn out with my tears.

Late into the night, after the one-thirty M & O but before the three-o'clock Frisco, Daddy'd come back, dragging behind a smell that was sharp and mustardy. Sometimes on top of that he'd smell like gas and woodsmoke, the way people smell at a barbeque. I'd have my back turned when he got in the bed. I breathed long and slow, playing dead until he started to snore.

When he wasn't gone at night, he was on the phone. Big

Dan or Mr. Jenkins or some of the other misters. "Honey," they'd
breathe into the phone, "run get your daddy. Tell him it's Mister
So-and-so." I never remembered the names. After I told Daddy, I
lost track. Now that Mama was gone, Daddy was talking ugly into
the phone. N_____ this and n_____ that. The word buzzed
around his mouth like a biting horsefly. If Mama'd been there, she
wouldn't have stood for the word in her house. She wouldn't have
swatted at it either. She would have just walked out the front door
and left it buzzing. Let it have the whole place. She'd have been
long gone, which, of course, she already was.

One morning when we were standing out in the yard with
Big Dan, Daddy said right out of the blue, "They going to take us
over, take our women, pollute the race. And them pinko communists are in league with them. They want to take us all down the
toilet with this civil rights crap. Did you hear about them starting
things up over in Clinton?" He said it like he was saying nice day,
how you doing, or some such.

Big Dan's mouth hardened up. He slapped his straw hat on
his leg. His raw head turned even pinker around the curl he'd
drawn up from behind and plastered on top. "Got to stop it now.
Nip it in the bud. Good thing we got a firm hand in this town. A
firm hand is sorely needed these days. Sorely needed."

I was thinking about Ray and my dream about the burning
tree. Ray didn't seem to have any interest in any woman at all
except Zenie. He was mightily interested in her. He never even
looked at white women, much less bothered them. It was almost
as if *he* was scared of *them*.

I had to take up for Ray. I pulled on Daddy's pants. "*Ray* isn't
bad, Daddy."

I didn't like the way it came out. I didn't mean Ray was the
only Negro man who was nice. I knew of others. Mr. Lafitte, for
instance. The old men on the benches at his store. L Junior.

I was thinking there had to be hundreds, thousands, millions more.

Both of them looked down at me, then rolled their eyes at each other. "Well. Got a smarty britches here," Big Dan said. "What you going to do with Miss Smarty Pants?"

Daddy's mouth twitched like he was going to laugh. "Sister, what you got to understand is that there are niggers and there are good colored people. Ray and Zenie, they're good colored people. They know their place and they're useful. They don't step over the line. That girl of theirs is another story. The one staying with them. A nigger, well, a nigger's a nigger. Nothing good to say about them. They're trashy and they don't know their place. There's a difference. These outside agitators, Jews and homos and all, they're niggers too."

Big Dan nodded. "White outside, black as pitch inside."

"You got that right." Daddy waved to Big Dan, and we started up Mama's path to the Chevy. On the way to Mimi and Grand-pops' Daddy looked over at me like he didn't know exactly who I was, riding along with him. I didn't look him in the eye. I was scared I'd made him mad when I said Ray was nice. Now I was wishing I hadn't said it.

Instead of mad, though, Daddy seemed interested. "You get-ting pretty grown up, Sister."

"Yes sir." I looked down at my feet, brown from the layer of dust that had built up on the floor of our house.

"Maybe it's time you got yourself *educated*. Learn a few of life's lessons." He threw the word out like a worm on a fishing line.

"I'm going to school in September."

"I'm talking about a different kind of school."

He didn't say anything else about it and I didn't either. Much as I wanted to go to school with the regular children, I wasn't wild about having to go earlier than I'd planned, which was the end of September. I'd been putting off the multiplication tables, which were deadly dull, and now Eva'd gone and scared my pants off about diagramming. I didn't want to get caught short. Mainly, I was dearly hoping that Mama'd be back before September so she could get me some clothes. I'd outgrown almost everything and what I hadn't was getting tighter by the day. Mimi tended to buy me prissy dresses, which I had no use for except for church. I needed outfits, but not prissy ones. Just regular ones. Crop tops and plain skirts. I also liked jumpers. You could wear them with short-sleeved shirts at the beginning of the school year when it was hot, then put your long-sleeved shirts under them when it cooled off. They were versatile, which Eva had said was important in a piece of clothing.

A few nights later when Daddy got a call, it was earlier than usual, more light than dark. I went on down to get the box and the headache stick. When I got upstairs, Daddy was still talking. "All right," he said into the phone, "I'll bring her." Then he hung up and turned around and gazed down upon me like I was a pleasure to behold. I handed him the box, but he didn't take it.

"Got a surprise for you, Sister, if you can be good." His eyes had a shine to them.

I perked up. I'd missed my milk shakes. Maybe he was going to take me to Joe's.

"How'd you like to go to a meeting? A get-together. You can carry the box yourself. Get yourself a little education."

A meeting wasn't nearly as good as a milk shake, but it wasn't as bad as having to go to school early either. "All right." I tried to sound pleased to be invited the way Mama taught me to do when the Greats made me come over and sit in the dark parlor with them right before Christmas. The Greats were two of Mimi's sisters who lived together across town in a house with peeling paint. They had lost most of their hair and smelled of camphor and offered peppermints in plastic wrappers and lukewarm water in paper cups. They always wrapped up something they already had and gave it to me at Christmas. One year it was a salt shaker in the shape of a reindeer. The next it was the matching pepper. Mama and I always brought over a perfect whole lemon cake just for the two of them, which they made much over, but hustled directly into the back like it was something private and shameful. Instead of offering a slice like you'd expect, they passed a little jagged white china bowl with peppermints in plastic and I had to act like they were the biggest treat ever.

So between Mimi's too-loud hats and the Greats' peppermints, I'd had practice in acting enthused when there was nothing to be enthused about.

"Hold up now. You don't sound too happy." It was a warning. I looked up at Daddy, but I couldn't quite see him the way I used to. It was odd, but as time went on without Mama in the house, I was beginning to see him as if he were a ways away. Even if he were right in my face, which he was most nights, he seemed far away. The sheets and pillowcases had slicked up with the shape of us, but seeing him was another story. He was like the little letters at the bottom of the eye chart. You could make out their shapes enough to say one was E and the other F, but you couldn't really see them well enough to know them truly.

"Oh boy." I wanted my words to fly. Instead they hopped around on the ground like a pair of fat lazy doves.

"Get some shoes on." He eyed me up and down. "And go get on a better shirt." He took the box and stick out of my hands and put them down on the coffee table. "Make it fast. I'm going to wash up. We got to get a move on."

He went on into the bathroom. I heard the water. When Daddy washed up, he splashed up a storm. It made puddles on the sides of the lavatory and puddles on the floor since Mama wasn't there anymore to mop up his splashes. When he came out, I could see the grooves of the comb in his hair running in little lines across and down. He'd made a line part on the left side. Not a hair on the wrong side of the line. I'd put on my best everyday shirt, though it was getting too little in the shoulders and chest. It was blue with little pearl buttons and eyelet around the neck and sleeves. "Nice and cool," Mama said when she brought it home all new and fresh last summer. Now it was faded and soft and wrinkled, though Mama would have ironed it if she'd been here. Not that I'd be going at all if she'd been there. The little pearl buttons were pulled tight.

We went along the stepping-stone path to the car, me bringing up the rear. I carried the box and the stick, Daddy's lady slave. By then it was just about dark and Miss Kay Linda's night jasmine was revving up. Some of it brushed my face. I took a big whiff. It was so sweet it made me want to suck it like you suck honeysuckle. I was starting to feel not altogether bad to be going out with Daddy on a summer night, instead of getting left behind in a hot dark house all by myself. Enjoyable once I got into the spirit of it. Uncle Wiggily heading out on another adventure. The box was my valise. The headache stick my crutch. In my mind, I hopped up and down.

When we got to the car, Daddy came around to my side to open the door for me. Just as I was getting in, he touched my shoulder. When I turned around, he was standing there with his finger under his nose again. "Do you remember what this means?"

"Don't tell?"

He nodded. "Everything's a secret from now on, Sister. Lips sealed."

I didn't say anything, just nodded in a serious way.

"Show me."

I put the box down on the seat, and put the first finger on my left hand up under my nose in the sign.

He shook his head no. "Wrong hand."

I changed to my right and made the sign again.

"Good. Now it's a promise you can't break. Nigh unto death. Swear it."

"I swear."

The dark was crowding Daddy's face, drawing a veil across the little space between us. I tried to see into his eyes to tell whether they were smiling. His mouth wasn't. I couldn't see his eyes. I stood there and waited for what was next. I didn't see him move, but he must have because then he was opening the door on his side. I picked up the box and got in the car, closed the door. The box was riding in my lap. I had a good strong grip on the headache stick.

I thought we'd have to ride a long way and end up out in the country on dirt roads, like when Mama took me to the bootlegger, but we just bumped across town on regular streets. Daddy pulled into the Phillips 66 where he always bought gas. It was dark, closed for the night. There weren't any other cars around. Next door was a big garage. When he turned off the engine, everything seemed quiet for a minute and then the night sounds came rushing in, nearly as loud as Daddy's muffler but peaceful and settled. Daddy got out on his side and came around. When I handed him the box, he reached down and got the stick too. Then I got out. The back of my shirt was already wet with sweat and sticking to my back.

"Come on," he said, and started toward the garage. "I got stuff to do. Got to open this place up." There was a door on the side with a padlock. He pulled a key out of his key chain and opened it. The door was big and heavy and had a spring on it that made it swing shut if you didn't hold on to it. He backed up against it to hold it open for me. "Get on in."

After I went through, Daddy let go of the door and left us in pitch black. Then he reached up and pulled a chain. A bare bulb shot up light and there we were, in a little room with another big door. It had a peephole on it. That door was locked too, but Daddy used another key to get it open. "There're only two people in the whole world who have this key," he said, "and I'm one of them." Then we went into a big room. The place was swampy and close. Daddy turned on a switch and a big attic fan started up so that the night air, which had seemed so hot outside, came rushing in sweet and cool.

The room looked like a Sunday school class getting ready to commence. It had a gold shag rug that felt soft the way grass feels soft. Folding chairs arranged in a neat square all facing the middle raised-up part, which had a cross that stood up taller than me. It was made out of two pieces of wood and a whole bunch of red lightbulbs. There was a poster tacked up on the wall of somebody in a white hood and robe on a rearing up-horse that was wearing a skirt and a hood too, which was probably why it was rearing up, it couldn't see where it was going. The horse person reminded me of the Queen of Palmyra heading into battle, except she was covered up in the white robe, with two crosses on its front where the queen's bosoms would have been. At first I thought I saw the moon curve of those bosoms under the white, but when I looked again, I could see it was not a woman but a man, with a look on his face that said I'm as pure as the driven snow, don't mess with me.

Daddy fished the little key to his box out of his shirt pocket. He unlocked the box and pulled out the Bible, the little sword, the vase, and his two flags. He handed me the Bible. "Find Romans," he said. "It's in the New Testament."

Of course I knew Romans was in the New Testament. Right before Daddy'd absconded with us, I'd dedicated my life to Jesus at the First Methodist Church, along with a bunch of other children. The preacher had given each one of us our own King James Bible. After the service he had gathered the children together and got us to open our Bibles to the first page. Each one had: I, [YOUR NAME], took Jesus Christ as my savior and Lord on March 2, 1961, and I am saved. He told us to write in our names, and the deed would be done. When I wrote in *Florence Irene Forrest*, I felt a fluttering inside my chest and I figured it was the Holy Ghost coming in for a landing.

Later, when I got home, I added my own personal PS, which said, "Get thee behind me, Satan." On the facing page, I drew the outline of my own hand and wrote inside it THE FINGERS OF GOD. I'd labeled each finger the way we'd been taught in Sunday school. The thumb was the saving finger, the pointer the warning finger; then there were the guiding finger, the judging finger, and the keeping finger. I wondered which finger had tabs on me tonight.

I was glad to have something to do while Daddy was getting the place set up. While I was pouring through the Bible looking for Romans, he went over and plugged in the cross. A few of the bulbs were gone, but it looked pretty anyway, Christmas and Easter all rolled into one, though witchy. Daddy put the two flags into pole holders on either side of the cross so that they draped down on it. It made a pretty sight. Each flag hung over one arm of the cross so it seemed safe and at home underneath them. Then he went over to a sink and filled up the vase with some water. I was thinking this was going to be some kind of party, with flowers no less, but then he just put the vase on a tall table next to the cross and laid the sword next to the vase. He turned off the overhead light and looked over at me. "Did you find Romans, honey?"

I hadn't found it. It was now dark in the room except for the lit-up cross, which was red, in any case. I'd started singing in my head the books of the Bible so I'd know where to look, but when I got to Romans I didn't see it in my head because the song went "Matthew, Mark, Luke and John, Actsandepistlestotheromans, so I didn't catch the Romans part of it. I was almost to Revelations.

"No, no, you passed it up." Daddy grabbed the Bible out of my hands. He was in a hurry. "Here, right here. Now Chapter Twelve. Right here." He put the Bible on the table too and then took a quick look around. He was sweating, but he pulled his black robe and hood out of the box and put them on. In the witchy red glow it seemed as if he'd just left the room he was so invisible under all that black. When he spoke to me from behind the hood, it didn't sound like him, but just a muffled voice from way out yonder. "Come here," the voice said and Daddy's arm reached out and took my elbow and pulled, which hurt on account of my scars. He corralled me over beside the front door just as there was a bang on it. Then a scratching sound.

"Who is it and what is your business?" The question came from behind Daddy's hood, but it didn't sound anything like him.

From behind the door came "I am Klansman Chisholm. I seek entrance to the Klavern to meet with my fellows."

"Password?"

"Rose."

"Pass, Klansman." Daddy opened the door. "Hey Big Dan, you're the first." Daddy's voice was back to normal. "Here, take her till I get everybody in." He shoved me at Big Dan like I was a plate of cookies.

That's when I got it. Daddy was in a club, like Eva's girl club except it had a clubhouse and a password, and he'd asked me to join. Suddenly I felt like a queen. You didn't see Little Dan or May here. Just me.

I was relieved to see Big Dan looking like his normal ugly old bald self, no robe or hat or hood. Between the red glow the cross made and Daddy in the black, I had been feeling a little put off.

"Sure, Win, plus I got a surprise for her. Look honey, Miss Kay Linda made it for you." Big Dan pulled out what looked like a white brunch coat with long sleeves and a tassel tie and a little pointy hat made out of a white paper sack. "Come on, let's put it on."

Daddy's voice came back again. He sounded choked up he was so happy. "Look at that, Sister. Miss Kay Linda made you your own robe. How sweet is that? Say thank you to Big Dan, Sister."

"Thank you." I said it but I didn't mean it. The last thing I wanted was something else to put on. I'd already sweated through my nice blue shirt, plus I'd popped a button and lost it to boot. If Mama ever came back, she was going to be aggravated. "I'm hot as fire." It came out whinier that it should have.

"I'll take care of Little Bit here. Come on, honey." Big Dan took my hand. His hand was squishy. I felt like I was holding on to a piece of raw beef liver. It was sticky too, and wherever you pushed, it gave. He took me over into a far corner of the room where it was dark. He squatted down in front of me. "Let's take off your shirt," he said. "That way you won't be so hot underneath."

I was counting my blessings not to have to wear the thing like a choir robe over my clothes. I was going to unbutton myself, but he reached over and started on the buttons. I could have done them faster. I didn't like him doing them, but I didn't worry he could see me because it was dark except for the glow of the Christmas-lit cross, which his back hid. He was slow as Christmas himself, taking his time with each one. Fumbling around because it was so dark. Once he tickled me in fun, which reminded me of Mama's electric shock treatments in Jackson. Finally, my blouse was open and he drew it slow over each arm. He was nice and careful. "Do you want to keep it off for a minute, just to cool off?" His question was a nice little breeze blowing over my front. "I can fan you with it."

He was already fanning my front. It felt cool and refreshing. I was the queen and he was my slave with a palm.

Meanwhile, men galore were piling on in. It was old home week. I could see them over Big Dan's shoulder, but they couldn't see me. They were having themselves a good time jawing and patting this one and that one on the shoulder. Some of them I knew. Mr. Jenkins, who owned the drugstore. The little man in a neat uniform who filled us up at the Phillips 66, Daddy called him Sam. Daddy was the only one dressed up in an outfit. He was still at the door taking the password. In the dark I didn't recognize anyone else. They were all ages and shapes, but they had the same glad look on their faces, as if this party was the highlight of their year. They were milling around. There was a little table over the side, and one man was pouring out of a jug into paper cups.

A few of them noticed me and Big Dan and started over. I was feeling less than private. I grabbed the sack out of Big Dan's hand. "Let's get me dressed now."

"Sure, honey. You cooled off?"

I looked down at myself. My chest was glowing red from the cross. I looked like a piece of raw meat. "Yessir." I crossed my hands over my chest.

"All right then. Let's see. Miss Kay Linda said she made it up a little large so you wouldn't outgrow it so fast, but whoa, looks just right." He held up the white robe. It had two ties in the front, one at the neck and one at the waist. He helped me put one arm in, then the other. Then he tied the ties in little bows, his fingers busy little butterflies. He pulled out the pointed hat. "Let's see now. How does this work?" It had a pretty little white satin ribbon that tied under the chin. He put it on my head and tied the ribbon. "Oh, look at *you!*" Then he gathered me in his arms and gave me a big bear hug. I hugged him back because I could tell how much he liked me. Which is not something I took for granted in my situation. I couldn't remember the last time I got hugged, much less bear-hugged. I hugged him hard. I didn't want to let him go.

"Bet you still hot, right?"

I nodded. The robe wasn't heavy, but it was head to toe. I was steaming.

"Let's get off those shorts then. That'll help."

Before I could say no thank you sir, I'll keep them on, he opened up the robe in front and gave them a quick little jerk. They came down fast because they had elastic in the waist. My underpants came down too, but I grabbed hold of them and pulled them back up. "Oopsy daisy. Step out now, honey." He leaned down and pulled the shorts away from my feet. "Here, now, honey, I'll put your clothes in this sack. Isn't that better?" He reached under the robe and rubbed me up and down on the leg.

It was airier underneath, though now I was sweating more than ever.

"Where's my daddy?" It came out fretful.

"Sure, honey, let's go find him. See if he's done with his work. This is just a social meeting. You so cute in that outfit everybody's going to want to get a look at you."

I saw Daddy across the room. He'd taken off his hood so he just looked like a member of the church choir in his black robe. He had a cup in his hand and he was laughing. I ran over to him.

"Well, hey now, look at my girl!" He put his hands on my shoulders and pulled me over in front of him. "Look at my girl!" The second time he hollered it, all the men stopped talking and looked. I stood there, my back pressing into his dark middle, his fingers digging holes in my shoulders. "Wave at everybody, honey," he hollered. I waved and everybody clapped and cheered like they were at a parade.

Then they all crowded round. One of them pulled me over, and then they started passing me around like I was the body and the blood, the communion cup everybody wanted a sip of. After a while they got their paper cups from the table and sat in little groups sipping and laughing and got me to walk from one to the other. One with brown teeth and a cheek of tobacco reached through the place between the ties of my robe. He tickled me till I wet my pants a little, then a little more. I was screaming bloody murder by then, Daddy way across the room, he looked over once but then just smiled real big at me. You know how you scream when you're getting tickled. It sounds like you're excited and happy. "Look out," the brown-tooth man hollered. "She's wetting like a baby. I'm getting rid of this one." Then he passed me onto the lap of a real old man with yellow skin. He rubbed his scratchy face on me. Then he shoved me over to the next one, who opened his knees and pulled me in and gave me a big old hug. They were thick as bees. I went around once, then again. "Let me have her back," the really old one kept hollering. One of them pulled me onto his lap and bounced me hard. My teeth snapped and kicked. I bit my tongue and tasted blood. Daddy kept on with his laughing and smiling across the way.

After a while there came up a fog. It rose in front of my eyes so that I didn't see any of them anymore. It was so thick that I had a minute when I thought I was somewhere else, out on the street, and the mosquito truck had just passed by. Or maybe I was in a black dismal swamp and the gases were rising fast. All of them floated back and away before my eyes, though their hands still reached through the fog.

When I got home that night, somebody had taken off my wet underpants and put my shorts and top back on, so I was dry at least. When Daddy lay down in the bed and reached for me, he said, "You were real good tonight, Sister. I was proud of you. Look at me."

I was too tired to roll over. I turned my face to look at him, but the fog was still in my eyes. All I could see was the outline of his head in the pearly light of the moon coming through the window behind him. A dark blank circle with a halo. He looked like pictures I'd seen of the angel of the Lord when he told Mary she was going to have God's baby.

"You know how much I love you, Sister honey?" The way he said it was like a song.

I was too tired to say yessir, so I just nodded. He felt it, though. My head was right there beside him. Precious Cargo.

12

The next morning I felt different. It wasn't the soreness. It was something else. Something that had the feel of long distances. It unfolded out ahead of me, world without end. I had gotten on the M & O going to Memphis but it had passed Memphis by. It had decided to go on and on. All I could see were tracks and the tracks didn't stop anywhere. I was in a story without an ending. Nobody was found, nobody saved. Nobody got out of the briar patch or made the alligator laugh. Just the never-ending tracks as far as the eye could see.

I woke up thinking about Miss Josephine counting leaves. Was she thinking about long distances, what numbers were so far out there ahead of her that she'd never get to them? They kept pulling her on, though. They wouldn't let her stop and say this is it, this is the end of the line. This is my house and I am home now.

That morning, for the first time ever, my father made me some breakfast. He put some butter on a piece of bread and stuck it under the oven broiler. Then he poured out a glass of milk and handed it to me. The milk had turned, but I drank it anyway. I hardly tasted its bite. The toast burned black, but I ate it. I was happy for it. He kept telling me how much he loved me, right down to my bones, he said, and when he said it, he came around and gave me a bear hug like the one Big Dan had given me. It hurt but it felt good too. We made the finger sign because we had secrets. I was a member of his club.

When he dropped me at Mimi and Grandpops' like always, instead of opening the car door and hopping right out like I was supposed to, I held on to his arm like a lady with her partner on the dance floor.

"I want to go with you." Just as the words came out of my mouth like sickly sweet syrup, I heard the seven-thirty train. It called out *no, no, no, no.*

"Sister baby, I'll see you tonight." He smoothed down my hair on top. It was the first time he'd ever done that. My eyes started up. "Now you go on in like a good girl. I know you a good girl. Now remember . . ." He put his right finger up under his nose and smiled so sweet it almost broke my heart.

"Yessir." I put my finger up too. The right one.

He reached over and opened the car door, and out I went. Plop on the curb. The thud made my legs ache all the way up into my backside. I felt the jarring in my bones. I watched him drive off the way Mama had, but I knew he'd be back. I ached all over, felt hollowed out, but I had a full and satisfied heart because I didn't have to worry about him coming back for me. *He* loved me too much to leave me high and dry.

After noon dinner I dragged on home with Zenie. By the time we got to her house, her legs had made brown spots on her support hose so that she was in a hurry to soak them in a tub of Epsom salts. The longer they stayed like that, the harder it was to get the hose to let go. For once, she pulled me along instead of the other way around. She cast an irritated eye at me. "What you so lazy for today, girl?" My arms and legs didn't feel like they belonged to me. They were logs I was carrying. Even my insides felt sore and used up.

That afternoon it seemed as if I'd just gotten to Zenie's, much less settled there, when here came Grandpops to pick me up. I popped up off the couch and saw little blackbirds flying before my eyes. They looked like pieces of dark gauze, torn with a rough hand. Zenie and Grandpops made me sit back down and pushed my head between my legs until the blackbirds flew away.

"She's acting poorly," Zenie said. "She act like she got the weak blood, sleeping all the time. Maybe she need to go to the doctor. Maybe she need some of the iron medicine."

Grandpops leaned over and fanned me with his hat. He always took it off when he came in, but he never sat down in Zenie's house. She never asked him to. She'd bring him a cold glass of water and he'd drink it in a few quiet swallows standing in the middle of the room.

"All right, then. Thank you, Zenie," Grandpops said when I could hold up my head. "We'll get her some vitamins." He opened the door and nodded his head politely to Zenie. He had to look up to talk to her. She was so hefty and tall she made him look like a little old boy, wrinkled and wizen.

"Good-bye until tomorrow," Zenie said.

He put his hand on my shoulder and tapped. "Florence." I knew that meant to tell Zenie thank you.

"Thank you." I looked down at the floor when I said it. It shamed me to have to thank her for keeping me when I was old enough to do for myself.

"You welcome." She still had on her white outfit from work, though her stockings were soaking in the kitchen sink. She nodded and smiled, arms crossed over her bosoms, standing on one leg and then the other, willing us out the door so she could sigh and sit in her flowered easy chair with the foot stool to match. Looking back through her front window, I could see her settle in, her face framed by the geraniums on the sill.

"You dragging, girl. What's wrong with you?" Grandpops asked on the way home. I couldn't seem to put one foot in front of the other.

"Nothing except getting dragged from pillar to post every day of the week."

He touched me on the top of the head. "How's your daddy doing?"

"Fine." I pulled my head away.

"Y'all getting along all right?"

"Yes sir."

"You heard anything from your mother?"

"No sir." Daddy had said not to tell anybody about the letters from Mama.

He patted me on the shoulder. "It'll be all right. Your mother will be back soon and you can stay home. School'll be starting up sooner than you think—less than three months from now—and you'll find some friends to play with. You'll see. It's going to all work out. You just been having a hard summer. We all have." His voice sounded like salt hitting a hot frying pan. Scratchy and brisk.

Nothing he said impressed me. I didn't have high hopes for Mama. Judging from her letters, she was getting more mental by the minute. Plus even the word *school* made my heart skip a beat. I'd been telling myself I was making progress on my studies, but Eva's remark about diagramming chilled me to the bone. I could read, thanks to Grandpops, and I was making progress in social studies with Mimi despite the hat business, though I knew she was teaching me what she taught in high school, not what I needed for fifth grade. Sometimes I watched Ray add and subtract, but I still needed to memorize the multiplication tables, which Miss Josephine said she'd drill me on, but she kept falling asleep and so did I. All in all, I didn't have high hopes about how the fifth grade was going to turn out. Plus I dreaded the morning I had to try to find an outfit that still fit and walk down the sidewalk with all those girls with shining hair in their color-coordinated sets. Would they still look right through me like I was a ghost? I'd rather sleep on Zenie's couch the rest of my life, world without end.

For supper, Mimi had her tomato aspic and a cooling tuna salad with celery and sweet pickles ready for Grandpops and me. Then at long last the day was over, and I was at the curb swatting mosquitoes waiting for the firecracker pop of Daddy's Chevy coming for to carry me home. Mimi and Grandpops crouched in the burrow of their living room waiting for me to leave so they could go out on the front porch and enjoy the evening without having to talk to Daddy. They never turned on the light. When Daddy was pulling away from the curb, I looked back and saw their double shadow shading the screen door. The door opened just a little before we got all the way down the street.

The days went on. Daddy and I were like one piece of water that parted in the morning and flowed back together at night. I wasn't sad like I'd been before. I didn't think about Mama as much. Her not being there had settled in on me. The places where she wasn't, the things she wasn't there to do, they seemed to shrink, and after a while they began to dry up like puddles in the sun. Daddy had put her pots and pans and beaters and measuring cups back up in the cabinets. If you opened the doors, they all came falling out. As long as I didn't open them, though, our kitchen seemed regular, not a cake lady's kitchen but any old body's, except of course nobody ever cooked in it.

Eva was laying low, but she was busy. She'd given up on being the policy lady after getting roughed up by the peckerwoods. She had other plans. She had decided what the folks in Shake Rag needed was literacy. I asked her what that was and she said it was reading and writing and she was going to work in her spare time to help grown-ups learn to read. She'd gotten some books in the mail on teaching people to read by the sounds of words and she'd read them cover to cover, turning down every other page. It was called Phonics, though the word itself didn't seem like a good advertisement for the idea of it. It wasn't that hard, Eva said. All you had to do was learn the sounds of all the letters. Then you could sound out anything but the trickiest words. And even those had rules to go by.

Every Sunday after church she was down at the AME Church signing people up for lessons, which she said would make them better citizens. The AMEs were more forward thinking than the folks at St. John the Baptist. A change was coming and many of them wanted to pass the literacy requirement so they could sign up to vote, which was easier said than done, no matter how literate you were. Eva had gotten a copy of the Mississippi Constitution, and they were studying it like the Bible. The law said you had to be able to copy out a passage from the Constitution and explain it, though Eva said the passages given to the people from Shake Rag were so complicated Einstein couldn't explain them, which was the whole point. But they kept trying. Every few weeks a group of Eva's pupils would go down to the courthouse like they were going off to fight World War III and walk through the dopers on one side and the guns on the other the way Mama and I did when we visited the sheriff. They tried again and again to register, but they always came back shaking their heads. Word got around that over in Harmony, in Leake County next door, Winson Harmon, who'd raised a ruckus in Washington about not getting to vote, got the Justice Department to come down and stand with her to register. She wrote out her passage from the Mississippi Constitution and when they asked her what it meant for the umpteenth time, she answered, "It said what it meant, and it meant what it said," and they finally let her register. The AMEs tried that, but it didn't work for them. No surprise, Eva said, since the Justice Department seemed to think everything was just hunky-dory over in Millwood.

Zenie and Ray and Miss Josephine had all about given up on getting her to go on back to Raleigh. She was being mulish. Worse than mulish. She was like a nesting owl in a hollowed-out tree and nothing short of a stick of dynamite was going to budge her. They begged and pleaded. They got ugly with her. They told her she couldn't live with them anymore, but she said she wasn't studying leaving whether she lived in their house or not. She said, "It's not like I'm going to be here forever, only till school starts in the fall. You going to put your one and only niece outdoors?" That one always kicked the wind out of Zenie. Then, to finish her off, Eva would cock her head and wink and say slow and sweet, in a dripping voice that didn't sound at all like Raleigh, "Lordy mercy, I just got here and you-all kicking me out already!" They couldn't do a thing with her, but they stopped short of buying her a one-way ticket and taking her down to the station. I heard Ray tell Zenie maybe that's what they ought to do, but Zenie said Eva was so stubborn that even if they managed to get her on the train, which would take all the deacons at St. John's and the AME combined, she'd just get off in Memphis and buy herself a ticket right on back to Millwood. So why waste good money?

The one thing nobody threatened to do was to tell her daddy. I heard Ray and Zenie stew about it. Whether to go down to Lafitte's and call Marie without Jake knowing, but everybody who knew Marie knew she was a fool with no spine. She'd tell Jake and he'd be on the doorstep snatching Eva bald-headed for raising a ruckus. That was something nobody wanted to see.

Meanwhile Eva was charging out of the house every morning loaded down with books and magazines and pamphlets. She had a determined look in her eye. I thought all grown-ups knew how to read. I thought it was like walking on your own two feet and using the commode. The stories just grabbed you and you just fell into them after a while, which is what had happened to me when Grandpops read to me. It was a mystery to me how I'd learned to read, but one day I just started reading along with Grandpops, surprising us both. That's just it, Eva said with a gleam in her eyes that matched the rhinestones on her glasses, you had to get somebody to teach you, to *facilitate*. Literacy wasn't like a piece of my mama's lemon cake you handed over to somebody on a plate. And if nobody at home could read, you had to learn in school, but some people had to quit school and go to work before they learned what they needed to know. So they needed extra help to get caught up.

Eva said that literacy wasn't just about stories; it was about structure and logic and how words belonged to each other. One afternoon she and Ray were sitting at the table working on his vocabulary. Ray'd told Eva he wanted more words. Since she'd been in town, he'd started reading the old newspapers and *Saturday Evening Posts* Zenie brought home from work; now he'd pilfered *The Hunchback of Notre Dame* from Eva. She caught me hovering in the doorway between the kitchen and living room trying to pick up as much of the lesson as I could.

"How much school you say you missed last year, Miss Nosy?" she said.

"Pretty near all of it, I guess."

"Shame to have good schools to go to and not go." Her glasses had crawled down on her nose so that I could tell what she was going to look like when she got to be a prissy old-lady school-teacher.

"I was sick and we moved a million times."

She looked me over. Then she frowned and said, "Well, you can look on if you want to. But don't stand between us and the fan. And don't breathe all over me."

That was the day Eva got it into her head to teach us how to diagram sentences, which she said would help us with our reading, and more important, our writing. I was all for it. I'd heard that you had to write themes in fifth grade and stories too. Ray, I think, would have much rather read *The Hunchback of Notre Dame* but was too polite to say so. He sat at the kitchen table watching her work with pencil and paper to map out the sentences, and I looked over his shoulder. Eva loved diagramming. She said it was a way to tell what something is by what it belongs to. If there's nothing for a word to belong to, you have to let it go. Cut the rope. It is a dangling modifier.

The first sentence Eva diagrammed for us was about a girl and a rose. *The girl carefully touched the beautiful rose.* She said beautiful belonged to the rose. It got its life from the rose. The other side of the story, she told us, was that the rose became what it was by being beautiful. So the modifier and the thing being modified, they each made the other what it was, until they were both like Miss Josephine counting mimosa leaves, going on forever and ever until belonging to the thing made you become it. All of that just tumbled out of Eva's mouth like a poem. Though I didn't understand a word of what she was talking about, I could see how she loved the way words lined up and belonged to one another like the ingredients of a perfect cake, right down to the last grain of salt.

She made one long line and hoisted the subject and verb onto opposite ends of it; then she drew the slanted lines for the modifiers. Just when Ray and I had gotten it straight about what was where and why, she smiled and said, "But what if . . . " and wrote out another sentence with almost the same words: *The careful girl was touched by the beautiful rose.* Ray and I groaned together.

"How can a rose touch a girl?" I asked.

Ray chuckled. "What'd it go and do, reach out and grab her by the hair of the head?"

"There are many kinds of touching," Eva answered with a frown, and shoved the dictionary at us. "Look it up and read it to us."

Zenie, who was all the time fussing at Ray for not reading lo these many years, was now stuck with the job of picking up books and papers and magazines all over the house. Finally, she said to Ray, "When you're through with something, just drop it on the floor so I'll know what to throw away and what to keep." She'd go through the house picking up papers and books here and there, singing and humming little snatches of church songs under her breath. Shadrach, Meshach, and Abednego in the fiery furnace with an angel. Were you there when they crucified my Lord? Sometimes it causes me to tremble, tremble, tremble. Her singing and humming folded around the house like pretty paper around a present and made us feel everything that happened inside was strangely momentous.

Listening to Eva's pretty talk about words and looking over Ray's shoulder while he sounded out the long words in his books and diagrammed sentences was the closest I'd gotten to being a part of the goings-on at Zenie and Ray's. Most of the household happenings I watched as if I were peering through a piece of cheesecloth. I saw the life they lived that summer, but just a gauzy, dimly lit version of it, as if I were seeing it as a grown woman looking back in memory rather than being there in the moment. They had their secrets. When they wanted to say something they didn't want me to hear, they turned their faces away from me and mouthed the words, or they took it outside on the front stoop and whispered it back and forth. They held themselves apart from my prying eyes and kept their privacy even though I was eternally present and watchful, taking up the living room with my hungry self. I wanted to be in it, what it was they had together, but I was always scratching on the door.

So it was strange when one afternoon Eva came over and sat down beside me on the couch. I was just waking up from a nap and still half asleep.

"Hey Flo," she said, "I have an idea. What would you say about me *tutoring* you in reading and grammar? I'm almost a teacher, you know, and I'm going to teach junior high when I graduate."

My eyes popped open. This was the first piece of luck I'd had all summer. "Is tutoring the same as teaching?"

She winked. "It sure is, except better because it's just you and me so you get *personalized* attention."

The way she said *personalized* made my heart rattle about in my chest.

"Why you wanting to do that for? You got other fish to fry."

She pushed her glasses back on her nose. "Money, pure and simple. I need money. Plus, girl, whether you know it or not, you need me."

My eyes filled up, which mortified me no end. "But I don't think Daddy . . ."

"Don't go asking your daddy. Ask your granddaddy. Tell him I charge a dollar an hour for my services. Tell him I can start tomorrow. We can meet every day if need be. It can be our secret."

"When are you going to sell your encyclopedias if you got to tutor me?"

She stood up. "You just worry about talking to your granddad. Let me worry about selling my encyclopedias."

Eva had gotten on with another company, this one in New York City. She was trying to sell encyclopedias, which was another reason she wanted people to learn to read if they didn't already know how to. A week ago the sample set had arrived at Zenie and Ray's.

The encyclopedias were the color of blood that's almost dry but not quite. A dark pearly red. The color seemed heavy and full of portent. There was one book for almost every letter of the alphabet except some that were combined, like XYZ.

That morning Eva had taken them all out and put them in order on the living-room floor. They made a good-sized square.

"Don't get them out of order, and wash your hands before you dare touch them," she said in her queenly way. So I parked myself in front of A and started in on it. I was a dog with two dozen bones. My first time through the books I just looked at the pictures. Africa was a pretty shape with a big fluffy tail and lions and tigers and elephants galore. Babylon was a city on the Euphrates River with palm trees and gardens. California was the state that hung out into the Pacific Ocean and had artichokes growing down to the water and earthquakes that brought down skyscrapers. I began to think I didn't need to go to school, just read Eva's sample set and I'd know more than most people ever do.

At the bottom of one of the boxes the sample set had come in was a booklet of directions on how to sell them in "economically slow areas." The trick lay in selling the books in three sets. Cash in advance. The layaway plan. Folks paid a little at a time and then finally they got A through G. Then they laid away more and got H through O. And then finally the P through Z. I had a picture in my head of a little girl's mother and father starting out with paying for A through G, then working their way to H through O, by which time the little child had grown into a woman, knowing everything there was to know about anything that started with A through G. Nothing about anything else. Leaving home and going to work. Meanwhile, her mama and daddy would be putting away for P through Z.

With the encyclopedias Eva got a white man named Frank. He was so big and colorless that he looked like a polar bear without fur. He was called a team captain and was supposed to be training her to sell encyclopedias in the Negro community, which was a joke. Eva said he didn't know the first thing about Blacks, which is what she'd started calling Negroes in the past few weeks. When Frank arrived a week ago he wanted to go knocking on doors with her, but after the first day, she wouldn't let him. "He just plain scares folks," she said. "He doesn't know how to meet and greet. He's big as a barn and looks like he's got a sheet for skin. He'd have to put a gun to their head to get them to buy anything from him. I'll do better on my own. They know me." Plus Frank slowed her down. He was so heavy and white he couldn't take the sun. He was always huffing and puffing and wore a wet white cloth on his head that made him look like the men in Daddy's club. "Going to drop dead at my feet one day, and nobody's going to lift a finger," Eva said. "Expect me to carry him to the funeral home. Ha!"

But she kept Frank close. You could tell he loved her to death. He drove her up and down the little dusty Shake Rag streets in his blue Chevy with its big backseat for all their sample sets and sat in the car fanning himself and drinking Orange Crushes while she went door to door, his upper lip getting brighter and brighter orange as the day went by. His eyes followed her to every door, but Eva told Zenie he kept his hands to himself. He lived in a boarding house downtown and went over to Indianola to see his mother twice a month. Eva had the good sense never to travel in the car with him outside Shake Rag. In fact, she never went outside of Shake Rag herself. "Enough right here to keep me busy till the end of the summer," she said when Zenie told her it was no kind of life she was living, being cooped up like a chicken in a wire cage.

Soon Eva had sold so many layaway orders she needed to spend part of her afternoons filling out forms and sending them off to New York City. The encyclopedias were a big hit. Folks liked them and the idea of them. In the past week she'd started wearing bright little scarves around her neck. Nice rows of bracelets on her arms. She bought Zenie some Dr. Scholl's pads for her shoes and made Ray pick himself out a good shirt in the Sears catalog. She measured the space where the bathroom door should be and got Frank to go into the lumberyard and buy a rough wood door and then sent him to the hardware store for some hinges. Ray planed, sanded, and shellacked the door, then put it up and sanded and shellacked it again. It was a perfect fit. Now everybody could have privacy.

Eva would sit at Zenie's kitchen table with a nice glass of sweet tea and all her layaway tickets and money stacked up in neat little piles. While she did her paperwork, she turned the radio on low so as not to wake Miss Josephine and Zenie and hummed little snatches of songs. Sometimes, while I lay on Zenie's couch with my eyes closed, I would pretend I was in my bed at home and Eva was my mother baking in the kitchen.

Which was fine with Zenie, who lay down on her and Ray's bed and propped up her legs like the doctor said to do, each one on its own pillow, sores scattered up and down like seeds in the earth, some deep and wide and crusted over, some just getting started. Her veins came together in dark little hills rising up here and there amongst the sores. Her feet had big bumps and humps all over. You couldn't tell where her ankles were. She put a fan up on her dresser so it blew right on her feet and legs. When she lay there spread out like that, she claimed the whole bed. She slept so deep that she looked dead. She was sure enough dead tired I could tell, and I tried my best to be still and good while she rested.

Zenie dreamed in the afternoons. She said one minute she'd be swimming through the air the way she used to swim in Jasper Creek when she was a girl, breaststroking her way back and forth over Millwood, looking down on everything happening. Sometimes, up in the air, she'd follow the straight paths of the train tracks. Other times she'd make her own paths over the mill and fertilizer factory through puffs of black soot through Milltown with its peeling doubles and peaked-looking white folks, over the nice parts of Millwood with their solid two-story houses like Mimi and Grandpops', by Crosstown where Mama ran into the train, over the cemetery where the tombstones in the white and colored parts looked like dominoes in a lopsided game. Full circle and then she'd glide back down to her own home sweet home. Her own good bed. Light as a feather, cool as a cucumber on vinegar ice. When she flew like that, everything became clear as glass. Everything there was to see she could see. The good, the ugly, and where they came together and got mixed up. When she woke up from her swimming dreams, her legs felt heavy as lead, slip sliding on the sheet, like she'd been running all afternoon (Ha! she said, as if she could run for one minute even). All she'd want was to fly back into that dream and steal away over this good earth with a cool loose heart.

While everybody slept, Eva worked and hummed along at the kitchen table in the peace and quiet of the long afternoons. She took off her shoes and curled her toes around the bottom rung of the kitchen chair. Bent over her paperwork, she twirled pieces of her hair, and her bracelets would jangle soft and sweet like wind chimes in the distance.

At first Eva and Grandpops had been stiff with each other when he came to get me in the afternoons, but when I told him she was teaching folks to read over at the AME, he said he couldn't fault anybody for that. Then I told him that Eva was teaching me and Ray how to diagram sentences and he said good, it's time somebody taught you something. The afternoon Eva offered to tutor me, the encyclopedias were stacked up in a corner of the living room when he came to pick me up. He leaned down and picked up A and started reading, standing there in Zenie's living room.

"Those are good-quality encyclopedias," he said in a surprised voice after he'd thumbed through them. He picked up B and C.

Eva slowly raised her head from her paperwork in the kitchen. "Good as they come," she said in a prissy voice. "Wouldn't be selling them if they weren't." Then she went back to her work, the late-afternoon sun pouring over her, turning her to gold.

"Grandpops," I burst out. "Eva said she'd tutor me! She's going to teach junior high and she knows what I need for fifth grade."

Eva had gone back to her paperwork and didn't lift her head.

Grandpops raised his eyebrows at her. "Is that right, Eva? You're willing to do that?"

She raised her head again, nodded and went back to her paperwork.

Then he looked over at me. "That sounds like a pretty good idea to me, if Eva's willing. And maybe we ought to get you a set of these books too. Should have done it a long time ago." My chest set to chasing rabbits when he said that. "What do you think? Would you use them?" He looked down at me. What was left of the mimosa tree out front after Miss Josephine's counting fanned out behind him in the window. He looked like he was in a picture frame.

"You mean all of them? A through Z?"

Grandpops laughed. "Well, it wouldn't do you much good just to have A through F, now would it?"

"That's the way a lot of people *have* to buy them," Eva piped up from the kitchen, waving a fistful of forms. "Can't afford to do it any other way. Some people aren't as well off as others. Can't even make the rent. Or the burial insurance." Her voice sounded like she'd just pulled it out of the icebox.

Grandpops looked down at the floor for a minute, then said quietly, "Yes, I know that, and I'm sorry."

I was thinking Eva was the worst salesman I'd ever seen. I knew for a fact that she had yet to sell a full set, and here she was acting like her encyclopedias were too good for the likes of us. I opened my mouth to say I wanted the encyclopedias more than anything in the world, but that wasn't true. I wanted Mama home more. I wasn't averse to lying, but I didn't want to jinx her from coming back, though as the days rolled on, I'd pushed her as far out of my mind as I could. She was a passenger on a train, getting smaller as it left the station.

Grandpops grinned at me. "I'll talk to Mimi about all this," he said to me. Then he raised his voice. "How much do you charge for tutoring, Eva?"

Eva stirred in her chair. "A dollar an hour."

"That sounds more than fair. We need to get this girl ready for school in the fall."

Eva raised her chin and eyeballed me. "I can do that. She's got a lot of catching up to do, though."

"All right, then, y'all go ahead and start tomorrow, and save us a set of those encyclopedias, if you don't mind." Grandpops laughed a little. "We'll get this girl educated yet."

Eva was chewing the corner of her mouth like it was a new wad of tobacco. "I don't mind." Then she half smiled at me. "No more naps for you, girl!"

The next morning I sat in the fork of the tree outside Mimi and Grandpops' kitchen. Sometimes now I could step outside myself and see a girl too old to climb trees and too old to combine stories and pretend I was Uncle Wiggily hiding out from Br'er Fox, though that very idea had just crossed my mind. I tickled my nose with a powder-puff blossom and watched Zenie at the stove. Her hair was in her regular bun and as usual, there were little curls galore pulling out around her face. She had on her white outfit with the white apron over it. She was frying bacon in an old iron skillet. I was prepared to jump down and come in to breakfast as soon as I saw the bacon come out and the eggs slide in and start to glisten in the grease. Mimi had gone out to the Curb Market for some butter beans. Grand-pops was still in bed, which was odd given it was a weekday.

Suddenly Zenie's head went up. Her eyes popped wide open like somebody had poked her hard in the back. She dropped her long fork on the floor and started moving fast. I blinked and when I looked again, she'd disappeared. The bacon sizzled on. I watched it for a while until I started to see smoke. Then I climbed down and ran up the back-porch steps into the kitchen. The fork was where Zenie dropped it and the bacon pieces were black lumps in a float of smoking grease. I turned off the eye, but knew better than to move the skillet back. I'd learned my lesson on that score. It smoked on, the bacon shriveling up even blacker and smaller. I figured I'd just evened myself out in terms of fires, since now I'd stopped one from happening instead of starting one up.

Then I heard a thump and a bang upstairs, then Zenie hollering Oh Lord have mercy help us, Oh Lord have mercy help us, on and on. I ran up the stairs so fast I don't even remember doing it and followed her hollering into Grandpops' room at the top of the steps. He was folded up in a heap on the floor, looking like a neat pile of dirty clothes. Zenie went for the phone in Mimi's room next door, but I just stood over him not knowing what to do. Then I saw how he'd settled himself, like he'd climbed into a box and had to arrange his bones just that way to fit. It was careful, the way he laid himself down, like everything else he'd ever done in his life. He didn't want to cause any trouble or take up any more space than necessary.

The way Zenie told it later, he'd called out to her and she'd gotten upstairs as quick as she could, given her leg situation. There was something wrong, she knew it by how many times he called her name. If he'd just called once or twice, she wouldn't have thought much about it, but here she was frying bacon and heard Zenie Zenie Zenie Zenie in a wave of sound that just wouldn't stop till she got there. When he saw her coming up the last step, he rose up from the bed and hollered out Zenie one last time. Then he started to fall, then she caught him. He was cold and slimy like a fish. She tried to let him down easy, slippery and heavy at the same time, but her back gave out at the last and he slid into a pile. Then he turned himself just a little as if he were tucking himself in, and expired.

When she got back from calling, Zenie said, "Get on down to the street and watch for the ambulance. Wave at them when you see them coming so they'll know where to stop," so I went running down the steps and out to the porch. I got down to the curb and started looking down the street both ways. I would run right out into the middle of the street and wave them in when they came. I waited under the oak tree at the curb, jumping from one foot to the other, root to root. They didn't come and they didn't come, so I started crying and came on back upstairs just to make sure Grandpops wasn't sitting up and rubbing his elbows and saying what happened? like Freddy Ives did in school when he had his fits. Something made me tiptoe up the steps. When I got to the top of the stairs, Zenie was mopping up the floor next to Grandpops with a towel. She was doing it with her foot so as not to have to kneel down. She was humming a long drawn-out sigh of a song.

She'd rearranged him into a long line of himself. He was

stretched out with his bare toes sticking straight up, and he had another towel over the top of his pajama bottoms. His hands were folded in a little mound on his chest. There was another little mound between his legs. I knew what that meant. I'd seen Daddy in his shorts when he got up in the morning. When it comes up like that there's not much a body can do but push it down and hope it goes away. "Close the barn door, the pony's out," Mama used to say to Daddy.

I stood in the door to Grandpops' room crying quietly. Zenie's back was to me while she was mopping with her foot, holding on to the bedpost for balance.

"What you doing?" She jumped a little when I said it.

"Fool, didn't I tell you go watch for that ambulance?" she said, not turning around. "When folks pass, the bladder going to empty. Get on back down there."

That's when I got it. Mr. L was right. Dead's dead. Grandpops would never do anything like peeing on the floor or having his pony out if he were alive. He would be embarrassed beyond belief. The little wren Grandpops and I kept seeing on our way home started flying around my head. I couldn't see it but I knew it was there just beyond my sight. I could feel the flutter of its heart inside my chest, and its little brown tail brushed my face.

I was starting back down when here came two red-faced men running up the stairs only to stop short at the sight of Grandpops lying there in a line and Zenie shaking her head and humming even louder when they came in. One of them, he had a belly and was huffing and puffing, said, "Out of the way, auntie." Zenie flashed her eyes and walked over to the corner of the room. The other knelt down and moved Grandpops' folded hands and planted a stethoscope over Grandpops' chest, then put his finger on Grandpops' wrist, then shook his head like Zenie had. That was that. Dead's dead and nothing else but. They lifted him like he was nothing but a pile of dust and laid him on a stretcher, covered him, all except for his face, with a long gray cloth, and strapped him in. They carried him down the steps like that, but when they turned on the landing, one of his arms fell loose and his hand dragged the step.

"You," Zenie pushed me to the stairs, "get hold of that hand. Make them put it back."

So I ran down the steps and caught up with them. I reached down and took Grandpops' page-turning hand, the faithful one, which was heavier than I could have possibly thought, and lifted it up to the men. They didn't stop until they got down to the living room, but then they put him down again, and tucked his whole arm under the strap. After that they were more watchful to keep him tucked in.

When they got him down the walk, they laid the stretcher with him on it under the oak tree while they opened the back doors to the ambulance. It was bright morning by then and the new oak leaves fluttered over his face. When I first saw them move, I thought it was his face coming back to life, but then I saw his stillness beneath the leaves' pretty scallops.

After they got him in the back of the ambulance, the fat man who'd called Zenie auntie turned to me and said, "Tell your mamaw we're taking your papaw to the hospital. Tell her to call the hospital."

I hated the sound of those names. *Mamaw. Papaw.*

When they pulled off from the curb, it was slow and careful. No siren. The ambulance looked smaller and smaller as it went on down the long street under the drooping oaks and sycamores. After a while it became the period at the end of a sentence. Then it disappeared and all I could see was gray pavement and dust.

When I went back inside, Zenie was still moving around upstairs. She was singing loud now. Oh Lord, it causes me to tremble, tremble, tremble. I was trembling myself, and something loud had cannonballed out of my chest. I started up the steps just about the same time she started down, one step at a time then stop, one step at a time then stop again. She was dragging, I could tell. When she rounded the bend of the landing, I could see she was carrying sheets and towels so I ran up to help her bring them down. She'd wrapped up a neat package of them, the regular sheet package for Uldine except smaller. Damp coming through.

When she turned on the landing, I saw that she was crying too. Zenie wore lightish powder and the tears had plowed dark rows from her eyes to her jaw line. Suddenly, she raised her head and sniffed the air.

"Hell and damnation, the bacon!" She dropped the sheets and started down faster.

"I turned off the stove. I turned it off." I ran up the steps to help her with the sheets, but she kept on thundering down the steps like she hadn't heard me.

I grabbed her arm. "Zenie, I turned off the stove, it's all right, it's all right!"

When I got up next to her on the stairs and reached out for the sheets, she grabbed hold of me behind my neck and pulled my face up next to her chest. I smelled a smell on her that wasn't her but something that had brushed her and stuck. It had a sweet bite that was old and strong and ripe. I grabbed hold of her waist, scratching the tender insides of my burnt arms. She said, "Oh Lord, girl, what we going to do? What we *going to do?*"

When she held me like that on the stairs, heart to beating heart, I thought I knew what she meant. How were we going to live without Grandpops? There was no imagining it. But then I looked up and saw something in her eyes that wasn't that at all, not sadness but something else that had set forth across her face like a rabbit running zigzags across the open field. She was scared. Not of Grandpops' dying, but of his not being there anymore. He had held something back.

13

There are peculiar days in June when the light turns and you can see that some piece of the world has given way. The day we put Grandpops in the ground, the light cut through us and bounced off. It made us bright and hard to the eye, split between outside dazzle and inside dark, so that when we turned to look at one another, all we saw were strangers. I could look up from my seat in front of the grave and see the tiniest things. The crust of dry lather on the preacher's cheek as he stood before us. The powdery fuzz on the underside of Mimi's chin. But I could not see into the life of things. I could not see what waited to be turned over and uncovered. My eyes ran wild along the surface of the world. There were no places to burrow in.

The afternoon was so hot the metal folding chair burned my butt when I took my seat under the little gray tent next to the grave. The men in coats and pants were flinging sweat, their faces the color of ripe peaches. They stood clumped together around the edges of the green rug that had been put over the pile of dirt. The red clay hole had smartly cut edges. Someone had taken time neatening them up, making them plumb, though the care-taking was barely worth the trouble since the box was sitting on a platform right on top of the hole. The coffin—Zenie said not to call it a box—was a dark wood with a high coppery shine. It was covered in red carnations. His favorite color and his favorite flower, but cheap, cheap, cheap, said Mimi when she ordered them. Red would have been all right, but those carnations, they mortified her. Were they dyed that color? Regardless, they were tacky as all get out, but what could she do? Everyone who knew Grandpops knew he loved things that were red. Holly berries, carnations, red velvet cake. "Wear the hat with the cherries," he used to tell Mimi, but you can't put cherries on a coffin. And he didn't like red roses. He thought they were a cliché; roses in general were, he said.

The grass all along the ground was green but not the greener-than-green of the rug. The light was a pair of scissors cutting through the open ground and across the surface of us as we sat under the tent next to it. It sliced pieces of us into long lemony strips, while the other parts, half a face, an arm, one leg, stayed in deep shadow. We looked like devil's food cake, with stripes of lemon icing.

My mother had gotten sprung from her nervous breakdown to come back from Jackson for the funeral. Daddy had gone to Jackson to get her the day before. All afternoon I'd been at home waiting for them to come through the door. I'd planned it. I wouldn't squeal or cry like a baby but would walk up to Mama quietly quietly so as not to spook her. I would give her a quick businesslike hug, the way I used to when I'd come in from spend-ing the night up at Mimi and Grandpops'. I had made some nice egg-and-olive sandwiches, with a good kick of mustard the way she liked. I'd sliced the green olives just so, keeping the pimentos inside each little slice. I'd put them into the egg at the last minute and tried to keep the pimentos from coming out of the olives. I was forbidden to cook on the stove, but Daddy had let me boil the eggs that morning before he left. We had some fresh buttermilk in the house, and I'd gotten Daddy to get me some lemons for lemonade the day before, plus some nice rainbow sherbet for refreshment in the heat. I made the sandwiches and cut them into diagonal halves. I covered them with a damp dishcloth the way Mama taught me to keep them from drying out. I put them on the top shelf of the refrigerator. I wished I'd had two pretty sprigs of parsley, but that was the last thing Daddy would think to buy. He probably didn't even know what parsley was.

What I had in mind was a nice light supper. Of course she'd be tired, but she'd want to have a little something while she rested up and visited with me before she went on off to bed. After she got on her nightgown, she'd come in and sit beside me as I lay in bed, and I'd move my stack of library books over. She would have a big day coming up so she wouldn't stay long, just long enough to say she was feeling better and everything was going to be all right, she'd be home soon. Maybe she would tell me Grandpops had gone to his Heavenly Father, and we would see him again one of these days, don't worry. Then she'd need to get her clothes in order. Instead of the smells of baking while I drifted off, I'd smell starch and hear the sizzle of the iron on her best white blouse over the trains' friendly comings and goings.

When Daddy came through the front door, I was expecting him to holler out, "Hey, Sister, come see your mama!" Or just "Sister!" I was in the bathroom but I had the door open. I'd had my bath because I expected Mama to want one and I didn't want to get in her way. I had patted under my arms with some of her Mum and put on a nice shirt, which was faded but not too small like most of my clothes were getting to be. I didn't want to have to explain the scars on my arms, so I'd pulled from the back of my closet a long-sleeved shirt, which was as hot as blue blazes. The morning paper said it was going up to right around 100, which if Grandpops had been alive he would have looked up in his almanac to see whether it was a record breaker. I'd washed my hair too, because of the funeral and all. In the tub I'd cried myself out for Grandpops. Lying in the lukewarm water, I just let the tears roll down, washing my face every so often when it got too raw feeling, and then starting all over with the crying. After a while I felt like I was bathing in my own tears. What tore me up was how little he had seemed, how light and thin. Like he'd never been here at all, that it was all a dream, him walking in his seersucker suit and bow tie to work and back and picking me up at Zenie's and reading me Uncle Wiggily and not wanting anything back except to make me into a decent human being. I'd made him my shining star. But he was only a fleck of dust.

The screen door squeaked open. Then flapped shut. I heard Daddy walk through the living room, his shoe dragging on the floor. A worn-out, down-and-out sound. I listened for the other footsteps but didn't hear them. Then I heard the faucet run in the kitchen. I walked out of the bathroom. Daddy was standing with his back to me at the kitchen sink. He was leaning against the sink drinking a glass of water, standing on his good foot, resting the other toe pointed down to the floor. I could see that the edge of his heel had worn down. He needed to get them resoled.

"Where's Mama?"

He didn't turn around. Then he put his glass down in the sink. He stood there with his back to me still.

"She wanted to stay up at your Mimi's tonight. Wanted to be up there in the house with her. Didn't want her to sleep there by herself with . . ."

With Grandpops, I thought. With the body.

Just when I thought I'd cried myself out, here I was revving up again. "I wanted to see her. I thought she was coming on home. I wanted to see her. *I* want to see her." First it came out like a whine, then it changed to a wail.

"You'll see her tomorrow." He still didn't turn around. He was holding onto the sink. I could see his arms muscle up like he was lifting something heavy and it was a terrible strain. I walked closer and just stood there behind him with my head pressing on his back. My arms ached, and when I felt him quake with his own sadness, I put my arms around his waist. I could see the little white lines on the insides of my arms when I stretched them out. He caught my hands and pulled them to his chest like a lifeline.

We stood like that for a long time. He had my hands and pulled me closer and closer into his back so that I melted into him. He cried and cried. The more he cried the more he quaked, pushing back and forth on the edge of the sink, faster and faster, breathing deep in his chest until he let out a groan and let go of my hands and just stood there gasping and leaning over the sink. He didn't turn around, just stood there panting. Then I felt his stomach ripple like a big fish had just swum through it, and he upchucked in the sink. I let go of him and let him finish. Then he ran some water and threw it on his face and rinsed his vomit down the sink. He didn't turn around.

I sank down in Mama's chair at the kitchen table. The sky had gone dark in the window behind the sink. We heard the whistle of the nine o'clock in the distance with its old *no no no no* and the katydids started up with their *yes, yes, yes*-ing. I could see the lightning bugs begin to touch the screen and blink with surprise. As night drew its curtain, the outline of my father's face rose up before me, reflected in the window. His face was dark against the kitchen light behind us, but the lightning bugs outside played and sparked in front of it as it reflected in the pane. His face was not really real but only a reflection, and they were real, the lightning bugs, right outside the window drawn to the light inside; and yet the two of them, his face and the lightning bugs, seemed to touch, as if he were out there with them like a peeping tom instead of being on the other side with me, which goes to show how seeing can fool you. Finally, his breathing was quiet, and I knew he wanted me to turn around and walk away from the dark and go on to bed, so I did. I got on my pajamas and started my fan on medium and got into bed. I arranged the sheet over me and threw the rest of the cover to the side. I lay there waiting. I was thinking he would come in and sleep beside me like he'd been doing off and on since Mama left, but after I heard him moving around in the bathroom and flushing the commode, the bed in his and Mama's room squeaked with his weight and I knew he was going to sleep in there.

After a while I started to drift off. Every now and then a moth or lightning bug would bat the screen on my window. In truth, it was a comforting sound, the fluttery touch. I wanted to unhook my screen and let them all in, but I knew all they'd want to do then was to get back out again.

The next morning up at Mimi's, Mama gave me a quick everyday sort of hug with her good arm. The other was in a dirty cast. She said hey honey, but she didn't look into my eyes. She didn't even speak to Daddy. He went back outside on the front porch and took up residence in the swing. She seemed distracted by Grandpops lying in his coffin up on the buffet table like a slab of beef. "What's he doing up *there?*" she kept on asking everybody, but no one answered her question. Mimi had been in bed for a day and a night and wouldn't get up for nothing. When the funeral men had knocked on the door, Zenie had told me her legs were on fire and she was trying to get the damn house clean. She said for me to run upstairs and tell Mimi come on down, but when I knocked at Mimi's door, Mimi didn't answer. The men had Grandpops out in their hearse and wanted to know what to do with him. Zenie couldn't very well send him back. So it was just the two of us present and able to say come on in, just like we'd been the ones to send him off in the ambulance. Zenie took one look at the little rickety thing they had for the coffin to stand on and didn't take to it. If somebody bumped into it, that'd be all she wrote. He'd come tumbling down, box and all, and pop right out and it would be a sure-enough mess and Mimi would skin her hide. So Zenie had swept off the big buffet in a split second, whipped the white linen cloth off the dining-room table—not the best one, but starched and clean, thanks to Uldine—and said, "Put him there."

One of the funeral men said, you sure you know what you talking about, auntie? Was that all right with the lady of the house? Zenie said she didn't know, seeing as how the lady of the house wasn't there, but if Mr. T fell on the floor, she was going to tell the lady of the house the funeral men had put him there. They shook their heads. They had seen stranger things, plus they felt like they were going to faint between the putrid sweet of the gladiola sprays all over the place and the heat and humidity. All they wanted was some blessed ice water so they did what she told them to. It wasn't their little red wagon. After they left, she moved the glads around to the front of the buffet and placed them like choirboys, tall in the back, shorter in front. She looked Grandpops over, then muttered something to herself and went hobbling upstairs. In a minute she came back down with his comb. The funeral-home people had given him a side part, which made him look off center. She wet the comb at the kitchen sink, drew the line down the middle of his head with the comb, and set his part in the middle so that he looked more like himself. She smoothed both sides nice and neat.

Then she put her hands on her hips and looked at him hard. "He look all right for a dead white man," she said.

I shot her a look. "Don't talk that ugly white talk when he's up there dead as a doornail." It was the meanest thing I ever said to her, and I was thinking she better listen up.

I was expecting her to get mad as fire, but she just looked surprised. "Hey now, I wasn't casting aspersions. Nobody's fault white folk lose their color when they die. They fade out. Then the undertakers color them up like they in the circus. Too pink, or yellow-like. The pigment don't hold."

After a while, when people started bringing over food, Zenie got Mimi out of bed by telling her enough was enough, she had to get up and get herself ready for visitation, they couldn't put it off forever. They came down the stairs together, Zenie holding Mimi's arm, Mimi in her brunch coat with her white webby hairnet still on her head. They made a slow little parade into the dining room. When Mimi saw Grandpops perched up there, she didn't seem to notice the buffet. She just went over to him and started crying and patting his folded hands. "You sweet man," she said, "why'd you go and do this? Why'd you have to go and leave me like this? Now what am I going to do, you old fool."

At the grave, Mama sat still as glass in a folding chair, her broken arm in its cast lying across her lap. She was eye level with the coffin as it hovered over the hole. Her hair had grown while she was in Jackson, partly hiding a long red scar that flamed down the side of her face. The tips of her bangs tickled her eyelashes and hid her eyes, though they flitted and darted beneath, little brown animals watching from the woods. She had on a suit the color of smoke. Her hands looked sunburnt and chapped and all scratched up, like a country woman's, as if she'd been put to work in the fields. I pictured her moving slowly over rows of cotton like a convict from Parchment Penitentiary, bent over with a long knapsack tied in a sling and dragging out behind her, pulling at the white tufts with her good hand, cutting her fingers on the sharp points of the bolls.

She held a handkerchief with lace around the edge, but she wasn't crying like Mimi, whose sausage bosoms were syncopating up and down, the brooch between them sinking lower and lower into the cave they made in the middle. The three of us—me, Mama, and Mimi—were lined up on the first row so that we had a sideways view of the packed red clay under the box. The Greats sat directly behind us, their white hair so close to invisible in the bright sun that they looked bald. I was wishing for more family to sit with us, sisters and brothers and aunts and uncles and cousins, but we were precious little, and now smaller than ever. Mama stared off into space like she was having peaceful thoughts and please don't bother her. There was a stillness about her that called attention to itself, though people would have been looking her over anyway, her just taking a break from her nervous breakdown to attend Grandpops' funeral. She sat old-woman-like, bent over a little, her head just forward from her shoulders. In the short time she'd been gone, a little hump had come up at the back of her neck. Nothing about her moved except those scurrying creature eyes beneath the bangs and her beat-up hands, which were busy busy with the handkerchief. She would pleat it in neat little pleats, then let one end go, holding the other, so that it fanned out and looked like a pretty white bird that had been shot down, and had landed right there in her lap. Alive but broken. Then she would take it up and smooth it out and start to pleat it again.

When I looked at her, I thought *Mother*, not *Mama*, because she didn't look like anybody's mama. She looked like she was walking fast on up ahead in her mind, not even caring who fell far behind.

It was getting later and we were facing west. Suddenly, the sun fell forward like it had been spilled out of a cup and lit up one side of her face, the other side made dark by contrast. She looked as though she had been sliced in half by a sharp knife, like her cakes.

The service was going on, but I couldn't hear. My eyes were everywhere, but my ears weren't working at all. The preacher's mouth moved, then the people came up and hugged us and their mouths moved as they leaned over us. Me they petted on the head, Mother they just nodded at and spoke a few words to. Through it all, the petting, the mouths moving up and down as if the words were food to be chewed, I just sat there next to my mother and watched her sideways out of the corner of my eye like an old hang-headed dog who watches the one she follows down the street, not staying too close but not letting the one being followed out of her sight either. The person the dog follows isn't her owner, who is long gone, but just someone who might have a spare bone, some water in the heat, an easy hand.

While the preacher was talking, I turned around and saw Zenie and Ray standing up under a big ginkgo tree behind the tent where all the white people were sitting. They had been up in the balcony of the First Methodist Church too. It was all right for black people to sit up in the balcony if they were invited to white folks' funerals or weddings. The women who maided like Zenie wore their holiday serving outfits; the men buttoned their shirts to the top and had on pants and suspenders instead of overalls. The ginkgo's fan leaves were so paper thin that the sun burned right through them, making them invisible except for their spiderweb veins. The leaves were a young creamy green, just barely tipped in the color of the lemon jell Mama used to put in the middle of her cakes. The lemon would wash over the whole tree in October when the ginkgo would upchuck its fruit in splatters all over the ground. The mess stunk to high heaven. For that reason I was glad Grandpops hadn't died in October, though he'd loved that tree, stink and all, especially in fall. When I was little and we'd walk past the cemetery on the way home from Zenie's, he'd stop short on the dusty path and take off his hat like he was in church. The tree would be a lake of yellow, splattered across the sky. He'd stand there long enough for the mosquitoes to start in on my ankles. "Aren't we the lucky ones?" he would say. His whole face would light up and glow as if the gold from the tree had shaken loose and dusted him.

Now the sun in its brightness made everything it didn't hit seem blacker than darkest night. In the ginkgo tree's shadow, Zenie's and Ray's faces were lost to me. Only their clothes seemed to stand there, straight up and purposeful. Zenie had on her Christmas uniform without the apron. White and starched enough to stand up by itself. She had food to serve later up at Mimi's. Ray looked like a going-to-church version of himself. He had on a suit coat in addition to having his shirt all buttoned up. He held a hat in front of his midsection like a shield. I saw it was one of Grandpops' old felt hats, gray and soft and folded in on itself.

Eva was there too. But she stood a few paces from them, away from the tree and closer to us under the tent. She was in full sun. She wore what the white ladies were wearing. A dark dress, her navy blue outfit it looked like, a little pillbox hat with a snatch of a veil, and some high heels. She had a little clutch purse under one arm. She opened it and took out a handkerchief and blotted her face.

I didn't see Daddy. Back at Mimi's house later, with people shoveling in the hams and roasts and asparagus and green-bean casseroles and cheese straws and Mrs. Polk's pies, he sat by himself at the round oak table in the breakfast room, drinking coffee. He spent time fixing each cup, just this much milk from the pitcher, no, a bit more, one teaspoon of sugar, then two, maybe a half more. He kept looking down at his cup as if it was a hard puzzle he was trying to find the right pieces to finish. After he'd drunk the first cup and poured himself another out of Mimi's silver coffee pot, he went through the whole thing all over again. He sat in the midst of everyone, not speaking, his head down, his eye on the cup. Sometimes he picked up his spoon and stirred the sugar that had settled to the bottom. A greasy lock of dark hair had separated from the rest. It hung a bit down and to the right side of his forehead. It gleamed with Mr. Holcomb's oil. One of Mimi's revolving fans was on the buffet, and each time it turned his way, the lock of hair shuddered in the disturbed air. When I went over and stood beside him, he reached out and grabbed me around the waist and held on. I leaned into his side, staked out and claimed.

Mother had betaken herself onto the back screen porch to get away from the crowd, but her cake ladies had followed her out there and fidgeted her into a corner. When I went to the back door, she was standing in the middle of them in her gray suit looking like a single dove in a covey of blackbirds. They fluttered around her, patted her and tried to fluff up the flatness in her hair. While they made over her, she just looked down at the wood floor like she was counting the boards and wrapped her own arms around herself as though she was chilly. The late afternoon sun bore down on her head, and I could see the dandruff on the surface of her hair. There was no shine to it, just dullness and weight. It looked a couple of weeks' worth of dirty. Moreover, she didn't smell right. She didn't stink, but she smelled heavy like oil or metal, not breezy and sugary and sweet.

Navis stepped toward Mama and touched her elbow. "Martha, we're so sorry about your father. We just want you to feel better. I'm going to take you to the beauty shop on Monday. Get you a nice permanent wave."

Mama brightened up a little and touched her hair. "I need fixing up," she said.

"Yes, you do," Navis said softly. "I'm going to take you to the beauty shop on Monday. Get you a haircut and a nice permanent wave and buy you a sandwich. I'm going to take the day off. Then we can go over to your house and sit on the front stoop under the clematis and have some coffee like we used to."

"Get her a manicure too, Navis," another lady said. "Get her nails done. Always gives me a perk to get my nails done. Poor little thing, losing your daddy who you loved so dearly."

Navis frowned at the lady.

At that point, Mama turned around to them. She started backing up toward the screen door to the back porch steps. She put her arms straight out in front of her. You could tell she just wanted to fly away from the cluster of ladies and their pushy ways. "Now you-all listen to me." Her words seemed to come not from her mouth but from somewhere behind her head. She looked like a puppet whose voice belonged to somebody behind the curtain. "I'm going to go on home and make some of my cakes now. Just go on back inside and I'm going to make you some good cakes. Going home right now. See you in the morning. Pickup between nine and ten."

Navis reached for Mama's arm again, and Mama flinched like Navis's touch burned and jerked her arm away. She rubbed her arm.

"Martha," whispered Navis. "You don't need to make us anything. You just need to rest and get well. You're going to be just fine. You are."

"Don't I know it," Mama said, and put her arms behind her so Navis couldn't get hold of her again. Now the voice that wasn't hers but came out of her mouth sounded like a little girl's. Whiney and fretful. "Now you-all just give me a little bit of time. Everything's going to work out. All right now, you-all do me a favor and go on back inside and talk to my mama. Go on now. Go, go." She clapped her hands in front of her, and they flew. All except for Navis.

"Martha."

Mama was on her way out the screen door. She stopped when Navis said her name and turned around and said in her regular voice, "Navis, I just need to get on home right now. I just need to have some peace and quiet."

When she said that, Navis stood looking at Mama for a while. Mama looked back, her chin up. Then Navis sighed, touched Mama's dirty hair, and turned around and went inside with the others.

I was watching and thinking not me. You not flushing me that easy, missy. I'm sticking to you like glue. Something clicks into place in my mind. I pull a big stiff bow out of a pot of mums on the porch table, twirl it on its sharp little pointed stake.

She shoots me a look. "You too. Get on back in there and help Mimi."

I eye her back. I'm not a bit scared of her, she's done to me the worst she can do, at least so I think at the time. I'm that old stray dog. I'm not about to let her out of my sight, even if she kicks me in the ribs. I hunker down beside the big table on the screen porch that has the red-and-white-checked oilcloth on it. I'm half under it, the oilcloth drapes my head. For a second the weight of it reminds me of the outfit Miss Kay Linda made me. I'm thinking all this and humming "Lead on, O King Eternal." It's the song in my mind because they just sang it in church when the preacher said Go forth in peace, and Daddy's friends took Grandpops back down the aisle and out the door. I hummed on, waiting for Mama to make her move. In my mind I made it Queen Eternal, as in Zenobia Eternal Queen of Palmyra. Where my Queenie leads I will follow. Lead on, O Queen Eternal, the day of dark's at hand.

"I want to go on home with you." The sweat that's been rolling out of my hair all afternoon has finally found its way into my eyes. It burns like fire, but I'm not crying, no ma'am.

Then Mama looks behind and above me. I turn around and

there's Zenie standing in the doorway. Her uniform has long half-moons under her arms, and her apron, a lace one she only wears at Christmas and Easter, looks droopy and stained. She props her arm up on the doorjamb, looks at Mama for a minute, and then says, "Hey." That's all, just that.

Mama stops in her tracks. "Hey."

Zenie ignores me, and walks toward Mama. "How you doing?"

When Zenie asks the question that is really a question, Mama's face starts to crumble like the bone has given way. "He was right, you know, about Win. My daddy was right all along."

Zenie looks at her steady and sad, but doesn't say a word. Then she pats her side pocket and takes Mama's arm, like she was a little child.

They walk out the screen door to the back stoop and then down the back stairs. Zenie looming large and moving slow, swaying a bit from side to side. Mama, looking like a frowzy baby bird on stick legs next to her, letting herself be led forward into the yard for a tidbit of worm or bug, down toward the back of an old peony bed, to the speckled shade under the pecan trees on the back lot.

They stand there for a while with their backs to the house. Zenie takes a little brown paper sack out of her pocket. She passes it to Mama, who tips it to her mouth. They stand side by side. Mama's head the level of Zenie's shoulder. Mama passes the sack back to Zenie and Zenie takes a sip and passes it back. They stand there for a while, just passing the sack every now and then. Then Zenie takes a cigarette out of the pack she keeps in the breast pocket of her uniform and hands it to Mama with a pack of kitchen matches. Mama lights a cigarette, takes a few long drags and then hands it back to Zenie, who smokes the rest of it. Then, after a while, they turn around together and come on back to the house.

Zenie looks at me standing there waiting. Then she looks over at Mama. "Take her on home," Zenie says to my mother. "Take her on home now." Zenie goes on through the back porch and into the kitchen.

Mama comes onto the porch after her, but doesn't follow her back into the house. When Mama climbs the steps toward me and stands in the open screen door, her back is to the late afternoon sun. I can't see her face and greasy old hair anymore. They're dark as a swamp. I can't see her mouth move when she says, "Come on then." I wonder if I hear the words at all or if I just thought them up in my head. They don't seem to be coming from anybody or anything, even when she sighs down deep and says them again. They just appear to me heavy and hard, like Moses had brought them down the mountain from God carved in stone. There they were. I could put my fingers inside them and feel the cut of the knife that made them. Stone words. One commandment: Come On Then.

I shut my eyes and rub them to get the sting out. When I open them, she's back out the door. I can hear the gravel crunch in the driveway as she walks away. I leap up and run through the door just in time to see the back of her turn the corner by the big bush at the side of the driveway. I start to run, thinking that if I let her out of my sight, I'll never see her again. When I round the corner by the bush, I see her gray shape moving on down the sidewalk, walking as fast as it's possible for a person to walk without running. I start running.

"Mama, wait!" When I holler to her, she stops, which seems like a miracle in itself, but she doesn't turn around. Whatever it is she's so bound and determined to do, bake a thousand cakes or fly to the moon in Uncle Wiggily's airship, her plans don't include me. I don't care. I'm gaining on her fast and furious.

"What you running off for?" I huff along beside her.

She doesn't let up her pace or look down at me. "I got work to do."

"What work? Good Lord, Mama, what you got to do that's so all-fired important right now this very minute?" If she's crass enough to run off from her own daddy's funeral party, at least I need to call attention to her malfeasance, which is a word I learned from Eva. It's not only mental, it's embarrassing. Since Mama had run into the train, which started people clucking and shaking their heads when they saw me, I'd taken to serious worrying about what people thought. It was bad enough up at Mimi's. There were Mimi's friends and the cake ladies clumped up together in the living room murmuring low about why Daddy had the nerve to get all his low-class friends to carry the coffin of such a man as Grandpops, who wouldn't have given any of them, including his own son-in-law, the time of day while he was alive. Daddy's friends were trash. They scared the colored to death, ran around at night, didn't stay home with their wives. Look what happened to poor Martha. I knew what they were saying just by looking across the room at the shapes their lips made. Meanwhile my daddy sat in the breakfast room trying to get the sugar and cream in his coffee right. When he had claimed me with his arm, rough yet gentle at the same time, I wanted to hug him. Walking beside Mama, who didn't claim or even want me period, I thought I ought to go back.

But I stuck by Mama. I could see she was heading home, back to our little house behind Big Dan's and Miss Kay Linda's. It was only a few blocks away. We walked together as in a parade. Her first, me after, skirting the crape myrtle bushes that grew between the sidewalk and the curb. *Thrum thrum* went our feet on the sidewalk. The crape myrtles weren't blooming yet, but I grabbed the round buds as I walked by and popped them open, firing off little pink explosions of blooms under my fingers, then dropped them in the dust.

When we got there, Mama cut straight across Miss Kay Linda's side yard instead of using the stone walkway. The second she got inside the front door, she headed left into the kitchen and looked around like she was expecting it to say hello Martha, welcome home. Then she stopped short. I'd gotten used to the bare kitchen, but I could see it through her eyes. A shock. No pots and pans and measuring cups. Not even her apron on the nail in the wall inside the door.

She turned around and looked at me like the barrenness was my fault. "Where's my stuff? How am I going to make cakes for all those ladies if I don't have my stuff?"

"I didn't put it up. Daddy put it up."

"Ha!" she said. "I guess he didn't think I'd be coming back. Thought he'd locked me up and thrown away the key. I guess my stuff was just in his precious damn way while he was busy cooking all those wonderful meals for you-all."

"We can put them right back out. Look here." I opened the cabinets and grabbed some bowls. Then I pulled out the tray at the bottom of the stove and got the pots and pans. I opened the drawer and dished out spoons and whisks and forks and dumped them in one of the bowls.

"Everything's all messed up," she whined. "Where's my apron?"

"No, look right here Mama, it's all here. It'll just take a minute." I snatched open the cabinets and pulled out measuring cups. I got the recipes out of the drawer just in case the shocks had scrabbled up her brain, which I guess would scramble up her recipes in her head, which would be a terrible mess. Egg yellows in the divinity icing, almond extract in the lemon jell filling. Nobody would eat a thing. I found an old apron, not too clean but still usable and at least not burnt up, hanging on the inside of her closet door with her nightgown. I handed it to her, and she pulled it over her head. She forgot to tie it in back, so I went around behind her and tied it in a nice tight bow. We had a long night ahead. I had just set the stove for 350 when she went over to the kitchen cabinet and opened the door. There was a long silence. Then she shut the door and turned around.

She opened her mouth to say something and then closed it. She reached over and opened the refrigerator and looked inside. Then she shut the refrigerator door and turned around.

"He threw away all my ingredients." Her voice was thoughtful now. "He even threw away my vanilla."

I'd forgotten that Daddy had gone through the kitchen with a paper sack the day after Mama had been removed to Jackson. He'd pulled out everything Mama used to make her cakes—Crisco and flour and lemon Jell-O and cocoa and vanilla extract—and dumped it all in the sack. Then put the sack in the garbage for pickup the next day. He did it the way he put up the pots and pans and bowls, fast and all business, like it was something he did every day. Like he was the putter-upper in the family, and good for him. Under his hand, everything disappeared and you'd never have known there had been cakes even conceived of, much less baked, in that kitchen. No crumbs or drips. No stray flour siftings around the kitchen floor.

Mama had started to untie her apron. She looked distracted. Her eyes bulged a bit, red and worried. "Got to make a list. Got to get to the A & P before it closes. Oh Lord, everything is just too hard."

"The A & P closes at six," I said. The kitchen clock said 5:15.

"Oh dear." She stood in the middle of the kitchen and put her hand over her eyes.

I reached up and grabbed her hand. "Daddy's car's out there. We rode to the funeral with Big Dan and Miss Kay Linda. You can make it if you hurry." I opened a drawer and grabbed a piece of paper with a pencil. "Let's make a list real quick. What do we need?"

She didn't answer, so I started in. "Regular sugar, confectioners' sugar, sweet milk, buttermilk, flour, butter, vanilla . . ." I took a breath.

"Salt, cocoa, butter," she snatched the list from me and started writing as fast as she could.

"I said butter."

She scratched it through. "*Eggs!* Almond extract, baking powder, he might have at least left the baking powder!" She started toward the door.

"Tartar!" I sang out to her. "Soda, vinegar!"

"*Brown* sugar," she hollered back, still writing as she opened the screen door.

"Crisco. Don't forget the Crisco. Write it down. Oh, I know we're forgetting something, Mama." I was on her heels. "I'm coming too!"

She stopped short, door half open. "No ma'am, you stay here and get this kitchen *organized*! Wash and dry my stuff. Get everything in order. Devil's food first. Lord, I'm going to be up all night as it is!"

I kept up with her. I didn't want to let her out of my sight. I snatched Daddy's car keys from the nail he hung them on.

Then she whirled around and pointed one skinny finger at me. "You *stay*." She snatched the keys from my hand and made a fluttery motion over her face and body as if to gather herself and make sure all of her was still there and attached. Then out the door she flew.

It wasn't until I heard the Chevy start up that I realized that she had left without her purse. I ran in and opened the top drawer where Daddy kept his underwear and rummaged out a handful of bills. I ran out the door to give them to her, but way up at the curb I heard her scratch off. Even then I didn't worry. They knew her at the A & P, they'd let her have credit the way they always had.

Then I remembered we hadn't written down lemons. I just hoped she'd remember the lemons.

—*Part III*—

14

What do you do when you turn the page and come upon a giant with snaggled teeth and a big appetite? You close the book without a sound. Tiptoe out into the dead of night. Take to the sky like a pretty red-winged blackbird. Then you can blaze far above the sticky earth until your wings give out and then it's *kerplunk* into the marsh and tall sweet grasses of a whole other story.

Sometimes I dream I'm a lady teacher like Eva. I live in a far place, tucked away in a little house so covered over in trees with leaves like Big Dan's fig tree nobody will ever find me. I draw lines on the blackboard and tell children to trust the girl who touched the beautiful rose. I tell them there are things to be afraid of, but sentences will stick by them. Sentences don't up and run off from you.

There are ways to leave your own story. You can leave the place it happened, though be forewarned, if the place is too sad about you leaving, it won't think twice about packing up its valise and hopping the first Frisco through town to follow you. It will be your faithful sidekick. At night when you are sleeping, it will tiptoe straight to your bed and kiss you on top of the head. Its sadness at losing you will burrow down, through brain and flesh and bone, straight to the heart, where it finds its own true home. Then the only thing left is to stop thinking of yourself as the one who had the story, who was in the story. You push that one under the train and start out again.

The first thing I did after Mama drove off was to rinse out the mixing bowls and pots and pans. You never know when things sit awhile under the counter what's been crawling over them. I wanted everything nice and clean for the giant baking we were getting ready to undertake. I was thinking too that we ought to have a little supper before we started baking so I checked on my egg-and-olive sandwiches from the day before. I was wishing we'd taken some of the food that people had brought up to Mimi's, but when you walk out the back door without saying a word the way Mama did, nobody says wait honey, look at all this food! You got to take some of this good food home, we can't eat this much in a million years. So here I was, staring down a pile of day-old sandwiches. They were all right, a little soggy on the tops from the wet cloth. They needed eating. They couldn't go another day. I laid them on the kitchen counter to dry out.

By the time the clock on the stove was straight over to 7, I had eaten four triangles and left the other four for Mama. No thoughts of parsley; I was well beyond that. I had decided to wash the spoons and measuring cups and whisks and so on. I'd dried them all and left them out on the counter. At seven thirty I decided to grease the pans and cut the waxed paper to fit and put it inside them. Then, why not, I greased it too. This I did with a paper napkin, which I dipped in a little butter that was left in the refrigerator. Not having any Crisco, which I know from Eva is not only a dangling modifier but also a sentence fragment. All of the pans would be ready when Mama came back. The stove had been on since she left, and the kitchen was blazing hot. Then there was nothing left to do, so I went and sat on the couch and waited. At eight o'clock I went outside on the porch stoop to cool off, and then walked up to the street so I could help with the groceries when she came back with them. She must have stopped someplace on the way home. Maybe she went back by Mimi's to see how she was doing and pick up Daddy and some of the piles of food. Maybe she swung by the bootlegger, which aggravated me because I'd have been happy to take the evening ride. A chocolate milk shake would hit the spot about now. I sat down on the curb under the streetlight and settled into myself to wait.

I waited a good long time. I was hopeful. I was full of care. I was trying to keep my mind open and free to roam, enjoying the shapes and lines and shadows of the growing dark. I was trying not to think about Grandpops under the ground or Daddy above it. I was actually reciting Mama's cake recipes over and over in my head so I could barrel full speed ahead into the baking and impress her when she got back. Devil's food was one and a half sticks butter, one and a half cups sugar, three egg yolks, lightly beaten. All creamed together. Add two ounces bitter chocolate, melted in a double boiler. I was trying to think whether there were one or two teaspoons baking powder that went into the sifted flour and salt when I noticed the roaches. Maybe they were reading my mind and I drew them to me with my conjurings of sugar and flour and cutting in the Crisco. Maybe it was just the time of night right after first dark when the little day breezes stop and nothing moves. In any case, there they were, scudding everywhere, gangs of them clumped and peckish under the streetlight, bustling about up and down the sidewalk behind me on errands here and there, busy and nasty, bumping into each other, antennae waving. I'd never realized how many of them ran around at night until I got down on their level and paid attention. I'd taken my shoes off when we got home from Mimi's, and now the roaches thrust themselves like little soldiers up against my bare feet. I lifted my toes up off the ground. I didn't want to move, but they were edging around me everywhere. They were getting ready to climb me like a tree and see what tidbits they could find.

Something had to be done, so I got up and tiptoed back into the house, trying to avoid them on the sidewalk and walkway. They were on the front stoop too. I knew they wanted to get into the house and be ready to pounce when Mama came back with all her ingredients. I went into the kitchen and looked under the cabinet. Mama's poison bottle of moonshine was gone, Daddy had seen to that, but her blue plastic spray bottle of Sevin dissolved in water was still there. She mixed the chalky Sevin powder with water and sprayed the mixture on monster tomato worms when she used to grow tomatoes along the barbed-wire fence in the backyard. The big green caterpillars would rise up on their haunches and fight the spray but then they curled up in horrible semicircles and died. Within hours their juice had oozed out and they had dried up. I figured it would work with roaches. The bottle was almost full when I shook it, and for that I was thankful. I went into my room and put on some knee socks and saddle oxfords. Then I got the spray bottle and headed back outside.

The first thing I did was hit the ones on the front porch. They took their own sweet time dying, flipping and kicking and carrying on. The Sevin left milky streaks everywhere, but I figured I could hose down the porch later. When I was convinced I'd gotten all the roaches on the porch, I headed out to the street and started in on them there. I chased them up and down the sidewalk and then went for the curbside under the light. When I'd killed them there, I shook my bottle. I had plenty left, so I started up the street. There had to be a lot more roaches in the neighborhood. Why hadn't I thought of this before? I was going to get them all. In the morning everybody would walk out to get their papers and find zillions of roaches stretched out up and down the street as far as the eye could see, from here to Kalamazoo and back, belly up with their feet curled in nasty little quotation marks above them. People would holler glory be! Who saved us from the roaches? Who knew how many there were?

I went on up and down the street spraying and watching them flip and die. I covered about half a block side to side, streetlight to streetlight. Then my bottle ran dry. Which is when I started stomping them. A hopscotch sort of game up and down the street, seeing how many I could squish with two feet at the same time. Once I counted five, three under one foot and two under the other, but mainly just managed one or two at a time. Up and down the street I hopped, from one streetlight to another, because that's where I could really do some damage. The lights threw my shadow ahead of me; it looked like Sodom and Gomorrah all rolled into one devilish dance. I hopped and stomped, every now and then bending down low over the ground to see their guts.

It got later and later, but I kept on for a good long time. I heard the nine-o'clock Frisco whistle call out. Every now and again, I'd see headlights and think Mama was finally back. I'd run back to the light in front of our house, but then the car would pass with other people in it, and they would stare at me the way I'd stared at the mental girl on the porch. What was I doing out in the road like that? Why wasn't I safe in my bed at home with my mother and father like other girls? You could see what they were thinking: that I was Trouble with a capital T and maybe mental in the bargain. Not Precious Cargo.

Even with the streetlights, the night got darker and darker. The swallows had disappeared. You could see moths and lightning bugs and some big old noisy beetles. Every now and again a bat would whoosh by faster than the eye could trace.

Then a car came on down the street slow, like it was going
to turn into Daddy's parking spot in front of our house. Instead,
it came to a cruising stop in the middle of the street and a back
door cracked and out slid Daddy in one long easy motion. He
came on walking down the street toward me, and the car coasted
on. I could see a big pile of men sitting shoulder to shoulder inside
as it glided by quiet as could be. I wondered why they didn't let
Daddy out in front of his own house instead of half a block up the
way. Walking wasn't Daddy's strong suit. He came on down the
street, rocking back and forth like he was riding a horse.

When he got nearer and saw me, he started walking faster and
hollering at me down the street, "What the hell you doing out
here in the dark at this time of night? Where's my car? Where's
your mama?" When I told him she had gone to the store to get
her ingredients, he said, "Bullshit, it's eleven o'clock at night, A
& P's been closed five hours. Goddamn her hide, she's gone and
flown the coop and stole my car again."

"She made a list," I said, but the minute the words came out
of my mouth, it was as if they didn't really parse. They weren't a
complete thought the way a sentence is if it's true and good. They
dangled in the still night air, like the strands of a torn web that
touches your face in the dark and then flies into pieces.

Daddy kicked the big old oak tree he was standing under.
His brick shoe made a soft thud like a baseball being caught in
a mitt, and he jumped up and down on his good foot holding
the other and yelling, "Fuck that bitch! Goddamn her sorry ass."
Then he hobbled as fast as he could back to the house. I kept up
my work of stomping roaches in the street. I'd become a roach-
stomping machine. I wasn't thinking about anything but murder
and mayhem. Finally my legs and feet numbed out on me and I
had to quit.

When I dragged myself back into the house, Daddy was on

the phone describing the car, but he wasn't talking to the sheriff; he was talking to his buddies, calling them one by one, telling them to get out there and find her. Red 1957 Chevy. Mississippi V78863. Big dent in left back side. Makes a racket. Try the bootlegger, the county roads. Fan out. Hunt her down. One greasy-headed scrawny white woman. Crazy as a loon. Bring her in.

I figured they'd be looking for her at the white bootlegger, but I didn't say anything about the black bootlegger, which is where I figured she was headed. A picture of my little scraggly-haired mother had come into my head. She was Br'er Rabbit hightailing it through the briar patch in a car that had the look of a fire truck with fins and sounded like the Fourth of July. She'd be hiding her features under her bootlegger scarf if she'd thought to bring it. The foxes were after her. She'd be easy enough to find, I thought, either they'd hear the car or see it. I was having trouble knowing what to hope for. Did I want the scratchy-faced, yellow-toothed ones to find her? Or Big Dan with his beef-liver hands? Did I want Daddy to have her back, in his current state of pissed-offedness? Didn't I want her to find herself an airship and fly off to the next adventure?

What got me was not the fact that she had run off, but that she had left me behind. I wouldn't have been any trouble riding sidekick. Uncle Wiggily always had somebody tagging along on his adventures. Why didn't she just take me and her recipes and we could set up a nice little cake business in Jackson or down on the coast? We could pick up Eva and head for Raleigh like in my dream. Mama had seemed so intent on coming back when she left that I actually wondered whether she didn't make up her mind until later on, when it was too late to come back for me. Maybe she was circling the block right now trying to pick me up. If she was, she'd sure enough get snagged in the trap Daddy and his friends were setting up.

When I stood right outside the open front door and heard Daddy on the phone, the *no, no, no, no* of the midnight train whistle took hold of my insides and I was nothing but the sound of those two perfect Phonics letters. Eva said to put the flat of your tongue onto the roof of your mouth and moan: that's the N. Make a circle with your lips and push the air through for the O. No to Mama having flown the coop again. No to Daddy sending out his buddies like mean dogs ready to tear her to pieces. My hand was on the handle of the screen ready to push it open and go inside, but I dropped it like a hot potato and turned around to face the outer darkness all around me.

With the light of the house behind me and Daddy's voice (find that bitch, get her, track her down) fading in my ears, I entered the noisy dark outside and started walking. My legs and feet hurt from the roach stomping, but I decided to put my foot in the road. I moved like a ghost alongside Miss Kay Linda and Big Dan's house and up toward the street. Their kitchen light was on; Daddy had woken up Big Dan. As I glided past, I heard Big Dan call out, "Who's that? Who's out there?" I could hear him opening the door, so I crawled up under a fig tree by the side of the house. Just a few days ago, I had sat under the tree and eaten figs. No one knew I did it. Little Dan and May walked so close by me I could have reached out and tickled their dirty feet. They never knew I was there. It had been my secret place, my fingers sticky with the white pulp that oozed from the stems. The wasps were having a field day, made heavy and slow with the sugar, but there was plenty to go around for everybody. I didn't bother the wasps and they didn't bother me. Nobody could see me for the furry elephant ear leaves of the tree, which bowed all the way to the ground. They made a cave, and I'd stayed hidden in the cool darkness for hours in broad daylight.

Big Dan came out of his back door, which opened into our

front yard, and went striding around the yard. "Who's there?" He carried a headache stick of his own and used it to part the shrubs around the house. I was sweating bullets that he was going to find me, but the tree had several layers of branches and leaves, so that when he pushed some aside, there were the friendly others to hide me. He stood just a few feet from me and hit the side of his leg with the bat. *Thump, thump*. I shuddered and shook. I felt like Bomba up in the tree with the cannibals all around and about. Finally, though, he gave up and went on back into the house.

I waited a good long while and then took off running from shadow to shadow, house to house, making my way up the street, steering clear of the streetlights. I went on back up to Mimi's first. The house was pitch black. I figured Mimi would be dog tired from the funeral and dead asleep. She had a stash of pills from the doctor. It would scare her to death if I rang the doorbell or threw rocks up at her window. I thought I might get into the back screen porch and lie down on the floor, but the latch was locked. I sat on the back steps for a while, wondering whether Grand-pops still wandered the house. I thought anything's possible, so I prayed to him, having given up on God and all his fingers a while back. Help me figure out what to do, I said to him, or what was left of him. The more I asked for help, the more agitated Grandpops seemed to become. I even fancied I heard him from deep inside the house, pacing back and forth, back and forth, the way he used to when something was worrying him. But he didn't answer me or give a sign. When I looked out onto the backyard, the dark seemed darker. Even the lightning bugs had gone to bed. I wondered if Daddy had figured out yet that I hadn't come in to bed. Maybe he was so aggravated about Mama flying the coop that I had slipped his mind. He was out cruising with his friends looking for her, expecting me to take care of myself. Maybe they were looking for both of us.

Given my lack of options, I decided at that point to go on up Goodlett Street to Shake Rag. I reasoned that it would just be a case of Zenie taking me a little sooner than usual. I could take an early nap on Zenie's couch and nobody would know the difference. I set on up the street. The moon was shining, but just a sliver of one. I felt light and floaty. My feet barely seemed to touch ground. I made a wide berth around the cemetery, though I could see the outline of bloated ground and the pile of flowers with stand-up sprays of glads all in a circle. Their spikes looked like spears in the shadows on the ground. There was a white cross of carnations. Daddy's friends had sent that. At first it stood out in the moonlight like God had come down from heaven and placed it there. Then, even as I watched, a cloud floated over the moon and the cross turned evil. It looked like a ghost with his arms flung wide, ready to hug you tight, make you hot and sweaty and afraid. The Holy Ghost. As I stood there, the pukish stink from the ginkgo tree seemed to rise like a wave in the night and wash over me. I could taste it on my tongue even though—and this was the scariest part—I knew the smell wasn't real but only a story I had made up. The tree made its mess in October, not June. Story or not, it was a horrible sight and a horrible smell. I started walking fast, too tired to run, but walking as fast and furious as I could. My feet and legs quaked. I could feel myself wobbling from side to side like Daddy. I panted hard, my heart felt like it was about to jump loose from my chest, and my face was wet like I was walking right into a rainstorm. I wished I'd never left Daddy. I wished I was home in my bed with his hand, I don't care how heavy, holding me in place.

Just when I came to the top of the little rise in the road beyond the cemetery, I stopped in my tracks. Shake Rag was lit up like a torch. It had to be two o'clock in the morning because the one-thirty had come through a while back, but behind the blinds and curtains, everybody's lights were blazing. In a few of the houses you could see the TVs flash from picture to picture. Zenie's street and several blocks beyond were as bright as the white side of town was dark. Zenie and Ray's place looked especially lit up. Every room was bright. Through the green leaf curtains on the front window I could see the shape of four heads hovered around something. Was it the radio? Did the folks in Shake Rag always stay up this late? No wonder Zenie was so worn out all the time.

I picked up the pace, kicking dust and rocks as I got closer. The crunch they made sounded cheerful. The sound a person makes when she has a place to go and that place is coming right up. I was almost running by the time I got to the house and headed for the front stoop. I could hear the radio inside. In Jackson somebody was dead, shot in the back in his own carport in front of his own house. Blood everywhere and T shirts saying Jim Crow Must Go all over the driveway. That's all I could make out. Right in mid-step as I came up to the front stoop of the house, I had my hand raised to knock. Before I could bring my knuckles to the door, the radio and all the lights went off, almost all at once as if one giant hand had flipped a single switch. Dead silence inside. It was as if everyone had decided to call it a night just as my foot hit the front stoop. I knocked anyway. I knew they were in there and awake.

At first nobody came to the door, and when they didn't, I strained my ears for someone to call out just a minute, or wait up, or who is it? But nothing. I banged again. The houses on either side had suddenly gone dark too. The night was still and lights were going off everywhere.

"Zenie?" I said it slowly to the door. "Zenie, are you awake?" When nobody came, I yelled it out, "Hey Zenie, it's me, Florence. Are you there?" even though I was dead sure she was. Then I heard footsteps, and Ray opened the door a crack. In the dark I could barely make out his face, except for the mouth. There was a pucker to it, like he was sucking on a sourball that wouldn't turn him loose.

"Yes'm?" he said it out of the side of his mouth. He'd never called me ma'am before. I didn't know what to say back. I knew I must be a sight. I'd cried so much that day I felt like my eyeballs were falling out of my head. Standing there, I imagined roaches set on revenge were crawling up my legs and the gingko stink had stuck to me. But there was a lot of night ahead, and I didn't know where else to go. "Is Zenie here?" I asked.

"She gone."

"Gone where?"

"She not here right now. Go on home. Get on back where you belong now." With that, he eased the crack in the door shut and clicked the lock.

I didn't know what to do, so I sat down on the stoop with my back to the door. Lights were going out everywhere now up and down the street. Inside Zenie's I heard whispers through the open front window.

"She still there?"

There was a pause. "Um hum."

"You got to explain it to her. *Explain* it to her." This last sounded like Eva.

"Eva, don't you go out there." It was Miss Josephine's singing voice. High and worrisome. "Don't you go outside that door, Eva."

"Then she's going to sit there till morning. Till doomsday. What are we going to do then?" Eva said.

Well, you could ask her to come in and give her a place to sleep, I thought. You could be decent to her since her grandfather is spending his first night in the ground up the street, and she's worn out with her mean daddy and her mother's gone on the lam. Again. You could show her a little kindness, missy. I was working up a steam.

The door opened again. Such a slow *click* it made that I almost didn't hear it. I didn't even turn around I was so mad. I smelled rosewater and glycerin and knew it was Eva. She came out and closed the door real quiet and sat down next to me. I didn't look at her.

"Listen here, girl, you got to get out of here. Right now. There's folks would get mad at us for taking you in in the dead of the night. They'd hurt us. Do you get what I'm saying, Flo? We could get ourselves killed if we let you in. You've got to get."

Eva's voice sounded so ragged and hoarse that it made me shiver. She had been crying her eyes out, you could tell, like me, but I knew it wasn't over Grandpops dying.

I looked hard at her straight on. We were nose to nose, just a few inches apart. "What you crying for?"

She looked at me in surprise. "You haven't heard? They shot Medgar Evers tonight. In his own front yard, with his little children in the house. He's gone."

I knew Medgar Evers because his picture had been in the papers. Libraries and voting and Woolworth's and a boycott. My daddy called him one of those damn Evers niggers and said he and his brother ought to be shot for all the trouble they'd caused. When Daddy found out about Medgar Evers getting killed, he'd say one down, one to go. Medgar ran the NAACP in Mississippi, which was a communist front—everybody knew that, Daddy said, from J. Edgar Hoover on down. But I could see why somebody would cry over Medgar Evers. He had a kind face and three little children, and his wife was pretty like Eva.

"Did you know him?" I asked Eva. "Was he your friend?"

"I met him once. Shook his hand. Yes, he was a friend of

mine. He was a friend of the people." She started crying. "But they killed him."

"Who? Who killed him?"

"Crackers in sheets. Who else going to kill a black man?" Her voice was cold. "Lily-livered bastards. Shot him in the back in cold blood."

"Why?"

"Because he wanted us to have what white people have."

"Why did somebody shoot him for that?"

Eva hesitated a minute. When the words came out, they were like a snakebite. "Hell if I know," she hissed. "Ask your *daddy*." I couldn't see her in the dark but knew she had that sly look the sheriff had when he told Mama to ask Daddy about Eva getting burnt and bothered.

"You go to hell." I snorted up a whole bunch of air and started crying again. I was sick and tired of getting my daddy thrown up to me. Everybody always saying your daddy this and your daddy that with an ugly sneer to it. Looking at me like I was bad seed.

"You go *home*." She stood up and thumped me on the shoulder. "Where's your mama tonight anyway? Go on back to her. Here she is, first night back from that hellhole he put her in, and grieving, and you off midnight wandering. Get on home now."

Before I could say that Mama had flown the coop again, with Daddy's latest car and the grocery list, Eva had risen up and gone inside. End of conversation. The lock on the door clicked. It sounded like someone spitting loud in the street.

And that was that. Nothing else stirred. Nobody came out. Nobody said anything I could hear. No sounds but frogs.

But I didn't move on. I just sat. I looked up at the moon awhile and then I put my head down in my arms. Everything inside had quieted down and the lights were off.

After a long while, the door clicked open again. I looked up and it was Eva. "Lord, girl, we can't get rid of you," she said. "You're like one of those bad dreams I keep having over and over."

"Thanks," I said and put my head back down.

She sat down. "Well, there's no sleeping for anybody tonight. Let's go sit on the back steps. We might as well have our first lesson until the sun comes up. You've got to know already about subjects and predicates. So let's talk about clauses and phrases."

I shook my head woefully. "Let's start with subjects and predicates."

So we did. That night I learned more than I'd learned in my whole year on the lam all put together. Finally, after we'd made it through synonyms and antonyms and the birds had started in singing, Eva stretched. The moon was still up and I could see the streaks of dried tears tracking down her face. She said, "All right now. I'm tired enough to sleep. You go on down to your grandma's now. Tell her you're all right. Talk to her about the tutoring. Tell her your granddad signed you up. Tell her a dollar an hour. And *don't* tell your daddy you were up here. You understand that?"

I nodded. Then she touched my shoulder. "All right, go on now and let me take a rest. Lord knows what this day's going to bring."

I got up and went on down the street. I was moving slow and it took a long time for me to get to Mimi's. The house was still dark (what did I expect?), so I lay down in the front porch swing. It was hard and slimy with cold dew. I got the swing going a little by throwing my butt back and forth and I tried to think of myself as a baby getting rocked by some big invisible hand. A heavenly hope mother or daddy who was taking care I didn't cry or fret. I tried to think of myself as precious cargo on a long bootlegger run to morning. And when the sun finally came up all pink and golden and I unfolded myself and got up and rang Mimi's doorbell, she came down after a long while and took one look and sighed a big deep sigh. Her hair was mashed in on one side and her hairnet was hanging off the other. The lids of her eyes were so puffed out and her mouth so puckered up that she looked like a huge, white hooded owl perched behind the screen in the doorway. She had on a slip instead of a nightgown. Her bosoms were sausages lying flat from her shoulders to her elbows.

"Have they found your mother?" By the way she asked the question, I could tell she knew the answer. Daddy must have called her last night.

"I don't know."

"Where you been? You look like something the dog dragged in."

"On your porch, just resting."

"Why aren't you at home with your daddy." It wasn't a question, and she knew it.

I didn't answer.

She stepped out of the doorway and held the screen open for me to come in. She sniffed and made a face. "Girl, you need some Mum." I started to say I needed a lot more than Mum, but then she patted my nasty head and said, "I haven't slept a wink all night. I've got to lie back down a while before I can think straight." Then she turned around slowly like she was in a dream and went on back up the stairs.

I heard the springs on her bed squeak and sigh, and then I went on up too. I stood in the doorway to her room. Her back was to me in the bed. She had her knees drawn up tight and her feet folding over each other like flippers on a seal. No cover. I wanted to crawl in and hold on to her back, latch myself to her. She could be the tree and I could be Bomba. But then I heard the slightest little snore and I could tell that she'd fallen to sleep like a dog that's been lost and running around all night long. So I tiptoed out and went on downstairs to the kitchen and started in on the funeral leftovers, which were considerable.

Zenie usually came around seven thirty, but seven thirty came and went and so did eight with no Zenie. I went out and got the Jackson *Clarion-Ledger* that she usually brought in from the yard. No word of Medgar Evers getting shot that I could tell. Nothing at all. Screaming headlines about Governor Wallace, who had to stand down and let the Negroes come to school because the president sent in the National Guard. In the picture on the front page, the governor looked like a rooster on the side of the road, puffing himself up and twitching, but scared to cross. Plus, while I was stomping roaches last night, the president had made a speech and said we had to let the Negroes come on in. He said for white people to examine their conscience. We are supposed to be a free country. He didn't say he wanted us to be polite to Negroes, but I bet he says Mr. and Mrs. to them.

Bent over the kitchen table, eating the first thing I came to in the icebox, which was a big bowl of potato salad, I tried to examine my conscience the way the president said to do. Twice now I had been ugly to Zenie in that I'm-white-and-you're-not sort of way. I was mortally ashamed of it and of the evilness in my heart it must have come from. Where did that foulness come from anyway? I still had that dream planted deep in my head by Daddy about me being Bomba up that burning tree with the savages down below. Every now and again I dreamed it, and I think somewhere deep inside me it had grown underground and sent up shoots in unexpected places, the way poison ivy does, just popping up where you least expect it. I hoped I'd made it up to Zenie by getting Eva out of the bed after she'd got beaten up. Now that I could see the evil thing lurking in my own nature, I was going to watch my mouth better. The way I saw it then, it didn't matter about the ugliness in your heart if you just kept it out of your mouth. I thought maybe if you kept it locked inside you, unheard by anyone, it dried up after a while like a piece of rotten fruit, given that it's not how you really meant yourself to be. Not your true-hearted self but a web of something else all around you that crawls up into your insides and tries to make a nasty little nest there out of poison and ugliness.

I sat there eating this mountain of potato salad. It wasn't done right, not like Mama's. Not enough mustard, way too much onion, no vinegar whatsoever, no sweet pickle relish, but I couldn't stop shoveling it in. The more I ate the more I wanted. There was a big roast sitting out on the kitchen table and a row of desserts, but all I had a taste for was this bad potato salad. The house was quieter than I'd ever heard it. Just the *tick tick* of the kitchen clock and the sound of me crunching too many onions. Grandpops in the ground, Mama flown the coop, Mimi upstairs in her grieving sleep, and Zenie doing a disappearing act on the day we needed her the most in the whole world, having locked herself away for Medgar Evers. I ate on. After a while I was full to overflowing. Then I put my head down on the kitchen table next to the bowl of potato salad. In the growing warm of early morning the bees were starting up in the nandina bushes outside the kitchen window.

After a while I lifted my head from the table and felt the heat of the day settle over me like a blanket. Mimi was standing in front of me in her brunch coat. She said, "Well now," with a bit of surprise to find me asleep with my head on the kitchen table of all places. She put the potato salad back into the icebox and boiled herself some coffee. Then she sat down at the table and put two spoons smack-dab in the middle of Mrs. Polk's caramel pie, which was sitting right there along with two cakes and three other lesser pies and a plate of dried-up sugar cookies. With a sweep of her hand, she pushed aside the cakes and lesser pies and cookies and put Mrs. Polk's pie between us. "Well," she said, her eyes so red and swelled up she looked parboiled, "if we're going to eat, we might as well eat something good."

15

Some stories run for their lives. They zig and zag, moving so fast you can't find the secret path of their steps through the fields, only soft prints here and there to let you know something with a quivering heart and a soft belly passed that way or this. In what direction it ran or to what end, you will never know. Sometimes you see the blood or fur, and you know it didn't get away.

In the days that followed I hardly ever saw Eva except in the late afternoons when we had our lessons. Mimi was ponying up the dollar an hour, and Eva was teaching me up a storm. I'd gotten so good at diagramming that she was throwing foot-long sentences at me, sentences with compound this and complex that, adjectives and adverbs and clauses and phrases galore, sentences you could build a house out of and move right into. She was particular about semicolons and drilled me on them until I was bored to tears. She lit a fire under me with such pronouncements as, "You can't get into the fifth grade unless you know the function of the semicolon," and, "You won't make it through the first week unless you can spell *Mississippi*." When I'd build a mansion on the page out of one of her tangled sentences and all the rooms were in the right places, she'd flash me a million-dollar smile and say, "Now see how easy that was, girl?"

Especially when I diagrammed sentences, I could feel a little smile playing at my lips.

Sometimes Eva talked to me about being a teacher. "Words open the keys to the kingdom, girl," she said. "Words and sentences and stories. They're all we've got to get by in this cold world."

Meanwhile, she was always running in and out at all hours. The more determined she got, the prettier she became. She'd gotten herself a new pair of specs with pointy ends that turned up with little rhinestones on them. Cat eyes. She kept on wearing her little cowgirl scarves tied crisp and perky around her neck. Pretty bright colors, yellow and red and blue. Zenie had given up trying to talk her out of anything, though Ray and Zenie were always whispering in the kitchen about where was she going, and who with, and what would come of her doings. Since Medgar Evers, there was a stir in the house. The whole state was on full rolling boiling. Folks riled up and on the move all over. In Jackson, boys and girls getting bit by dogs, hosed down, put in garbage trucks, and dumped like trash in livestock pens at the state fairgrounds. It was worse than when, a few weeks before, in late May, some men had poured ketchup all over Eva's school friends at the Woolworth's lunch counter in Jackson.

One morning when Zenie was fussing about Eva putting everybody in danger, I heard Ray say, "We got insurance. Peckerwoods ain't lighting no fires under us long as we got the girl in the house. We in the catbird seat. Got the devil over a barrel. He find himself without nobody to see after her, he be in hot water. I got a good mind to get out there myself."

There was a long silence, then Zenie's voice burning fire. "You go doing that and you going to end up the next one six feet under and they ain't going to bury you in no Arlington Cemetery neither. Pieces of you be scattered into the next county. Never find all of you."

"These days they kill you just for breathing air, leastways I go a man." Ray said.

Late in the day, after Eva had finished with my lesson—about the time people came out to sit on their porches with fretful babies or water their flowers—she would go from yard to yard with her encyclopedias. There were four of them selling now, the albino-looking one named Frank and two other white boys who looked like a pair of Seventh-Day Adventists with long hair. They all belonged to the NAACP. Zenie said they did too much race work and not enough encyclopedia work. At night the four of them were always heading off to meetings together. Eva asked Ray and Zenie to take in two students from up north who had hooked up with the students at Tougaloo College to organize the voter registrations. Zenie said they didn't have room, plus Eva could play hari-kiri with them Freedom Riders, but she'd have to find her own house to do it in. Hurt and more hurt, Zenie said. That was what was going to come of it all.

"Watch your back," Ray hollered through the green leaf curtain to Eva when she was getting ready to go out one night. The lightning bugs were starting up. "Bunch of mean rednecks out there. They got your number. When you coming home, girl?"

"Won't be long," she called out from her and Miss Josephine's room, "be home in a while now."

Ray and Zenie were waiting for me to leave so they could eat. Zenie had warmed up some biscuits and ham left over from breakfast for Miss J, and she'd taken them on a tray to bed with her. That afternoon I'd come home with Zenie because some church ladies came over to get Mimi out of the house for supper and Daddy was collecting way out in the county. He was picking me up late. I told Zenie to let me just sit out on the front stoop, but she said no, too much going on. Just as Eva got all ready and was getting ready to head out the front door, Daddy's car pulled up. Eva stopped short in her tracks. "Well, if it ain't the devil himself," she said under her breath and turned around and headed back into her and Miss Josephine's room and drew the green leaf curtain.

Zenie had me out the door in no time, though she didn't need to worry. Daddy never came in. "He might have to pay you something if he knocked on the door," Ray said under his breath one time. Daddy would just sit in his car smoking and hit the horn if I didn't come right out. When he was parked by Zenie's, folks would disappear from their stoops and porches into their houses and Zenie's lively street would all of a sudden look like nobody lived on it.

Eva was back to sleeping with Miss Josephine, who was now in the bed more than out of it. When Zenie would fix Miss J's breakfast on a tray and take it in to her, Eva sometimes would still be asleep down under the sheet beside her. Miss J always said she wasn't hungry, and Zenie always answered just eat a little bit then and drink your coffee. Eva wouldn't budge. She had been out late. Zenie got Miss J up and took her into the bathroom for a good wash. When they finished, Miss J came hobbling out on her cane, nice and fresh in her pink brunch coat that Zenie had made for her with the peter pan collar trimmed in rickrack. When Zenie got her parked on the sofa, Miss J would close her eyes and have her morning nap. Then, when we got back in the afternoon from Mimi's, there she'd be, exactly where we left her, all bent over and looking as relaxed as anything. She'd blink and say, "Oh my, here you are, back already. I must have dozed off."

One morning Eva got up early, right after Zenie had taken care of Miss J. She came into the living room, where I was sitting on the sofa next to Miss J, who had already gone back to sleep. I was looking at Zenie's Sears catalog. Eva sat down in the chair right across from me. She propped her feet up on the coffee table.

"Hey girl, what you looking at?" she asked, all sweetness and light.

"Nothing. Just looking." The truth was I had been looking at those little hooks you put on bathroom doors. I was studying how they attached. I thought that if I could lay my hands on one, maybe even take one off a door at Mimi's, I could put it up on my bedroom door without too much trouble. All I needed was a screwdriver.

Eva leaned over. "What you studying hooks for? What you got needs locking up?"

"Not studying them. They're just there on the page I was on." Her nosiness burned me up. I wasn't messing in *her* business.

"How your arms doing now? They about healed up?"

Her question surprised me. I hadn't thought about my arms lately. I turned the insides up and looked down at them. Just webs of little white raised lines were left. They looked all right to me, though still tender to the touch.

"How about your face?" I asked her.

She shrugged and turned her cheek to me. "You tell me." The little pink circle had settled in. It looked like it was there to stay.

"It looks better."

"Still there, though, just like yours. Guess we both branded, Flo," she said. I didn't say anything. She looked me hard in the eye. "Guess we got something in common now." She sat back in her chair and sighed. We sat there for a few minutes. I could hear Zenie flipping corn cakes in the kitchen.

"Looks like corn cakes for breakfast," Eva said. "Hope she got some sorghum in there."

"She does," I said.

"Have you heard anything from your mama? She'll be coming on back before long, I expect."

I perked up. Nobody else would talk about my mother. It was as if she had never lived and breathed on this earth. I was one of the pagan babies they talked about at church. I had dropped from the sky into everybody's laps. "I ain't counting on her coming back." When I said the words, I knew them to be true. Eva was like that. There was something about her that made you want to tell the truth.

"Don't say *ain't*," she said quietly. "She'll come back. She will. She's just confused about herself. She'll come on back to herself and wonder why in the world she did it. You know, I did. You made me see myself lying there up in the bed like a big old toad frog squashed in the road. Feeling sorry for myself. I owe you one, girl."

I shook my head. "You got more get up and go than Mama does."

"Maybe, but when your get up and go just got up and went, you got to move off someplace in your mind before you can come back. And you need a reason to come back."

I kicked the sofa hard. "Seems to me she's got one dadgum good reason sitting right here."

Eva nodded. "She does, and she'll think it up before long. She just temporarily passed it by in her mind."

"You just saying that."

"It's true, girl. She's not going to leave you behind forever. You mark my word." Eva pushed her pointy glasses back on her nose and leaned forward. "So what you been doing long about evening? You got some girlfriends?" She paused, but I didn't say anything. "You been going out with your daddy and his friends at night? They take you to their clubhouse? Do you get to see them get all dressed up?"

The way she asked the last three questions all in a little excited rush made me know that they were the whole point. She didn't give a flip about Mama or who missed who. Priming the pump was all she was interested in. She wanted to know about Daddy and his club. The truth was I actually would have liked to tell her about the box and the Nighthawk and the password and everything else. All these secrets were weighing me down. I wanted to tell somebody the whole thing and be done with it all and have that somebody say, my goodness gracious, that's all very very odd, grown men in costumes pretending to be birds. Wonder why they do all those strange things. Are they mental? But in my mind's eye I saw Daddy with that pointer finger over his mouth.

"I just stay home at night and listen to WLAC," I said. "That's all. Sometimes I read. Sometimes go out in the yard to cool off."

She got up and looked down at me. Her eyes were burning. She laughed a short little laugh. "Lord, child, you got one boring life. Boring. Nothing better to do than that. Y'all don't even have a TV, do you?"

My life wasn't as boring as I made out. Watching Daddy to find out what he'd do next was keeping me on my toes. When he wasn't out gallivanting, he was ranting and railing about outside agitators descending on Mississippi like a plague of locusts. Communist mongrels and Jews. Mud people. They wanted to eat off our plates and marry our daughters, take everything we held dear. We'd all be brown before you could say Jackie Robinson. Dirty bastards coming down here just to get into our business, tearing down everything we hold dear, making little brown mongrels pop out right and left. Daddy and his friends fretted that the agitators were going to come over from Jackson and try to integrate the mill. The men down in Milltown who worked there had gathered themselves together. Now, every night, Daddy got calls to come to meetings. When I'd answer, they wouldn't even be polite. They'd just say, "Where you pa at?"

Which was a good question. He stayed gone all night some-times. With no Mama around to throw a fit, he kept the pretty wood box handy in the bottom of their closet instead of sending me down to the basement for it. There was another box beside it now, a rough pine box. No lock. Sometimes he took it along with the other one when he went out at night. I sneaked a look at it one night when he was gone. It held an interesting assortment of things. Some license plates, pieces of rope, a big hunting knife with a shiny sharp blade, the pieces of a broken-down shotgun and some slugs, a map of Mill County, a hatchet, some torches, a Westclox alarm clock. The whole box smelled of gasoline. He'd taken my white getup and hat out of the pretty first box and stashed it on the floor in the back of the closet. It probably had spiders making nests in it because the house was getting dirtier by the day, but I was getting bigger by the minute, so it probably wouldn't have fitted anyhow. He didn't ask me to come to meet-ings with him anymore, for which I was grateful. A little part of me wanted to go, the part that wanted to be paid attention to and told how pretty I was. Being at the meetings was like standing in front of a three-way mirror in a new dress, except for the rotten-smelling old men with whiskers who picked me apart from myself as if I were a pea to be shelled. But another part of me was grow-ing stronger and double-stitching me back into my shell in the same determined way Zenie sewed and then resewed the braid onto her band uniforms. That one wanted to keep herself apart and wait for something else to happen. For the Queen of Palmyra to come to the rescue in her chariot of gold. For Mama to come back with the ingredients and say she was sorry to have taken so long. For a new chapter in my story to commence.

When Daddy was gone after dark, I made the most of it. Mimi had given me the full set of Nancy Drew books Grandpops had bought and been saving for me. They were better than the library books I picked out for myself, better even than the encyclopedias that Mimi said she'd buy from Eva since Grandpops was going to. They were better because of the stories. Disappearing staircases, diamond necklaces, buried treasure. Nancy always rescuing people who were locked up in basements or turrets, or getting locked up herself. Stories that pulled me through the long nights and brought me out on the other side of a world where everything turned out the way it should because Nancy was brave and tough and smart. Though Zenie wouldn't have approved, I got to thinking of myself as Nancy Drew and the Queen of Palmyra rolled into one, with a bit of Br'er Rabbit thrown in. I got Mama's radio and listened to John R on late-night WLAC out of Nashville just the way she used to. I danced around and sang to the hits. "It's My Party and I'll Cry if I Want To." The little black fan I'd propped up on a chair at the foot of the bed kept me company with the little shocked screech it made when it came to the end of its lazy turn.

I had the idea that if my Hit-the-Road-Jack mother ever did come back, she'd wait until dark. She'd check to make sure Daddy's car was gone, and come to the window by my bed and bat softly on the screen, like a moth coming to the light. I read my books next to the open window so I would hear her when she came. I spent the long slow nights waiting. The trains called their warnings. The owls made the baby rabbits cry out for mercy.

I came to think of myself more as part of those dark comings and goings out in the hot shifting night than that other Florence who went through her humdrum days. I kept a sheet pulled up over me, though it kept me sweating all night long. Before I turned out the lights, I shut the bedroom door and shoved my night table in front of it. I slept on my right side, turned toward the door. If Daddy was to slip in to lie down with me, I wanted to hear the door creak and the table scrape before I heard his brick

shoe drop on the floor and felt his weight on the bed. I wanted
to be awake and prepared. Gone was the homey feeling I used to
have with my father lying there with me and telling white-knight
stories while Mama would be cooking and singing in the kitchen
and the door was open and the light shining in. Now when he
would go on about knights and agitators and brown mongrels
and communists, it got to sounding like a crazy song on a stuck
record. Sometimes he would turn away in the bed and thrash
about like an evil spirit had taken hold of him and was trying to
get out. Mama used to call Daddy back from my bed like he was
a little boy out playing Red Rover past dark. Now, when Daddy
dropped his brick shoe beside my bed, there was no one to call
him home.

In the mornings he took me up to Zenie's in an old Valiant
he'd borrowed from a man who spit tobacco juice right next to my
bare feet. When I'd knock on the door and Zenie would open it a
crack so that I could come in, she'd just look at me and shake her
head and tell me to go back to sleep on the couch, I looked like
something the dog dragged in.

One day, about a week after Grandpops died, Zenie took
Mimi into the kitchen and told me to go out and play. I didn't
waste any time getting up into my tree next to the window, the
one I was in when, unbeknownst to us, Grandpops was dying
upstairs while Zenie was frying bacon on the stove under the
window. In the kitchen Zenie and Mimi talked in deep earnest,
Zenie standing tall with her arms folded, like the queen she was.
Mimi sat in Zenie's high-back chair and tilted her head up to
listen. Then Mimi's face turned sour and she started to rub her
hands together like she was washing them. Then she reached up
and grabbed at her own face the way you see a cat go after a biting
flea. I expected Zenie to lean over and pat her on the arm, but
Zenie turned back to the stove. After a while, Mimi said some-

thing to Zenie and Zenie nodded in agreement. They looked at each other like they'd decided something and a weight had fallen off their shoulders. When Mimi walked out of the kitchen, Zenie flicked an eye at me in the tree, which let me know they were through and I could come back in.

The next morning Mimi calls me into her room and sits me down. She has made some phone calls. She has decided to send me to a camp for girls up on top of Lookout Mountain in Tennessee, where the nights are so cool you need a blanket and I can be a regular girl. I will ride horses and swim in lakes. I will do crafts. Camp Mentone. It isn't cheap, but it will give Zenie, who is plumb worn out, a rest and my mother a chance to see the error of her ways and come back. It will get us through July. Mimi has talked to Daddy and he says it's all right with him as long as he doesn't have to pay for it and it's only for two weeks.

For my camp clothes, Zenie measured me bottom and top. She made a pattern out of newspaper and sewed me up some new crop tops and shorts with elastic waists. "You getting big as a horse. You needs to get out and play like the other children," she said. "Why don't you get out and play with some them girls?" She went rummaging around in the bottom of one of the shoeboxes and came up with some chalk. She handed it to me. "Take this home and make yourself some hopscotch." I knew other children were out in their yards doing this and that, but playing didn't appeal to me. The heat was smothering, plus I didn't have any skates or a bicycle. Hopscotch and jump rope are about the only things you can play by yourself, and they get old fast. It was true that my waist had gotten bigger but so had everything else.

When Mimi started sewing name tags into my underpants and shorty pajama pants, she threw up her hands and said her grandchild was wearing rags, she couldn't even get a label to hold in them. She cried over the labels, and she cried behind the wheel, driving us down to Black's Department Store, where we got some more underpants in all colors of the rainbow and some pink pajamas with white ruffles. Then she cried while we had some rainbow sherbet at the counter at the Ben Franklin, and cried even harder when the Baldwin sisters saw us and came over to say they were sorry about Grandpops. Then she blew her nose and we headed down the street for the post office to buy some postcards. Later that day she sat down and addressed them to herself and put stamps on them and gave them to me so I would write and let her know how I was doing. Her eyes swam with tears as she told me to write her. "I depend on you," she said. "I'm going to miss your company. You're all I've got left in the world."

At the Ben Franklin, after we'd gotten some calamine lotion and a pink toothbrush holder and some Mum, Mimi turned around and looked me up and down. She frowned. "Hmm . . . your mother got an early start in life." She looked around, then went over to another counter where a silver-haired lady stood. "We need some supplies for camp," Mimi said in a funny sort of way. The lady nodded and reached under the counter. She came up with a box of Kotex and a belt and whipped them into a sack almost before I could see what they were. I wasn't born yesterday. I'd been thinking about when I was going to have to get on the rag along with the rest of the world. What I was going to do. Not that anybody had ever explained it to me. I'd sleuthed it out here and there, like Nancy Drew. It looked horrible and smelled like pennies. I hoped my time would never come, but I knew that was wishful thinking. I kept up my research. I had pulled used Kotex out of the bathroom at home when Mama lived there. Before she left, she had been thoughtful enough to leave some in a box under the lavatory in the bathroom. I had pulled one out and stuck it in my pants, just to get the effect. It had slid forward and then back, then all over the place, and it gave me that funny feeling, like scratching the poison ivy that time I got it Between the Legs. I was afraid that it would slither around like a slippery bar of soap and pop out *kerplop* right on the sidewalk if I ever actually tried to walk around in it.

When we got home and unloaded my stash on the kitchen table, Mimi pulled out the sack with the Kotex and belt in it and handed it to me. She looked down at her feet. "Did your mother tell you how to use these if you need them?"

She seemed to be holding her breath for an answer. I knew if I said no she would just turn on the waterworks again. Mimi looked bad. She needed a blue touch-up on her hair, which was growing out a yellowish gray. Her face was covered in red blotches and puffy to boot. Mimi was a neat dresser, but one of her garters had slid below her dress and her slip was showing. I wanted to throw my arms around her middle and bawl my eyes out too, but I knew that would just make matters worse.

"Yes ma'am." I tried to say it in a comforting way.

"All right, then," she said briskly. "Now Florence, you know you have your grandmother's ear if you ever have anything you feel you need to tell me."

It was an odd thing to say and an odd way of saying it. I tried to diagram the sentence in my head so I could follow the sense of it. What would I need to have her ear for? While I was trying to figure that out, she nodded and firmed up her lips. "All right, then, shoo fly," she said, "I'm worn out. Going to take a nap."

Right after Daddy picked me up later that afternoon and took me home, he went out in a hurry, with both of his boxes, one under each arm. In his hands he carried two paper sacks full of white paper. After he left, I took the belt out of the drugstore sack and fooled with it until I got the hang of putting the Kotex on and taking it off. I didn't need it yet, but it seemed smart to practice. I had the idea that girls gushed like geysers when they were on the rag, and I didn't want to be trying to figure all this out for the first time in such a state. I wanted to be prepared. Plus I had a feeling that it was exactly what I needed. In Eva's C encyclopedia I had read about a garb called a chastity belt, and that's what it struck me as. I imagined it as having a bit of gold on the tabs and some nice jewels hanging from it. The Kotex roasted me like a goose, and the hooks that held the tabs pulled and pinched my bare skin, but it somehow seemed good and right to wear it. It felt safe and true, a thick gauzy lock on the door in case I started up. I had plenty of other things to worry about, so I figured if I kept whole business on, I wouldn't get caught short. Plus if I didn't get to bleeding and took a bath every night, I could use the same one over and over.

When Daddy came in late into the night, he smelled burnt. I wasn't asleep and I caught his stink before he even opened the door to my room and made the night table scrape across the floor. When he sat down on the edge of the bed, I turned over on my back. He dropped his shoes and heaved himself in. He sighed and brought his hand, hot and heavy, down on my stomach. He was just about to say, like he always did, "You awake, Sister?" when his fingers touched the Kotex belt. He fumbled with it a minute, then jerked his hand away like he'd been nailed by a water moccasin. He made a little swallowing sound in his throat and in one scramble got his feet on the floor and leaned down and grabbed his shoes. I peered through the dark to see him bobbing out of the door in his bare feet as fast as he could go. I closed the door behind him and put the night table back.

The rest of that night I slept hard and dreamed of Mama coming to the window. She pressed her face up to the screen so hard it made her lips spread out in a blob so that I could see the pink underneath them. She just looked in at me, not saying a word, though it seemed to me as if she was trying to tell me a secret that would change everything.

Two days later Mimi took me down to the Greyhound station to put me on the bus to Chattanooga, Tennessee. Zenie came along, riding in back. Zenie stayed in the car while we got the ticket. Mimi and I waited in the side of the station that said, "Waiting Room. White. Interstate Passengers." I had wanted to ride the train, but that would have involved taking the M & O to Memphis and then transferring to another train bound for Chattanooga. Mimi didn't want me to transfer. She wanted me on the bus until the end of the line, where some camp people were going to meet me and drive me up the mountain.

When the bus came into the station, I ran back to the car to say good-bye to Zenie, but she was dead asleep in the backseat, her head resting against a partly rolled up window and her mouth a little open. I patted the part on the top of her head but she didn't wake up.

Mimi got on the bus with me to get me settled and made me sit up next to the driver. She fussed over me. Did I have a sweater now? If I had to get off the bus to go to the bathroom, TELL THE DRIVER TO WAIT FOR ME. TELL HIM NOT TO LEAVE WITHOUT ME. How was I going to know who the camp people were? They would have on tee shirts that said Camp Mentone. Plus the camp people would be on the lookout for me. The driver was standing outside and Mimi stepped down to have a talk with him. I knew she was saying to watch out for me. Then she came back and bent down over me and hugged me for a good long time. She didn't want to let me go, I could tell. I was her project, about to get launched. What would she do now? I was burning up hot under the never-ending hug. Zenie had made me a fried-chicken supper, which I was planning to eat just as soon as the bus pulled out.

"If Mama turns up, tell her I'll be back soon," I said with half a heart. I doubted the words were worth my breath.

"You just have a *good time*, honey." Mimi's face was gooey. Her eyes had misted up. "Just enjoy every minute. Don't worry about a thing. You are going on *vacation*."

The idea of going on vacation captivated me. At Mimi's bridge parties I'd seen ladies' pictures that showed them and their loved ones on vacation in Memphis or Florida or New Orleans. The ladies said they came back from vacation *refreshed* and more *themselves*. But actually I was going on vacation *from* my own real self, the one who listened for trains in the middle of the night and wondered whether her mother would bat on the window screen. The one that people's eyes scurried away from like little wild kittens when they heard her daddy's last name.

At camp I told everyone my name was Flo, and it was Flo this and Flo that. Flo, come here, I want to talk to you. Flo, do you think my nose is too big? I want to sit by Flo. Nobody asked my last name and nobody cared who my mama and daddy were. Nobody's eyes turned sly at the sight of me. In a few days I began to see for the first time how I had this gift. In the twinkling of an eye I'd gathered girlfriends galore. I seemed to know what they wanted before they even started to feel the want themselves. Girls wanted to talk to me and tell me things and have me close. They were afraid of getting their period. They had a pain here. It needed rubbing. Would I scratch their back? I laughed at their funny little stories about their mothers and fathers, or about being aggravated with them. Their parents' stupid rules and regulations to make sure they were safe and sound because they were Precious Cargo. How glad they were to be off at camp away from all that heavy loving.

Mimi sent me thick packed envelopes every other day or so and Zenie sent two thin letters, but I just put them in the bottom of my suitcase without opening them. It could have been the best news in the world, or the worst. I didn't want to know about it. I didn't want to think of myself as Florence Irene Forrest. I wanted to think of myself as a regular girl. Flo. I would live there forever among other regular girls. Somebody would pack me up in her suitcase and take me home by accident.

She would say, "Oh look, Mama, I mistakenly brought Flo home in my suitcase. She was my best friend at camp. Can we keep her? Please?"

And the nice mother would say, "Of course, dear, any best friend of yours is like a daughter to us. We'll adopt her and make her happy every day that she doth live. Welcome to our family, Flo honey."

At night, though, I slept on the top bunk next to a window and watched the stars divide and multiply. I went right to sleep, but woke up in the middle of the night and stayed awake for long stretches. I loved the night sounds and the soft paddle of the other girls breathing softly in sleep. I loved my bunk. Room for one only. Up there, I could breathe in the cool mountain air and think about nothing but stars and night sounds. No trains to mark the hours. I began to think of myself not as bereft, as I had before, but somehow floating out there by myself in the darkness, not hurt or bothered, just hanging out there peaceful and quiet among the stars, like the moon. I wondered if this was what it was like to be dead.

I had a bunkmate whose name was Jennie. Jennie had worried about God ever since her brother Matt had gotten run over on his bike while delivering newspapers. She doubted God was really up there taking care of business, and if He was, she hated His guts because He obviously didn't give a flip about Matt. When we said the blessing at meals, she looked straight ahead, her mouth in a determined hyphen. She slept in the bunk underneath mine, and sometimes in the night she would push on the bottom of my bunk with her feet and whisper, "Flo, are you awake?"

I usually was, so I'd say, "Um hum."

"I'm cold."

"Pull up your blanket."

"I did. I'm still cold."

I knew what she wanted. Jennie was always cold at night. She wanted to crawl in with me, which was against camp rules. No sleeping together in the same bunk, that was the rule and fine by me. I'd let her do it just once and I'd held her tight the way she asked, but after she'd stopped shivering and gone to sleep, I'd crawled down to her bunk and its cool sheets.

At camp I learned to dive, though it made my head hurt. I made pot holders galore and leaf imprints out of crayons pressed with an iron. I learned the difference between poison ivy and Virginia creeper and how to saddle up a horse. On the move all day, and never a worn-out feeling. We all had our chores. I'd jumped at getting kitchen work, for two reasons. I couldn't get enough to eat. Maybe it was the fact that I was running from one busy thing to another, maybe I was having a growth spurt. I ate all three of my meals but still wanted more. I figured if I worked in the kitchen, I could sneak a few bites here and there. Plus there were Negro ladies and girls my age working in the kitchen, and I liked the way they said some of the rich camp girls had their noses up their asses. The kitchen ladies were the only black people in the whole camp, and they didn't live up on Lookout Mountain, the reason being, they said, that all of their folks who had moved up there had had their houses burnt down. They snorted and said either there was a serious problem with white people up on that mountain or those Negroes were the most careless smokers in the whole wide world. I impressed the ladies by showing them how to make Mama's cakes. They were good cooks but they tended to make big dishes of cobbler and banana pudding for desserts. At camp, cakes were too much trouble and didn't stretch far enough. But the kitchen ladies wanted to learn the cakes for themselves. I told them how Mama had made a good business out of it before she ran herself into the train. They looked hard at each other and clucked like hens.

I watched the pie sliver of a moon get larger and larger each night until one night it was full. And when that happened, it was over. All of a sudden, we were standing around a farewell campfire holding hands and singing should old acquaintance be forgot and never brought to mind. That night, after I'd packed my pot holders, which I planned to give to Zenie and Mimi, and the leaf picture, which I thought Eva might like, and settled down in my top bunk, I could feel Daddy's heavy hand moving into place. It was a beautiful night with the moon so bright and full, but I had a taste in my mouth like metal. I could hear a raccoon getting into the kitchen garbage. I tried to count the stars, but I kept losing count. I whispered to Jennie to see whether she was still awake, but she didn't answer.

Early the next morning, I hugged all the girlfriends I had made and would never see again. Jennie held me tight and whispered something in my ear I didn't catch. Some of the girls cried when they hugged me good-bye. I would be their best friend for the rest of their lives, they said, but I just laughed and said come see me in Millwood, though I knew they never would; otherwise I wouldn't have invited them.

Then my counselor, Sherry, as in "Sherry, Sherry, Baby," put her pretty blond hair into a ponytail and drove me to the Greyhound depot in Chattanooga. She put me back on the bus for home with a ham sandwich. "Have a Great Year!" she said in her cheerleader way with a quick wave of her hand. And that was that.

16

When I got off the bus, it was dusk and Daddy was standing there waiting. I saw him out the window as we pulled into the station. He leaned against a post, his bad foot propped up behind him. He was taking drags off a cigarette and making puffy O's in the air. A slice of light played on his arm. He looked small from the window on the bus, like a country boy just hanging around. Compared to the other parents who had picked up their daughters at camp in big Oldsmobiles, he looked common. I could tell by his face that Mama hadn't come back. I went up to him and hugged him around the middle the way I'd seen the regular girls hug their fathers when they came to get them at camp. He didn't hug me back but just petted me on the head.

"You getting big, Sister."

I supposed that when he said big, he meant chunky. I had gotten thicker in the two weeks I'd been away. The shorts with the elastic waists were now tight around the middle, and Zenie had made them with room to grow. I was more interested in food than I'd ever been. I didn't worry about getting fat; in fact, I figured the more fat I had on me, the better I'd make out if suddenly I found myself without food. I was disappointed that Daddy had picked me up. The ham sandwich hadn't gone far, and I didn't count on him feeding me.

But he surprised me. "Let's go get us some supper," he said when we had wrestled my things into the backseat of the Valiant. The trunk on the Valiant wouldn't open because it was bashed in on one side from an old wreck. "Let's go down to Joe's and get us a hamburger."

I hated the idea of going to Joe's Drive-In with Daddy worse than I hated going hungry. Now that I had a clearer idea of what nice parents were supposed to look and act like, I couldn't abide the thought of being seen with him. There was something about Daddy, and it wasn't just the rusty bashed-in Valiant. He drew stares and whispers, whether he'd stopped at a light in his borrowed car or was knocking on people's doors. You could almost hear people saying to themselves, "That's *him*." He was the tough gun in the western picture show come into town to cause trouble.

"I'm not hungry," I said in a meek little voice as he started the car. I sat low in my seat, not looking out my window, which was, thankfully, stuck shut and coated in dust and grime. The words weren't out of my mouth before he caught me on the fat part of my left arm.

"You too good for a hamburger with your old daddy now you back from that fancy camp?" His hand squeezed my arm so hard my fingers froze into icicles.

I shook my head quickly. No.

"What'd you say?"

"No sir."

"No sir, what?"

"No sir, I'm not too good."

"All right then," he said, and let go of my arm so fast that it fell into my lap like a bird shot dead from the sky.

It was Saturday night and boiling hot. When he pulled the car into Joe's, there were high-school boys in shorts and girls in halter tops draped all over each other's cars playing their radios. "The Lion Sleeps Tonight" was in the howling part, and some of them were dancing around and howling right along with the music, like a bunch of hungry coyotes clumped up. They all turned to look when Daddy pulled up to the voice box with a little jerk and cut the engine. I kept my head down. I held my arm close in by cupping my left elbow with my right hand. My breath had come back and if I didn't move at all, it didn't hurt so much. On the ride to Joe's I'd decided I needed to go back to camp in my mind. I thought about weaving pot holders and diving into deep cool water and the quiet nights with stars and the living moon.

"Two hamburgers and two chocolate shakes," Daddy said into the box, which was dead because he didn't know he was supposed to push the button before he put his order in. That's how ignorant he was.

I didn't say anything. The teenagers were turning from each other and starting to stare and whisper out of the sides of their mouths.

Daddy leaned out the window again. "Two hamburgers and two shakes. Chocolate." He said it louder than the first time into the dead box. The teenagers started to snicker.

I put my head down and tried to toss my hair over my face. I had my mouth open to say push the button, you have to push it before you talk. But the words didn't come out. I just looked hard at the glove compartment. I sat there, my head turned down in a strange way. I could feel a funny little smile spreading over my mouth like warm butter.

"What's wrong with this stinking thing?" He reached out the

window and hit the box hard. "Ow, shit," he hollered, "goddamn that thing." The teenagers were elbowing one another and smirking. One let out a loud whinny.

That got his attention. He leaned out the window. "What you looking at, son?"

The boy tried to wipe the smirk off his face, but it didn't disappear all the way. He started getting back into one of the parked cars.

"You answer me now, boy," Daddy yelled out the window. "What the hell you so all-fired interested in?"

The boy turned his face away from us and got in the car with the others. Around us the radios started going quiet and the engines cranked up one by one. Daddy glared out the window. He looked like an old bear in a cage a man down in the country used to keep out by his store. You could look into that bear's eyes and know he'd kill you if he got out, but you and he knew he never would. Of course, the difference between the bear and my father was that Daddy was on the loose.

Then the car with the boy in it slid out of its parking place slow and easy, and one by one, the others followed. In a few minutes, our car was the only one left sitting in the whole front lot.

"All you have to do is push the button," I finally said. "You just push the button, see?" I leaned over toward his side and pointed. The way I said it was like the period you put at the end of a long wearisome sentence.

Before I knew what was happening, he had grabbed my left arm out of the space between us and wrenched it forward and backward so hard and fast that my shoulder gave a loud pop. It felt like a firecracker had gone off inside the socket. The burn it gave me exploded the breath right out of my chest.

I opened my mouth to scream and he pulled my left arm down with another pop. An arrow of pain sliced up the side of my neck and down to my elbow. My breath wouldn't come. I burst out in a cold sweat all over. Bits of white that looked like torn paper began to fall before my eyes. My arm dangled limp. He started the car. I tried to steady myself against the lurch I knew was coming, but when he threw the car in reverse and it jerked backward, I screamed.

He latched onto my knee and dug in with his fingers. "I don't want to hear nothing out of you. Nothing. Thinking you so smart." He rammed the car back from the box and into the street. Then he cut the wheels hard and headed for home.

After he scratched off from Joe's, Daddy didn't say anything else. He drove fast, taking the corners with a squeal of tires. I held on to my left shoulder and braced myself with my feet. He bent over the wheel looking like the thing he wanted to do most in the world was get me on home and get shuck of me. Riding next to him, I felt the giant hand of his anger pressing me to the seat of the car, not like I was precious cargo to save and protect, but like the crush of a wreck happening in slow motion. The lightness I'd felt at camp was gone. I'd been happily swimming in camp life where I was nobody's bad seed, no weight to me at all, no last name of Forrest with two r's. Now I felt the logginess of stepping out onto land. Daddy was back in charge of me. The Frisco was pulling out of the station with no stops planned.

The car was roasting. I could barely get a breath. The invisible hand on my chest pressed harder. I thought it might be God's judging finger, my punishment for not loving my father the way I should. For liking to see him made fun of. Showing him up for a fool. I was pouring sweat. The car window on my side was broken and wouldn't roll down. I pushed out the bat wing flap all the way to get some air. My shoulder burned.

When we got home, he carried my bag down the path and then told me to go to bed, he'd be late coming in. When he un-

locked the front door and I walked into the living room behind
him, my mouth dropped open. The place was a white sea of paper. Stacks and stacks of it piled up on the couch, the floor, the
coffee table, Mimi's backstabbing rocking chair. Mama's drop-
leaf table had been opened wide in the middle of the room and
was stacked higher than I was tall with typing paper, so much of
it that it made the place look like Spight's Office Supply Store,
which had been under Grandpops' office downtown. Below the
front window where the drop-leaf table used to sit was a rat's nest
of newspapers and magazines.

Daddy didn't explain the mess, and I didn't ask. He went
straight to his room and I went to mine, holding my trembling
left arm close to my chest. I could hear him rummaging in the
bottom of his closet. Then he came back through the living room,
and when I looked up, he was heading out the door with both of
his boxes, the pretty old one and the plain new one, one under
each arm. He had his headache stick in his hand. I heard him
lock the door from the outside. He had put a deadbolt lock on the
door, inside and out, no key in sight. It was the only door to the
house. He had locked me in and Mama out. My first thought was
of fire, since I was so good at starting them, but I knew I could
climb out a window, thanks to Mama, who always made sure that
wherever we lived, the windows opened and shut.

After I heard the Valiant take off down the street, I experi-
mented with my hurt arm, moving it this way and that just to see
if it still worked, which it did. If I held it close, it didn't hurt too
bad. I thought Daddy had pulled it out of the socket and then
jerked it back in. At least that was what I was hoping for. I went
looking for Bayer and found some in the bathroom. I took three
and started looking around through the stacks of papers all over
the living room. The papers in each stack had something different printed on them. One had little pictures of different people's

faces on it. They looked like school pictures of boys and men, white and Negro. Some of the pictures had an X through them. One was of a light-skinned Negro boy named Emmett. One was a darker man named George Lee, whose features I couldn't make out. The only one I knew was Medgar, just because I'd seen his picture in the paper and his grieving wife and little children in *Look* magazine. I remembered his neat mustache and the way his eyes looked like they knew something important. His picture had an X through it too. Another stack had papers with the same letter typed on them. It said:

Dear Editor:

It has come to our attention that a Negro boy attended services last Sunday at the First Presbyterian Church in Meridian as part of a visitation by a so-called Boy Scout Troop from New Jersey. WE CANNOT HAVE RACE MIXING IN OUR MOST SACRED OF ALL PLACES, OUR HOLY SANCTUARIES! This is POLLUTION OF THE WORST SORT BY OUTSIDE AGITATORS to bring the beast into the most hallowed places of our culture, the sacred white communities of our churches, the place where we come to be baptized into the spirit of Christ, ingest our first communions, take vows of sacred matrimony, and are carried into to have our last rites. If race mixing is allowed in the church, then racial purity is doomed. The church door opens to the white woman's bedroom, and the virus of integration will manifest itself in the pestilence of miscegenation and thus the death of life as we know it.

Sincerely,
Winburn Forrest III
Millwood,
Mississippi

I didn't know what *miscegenation* and some of the other words meant until I had looked them up in the dictionary later that night, but the whole letter and the pictures made me feel scared about Daddy in a way I hadn't been before. Yes he could be mean and ill tempered and hurtful when you aggravated him, and yes I was sick of him coming into my room at night, and yes I knew it was him that Mama was running away from. But this was somehow different. Seeing those papers was like being the lady biologist who'd discovered the new breed of spider, the brown one, the reclusive one. Something poisonous lurked under all these mountains of papers. A poison disguised as love. Who was that love for? It seemed it was for me. My skin. My girlhood. But I knew it wasn't for me. If it was, would he be hurting me on purpose? It was for something I stood in for, and that thing wasn't me but a picture of me in his mind. Not X-ed out like the Emmett boy or Medgar Evers, but glorified with an angel halo and wings, made into something I wasn't and could never be.

I backed out of the living room into my room and shut my door to what I'd seen. All of a sudden I felt queasy, but it wasn't just from my shoulder hurting, or even from fear and disgust. It was from being mad. I felt such a train wreck of madness plow right through me that it made me want to rip my own self to pieces because I couldn't live inside the girl he saw me as. I was so stretched between what I had been thinking I was on the inside and what I meant to him that I had to sit down on my bed to keep from fainting. I wanted to cut myself open and step out of my skin and leave it like a pile of dirty clothes on the floor. Then I could say to him, here, take it and give me the rest, give me the inside part and let me be.

I sat on my bed in the dark holding my arm in place. When I heard the ten-thirty M & O in the distance, I started to cry. I cried hard and loud for the time it took the train to come and

go and call out to me. I drowned out its *no, no, no, no*s. Then I
turned on the light because the train had come and gone and
a person can't cry forever. After a while you just flat run dry. I
wiped my face and blew my nose on my shirt and looked around.
I hadn't unpacked from camp because I had in mind taking my
dirty clothes up to Mimi's for Uldine to pick up with the sheets.
The pajamas in my duffle bag smelled moldy so I pulled an old
shirt and a pair of ratty shorts out of my drawer to sleep in. My
bag was a mess, everything wadded up and damp from the wet-
ness in the mountain air. I dug down to the bottom and found a
loose Kotex and the belt and tried to put them on. All this I did
with my one good hand, which wasn't easy, especially hooking up
the Kotex. I finally took the belt off and put it in my lap, hooked
it on the pad, then put the whole thing on at once, in one piece.
I hadn't been wearing it at camp, so it felt like a lumpy pillow
between my legs. I was too tired to read or brush my teeth, just
turned the fan on and got into my bed. The sheets stank and felt
slick. They hadn't been changed since Mama ran herself into the
train. At camp we'd had to strip the beds once a week. We piled
the sheets up on the front stoop to our cabin. Then, like magic,
in the afternoons when we came back to our cabins after a long
hot day, our bunks were made up all nice and fresh with cool
white sheets and light cotton blankets. I had gotten used to clean
sheets. I made up my mind that first thing tomorrow I would get
my stinky numbers off the bed and take them up to Mimi's too. I
thought about going to the Laundromat the way Mama did, but
it was too far away to walk.

I got into the bed and pulled myself over to the side where the
window was. It seemed hotter than ever. My skin was crawling
and itching. Maybe I'd gotten too used to the cool mountain air.
I was on fire from the monster Kotex, smelly from the stale air in
the bus, and sweating that kind of nasty sweat that comes with

being hurt and plumb wore out. The dirty sheets felt like waxed paper wrapped around me. I couldn't move much or lie on my left side because of my shoulder. I had to turn away from the door, and I didn't like the feeling of having my back to it. My eyes kept popping open because I would think I heard something outside my window, a consternation that hadn't been there before. I tried to tell myself it was all in my head. I was used to the safe buzz of a room full of sleeping girls and the night glowing peaceful and quiet out the window before me as I lay up in my high bunk in the night air of the mountain. I had forgotten what it was like to be the me I really was. The life that I was getting ready to have to take back up stretched out before me. I'd always used words and pictures and stories to think my way through the summer nights. Now, in my mind the stories wilted in my hands and fell through my fingers like Miss J's ruined leaves. There were no words for this story I was living, or at least not any I knew yet. When the train called out its *no, no, no, no*, that was the only word that came to mind. No.

I saw where I was. At the edge of a deep dark place, barely holding on. The worst part was I now saw how my mother was to blame. She had saved herself, bully for her, but she'd left me to Daddy so he wouldn't come after her. She'd absconded, casting me off like the extra scarf she'd kept in the glove compartment of the green Ford. I was her ransom. If she'd snatched me up with the grocery list that night she never came back, he'd have tracked her down for sure. I tried to bury what she had done in a dark basement of my mind. I tried to lock it up in a box, the way Daddy locked up his Nighthawk things. But you always knew the box was down there and that the spiders were building their messy webs all around it. It was not something you could forget or make to disappear. It was real and it always waited for you in its secret place because it always knew you'd come back for it.

That night I knew for the first time that I could just let go of the edge and fall in and sink to the bottom and never come up. Once, many years ago, it happened to a girl who went to my camp. They tell the story of how she just jumped into the lake one bright morning like everybody else and then, no girl, just a disturbance in the water, and after that, nothing. The lake folded over her like a fresh sheet over a bed, smooth and untroubled. It was a mountain lake and deep. They never found her. Now, sometimes campers think they see her floating on her back right under the surface of the water. Her mouth is open and she looks like she is trying to tell them something.

But I have another story for the lost girl. She was a fine swimmer who could hold her breath for a good long time. She swam underwater to a far island, and she came up on a golden shore where camp went on forever and ever, and there were no parents and no boxes and no headache sticks and no hot hands. She took up her new life like a queenly mantle and lived happily ever after.

I held my arm close, and I tried to think small. I tried to think about tomorrow. I'd see Zenie and Mimi and maybe Eva too. I could tell Mimi thank you for sending me to camp, which ought to make her day. I figured I could hide my shoulder from Zenie and Mimi, but I ought to avoid Eva because, being left-handed, how could I write or draw diagrams? When I moved, it felt gravelly inside like a little mouse was in there gnawing away. My shoulder felt like it had set in to throb all the night long, but I was betting that out in the daylight I could do almost everything else in a normal-looking way. So I fell into a jittery sleep thinking about how to fool them. Make them think I was all right. I was thinking too that if I pretended enough to be all right, maybe I would get that way. The Power of Positive Thinking, Sherry the counselor would tell us when we were trying to do something that was hard, like hike up a mountain or saddle a biting horse.

Her ponytail would bounce when she said it. Maybe I would grow a ponytail.

The next morning Daddy had to go over to Greenwood for a meeting of Mississippi Assurance agents, so he woke me up at the crack of dawn to drop me off at Zenie's. It was barely light and he looked like he'd just gotten home. The clothes he'd had on the night before had smudges on them. There were half moons under the arms of his khaki shirt. He smelled like vinegar and smoke and whiskey; and his hair, which had gotten too long, was weighted down with oil, though not Mr. Holcomb's sweet oil, but the oil of Daddy's own dirty head.

He stomped into my room. "Get up, Sister. Come on, let's go." That's all he said. When I turned over in the bed, my shoulder gave out a sickening crunch, which woke me up good and proper. I was so worn out I could barely pull myself out of the sack. I didn't brush my teeth or wash my face or pull the sheets off the bed the way I'd planned. I was already sleeping in my clothes so I just crawled out of bed, grabbed my sack of dirty clothes with my good hand, and followed Daddy out of the door without a word. He didn't look at me, nor I at him. As I followed him down the path to the car, my arm and shoulder revved up again, throbbing each time I set foot on one of Mama's stepping-stones.

I had gotten Daddy to let me leave my bag on Mimi's front porch on the way over to Zenie's. When he dropped me in front of Zenie's and scratched off, his elbow out the window and a Lucky Strike in his mouth, I hoped he would have a fiery wreck and die so I'd never have to see him again. That is your father, I said to myself. Your *father*, I said again, just so my murderous self would listen up. Honor thy father and thy mother that thy days may be long on the land the Lord Thy God hath given thee. But the man who drove away didn't seem like anybody's anything. Much less a father.

I could tell by looking at the front of the place that Zenie and them weren't up yet. The new day's sun was just now creeping out with its heat coming on before it actually broke through. It was too early to knock, so I sat down on the front stoop and waited for some sign of life inside. I held my arm down to my side. I needed some Bayer bad. I hoped Zenie had some. Even Ray, who left early in the mornings to beat the heat while he did yards all over town, seemed to be still in bed.

All I wanted was to crawl onto Zenie's couch. What sleep I had gotten the night before seemed snatched by the hardest from the heat and the trains and the agitated night outside the screen of my window. I kept thinking I needed to pay attention to something out there in the dark, but whatever it was, it seemed to be hiding itself Bomba-style in thickets of nandinas and crape myrtle, which were now blooming their hearts out, it being well into July. I couldn't depart from the feeling that I needed to listen harder and be more watchful for what was coming. I wondered if Mary and them felt like this while they were hanging around Jesus' tomb waiting for him to make good on his promise to come back to them. One thing I'd gotten to be an expert in by this time was waiting, like right now what I was waiting for was just a flick of the curtain at Zenie's front window. You had to wait with your heart and eyes and ears all open. Otherwise you might miss The One when it tiptoed in, and it might tiptoe right back out. You were supposed to be ready with a smile and a glass of iced tea with mint. You needed to be ready to help it come on in, if it needed help. In one of the *Clarion-Ledgers* Daddy had stacked up in our living room I'd read about how Medgar Evers's wife and little children had waited up for him the night he came home and got shot in his own driveway. When Mrs. Evers and the children heard the shot and came running out, they found their dear one in a pool of his own blood. But what if they had listened so hard for his car that they would have heard it driving up the street? What if they had opened their side door to the carport just a second sooner, right at the very moment their beloved drove up, would the murderer have said calf rope, called it off, for worry of hitting two boys and a girl and their mother? Just a second can be life or death. Off and on I worried that my mother would try to come back for me and if I didn't wait with enough care, I would miss her tapping oh so lightly on the window screen for me. Then she would leave and I would miss her forever.

I walked out into Zenie's yard and folded myself up under Miss Josephine's mimosa tree, which had new green shoots of leaves coming on strong to replace the ones she'd pulled off to count. I lay down under it, my head on my elbow, and watched Zenie's front window. Then I must have dropped off because I began to dream that Medgar Evers's black blood and my white blood had gotten mixed together. Now that he was gone, it was his blood I carried inside of me. I felt it move, slow and sure, heart to legs to belly. That's what Daddy and his friends thought: that Medgar Evers had to die so my white-girl blood could flow easeful. Top to bottom, in and out. But why and to what end?

Now, the flick of the curtain. Such a little thing that I almost missed it. Zenie opened the door a crack. She was still wearing her nightgown, her face in shadow. Then she moved forward into the dim morning light. She had a frown on her face, then a half smile. "What it doing out here?" she demanded. "Sleeping under my tree like a tramp." When I got up from the ground and went over to her, she actually gave me a big hug, which sent a jolt through my shoulder. I didn't want her to see me wince, so I burrowed my face into the front of her nightgown. Once I got in between her bosoms, I didn't want to leave. She smelled like Alba lotion and sleep. "Whoa, horse!" she said in an aggravated whisper. "Get off of me, girl!" She pushed me away and frowned.

"Weren't expecting you this early in the morning. We got company. Now be careful and don't wake nobody up. They all dead to the world."

That's when I got a good look at her. I'd gotten a vacation at camp, but it looked like she'd been wallowing in hell headfirst. There was a big exclamation point between her eyebrows, a long up and down line with a hole under it, right between the eyes. There were two parentheses that ran down the sides of her mouth to her chin line, and dark smudges under her eyes. Now, with the sootiness around her eyes and the creamy brown of her cheeks, her face had turned into two different colors. In the two weeks I'd been gone, she looked as if she'd grown a permanent mask.

When I tiptoed through the front room to the kitchen, I could see in the dim light that people were sleeping every which way around and about on Zenie's living-room floor. I almost tripped over them. Young people. Eva had sure gathered a lot of friends in the time I'd been gone. Then it hit me. Maybe they were here to learn the trade of selling encyclopedias in Millwood before hitting the big cities, like Greenwood and Jackson and Meridian. Eva had a knack. She'd won bonuses for selling. She must be teaching them the trade.

Zenie came in right behind me. "Don't worry about them there. They just visiting."

I sat down at the kitchen table and she started boiling the coffee. "They selling encyclopedias too?" I whispered the question.

Zenie's back was to me. She finished setting up the percolator on the front eye of the stove and came over to the other side of the table and sat down. The water under the coffeepot started to hiss. "They just visiting is all. One thing you got to promise. Don't tell your daddy we got all this company up here."

"Why not?" She didn't have to worry, but I was curious.

"He think too many folks in this house he might not let you come up and see me no more." Her face slammed shut, and I saw how the lines had come about. "He might not like you being in the house around so much black."

She was right, I'd gotten wise to Daddy's ways. He would hate me stepping over Negroes scattered about on the floor like branches cut from a tree. He might decide they were outside agitators and would just love the excuse to come riding up on his white horse and save me from them. Which would cause Zenie and them no end of grief. That much I knew.

"I won't tell him."

"You be sorry if you do. We all be sorry. You not supposed to be up here this early in the morning no how." She glared at me for a minute.

"I won't tell him. I swear on the B-i-b-l-e." I spelled it firm and clear and stared deep into Zenie's penny eyes. Grandpops had told me to only make promises you could keep. I could keep this one until hell froze over.

She could see that. She stood up from the table. "All right now, what sound good to eat? You get any supper out of that daddy of yours yesterday evening?" She kept her voice low.

"What do *you* think?" At camp, I'd discovered that the smarty-pants voice I heard in my head was starting to come out of my mouth more and more often, in little punctuated puffs blown out like cigarette smoke.

"Shhh. Don't wake up the world. Guess you good and hungry then. Let's see what I can find to tide you over. Want to get some sewing done before we go on up the street to you-know-who's."

She left me sitting at the table while she went back into her and Ray's room. A few minutes later, she was back in her regular white outfit and the white elastic hose she wore to work. The ringlets were gone from her hair. It was slicked back with oil. She smelled like fresh Alba. She set about warming some cold biscuits from the night before and stirring up a batch of milk gravy she made from lard and milk and flour in her iron skillet.

The gravy was bubbling when Eva glided into the kitchen without a sound. She was wearing a seersucker robe and had big blue rollers all over her head. Her face was scrubbed and shiny, no lipstick or rouge. She looked like a high-school girl.

"Look here what the cat dragged in." She whapped me on top of my bad shoulder. It was a friendly whap, but it sent sparks flying through my shoulder and I flinched from the hurt of it.

She peered at me through her cat-eye glasses. "What's wrong with you? You jumpy, girl."

"Shhh," Zenie said.

"Nothing's wrong with me." I pulled my elbow into my side and grabbed it to hold back the throbbing. "How you doing?"

"Staying alive, girl, that's about it. Worn out though, I'll tell you, worn out sure enough." She pulled out a chair and plopped down.

Zenie looked down at Eva and made a sound in her throat.

When Eva sat down at the table, I didn't get up to go to the living room the way I usually did to let her eat her breakfast in peace. Usually, if I were sitting at the table, Zenie looked at me a certain way when Eva came in for her breakfast, which meant I was supposed to go sit in the front room and not bother them while Eva ate fast and Zenie sat with her and drank coffee. But that morning there were so many people on the floor I couldn't even get to the couch. I hoped she and Zenie wouldn't notice I was still there and keep on talking. I didn't want to go out on the front stoop again, and there was no place else to go, unless they wanted me to go hop in the bed with Miss J or Ray, which, to tell the truth, I wouldn't have minded doing. My old tiredness had come back in spades, and my stomach was doing flip-flops. I felt dismal.

Eva eyed me. "So, Flo, don't guess you did any studying at that fancy camp of yours?"

I grinned. After two weeks at camp where it was "Flo" this and "Flo" that, it was homelike to hear Eva speak the new name she alone had christened me with. To my mind it was snappy and smart and sounded like the heroine of a story. Zenie never called me anything but *you* or *it*. I said, "I read some books."

"You lying."

I was too tired to lie a second time so I didn't say anything.

"Well, get your pencils sharp, girl. Your vacation is over," Eva said with relish. "We start back to work this afternoon when I get home. Hope you didn't let everything I taught you fly right out of your head."

My arm throbbed as if the very idea of writing pained it. "Let's start tomorrow. I'm worn out today."

Eva's eyebrows went up. "What time you get in last night? You look like roadkill. Smell like it too."

"Late," I lied for the second time.

Eva shook her head no. "Flo, we got to get the move on, girl. It's now or never. You're behind schedule and I've got to catch you up. It's already July." With that, she put her head down on the table and in a second was back asleep.

When the coffee was ready, Zenie poured herself a cup and finished the gravy and poured it over the biscuits. She made two plates. Over in the corner of the kitchen was her sewing-machine table and beside it the card table she kept for her sewing paraphernalia. The card table was piled high with braid and rickrack and blue serge. I knew she was up early making some Carver High School band uniforms because she did it every July about this time for the new children in the band. I wondered what it would be like to wear the scratchy material buttoned up to your chin and blow on a big instrument, maybe a tuba, and jive march around a football field in a perfect formation. For me, it was like trying to imagine flying.

Zenie took one chair from the kitchen table and pulled it over to the card table and pushed her stack of stuff off to the side. She got one plate, steam rising, and put it in the bare spot. Then, wiping her hands on a dish towel, she cut an eye at me and whispered, "You. Come on over here and eat this before it gets cold. Don't spill anything on my stuff." I got up and went over.

Then she plopped the other plate down on the kitchen table in front of Eva and thumped her on the head. Eva rose up bleary eyed and looked at her plate on the kitchen table and mine next to it on the card table. Our chairs were so close they were almost touching, but we were back to back and eating at different tables. She looked back and forth between them. "If this doesn't beat all," she snorted. Then she hit the top of the table. "If this isn't ridiculous, I don't know what is!" She glared at Zenie and rolled her eyes.

Zenie ignored her and sat down at the sewing machine. "Five down, five to go," she said, and started in on another uniform she had pinned up and laid out on top of the sewing machine. It wasn't even seven o'clock, but already so hot I could see sweat bead up in the creases around her mouth.

Eva put a bite of biscuit in her mouth and got up and poured herself some coffee and sat back down. She looked over her shoulder at me. "You're not much company this morning."

I had biscuit in my mouth and was chewing fast because it was too hot. Otherwise I would have mentioned the fact that you can't very well talk to somebody who's asleep.

"What kind of fancy camping things did you do? Have yourself a bonfire and cook up some weenies on a stick? Tell ghost stories? You sleep on the cold ground? What they feed you camping?" She gave me the once over. "Look like plenty, whatever it was."

Zenie stopped sewing and gave Eva the evil eye. I looked down. Below my dirty shorts my legs were spread out and lumping over the sides of the chair like blobs of bread dough. Between them was the now-sweaty lump of Kotex, which I needed to get rid of now that it was morning. I shoved another mouthful of biscuit and gravy in my mouth and chewed.

"Gone to camp a chatting fool, come back the Sphinx. You too full of yourself to tell some camping stories? Man alive, must be nice to get out of this place here. Got yourself a nice change of scenery."

The questions were darts and I was the board. "It was nice," I said. "It was better than nice. I wished I could have stayed there forever. I didn't ever want to come back here. I hate this place."

Eva and Zenie both looked hard at me and blinked.

"Well, it's delightful knowing you too, girlfriend," Eva hissed. "And I expect that's your way of saying thank you so much, Zenie, for the delicious breakfast."

Zenie looked hard at Eva. "She tired. Leave her be."

"*She's* tired. She doesn't know the name of tired. Walk in my shoes all day trying to sell knowledge door to door in this heat and you know tired."

"Maybe tired folks ought to stay home nights and get some rest for their tiredness." Zenie's mouth went thin and tight. "Maybe then they not get out of bed on the wrong side."

Eva took a big slurp of coffee. "Maybe those ones that got some backbone need to get out at night and work for them that don't. Maybe that's what's making the working ones so tired. They're carrying all of the rest of y'all on their shoulders."

"Nobody carrying *me*. Nobody carrying *me* no place. Truth be told, if anybody's getting carried around here, it sure ain't *me*." Zenie stood up straight and tall from the sewing machine, knocking over the stool she was sitting on and leaving part of a half-sewn uniform hanging by a thread on the needle. She turned to me. "Come on, you." Then she stormed out of the kitchen, stepped over a couple of pairs of legs on the living-room floor, opened the front door, and looked back at me. "Come *on*."

I shoved the rest of the biscuit in my mouth, grabbed another, and followed. Here I had to get up from eating a perfectly good breakfast! Meanwhile, the cause of it all, Miss Ugly, fell back to her breakfast and ignored the fact that we were walking out on her.

"Bye, Eva," I said under my breath to the blue rollers as I went past the back of her head. She didn't turn around and she didn't answer. Maybe she didn't hear me, or maybe she was too mad at Zenie. Whatever she might have said, could have said, she didn't say it. She didn't say a word.

I was half out the front door when I looked back one last time at Eva sitting in the kitchen. In that moment she turned her head and eyeballed me dead-on. "You. Flo. Miss Smarty Pants. Don't think you're getting out of that lesson this afternoon." She wagged her finger in my direction. "I've got some sentences that are going to knock your socks off. You'll be diagramming till midnight."

I smiled and waved with my good arm, relieved that she wasn't mad at me too. Maybe I could diagram with my right hand.

By the time I got out the door, Zenie had already headed for Mimi's. She was huffing and puffing. Her nurse's shoes kicked up dust in the street. I followed along but stayed a good house length behind her. I didn't want to get mixed up in her fuss with Eva. I was back to being worn out.

My stack of dirty clothes was still sitting on the front porch. Zenie sighed. "Sheet day," she said under her breath.

"I'll do it," I said. Zenie would think it strange if I didn't help with the sheets. I was already wet in my head and under my arms. Way past needing Mum. "Let me get a drink of cold water first."

Sheet day wasn't much of a to-do anymore. Just Mimi's bed and a few of her clothes and towels. No shirts for Grandpops to come back starched and stacked and folded just so, one for each day of the week except Saturday with an extra for a wedding or a funeral or if he spilled something at noon dinner.

Upstairs, the door to Grandpops' bedroom lay open just a crack, but not so you could see in. I touched the door to open it more and saw the dark bed with its knobby white spread. The bed seemed to stretch out longer and wider than it did when he was alive. I pulled the door back to where it had been and went on into Mimi's room. She'd left a note saying she had gone to school for a summer teachers' meeting. Her bed was unmade because of sheet day, so I just pulled off the sheets and pillowcases with my right hand. I went into the bathroom and got her laundry basket out of the closet. There weren't as many clothes in it as there used to be. Since Grandpops had died, Mimi dragged around the house in the same old blue polka-dot brunch coat. Zenie said she was sick to death of that ugly-as-sin brunch coat. She said that Mimi was so attached to it, she wouldn't be surprised if Mimi wore it when she went back to teaching school in September. I pulled the towels off the racks, laid the sheets out on the bathroom floor, put the rest of the stuff inside and, taking care with my shoulder, tied it up like a picnic sack. I kicked it down the steps and out the front door. I untied the knot and put my camp clothes inside with Mimi's things and then tied it back.

Zenie appeared behind the screen door. Her arm came out with some cup towels. "Here, put these in too."

I untied the knot again and stuck them in. The white pile stood ready for Uldine to pick up. She'd be getting all my stinking camp stuff, more than she bargained for. All wrapped up like a bad surprise in the lavender-scented sheets from Mimi's bed.

While Zenie was fixing midday dinner, I went upstairs and

started rooting around the bathroom for more Bayer. Nothing on the lower shelves. I got a stepping stool from Grandpops' study and brought it in to stand on so as to reach the top shelf. Behind a bunch of cough syrup and, glory be, the Bayer, was a little row of empty paregoric bottles. Somebody had spent time lining them up just so. They were so neatly lined up, they looked like they belonged in a communion tray. Somebody had been doping, the way Uncle Nash, Mimi's wounded brother, used to do before Mimi and Grandpops sent him back to the veterans hospital, where I guessed he still was. In his heyday, Uncle Nash specialized in drinking from little brown sacks in public, lolling about with the other dopers under Nathan Bedford Forrest's horse on the town square. If he recognized you, he'd holler your name at you when you walked by. This was a secret doper, though, and I wondered why he or she hadn't thrown away the bottles and how long they had been there.

My shoulder was hurting worse plus my stomach was turning over in an odd way, so I snatched up the Bayer. I munched three down, ran some water from the lavatory into my hand and swallowed it with the grit. Then I ran water in the tub and got in. I scrubbed myself from stem to stern and then, surprise surprise, went right to sleep in the tub now full of brownish-gray water. I dreamed something was coming. It was coming sure enough and soon. I saw the word *Apocalypse*, which, thanks to Eva and Phonics, I could sound out, blazoned across a dark sky. I saw fiery furnaces and misshapen monsters and terrible renderings. Then all at once my mother appeared before me in an angel getup, wings and all. She looked silly but she wasn't smiling. She was saying something about packing my bag. "Hurry. Get ready," she said, "there's a terrible storm coming." Then I heard it roar, then it was upon us, calling out for Medgar Evers's blood and then for my blood too, and I knew we were all lost forever in the storm.

17

I'd slept in the tub awhile, I don't know how long. I woke up to Zenie standing over me hollering Lordy Mercy, which made me wonder if I was dying like Grandpops had. Mimi was just coming into her bedroom next door with a stack of books and she dropped them with a crash and came running. She burst in on us, me just waking up in the water and wondering what Zenie was having such a fit about. I'd woken up in a shiver. The water had gone cold.

Mimi took one look. "It's her shoulder. Look at her shoulder! She's knocked herself out! Don't let her go under!"

Zenie hollered back at her, "Call the doctor! Call the doctor!"

When I opened my eyes and sat straight up in the tub and said "What's the matter? What are y'all yelling about?" they jumped back like I was Lazarus rising from the dead. The water in the tub was still a brownish gray and, when I looked down, what I could see of my shoulder was a deep purple with red streaks running down my arm like blood.

When I saw them staring down at me, I covered myself as best I could with the washcloth.

"Oh Lord," Mimi whispered.

"Get on up out of that bathtub," Zenie said. She took a towel off the rack and handed it to me. They trooped out in single file.

When I came out of the bathroom in Mimi's brunch coat, they were waiting for me in Mimi's room. She was rocking in her rocker hard and fast. Zenie paced the floor in front of the little fireplace. Their mouths were one thin line with no subject and no predicate.

"Come here, Florence," Mimi called to me from the rocker. "Come in here to me."

I walked into the room and stood before them. The way they looked at me made me sweat.

"Come on over here by me," Mimi said. She was rocking so hard her chair was moving across the floor and making the rug pucker up in its path. Zenie kept on pacing. I went on over and stood beside Mimi, keeping my toes back from her rockers. Zenie walked over to us.

"Let me see that shoulder again," Mimi said.

"It's all right," I mumbled, backing up.

Zenie moved in behind me. "Let her see it."

I unbuttoned three buttons of the brunch coat and let down the side over my hurt shoulder. Zenie reached out and took the brunch coat down farther in the back. I held it over my chest while they looked.

"Turn around." Mimi's voice was like ice on my bare skin.

I turned around and there was a deep silence. Mimi stopped rocking and stood up and walked around to my front again. Then she went back around. She touched a place in the middle of my back and I flinched. Suddenly Zenie came up on my left side and took hold of my left arm and held it out for Mimi to look at. On it the marks of my father's hand were outlined finger by finger in bluish red.

Then the two of them started up. Mimi started it with clicking her tongue; then Zenie started humming, not a song but just a low hum like a motor. They stood there for a minute like two strange insects tuning up for the long night ahead, clicking and humming. Then they stopped all at once. Zenie smoothed down my hair, which was drying every which way, and Mimi took my arm between her two soft hands. She took it in the careful, even way you'd take a little baby from another person.

"Honey, does it hurt when you move your arm?" Mimi asked.

"Not too much."

"Can you move your shoulder around all right?" She touched the front of my shoulder with her fingertips. I moved away from her hand. "It's not broken, is it?"

"No ma'am." I was as quiet and gentle with my answers as she was with her questions. I moved my arm in as much of a circle as I could stand. "It's all right."

I was holding my breath for the big question. I had my story ready to roll out the way they rolled out the Bugs Bunny cartoons down at the Lyric Theater. It was exciting and funny. I'd heard a scary noise in the night, so I got up to see, and then, *bam*, I ran smack-dab into the door going to the bathroom in the middle of the night. So hard I almost knocked myself down. It was so dark. No moon at all. As to the imprint of Daddy's fingers, I'd say he grabbed my left arm in the car when he had to slam on the brakes.

But they didn't ask it. They just looked at each other, then back at me. "All right now," said Mimi finally. "Go on and find something to put on. I'm going to call the doctor."

I whipped around and glared at her. "No! I said it's all right! See?" I gritted my teeth and wiggled my arm around to show her.

"I . . . I'll run away if you call the doctor." I knew that Daddy would kill me sure enough if a doctor got into it.

I went on out, and Mimi shut the door behind me. There was a rise and fall of voices, Mimi's unraveling like a ball of yarn, Zenie's firm and steady. Then they came out and Zenie went downstairs to finish up dinner, which was going to be late because of all the commotion.

Mimi hardly said a word during the meal, except, "Thank you, Lord, for these and all our blessings, amen," leaving out, I noticed, the *many* in front of *blessings* and the *In Jesus' name* in front of *amen*. She said the blessing all in one breath. The words ran together so that they seemed like one long drawn-out word. We ate fast, chicken and dumplings, which was one of my favorites, but Zenie's dumplings seemed to have too much Crisco. They fell heavy in the well and seemed to swell once they hit bottom.

When Zenie was clearing the plates, Mimi turned to me at the table. "Florence, I want you to carry you down to New Orleans with me for a week or so to see my sister Mabel. She's sick and she may need our help. I need you to go with me." The way she said it, the way it was a song she already knew by heart, made her sound like the little wren that sang to Grandpops and me on our way home from Zenie's. Busy and cheerful and full of vim and vigor. The hop, skip, and jump of her voice didn't go with the mouth it was coming out of, which looked like Mama's when she tasted a bad egg in the batter.

I knew what she was up to. She wanted to fly the coop with me, get me away from Daddy. The shoulder had had its own story to tell. I was all for the Mabel idea, except for Mama. What if she came back to Millwood for me and I was nowhere to be found? How would we ever find each other again? I was opening my mouth to ask those questions when they glided unsaid back down my throat like Zenie's burdensome dumplings. What did I care? Mama was the one who'd gone on the lam, left her only child with a batch of greased cake pans and no ingredients left in the kitchen to make so much as a simple pound cake. I'd like to be a fly on the wall when she came tiptoeing back in to find me absconded, lock, stock, and barrel. I'd take all my books, so she'd know I was never coming back.

While Mimi said her little speech about going to New Orleans, Zenie had been standing in the doorway to the kitchen, Mimi's dirty plate in one hand, mine in the other. I looked at her, then back at Mimi. They were waiting for my answer. My throat closed up, but I nodded. All right. All right.

"Good," Mimi said, "I'll talk to your father and I'll go out this afternoon and get the tires checked. How does tomorrow morning sound?"

I nodded again.

"All right. We'll start out right after breakfast. We'll have our clean clothes back by then and we can pack up here." She paused. "You stay up here with me tonight. I may need some help getting ready. Is there anything you need from your house you can't do without for the next few weeks? We can go get it right now, right this minute."

I almost said my books, but then I shook my head no. I could leave the books. There were other books and other stories. There was nothing there that I hadn't read a million times. I was sick to death of those stories. I felt like a leaf before the wind. I took a breath. It came out a sigh.

"All right, then. All right," she said. Then she looked over at Zenie. "And Zenie here is going to get her first paid vacation."

"Be my first and probably be my last," Zenie said scornfully, and then turned and took the dishes into the kitchen.

Mimi went on upstairs and I could hear drawers slamming

and her voice on the phone. She was calling her school, saying she had urgent business in New Orleans, she couldn't do the summer civics workshop next week, get a substitute. No, she didn't know how long. It was a family emergency. She'd let them know. Then she called the bank and told them she'd be coming by later and wanted to get into Grandpops' safety deposit box. She needed to cash out a bond. Then I heard her rummaging around in her closet.

In the kitchen Zenie had started washing the dishes. Unlike Mama, Zenie was a good dish washer. She didn't mess around. She used a rough cloth and lots of detergent and steel wool when necessary. I never had to send a dish back. I got up from my seat and went into the kitchen. I took up a dish towel to dry, but Zenie shook her head. "You better favor that shoulder for a while," she said. I sat down in her chair and watched her work. After she was done, I ran some water in a glass and took two more Bayer and headed for Grandpops' velvet chair in the living room. The chair held my imprint now. I turned to my right, curled up. I shut my eyes and the minute I did, I got a picture in my head of my mother in the kitchen baking. She had on her sweetheart rose apron and it wasn't burned and her bangs were standing straight up like she had been sweating and wiped her brow with the back of her hand the way she used to. She was watching a double boiler of icing that was almost ready to take off the fire. When I opened my eyes, Zenie had come into the living room and was standing in front of the fireplace. Behind her was a picture of a field of goldenrod in a scalloped gold-leaf frame. The way she was standing, her head was right in the middle of the picture. When I gazed up at her, her head looked crowned in gold.

"If your mama come back before you do, I'll tell her where you gone to," she said after a minute. "I'll tell her you down in one of them honky-tonks in New Orleans and she better get herself on down there and carry you home before you get yourself into trouble." She smiled at her own joke.

I sat up in the chair. "I ain't worried."

"Worried or not worried, I'm going to tell her to go down there and get you and carry you on home. Or maybe she just stay down there and keep you out of trouble."

"She ain't coming back I don't think."

"Some do and some don't, but your mama's the kind that do."

I couldn't see how Zenie would bet on Mama coming back. The way she was so sure made me want to smash a wall. Nancy Drew needed evidence to say something was true and so did I, and there just plain wasn't any. Not even a clue one way or the other.

"You tell her then, and we'll see what she does. We'll just see." I shut my eyes tight and curled up in the chair. I could feel tears slinking out of the corners of my eyes, clotting the velvet. I turned my face into the corner of the chair. It felt good and cool on my cheek.

"There lot worse things than taking a nice trip down to New Orleans," Zenie said. "Wish me and Ray could take a nice trip like that. Have us a second honeymoon."

I tucked myself back into the chair and shut my eyes. After a minute, I heard her go back into the kitchen.

Then I started seeing strange things in the golden field of flowers over the mantel. There was a jungle in it and the jungle was on fire. All the trees were burning. Everywhere there were people and poor frightened animals running before the fire, dangling from burning branches, until the glittery gold blaze took them and made them curl up like dead leaves.

The next thing I knew my eyes popped wide open and there was Daddy full blown before me in the middle of the living room pacing and stewing. I heard the back screen door squeak and close and I knew Zenie was long gone without so much as an all right now, good-bye until tomorrow, slipping out like a cool breeze before the storm.

He smelled like smoke and fried fish. His voice was hoarse, like he'd been talking nonstop. He said, "Come on, Sister, roll out of that sack. Don't you ever do nothing but sleep? Lazy as they come. I'm going to put you to work. I need you to fold some letters and put them in envelopes."

I didn't even try to imagine folding letters and getting them into envelopes with one hand. I hopped up like a chittery bird and sang out, "Mimi wants to talk to you, Mimi wants to talk to you."

He was halfway out the front door. "What for?"

I hopped around him and went for the stairs. "I don't know, but she does. I'll go get her." I said it as I headed up. These days Mimi was getting harder and harder to wake up, so on my way up the steps I hollered out, "Mimi, Mimi," just to get her started. I grabbed my arm to my side and ran on up the rest of the steps.

When I burst into her room hollering, she was curled up in her usual way in her slip, with a bit of the spread pulled over her fin feet. She had on her white hairnet. "What, what!" She rolled over and glared in my direction, her eyes pinkish and mean.

I was huffing and puffing. "Daddy's here! He's downstairs. I told him you wanted to talk to him. He wants me to go on home with him right now. Come on downstairs. You need to come on down and talk to him and tell him about taking me to Aunt Mabel's."

"All right, all right, go on down and tell him to wait. I'll be down in a minute, when I get dressed. Where's Zenie? Is she still down there?"

I shook my head no. I backed up but didn't leave her room.

She sat up and shuffled around with her feet for her bedroom shoes. "Go on now. Shut the door. Let me get some clothes on."

I shut her door and stood outside it for a while. I could hear Daddy pacing the floor downstairs. Then he hollered for me to come on, he didn't have all day. I came down the steps slow. I was trying to buy Mimi time to get dressed and get on down there.

He was standing at the bottom of the steps looking up. "Come on," he said, "she can talk to me another time. You got work to do."

"She's coming in a minute." I stayed on the midway landing where the stairs changed direction. "She said for you to hold your horses. She said to tell you it's important."

"If it's so all-fired important, why don't she get on down here?" He shifted from one foot to the other as he looked up at me. Then he clumped on over to the front door. "Come on. I'll call her on the phone."

"Wait. I'll get her." I flew back up the stairs before he could say no.

When I burst into Mimi's room for the second time, she had on the blue brunch coat. The hairnet lay on her pillow. She sat frozen on the bed facing the door. She licked her lips several times. "Come on," I said, "he's waiting for you but he's in a tearing hurry. Come on now. He's going to carry me home with him if you don't get on down there."

She was so still she didn't seem to be breathing. I took her arm with my good hand and pulled. "Come *on*."

Then she came to life and took a shaky breath. "All right, *all right*. Let go of me." She swatted at my hand and stood up.

We went down the steps together, her in front ready to scurry back up. I followed on her heels, collie dog to sheep, over the bridge out to the open road.

He was clumping back and forth in the middle of the living room.

"Win," Mimi said in a little girl's voice. "How you doing?"

"Fine." He looked at her and stopped pacing. "Listen, Miss Irene, I'm in a hurry here."

"Sit down, Win, I want to talk to you a minute." Mimi licked her lips again. "The thing is my sister Mabel. You remember Mabel, the heavy one down in New Orleans? She's been real sick. In and out of the hospital. I wanted to take Florence and go down to take care of her. I really need for Florence to go with me to help out with poor Mabel. I can't lift her by myself. Just until after Labor Day when school starts. Just a few more weeks." She said it the way you'd tell someone the best idea you ever had. "You don't mind, do you? It's a terrible situation, and Florence would be such a help."

Daddy had sat down in Grandpops' chair. He was trying to sit on the edge, which was close to impossible because it was a chair that took you in. Mimi was on the couch and I had pressed myself up against her soft hip.

Daddy's eyes narrowed. "No," he said. Just no. No excuse, no I'm sorry can't spare her myself right now.

Mimi colored up. "But Win, I really need her. And after all she's been through, a change of scenery would be good for her. Please think about it. *Please*. Just think about it."

Daddy glared at Mimi. "I want her here. She's all I got now."

I felt Mimi stiffen up. She turned to me. "Honey, step outside."

I gladly went out onto the porch. I sat down on the swing where I could watch them through the window. Mimi's back and the back of her head as she sat on the couch. Daddy's face. At first Mimi's voice quavered. Then it started to walk on water. I couldn't catch most of the words but I heard her say: either you do this or I do that. I saw Daddy's face turn sour then furious then sly. I heard him say: don't you tell me what. I know what you want

to do. You want to take my girl. Well, you just try it. Then he
came storming out the front door onto the porch and said to me,
"Come on, you." His hands were fists and the veins in his neck
were ropes. He looked madder than I'd ever seen him look, mad
enough to tear a house down and kill everybody in it. I thought
about making a run for it. I knew I could outrun him, but I didn't
know what would happen after that, after he'd called his friends.
I followed him like he'd put a choke collar on me, tail between
my legs, on the way to getting tied up in the yard again. As I got
up from the swing, I could see the back of Mimi's head, which
was bent down like a lily. She still was sitting on the couch. She
didn't turn around. The back of her hair was smushed flat where
she'd slept on it.

Daddy had the front seat of the Valiant piled high with papers
and envelopes, so I got in the backseat right behind him, which I
preferred anyhow so as to keep out of reach of his mean hands. I
looked out the window toward Mimi's, but I could barely see the
outline of the house, the back window of the car was so thick
with dirt. I looked hard at the back of Daddy's head. His neck
was a red clay brown, deep burnt from day after day of knocking at people's front doors and saying words they didn't want to
hear. Give yourself and your loved ones a decent burial. Only fifty
cents a week. Seventy-five a couple. Between his hairline and his
collar the little crisscross lines ran this way and that. Distances
traveled, miles and miles of tracks going and coming. When had
the first one been laid down? When he was the firstborn boy
gathering his mother's pretty speckled eggs on the farm out in
the county? Watching out for snakes in the henhouses? When he
took each of his four little brothers fishing for the first time? I'd
seen pictures of Daddy when he was little. He was small for his
age, with a shock of wavy tar-colored hair and one big shoe. He
was holding on to a little beagle hound with dragging tits. When

she'd get out of her pen, his dad would make him drown the pups. It was the right thing to do, Daddy told me once, because they had bad bloodlines. Who knew what was in them?

One day when his mother went to the doctor for a pain in her belly that had had her doubled over for a week and was sent straight out to Mill County Hospital without even getting to pack her own suitcase, never to come home again, his black-haired dad began to think the same thing about his younger brothers, the four of them being all towheads. My father's hair saved him, for it was the exact color of his dad's and had the thickness and the curl to boot. As the oldest, younger than I was now, he would stash his bright-headed little brothers around the house and barn when he would hear his dad's pickup whip up the long gravel driveway late in the night. His mother died before the next harvest, quilted through and through with lines and needles. Daddy visited her in the hospital just once with his brothers. They all lined up before her like crops in a row. She looked at him and rasped in a voice he didn't recognize, "Win, you got to take care of the boys. You got to. Promise me."

He promised and he tried, he told Mama, really he did try, but there were too many of them and not enough of him. He had to let them go to the state after a while. There was one he kept, Donnie the littlest, but it didn't turn out well. His father didn't get him, but Daddy stashed him in the wrong place one night. Daddy didn't know about the loose board in the loft or the bad nail. Of course Donnie was barefooted, Daddy had snatched him up from the bed the minute the gravel sounded (in those days Daddy slept in his shoes). He ran as fast as his bad foot would allow to the barn, half dragging, half carrying little Donnie. Shoved him up there with the hay bales. Donnie knew to keep quiet, even with a rusty nail in his foot. In a month he was gone, jaw locked shut, eyes hollow and surprised. Once Daddy told Mama he wished he'd just let the old man beat Donnie that one time.

But maybe, Daddy said to both of us one night out of the blue, Donnie was just not meant to live. Maybe his dad was right after all. Maybe Donnie wasn't a real Forrest and the blood will win out. When Daddy said that, Mama had looked nervously at me.

When we left Mimi's, Daddy had scratched off like he always did when he was mad. His hands clenched the wheel and he didn't even bother to light up the way he usually did. After a few blocks of squealing around corners the way he loved to do, he slowed down to a crawl. We were cutting across Shake Rag on the way home, though I didn't see the point of it. Shake Rag was out of the way. He cruised down Moses Street, past Lafitte's Grocery. The men sitting outside on the bench studied their feet when we drove by, their careful hats pulled down over their eyes, though anybody could see how crimped their mouths were.

When we reached a little alley of a street, Daddy took a left the way you make a nice long curve when you ice the edge of a cake, slow and easy and evenhanded. By now I was wishing he'd speed up again. The back window on my side was so coated in dust and grime that I could only see the shapes of things outside. It was stuck shut like all the windows except Daddy's. What little air there was in the car was coming in from his open window, and when he rolled along at such a snail's pace, the breeze from his window stopped. It was that time of afternoon when the heat gathers around your face like a tacky web. Shake your head, and it sticks.

I was thrown forward and then sideways when he slammed on the brakes and pulled over to the left side of the street in front of a vacant lot overgrown with weeds and wild bushes. At first I thought he'd dropped something because he leaned down and rummaged around under a pile of papers that had spilled off the front seat onto the floor below. He pulled out what he was looking for. Something metal, a tool. Now this, I thought. Now the car has broken down. Daddy never bothered to explain anything.

So, I thought, this is why he's been creeping along. I didn't want to stay in the car because it was so hot. It was beyond hot. The late-afternoon sun was ironing what was left of the day. Everything seemed ready to catch fire and burn. There was no air left to breathe in the car. I felt like a cake that'd just been shoved in the oven to bake.

Daddy opened the door of the car and got out. I was ready to follow but he told me to stay, so I stayed there behind the closed window in that oven of a car. When he got out, he left his door open a crack. Through my window's film, I could hardly see anything with the sun coming in at such a slant, but it looked like a woman standing on the dust path next to a big bush with little white flowers. I didn't really see the woman, just a shape that might or might not have been her. I could hear a buzzing through Daddy's window, maybe bees, maybe the woman, if there was one, speaking to my father, then him saying something back. They didn't exchange but a few words. I just heard her murmur something and knew by the pretty way the words lined up that she wasn't white. Then for just a second it sounded like she was singing.

But her face, if indeed she were there at all, it was hidden by his back, which was turned toward the car and me. Everything was so close, the street so narrow, and the dirty window was fogging up from my breath inside the mostly sealed car. Stupid Valiant and its stupid windows, I was thinking, I hate this stupid trash car.

Something, a quickness, caught my eye. Maybe the woman tripped or dropped something, maybe Daddy reached down to pick it up, though it hardly seemed something my father would do for a black woman unless she was paying him her burial money for that week and the coins fell between them on the sidewalk. Then the money would be his and he might pick it up.

In any case there was this quickness. Then he leaned over her and she seemed to disappear. And whatever encounter they'd had, it was over and done with in no time at all. A second or two was all, and maybe a flutter of color. Then he was back in the car, the tool nowhere in sight. When he got in behind the wheel, he turned around and looked me square in the face for a second. I seemed to be a surprise for him, as if I'd sneaked into the car while he was out of it, as if he'd forgotten I'd been there all along. I was relieved when he turned back around and scratched off and I finally got some air on my face. He wasn't even breathing hard.

It was all very ordinary, I didn't give it a second thought. All I could think about was being careful of myself with him. I was my own precious cargo. I watched how the beads of sweat trickled out from under his scalp and began to follow the crisscross railroad tracks that carved the back of his neck, which was even redder than usual from the afternoon sun. I thought, good, he's sweating, maybe now that he's hot too he'll drive faster. And he did. He tore through the streets like a tornado until he screeched to a stop in front of Big Dan and Miss Kay Linda's house.

When we'd gotten into our house, he seemed unaccountably excited. He left the keys dangling in the deadbolt lock on the door. "Sit down," he said, pointing to the kitchen table. Without looking around, he went to the bathroom. I could hear water running for a long time.

I sat on a stool next to the table and waited. I was thinking that since Grandpops was six feet under and Mimi couldn't get ahold of me and Mama was as good as dead, I was just going to have to be the most agreeable daughter alive to keep Daddy on an even keel. My plan was to say yes to everything. Absolutely every little thing.

His box was in a careless place—on the floor just inside the front door. I'd almost tripped over it when I came in. I thought I might offer to oil it for him to get him calmed down. I could do it with my right hand.

When he came back into the kitchen, he was scrubbed rosy from stem to stern; even his hair shone. He had on a new set of clothes. He sat down across from me at the table. He looked at me straight on, and his eyes flared up. He reached into his pocket. "Sister, you got a birthday coming up in September and I'm going to give you an early present." He pulled out a handful of quarters and started counting them and placing them in stacks of four, one next to the other, until he had twelve stacks lined up. Policy money. The stacks lay like soldiers marching across the table. Then he counted them again. "One dollar for each year and one to grow on," he said and, gathering the stacks between his hands, he pushed them slowly across the table toward me. "Here."

I couldn't believe my eyes. Mama and Mimi and Grandpops had slipped me some money every now and then, a shiny quarter here, a half-dollar there, a nickel or two from the tooth fairy, but Daddy had never given me a red cent, and nobody had ever laid this much money on me. My hands got to itching for those quarters.

"Happy birthday." Daddy rubbed his mouth hard, like he was trying to clean himself up after a meal. "You a good girl. You know how to keep secrets, don't you?"

"Yes sir." I put my right finger over my mouth like he'd showed me.

"That's it. That's the way. Anything you see or hear from being around your dad is a secret."

"Yes sir." I was following my plan to yes sir him to death.

"All right," he said in humdrum sort of way, as if he hadn't just given me stacks of money. As though he were saying all right, have some beans, or all right, take a nickel for an ice cream. Then he got up. "Take the money and go on down to New Orleans with your mamaw. Go to one of them big-city department stores and buy yourself something pretty. Take it and go ahead on."

"Yes sir," I whispered again. I stood and picked up the money, stack by stack. I divided it between the two pockets in my shorts. I watched his face the whole time to see if I was doing whatever it was he wanted me to do. It seemed like I was, so I walked sideways over to the front door. I didn't look straight at him but I kept him in the corner of my eye to make sure he didn't get up and go for me. But he didn't.

I was turning the doorknob when he said it. "You know what happens if you break the oath?"

I wasn't sure what I should answer. No sir seemed dangerous, but so did yes sir. I decided to move my head a little in a round-about sort of way that might be a nod yes or a nod no.

He came over to me and took my bad left arm between his two hands. His little spider hairs seemed to stand up higher on the back of them. My arm took on a life of its own and started quaking in his grasp as if I had a palsy. Fire shot from my shoulder down to the dancing arm.

Then he said the rest of it. "You die." He said it so quiet and peaceful that at first I wasn't sure I heard right. Then I looked into his face and saw the words burned across his mouth.

"Yes sir," I whispered.

He turned me loose and stepped back.

That's when two stories took shape all at once in my mind's eye. I could see them both clear as day and for a moment I stood frozen between them. The sentence that began both stories was this: Florence Irene Forrest's father tells her he will kill her.

In the first story scaredy-cat Florence slips out the door and walks slow through the yard and then starts to run and never stops.

The other was a different story with a different girl. Flo.

Flo is nobody's fool. She gets into the doorway and pushes open the screen, but she doesn't hop out like a scared rabbit saying yes sir, yes sir. She gets one foot out the door. Then she reaches down and all in one motion grabs her daddy's precious box off the floor with her good arm and pulls his keys out of the deadbolt lock with her bad one. No car for him! Then she says what she has to say; she hisses it.

"Catch me if you can."

He grabbed air for me, quarters flying this way and that, but I was too quick. I gathered myself and took a leap out the door and across the porch, barely touching Mama's stepping-stones on the way up to the street. He came after me with his crab crawl, but I left him in the dust, lickety-splitting it over Mama's little stepping-stones, the quarters jangling in my pockets. Just as I reached the street, I heard sirens, and when I looked behind me, he'd vanished into thin air.

I hightailed it all the way back up to Mimi's, my shoulder shooting off firecrackers each time my foot hit the street. The box jostled around. I dropped it once, but picked it back up and kept running. The sirens hadn't let up. They seemed to be coming from Shake Rag, though I paid little attention.

I ran up my grandmother's driveway and into her backyard. I headed straight for the row of pecan trees behind the garage and threw the box on the ground. The latch broke open, and out spilled Daddy's black garb and all the rest of his paraphernalia. Flags, cross, Bible, sword now flung loose from its holder, vase, cards, Zippo. Ordinary run-of-the-mill things scattered on the ground as if by a child playing some strange made-up game.

When I saw the lighter gleaming in the leaves, I remembered how easy it had been to start a fire. I also remembered how Ray killed the caterpillars with gasoline. With my right hand, I scraped some leaves and twigs into a pile around the box and piled up my father's stuff on top of it. I ran into the garage and picked up the can of gasoline next to the lawn mower. I was getting more and more used to doing with my right hand, and I used it to pour what was left in the can on top of the pile I'd made. I kept out Daddy's hood, which had fallen to the side and looked like a bat struck down in mid-flight. I flicked the Zippo and set fire to the hood. It made a nice flame, and I used it to start the twigs and leaves. They and the box caught in a loud *whoosh* that made me jump back.

The box burned for a while. I paced up and down watching it flame, then settle into a nice cheerful burn, and eyeing the driveway where, at any minute, my father might appear. I hoped Mimi would think the neighbors were burning leaves, and vice versa.

Nothing happened, nobody came. Before long the box and my father's things were nothing but a pile of reddish ash. With a big magnolia leaf I picked up the hot, smoky glass vase and threw it up against the side of the garage. It crashed to the ground in a million pieces. I took off for Mimi's back porch.

I burst through the screen door onto the porch breathing hard and yelling for my grandmother. It was coming dark by then, but she hadn't turned on the lights in the house the way she usually did this time of day. The door from the back porch to the kitchen was locked and the lights were off. I looked through the glass at the top of the door and saw Mimi sitting in the shadows at the kitchen table with her head in her hands. She scrambled to her feet when I banged on the glass with both hands. Then she peered out. I had my face pressed up against the glass. She jumped back when she saw me, then looked again, out into the dusk behind me. Finally, she unlocked the door.

"What, what?" she half whispered, half screamed when I burst in on her. She locked the door back behind me as soon as I got inside. When I told her what Daddy had said and the money he'd given me, she looked puzzled for a minute, but then she said, well then, we were going to New Orleans and we were going this very night, damn my clothes, damn the tires, damn the savings bond, damn her job.

We locked the doors and went upstairs. I helped her pack two big suitcases. One was hers and one had been Grandpops'. She got those into the trunk of the Plymouth by herself; she wouldn't let me help because of my shoulder. Plus, she said, I needed to watch her load the car and stay in the house by the phone. If anybody came into the yard, call the police. If I saw my father or any of his cronies, call the police.

After stashing the suitcases, she started snatching hatboxes from the top of her closet and piling them up on the backseat, all the way to the roof of the car. When she got as many into the backseat as she could fit, she squeezed some more hatboxes into the trunk, stacked two between us on the front seat, and put one on the floor of the car on my side so that I had to straddle it the whole way. There were still some hats left in the top of her closet, and she looked up at them and sighed. She took one last small box and opened it and brought forth a little number with a brown feather and a little half veil with butterfly designs. She plopped the hat on her head without even looking in the mirror and folded the veil back so that it wasn't over her eyes.

Right after midnight we headed out, fugitives into the night. She left a note for Zenie on the kitchen table. It said, "Dear Zenie, Gone for a while. Taking Florence you know where. Fox on our tail. Will write and send money for paid vacation. Take the food in the icebox and the sugar and flour and the pickled peaches in the crock. Take anything else the roaches would get and lock up the house. Please tell Uldine and the paperboy I'm gone. I will see about the mail. Thank you for everything. I'm sorry if I made you mad sometimes. I'm sorry I made you do the wash that time, truly I am. If you need to work for somebody else for a while, I will understand. I will miss you, Zenie. You have been a help and comfort to me all these years. You know I'd never leave like this if it wasn't the only thing to do. Yours always, Irene Calhoun."

I was worried that Daddy and his friends would appear in Mimi's backyard at the last minute, but when we ran for the car, the night was quiet and sweet.

Mimi had a map that she kept on her lap the whole way down to New Orleans. After a while it got soggy with her tears. She wasn't crying out loud, just drip drip dripping slow and sure as if she'd sprung a leak. I stayed awake long into the early-morning hours. My shoulder throbbed. I was panting the way a dog does when it knows it's lost. I couldn't seem to get my breath. We saw shadows of animals along the road. Deer. A warthog. A coon. All intent on getting some secret place only they knew about.

I kept watching behind us. When a car's lights would come into view, I'd start to sweat, but then it would pass us or turn off and we'd be alone again.

Mimi hummed hymns as the tires slapped the road. In the cross of Jesus I fain would take my stand. Let the water and the blood from Thy wounded side which flowed be of sin the double cure. In the sweet bye and bye we shall meet on that beautiful shore. After a while the hymns made me deeply peaceful, and my breath became slow and even. Finally, I closed my eyes.

It seemed as if I slept over centuries and great distances. I felt the earth's globe groan and turn beneath us, like the deep and invisible current of a powerful river. I felt us rising and falling as that current took us into a vastness that had no tracks to mark it, that seemed both land and water, earth and sky.

Mimi woke me up saying, "Look, honey. *Look.*" I woke to the sky just turning to rose. We were on a bridge coming in over dark water. On the other side, in the far distance, the lights of the city were shining before us like the halo of a giant angel.

"That wasn't so bad," Mimi said. Her hat had fallen forward so that the feather on it pointed straight ahead.

"No it wasn't," I said.

The rest was easy. Mabel was still asleep when we piled in so we had to ring the doorbell twice to rout her out. When she finally opened the door, she looked healthy as a horse in her bobby pins and white pajamas and said we looked like escapees from a chain gang.

Mimi rolled her bloodshot eyes. "You have no idea." She went into the downstairs bedroom and fell dead asleep across the bed before she even told Mabel why we were there or who I was, or took off her hat.

Mabel looked at me and said, "Well now, you must be Florence."

"Flo," I said.

"A name with some spunk. I like it." She led me upstairs to another pretty bedroom and said, "Maybe you want to take a nap too, Flo?"

I said yes ma'am and hit the hay.

In my dream (or maybe I'm still awake) I keep on moving. I am riding on a road that goes straight down into the dark water. No bridges in sight and no shining cities either. Now I'm flying because it's fly or drown. Not the breaststroke through the air cool as a cucumber, the way Zenie does during her afternoon naps. No. It's swoop and circle, riding the wind. On the ground below, the flutter of something bright yellow.

—*Part IV*—

18

It was all so humdrum. The way he stopped the car and jumped out, with her in the back. I thought he was going to get me to take her with me on my sales rounds. That maybe Zenie was off somewheres and couldn't be found. Or, maybe, I thought, as he clumped over toward me on that foot of his you can always see under his boogey-man sheets, he was going to get me to take her back up by Zenie's for him. He was in a hurry, that's for sure, and I thought that was what he wanted me for. To get shuck of her the way he was always trying to do, foist her off on the Negroes. I was thinking nobody here's going to be your mammy, peckerwood.

Then I saw the screwdriver, and I thought he must be having car trouble in that pile of rubbish he was driving. Clumping up to me with this easy glad look on his face, like he was real pleased to find me right there, right then. I thought he was going to say, hey girl, help me do something with this here car. Lift this or hold that. I wasn't going to help him do shit if I could help it, and I might've run on down the street and gotten away from him. Sure had every reason to, after the way he and his jerk-ass friends burned me and put their nasty hands on me when all I'd wanted was to make my tuition and a little spending money. I wasn't looking to be any Rosa Parks either, but he and his peckerwood sidekicks, they did something to me. They made me mulish, and I wasn't about to go hightailing it back home like a scared jackrabbit, no ma'am, because then they'd think they could just keep right on with their burning and touching and killing.

Truth be told, though, I was almost too chicken to run. I didn't know how fast he could move on that gimp leg. Even if I got away, I knew deep down I'd be running forever. I'd have to run all the way back to Carolina.

So I stood my ground waiting for him to get near me on the sidewalk and have his say. My scarf felt tight around my neck all of a sudden. I started sweating in my scalp and my glasses slipped down on my nose. I pushed them back. They'd fogged up a little so I couldn't see clearly. But I still wasn't worried about him starting up anything with me. For one thing, it was broad day still. Frank and the boys had just rounded the corner up on Moses. All I had to do was holler and they'd come running. Plus there she was in the backseat with her moon face pressed up to the glass (why the window was up in that heat I don't know). He wasn't going to do nothing to me with his own child looking on. Straight at me she was looking with those yellowish eyes of hers you can see right through. Lost as usual. She always looked lost. He probably wanted me to take her off his hands so he could get dressed up like Halloween and go lynch somebody.

I concentrated on how I was going to refuse him without him taking a hand to me. I'm sorry, Mr. Man. I'm in a terrible hurry. I feel sickly, sir. Going to upchuck any minute. That would be my contribution to the Movement for the day, keeping him from getting out of the house tonight, though if you ask my opinion, he was the cat at home too. I mean all you had to do was look at her when she dragged in in the mornings. Those burnt arms. He'd done that. I could see it writ across her face plain as day. With the granddaddy six feet under and the grandma'am crying and doping her way through the afternoons, Auntie felt obliged to see after the girl since that crazy cake woman had done so much for the people, warning them and all. But Auntie Z, she needed a rest from it. She was hoping the mental one would come on home and take care of her own flesh and blood, though I told Auntie don't hold your breath. That heifer's seen greener pastures, even if it's the inside of the loony bin.

He was keeping on coming. Galump, galump, on the bad foot. He put it down hard, and made the dust kick up in little puffs around that big ugly shoe of his. I was still standing there on the bucked-up sidewalk next to a nandina bush with little white flowers crawling with buzzing bees. Lord, big old bees everywhere. Sucking up the juice. I could see the black spots on their backs.

Watching him coming up the grass toward me, something deep inside me wanted to back up, but I was afraid I'd get stung by those bees, so I stood my ground and waited to see what he wanted. He still looked pleased, almost like he was going to say good evening and how are you and you have won a prize, missy. In the late-day sun, that dark oily hair of his looked like it had shoe polish dripping off it. I was facing the setting sun, and a beam of light blinded me all of a sudden. I couldn't see his face.

Then he was up on me and I saw his mouth.

"No sir," I said as quick as I could. The words were bees buzzing in the air. "No, sir. No sir. No, no, no, no."

He took me by the hair of the head. He pulled my head back with one hand and then I saw the screwdriver come up in the other, like I was a can he was getting ready to open. When I felt my pretty scarf tear and the ragged tip of the screwdriver dig into the hollow in my neck above the bone, between the two cords of muscle, I knew I was done for. It went in hard and it came out easy. When he was done, he let go of my hair, and my knees folded. I sat down in a heap and my head wouldn't hold itself up. It fell over to one side.

My throat filled up and when I opened my mouth to scream, all that came out was a river. I swam through it for what seemed like a long long time. And then I went down.

But when I went down, my eyes were still wide open. I could still see her. She was looking straight at me. I could see her looking out from the shore I wasn't going to get to.

— *Part V* —

19

The next morning Mabel handed the *Times-Picayune* to Mimi over a bowl of scrambled eggs. "Look what happened up in Millwood. A girl got herself killed. They say it must have been a spat with her boyfriend. Did you know an Eva Greene?"

Mimi gasped. She put her coffee cup back in the saucer so hard it cracked and the coffee sloshed over into the broken saucer. After she read the story, which was just a few sentences in the folds of a back section, no picture of Eva, nothing like that, she rose to her feet with the paper still in her hand. "Oh my God. Poor Zenie and Ray. I must send them a telegram." She went to the phone on the little table in Mabel's hall, picked it up, and then hesitated and put it back down.

I followed her into the hall. "Eva didn't have a boyfriend," I said.

"Flowers," she said. "I'll send flowers. Maybe I should go back. Oh my God. What monster would do such a thing? My Lord in heaven a *screwdriver*." She sat down in the chair next to the phone and didn't do anything. She just sat there and stared down at the floor. I came and stood next to her.

"Eva didn't have a boyfriend," I said again.

She looked up at me. In the dim hallway, her face seemed ashy; her eyes scurried over my face. She put her hand on my arm and searched my eyes as if she were looking for a lost piece of color in them. Then she reached over and hugged me around my waist. After she let go, she sat staring hard at a red rooster door-stop on the floor as if she had asked it a question and was waiting for an answer. It stared back at her with its little beady black eyes. Finally, she cleared her throat and said, "All right. Let me do this. Go on up to your room and let me do this." She said it sternly, as if she were correcting me for acting up.

I started to cry. "Say I'm sorry," I whispered. "In the telegram tell Zenie and Ray I'm sorry too."

Upstairs I sat on the bed and crossed my legs under me. Something fluttered at the back of my mind. Wash on a line, a scrap of paper blowing down the street, feathers. A bit of color. There were nubby tuffs on the white spread, and I started picking at them. I could hear Mimi talking on the phone, but her voice seemed to be coming from under water. I kept on picking threads from the nubs on the spread, piling them up like Miss Josephine's mimosa leaves. I began to count them, putting them in piles of tens. I thought I knew how Miss J felt when she counted. It was something that had to be done to quiet the flutter. Something had broken out in my chest, something awkward, then loose, a bird falling from the sky.

I tried to see Eva going home to Raleigh in a box the way Mr. Lafitte had said she would. Would they dress her in a bright scarf? Would they let her keep her cat-eye specs? Would they put her on a train? I tried to see that kind of stillness settle down upon her. But I couldn't. The stillness wouldn't stay still. It fluttered.

Even when the shock of Eva's death had dulled, I'd turn a corner and think I saw her sashaying down the street dressed to the nines in her navy blue suit. She remained alive in my mind's eye, popping up here and there as time went by, saying things like look what the cat dragged in, or bye, Flo, or hey, girl, when she passed through my thoughts in a pretty whirl. When I came to understand the work she did in Millwood, I saw her as the Queen of Palmyra, riding off to do battle against wickedness and save her people. I wondered if someone had killed her for that. I was pretty sure she didn't have a boyfriend, and if she did, she was too smart and sassy to choose someone who would stick a screwdriver into her throat. She would have chosen a man like Medgar Evers, someone with enough spunk to match her own.

The flutter, it hovered at the corner of my sight, always there but just outside my line of vision. Sometimes, when it got especially close, I wanted to reach out and close my hand on it the way you'd grab at a gnat that's buzzing around your head. Mostly, though, I tried to ignore it as best I could, though as time went on, the flutter wore on me, the way a recurring dream you can't remember but can't forget either wears on you. You have to either forget it or remember it; otherwise it will spin a web around you and never let you go.

But as time went on, Millwood and everybody in it began to fade like an old dress. Zenie I missed like crazy, but with Mimi and Mabel showing me how to ride the streetcars and what kind of snowball turns your tongue blue and where to cross Carrollton Avenue to get to school in one piece, Zenie too faded for me, just as my mother had.

My father loomed in my mind, but only because I was afraid he'd come after me and swoop me up, which he never did. Mimi heard he'd moved over to Greenwood soon after we flew the coop, and he'd started selling tractors for John Deere. I made up a story in my head that he'd become an ordinary man living an ordinary life. I started thinking that maybe he was just angry about something when he said he'd kill me. Maybe he didn't mean it and now he was sorry. He did send money from time to time. I came to dread those smudged envelopes with his handwriting on them. They made Mimi take a dark turn. She'd take them to her room and put them in her top dresser drawer like they were something dirty. Years later, when she died, I would find them, the checks still inside.

Though Mabel wasn't the motherly sort, she became my second mother despite her inclinations. She was not the proper lady that Mimi had been, and she was always saying she was teaching the two of us how to live. Mimi laughed more and was teaching social studies again. She had to roll up her sleeves and learn a whole new set of state laws and facts to get certified in Louisiana. When her school was integrated and a black girl was supposed to enter her homeroom, she got into hot water by telling her students beforehand that anyone who was mean to the new girl would just flat fail. No ugliness in her class. Her hats got louder and louder. She never took naps, and when she breezed out the door in the mornings, she'd say, "See you in the funny papers." On Sundays she'd fix herself up and put this little number or that one on her head, feathers and bows and veils, and she and Mabel and I would take the streetcar downtown and have shrimp remoulade and martinis at Galatoire's.

Br'er Rabbit always gets loose, and so does Uncle Wiggily. In the end my mother did too. While it seemed that she'd just flat vanished off the face of the earth without a red cent to her name, what she really did wasn't miraculous or even the smartest thing. But it worked. She went knocking on Navis's door. Navis had a garage, no husband, and a soft spot for Mama. She took her in and hid her and the car for months without anybody suspecting a thing. During tax season, folks expected Navis's door to be closed and her blinds drawn against the glare. They left her alone. After things died down, Navis drove Mama to Memphis in the dead of night and put her on a Greyhound bus to Navis's mother's house in Amarillo, Texas. And there my mother lived in the desert, helping Navis's mother carry water for her garden and baking cakes at a truck stop on the main highway.

When I was fourteen, Mama decided the coast was clear and it was safe to come out of hiding and make us a visit, which of course was a shock. Mimi, who had been secretly convinced that Daddy had murdered my mother and disposed of the body, almost fainted when she walked in the door from a full day at school and found my mother having iced tea in the kitchen with Mabel and me. Mama cried for days at Mabel's kitchen table and couldn't stop going on about how sorry she was. Her eyes swelled almost shut she cried so much, and her face stayed watermelon red from morning to night. When Mabel told her to buck up and brought her a shot of Southern Comfort, Mama said to get it out of her sight; she might as well drink poison. I got sick of her bellyaching and wished she would go on back to Navis or Navis's mother, I didn't care which.

Although Mimi never said a word against my mother to me after we got to New Orleans, probably because she thought she'd be speaking ill of the dead, she didn't exactly welcome my mother with open arms once she'd made her surprise appearance. When Mimi first laid eyes on my mother in the kitchen, she drew herself up and said, "Martha Irene, you ought to be ashamed of yourself. What a disappointment you have been to us all. Your father is rolling over in his grave." After that icy pronouncement, my grandmother would say good morning and pass the salt to her daughter, but that was it. At meals Mimi kept her eyes down and the rest of the time she was either off to school or in her room with the door closed. For her part, Mama hung her head and didn't press herself on us. But she didn't leave either.

Despite our lack of enthusiasm for her presence, she sent for her clothes and used her truck stop money to rent herself a little apartment with a big kitchen about eight blocks from Mabel's. Soon she was baking her cakes for debutantes and Mardi Gras balls and such. Then one day Navis came down from Millwood with a carload of stuff and didn't leave.

For years Mama didn't explain why she'd left me high and dry, and I didn't ask. For a while, whenever I looked at her, all I could see were roaches under the streetlights. Finally the roaches scudded under the floorboards of my mind, and Mama's never-ending trip to the A & P got to be more or less water under the bridge. By then I had come to understand that not everybody can be the Queen of Palmyra. For some people being afraid is the hardest thing in the world. I could see how such a person might do anything just not to be afraid anymore.

So I didn't hate Mama for leaving, though when she asked me to come live with her, I said no, I was with Mimi; Mimi was my mother now. This hurt Mama's feelings, which I meant it to, but she pushed back her bangs and said all right, she didn't blame me, she deserved that. Once, when I was in high school, she sat me down amid the pots and pans of her kitchen, laid down a thick slice of devil's food cake in front of me, and said, "Florence, you know I meant to come back. I really meant to. I didn't set out to leave. I just got to riding around in the dark, and then it got too late and I was afraid. I knew he was going to send me back to Whitfield, and I just couldn't go back to that. I was afraid I would die in there. You know I love you, don't you, honey? I always loved you." I said yes, but the cake stuck in my craw. I don't have much truck with love. It was not love that brought me over the dark water. It was something else. Something that didn't give way. Something that held. Mimi and Grandpops and Zenie and Ray and Eva had that something; Mama didn't.

In school I learned that a story is a weaving. At some point, the final thread is tied off, and the pattern emerges before your eyes in plain sight. You see what there is to see, and the story is complete. The end. This story goes on. Years passed and we got a phone call saying that Zenie had died from a clot that broke loose from one of the bad veins in her legs and traveled to her heart. Mimi drove up to Millwood for the funeral. I wanted to go too, but she said no; I was still only seventeen, a minor, and my father had rights. She said I had to stay out of Mississippi until I was of age. A few months later a letter brought news that Ray had died in his bed of smoke inhalation. The police said the fire was caused by Jim Walter's bad wiring, maybe the one thing Ray couldn't fix since he didn't know it was broken. I thought of Zenie's pretty green curtains curling and burning. Miss Josephine of course was long gone by then.

After four years at Loyola, only a short bus ride from Mimi and Mabel's, I got a job as a teacher at Crossman Elementary, the very school I'd gone to myself, except now most of the students were black. Full circle I went, all the while flying so far from home that nobody from back there remembers my name.

When Mimi died first and then Mabel, I took the money they left me and bought a little shotgun house on, believe it or not, Palmyra Street. Mama and Navis moved into Mabel's house. The neighbors on Palmyra liked me because I walked out on summer nights with two cans of Raid and sprayed roaches all up and down the sidewalk. My goal was a roach-free block. "Here come the roach lady," the children would say to one another and run for their porches. I bought the *Picayune Creole Cookbook* and made Sunday dinners. Some Sundays Mama, whose hair was now streaked with gray, and Navis, who had dyed her gray red, came to eat. They would ask me if I had any friends. I knew they were asking about men. I said I was too busy, which was true. Students want so much from you.

So if I were writing this story a century ago, I'd say, Reader, I am content, except for that flutter that troubles me from time to time. Chalk dust has seeped into my skin, making it seem drier and white. I chew cloves because I take a cig or two at lunch—what's wrong with that when your life is diagramming sentences for fifth graders who squirm and push against their desk like young horses? With families struggling to stay out of the projects, or to stay in the projects and off the streets, some of the children seem to dangle like misplaced modifiers. I know my job is to remain constant. Monday through Friday, end of summer to late spring, I am where I'm supposed to be. Most afternoons I stay late and tutor the ones who lag behind. I make them stay too, even if they don't want to. I tell them they're not getting out of the fifth grade until they learn what a semicolon does. How it holds things together but keeps them from touching too closely. How it balances and contains and keeps things from flooding over. For perfect assignments and good attendance, I give out roses from my little alleyway garden wrapped in wet paper towels and napkins. These the children handle with care.

"We watching your back, Miss Forrest," the boys tell me on their way out the door in the afternoons. "Don't you be worrying because we watching out for all your trees every minute of the day and night. Nobody going to cut down your trees on our lookout." When they laugh at their own joke and pull up their drooping pants for emphasis, I take this to mean they have a certain affection for me. Who knows? Perhaps they like to think I belong to them, that we are one another's precious cargo on a long ride to the future.

When the morning light cuts across the classroom, making a V across the linoleum floor, there's no turning back from the already steaming day, the school year, the chalk dust on my hands. And this is what I want most from teaching: it moves me through time. There is the beginning of the school year with its failing air conditioners and jumpy newcomers, the holidays glory be, then the victorious end of school and a blissfully empty summer. There are lesson plans, report cards, never-ending worries about Joseph with his druggy big brother or Mary whose mama wants all A's. This and that. The gravity of it all keeps the flutter under control.

The girl carefully touched the beautiful rose. Eva's sentence. I write it on the board. "Copy it down," I command, and they start writing, their heads bent low over their notebooks, scraping their pencils across the pages, noses sniffling and shoes tapping their desks. Then I begin the diagram: *girl/touched.* As I fill out the diagram with object, adjectives, and adverb, I plan the next sentence. It will be the other one from Eva. *The careful girl was touched by the beautiful rose.* I realize now just what a shrewd choice Eva made with this second sentence: not only does it illustrate the difference between active and passive voices and adverbs and adjectives, but it also shows how a word can mutate into metaphor. How the ordinary can become beautiful as well as ugly. How many ways one can touch and be touched. Or be full of care. The last sentence I plan is my own. It will be about thorns. How you have to watch out for thorns. But, of course, these children know that all too well.

Sometimes when I look back, I see a tangle of webs in the dark basement. I see Eva putting on her red lipstick, tying the yellow scarf just so. Zenie with her back turned at the stove, all the eyes on high, pots boiling, skillets splattering the wall with hot grease. Then Zenie turns and her face is wet with sweat but with something else too, something heavier than sweat.

I don't see Daddy so much as I feel his hand on the shape of me, molding me like clay. But the mold didn't hold. I was the bowl that broke. So when I see my life stretch out before me now like a long straight track, I am not happy but I am content with the view. I don't mind being on the train calling out *no, no, no, no.*

What I don't know yet is that one day, forty-two years from that night Mimi and I hit the road, I will be in the middle of diagramming a sentence on the board. It will be getting toward the end of August, and school will have just started that week. We are all roasting. The old window air conditioner is barely stirring the air in the room. I will have brought in my big floor fan, which is on low so that I can be heard. I will be standing in front of thirty students, who loll about at their desks, feet in the aisles, fanning themselves in various poses of impatience and discomfort. I don't know their names yet, but I have a seating chart. I've told them we are going to have our first test on diagramming, count on it, so most of them are taking notes.

I am known for starting hard, and like Eva I love diagramming. The sentence I have in mind today isn't the one Eva taught Ray and me about the girl and the rose; it is more complicated, more compelling. I like to think it is one of the knock-your-socks-off ones she promised me the last morning of her life. There is a collective groan when I write it on the board:

When the fireman broke in the window, the girl woke from a deep sleep; with barely a moment to spare, she was able to see her dilemma and jump.

A sentence with drama and flare, if I do say so myself. I chose it because I want them to learn a sense of balance and decorum. I want them to understand that a sentence isn't a story that can just go on and on. It can take twists and turns. It can offer surprise and pleasure and terror. But it has to end somewhere. There has to be a period. I'll admit too, I want to make them sit up in their seats and take notice. This class is not going to be a piece of cake. They are going to learn the difference between a subordinate clause and a prepositional phrase; they are going to know the function of the semicolon. You are going to be word architects, I tell them; but, to be an architect, you have to understand context. I've lost them with the context part, so I offer up my speech about how they'll understand what I'm saying through the diagram itself. The proof is in the pudding.

I start building the diagram on the board. First subjects and verbs. I call out to them, "Now then. What are the subjects of this sentence?" I am enjoying myself. It's almost lunchtime and I'm looking forward to the Winstons stashed in my lunch box.

On the front row, a girl who has been fanning herself with her notebook raises her hand. I can see the beads of sweat on her nose.

I nod. I am hoping she is going to whip out *girl* and *she*. I am hoping she'll be one of the smart ones. It's a strong beginning, I'm thinking: one hand in the air.

"Did that girl in the sentence die?" she asks. "When she jumped, did she die?"

This is not the answer I wanted, this is not the question I wanted. This is not why I chose this sentence. "No," I say curtly. "The fireman caught her. The fireman saved her life."

"Good," she says, and a smile plays at her lips.

Several students chuckle and murmur, "Um hum."

I turn back to the blackboard, and that's when it starts to happen. She surfaces out of my own web of chalky lines and words, emerging the moment I make the catty-cornered downward stroke for *dilemma* to rest on. The words *able to see* have just rolled off my tongue. The second of three verbs in a compound/complex sentence, I've just said to the students. They groan again, and I hear one of the boys on the back row snicker and say, "Shit. Compound *what*?"

I have my mouth open to say *complex*, compound *complex*,

when there she is. There she is. In the space between the word and the line it belongs to. She stares at me over a man's shoulder. The man seems to be leaning in to bear-hug her. Eva. Pretty Eva in her yellow scarf, looking at me through those cat-eye specs of hers. She seems to step out of the blackboard like a photograph that comes to life before your very eyes. Her face is the color of soot, not the pretty chocolate cream it once was. Our eyes lock. She nods at me, an odd sort of nod to the left: a slow-motion curtsy. Her arm comes up once, as if she is swimming, reaching for shore. Then she slides down out of sight behind the man, reluctantly it seems, like someone drowning, and there is only his back.

Then the man turns and I see his face and what's in his hand and a levee breaks deep inside my retinas and the river is coming in. Then I think no, it's not the river, it's the whole damn lake, it's the whole damn Gulf of Mexico. I squeeze my eyes shut to hold it back, but there's no stopping it.

When anyone faints in public, there's a fuss. And of course someone takes me home. I'm escorted into my darkened living room and put down on the couch. Someone gets me a drink of water, asks if I'm all right now, and leaves. I sit for a good long time and just try to breathe. I sit for hours looking down at my arms folded in my lap. In those hours, I come to notice that my hands are getting veiny, my forearms fleshy like my grandmother's. I come to understand that Eva has waited long enough. Forty-two years—it's 2005 by now—and she is tired of waiting. She has taken matters into her own hands.

When the light outside turns gray, I leave the house. I walk over to Carrollton and catch the streetcar up to Riverbend. There I cross the railroad tracks and walk up on the levee that holds back the Mississippi. The brush and trees grow in thickets along the riverbank. Men with bottles in little brown sacks come and go from those thickets; their trips seem purposeful, as if they are attending an important business meeting. There is a bend in the river by a transformer where the brush has been cut back and where I can see the water and walk down to it. At the river's edge there's an old rusted boat to the left and a broken-up wharf, gray and sharded, to the right, like the subject and verb of some vast and unfathomable sentence. In the coming dark I can't tell where the bank ends and the water begins. Without looking, I can feel the river rising.

The next morning I'm on a bus to Jackson and that same afternoon reading microfilm in the Mississippi Department of Archives and History. When I come across the reports of Eva's murder, I don't need to read them. After all, I was there. I am drowning in details. Broad daylight, yellow scarf, nandina bush, screwdriver, bees. And, of course, my father the Nighthawk. Furious at Mimi for trying to take me away, furious at my mother for leaving, furious at me for the hatred and fear I bore him, how he swooped around that corner so slow and smooth when he saw her coming down that side street. How he did that thing I couldn't see, didn't see. A willed, necessary blindness.

True stories happen, and then you tell them. But what you tell depends on what you see. And what you see depends on what you know.

What I don't know came later: a black boycott of white businesses organized by Rayfield Johnson, uncle-in-law of the victim, which made me wonder whether the fire that killed Ray was actually the result of bad wiring. Then a march led by Ray and Zenie and Eva's friend Frank when nobody was arrested for Eva's murder, even after a sheriff's deputy found the screwdriver in the nandina bush and some of the men from Mr. Lafitte's Grocery said they saw a Valiant with the policy man at the wheel go by. A small picture of the march, fuzzed by the microfilm, shows the three of them grim faced, Frank's white face and hair leaping up like a flame in the midst of a sea of black people with placards held high surging down Main Street, ringed by angry white men who looked like Big Dan. The caption under the picture reads, "Race Violence Breaks Out in Millwood."

By the time I get back down to New Orleans, a Thursday night, there is a storm brewing in the Gulf. Everybody on the bus is talking about it. It has hit Florida, turned around, and is heading back toward us. The joke amongst the passengers is that we're heading in the wrong direction.

The phone is ringing when I unlock my front door. It is Mama. "Damn it the hell, Florence, I've been trying to reach you for *two days*. When are you going to get a cell phone? Where on earth have you been? We've been worried sick we'd have to evacuate without you."

When she stops for breath, I say, "I went up to Jackson for a few days. Listen, Mama, I think it would be better for me to drive one of your cars out of here. We need to get all the cars out of here." I don't own a car myself, and I need one for what I have planned.

She draws a shaky breath. "Well, all right. I guess so. Damn this place. How the hell did we end up here?"

I think, well, after you ran yourself into the train and Grandpops died and you took the grocery list and left me with nothing but a stack of greased pans, and Daddy hurt me and killed Eva, Mimi had the courage and decency and good sense to throw me and her hats in the Plymouth and bring me over the dark water to Mabel because she didn't know where else to go. Then you came back because the coast was clear and there was smooth sailing. I say, "Okay, so can you bring me over a car, then?"

"Are you sure you'll be all right driving by yourself?"

"Of course I will. Just bring me the car."

"Why don't you just follow us? We've got two rooms in Jackson. We're leaving early in the morning. Crack of dawn."

"I need to see Daddy."

There's a pause. "Oh. Do you think that's really necessary?" Mama still hasn't forgiven me for stashing Daddy in Roselawn Nursing Facility down in Chalmette, just a few miles away. When they called from the John Deere place in Greenwood because he had started to carry his headache stick to work and whap it on his leg when he got aggravated at a customer, Mama had long since gotten a divorce, so it was my little red wagon. I told them to take the stick to him, but soon after that, he had a stroke right there on the sales floor.

The nursing home is a ranch-style house built low to the ground. It's flooded twice already and the one time I was there for the paperwork, it smelled like a sewer.

"Yes I do think it's necessary."

"You're not going to bring him with you, are you?" Her voice has iced over. There is only one possible answer to the question.

"Are you crazy?"

Mama breathed a sigh of relief. "All right, we're coming right over with my car."

I hang up and pour a shot of vodka. It sits on the kitchen counter like the beginnings of a little altar to a lost one on the side of the highway. I pick it up and drink it down.

I resist the temptation to pour again and instead pick up my suitcase and take it into the bedroom and lay it on my bed. I unpack dirty underwear and put in clean. Then I close it back up. I am ready to go. I light a cigarette and turn on the TV. The storm is back in the Gulf and is building strength. Florida was just a warm-up.

In a few minutes Mama hurries inside with the car keys. Navis is waiting out in the other car. They are thinking of leaving tonight. They've gassed up both cars. Will I be right along tomorrow?

Yes, I say, yes. I notice that Mama's hair is more white now than silver. Her bangs all white.

She stops in her tracks when I come out of the shadows of the kitchen. She peers at me. "You look terrible. What's the matter? What's wrong with you?"

Somehow I make the words line up. *I* is the subject, *saw* the verb, *Daddy* the direct object, the rest of the clause unthinkable.

She gasps and pushes her bangs straight up in that old lost gesture. "God in heaven, how could you have forgotten *that*? You remember *everything*. It's impossible you didn't remember seeing him *kill her*."

"It's not that I didn't remember what I saw. It's that I didn't know what I was seeing."

"You're not a fool, Florence. You must have realized later. Surely you must have figured it out." My mother's voice is cold. She looks shocked and innocent. A little old lady with nothing to hide.

I don't answer. What I remember about that time right after Mimi brought me to Mabel was my delighted dive into normalcy. Mabel's spacious high-ceilinged house with long windows and cool wood floors. School down the street and outfits that matched. A little room with a twin bed all to myself. No hot hand, no bootleg runs. I remember taking long naps in the quiet late afternoons, then doing diagrams on the kitchen table while Mabel cooked supper. Lining up the words the way Eva had taught me so that you could tell what belonged to what: where the sentence led and what story it was telling. Where that story began and where it ended. I remember eating scrambled eggs for supper and French toast with powdered sugar for breakfast. Moving from the middle of fifth grade, which Eva's tutoring had earned me, to the top. I remember my grandmother's hair turning to gleaming silver, how she let it grow out and wore it on top of her head like a crown. I remember getting to watch *Bonanza* and *Mr. Wizard's World*. I remember Mimi, Mabel, and me clustering around the TV and crying when President Kennedy got shot with poor Jackie in her bloody dress. I felt I'd come into the real world for the first time. It was a world that took its life from my mother's absence, and, I now see, from Eva's death.

I look straight into my mother's widened, blameless eyes. Something in me curls up to strike, to say maybe none of it would have happened if she'd *been* there. But then I don't say it because, even after everything, she still smells like burnt sugar, and all I can see is a woman half my age, her hair like wings, racing the devil to the bootlegger, rescuing someone else's precious cargo. I walk to the door and open it for her.

On the way out, she stops and looks at me as if she's seeing me for the first time. "You were afraid," she whispers.

"So were you."

She nods. "Eva was the only one who wasn't afraid of him."

"She was afraid," I said. "But she didn't run."

At first light the next morning I head for Roselawn Nursing Facility down in Chalmette. I head down Claiborne. People cluster in clumps up and down the street. They look at the sky and one another. They shake their heads. Some wait on their front stoops with suitcases beside them. The traffic is terrible and it takes me a good two hours to get there, though I'm going in the opposite direction of most people.

The parking lot at Roselawn looks deserted. Inside, all the breakfast things have been cleared away. Two old men sit at a table playing checkers. I continue down the long fluorescent hall. A woman clutching a frayed doll dozes in her wheelchair. Daddy's door is shut. I go in without knocking. He is in bed asleep. His roommate is out or dead. Here, I suppose, you never know. I go back out in the hall and drink a long time from the water fountain. My head is pounding. I get two aspirin out of the bottle in my purse and swallow them with some more water. Then I go back into his room and pull a chair up to his bed, in the process kicking aside his brick shoe on the floor. He's had physical therapy and now walks with a walker. Judging by the empty breakfast tray, he eats like a horse.

I watch him sleep. His thinness makes his nose loom large and beaked. With that nose and his bald head, he looks as if he's finally transmogrified into the Nighthawk of my imagination. Old and loony before his time, as if the swamp of ugliness in his head has turned into quicksand and sucked him in completely. After I stashed him down in Chalmette, I suspected they drugged him more than necessary since he'd lost most of his mind and strength but not his meanness. More power to them is what I thought.

Now I want him awake. I push the button on his bed to raise him to a sitting position. I poke his shoulder. "Wake up." I can't bear to call him Daddy though it's on the tip of my tongue. I poke him again, harder. He grunts and his eyelids flutter. There is a crust around them. "Hey, *wake up!*"

"What, what," he mutters, then turns over and looks at the door, confused and irritated. He hasn't been shaved today. The bristles on his cheeks and chin are white.

He struggles to sit up in bed. As he throws back the sheet, I smell his old man filth. I sit back in my chair. He peers at me in a predatory way. I cringe a little, still the rabbit.

"*What?*" he says fretfully. "What you waking me up for?" I can tell he doesn't know me, though I now have his full attention.

I lean forward into the stink of his excrement. His breath

is sour. There are deep pits in his face. "Daddy, you killed Eva Greene. I saw you do it. *I saw you.*"

He blinks a few times. Then, ever so precisely, he draws his gnarled right hand, stained brown between his judging finger and his warning finger, from under the sheet and lifts it slowly as if it is monstrously heavy and puts his finger in the position between his mouth and the beaked nose. The sign of silence. He reaches over and fumbles around for my hand. He knows me now. He knows I can keep a secret.

The hair rises on the back of my neck. "*You killed her.*" I whisper the words but I feel as if I'm shouting. I lean over him, down into his face and seek out his eyes under their hooded lids. I want some acknowledgment of the truth. A nod, a blink, a twitch. What I discover there is nothing at all. His pupils look like saucers somebody has poured milk into. I haven't seen him for so long that I didn't realize he had developed cataracts. He probably can't see much of anything.

Now he falls back on his pillow, almost instantly asleep. His mouth opens and he begins to snore softly, contentedly. I get up and walk out of the room. As I go down the deadly bright hall, I contemplate how beautiful the retina is, how it looks like a flower of a million colors. How those colors, the most vivid you'll ever see and a thousand shades of each, never stay in the same place but are always flowing one into another, becoming the inverse of themselves. My father's retinas must have looked like that; everyone's do. And what did those lovely retinas see when they saw Eva walking down that narrow dusty street? They, if not he, must have registered the yellow of her scarf, the neatness of the navy blue suit, the purposeful gleam in her eye. The way she had of putting one foot directly in front of the other when she walked as if she were balancing a heavy load. The backward slope of her shoulder under the weight of the briefcase. The curve of hip and breast. Glint of rhinestones from her glasses frames. And where did all this information from my father's beautiful retinas go, in the mind's locked box? What language did it travel to on its air-ship of innocent, deliberate synapses? Not to the words *beauty* or *strength*. Not to live and let live. Not even to lust, though there must have been some of that. The word, if he ever thought it, would have been his father's. *Impurity*. The foul and the feculent, corrupt and defiled. Sons who were not sons. Daughters who were more than daughters. Flesh and bone gone wrong. Tainted by blood. Ruined.

At the front door the nursing home manager catches up with me. She is huffing and puffing. "You're not taking Mr. Forrest? Most families are evacuating their family members. I thought you had come to get him."

"No," I say coldly. "I'm not taking him." I keep on walking.

My evacuation plan is to start driving, not north but east, east to the marshes and east toward the storm. I will cross the four narrow covered bridges, their overhead girders glittering like rhinestones, over water that is both fresh and salt, surly and choppy. The water will soon be getting higher, licking the bot-toms of the bridges. I will cross over inlets with alligator swamp tour signs, but no boats. At some point, I will take a right toward the Gulf. I will drive on forsaken roads past boarded-up houses until the road dead-ends into the Gulf of Mexico. Then I will sit on the hood of my mother's car facing the dark, uneasy water, and I will wait.

So I drive east, despite all the signs and arrows and roadblocks telling me to go the other way. The strip of flat swampland I drive on gets narrower and narrower as the expanse of gray water on either side grows larger. In the swamp on either side of the road, fingers of murky water make paths through the tall grasses as if giant hands are reaching out for something down in the marshes. As I drive, a sentence takes shape in my head. I begin to diagram it. *The girl saw everything through the dirty window, but she didn't say Daddy stop and she didn't tell.*

And what would he have done if I'd banged on the window and made him pause? Would he have turned the screwdriver on me? I was the one who zigzagged over the field toward home. He took Eva by surprise and she froze in the tall grasses.

When I reach the Gulf, the beach is deserted, not even any seagulls on the pilings out in the water. There is a beach road that turns left, following the sea. I ride on it for a few miles across a low bridge that the water is slapping over.

When I can, I pull off the road and get out of the car. Through the spray and drizzle I see a pelican sitting on a dead branch a ways inland. Perched on her branch, an awkward, hunched thing, she contemplates a still pool of water. We both wait for a good long while; I watch her while she watches the water. I think perhaps she is crippled; it is not a natural way for a pelican to fish. It has started to rain. Behind me the leaden sky and gray ocean have become indistinguishable.

Once, I watched Eva wash herself at the kitchen sink. The afternoon light had splashed on her wet arms and made them sparkle against Zenie's green leaf curtains. She had dried herself on a blue and white checked towel. Ray and I had sat at opposite ends of the table with our notebooks open, waiting for our lesson. Then she had turned from the sink and smiled at us and sat down between us, groaning that her feet hurt, and given us our sentence.

Now, in a motion both hesitant and sure, the pelican gathers her hollow bones and lifts, her pouch full. It is a heavy gathering, a splatter and a moment where it seems she will fail to rise. When

I follow her path through the fog and drizzle, I see another road up a ways. It turns left, away from the water. It is a sharp turn, the kind a story can make, but not a railroad track or the line of a diagram.

A story, who can know its secret night journeys or what precious cargo it might yet carry? Why it says you go or you stay, or wears its hat just so? As for the rest, here's how it begins: The girl, no, the woman named Flo gets back into her mother's car and cranks it up and turns the windshield wipers on high. She drives up the road through the fog and the rain and the years behind her and the years ahead of her, shivering, soaked to the skin, her hair in a tangle. In a few hours she will pass a family walking along the road—a man, woman, and boy—and she will stop and pick them up. In another month she will drive to Millwood and tell what she saw, though by then her father will be another untagged, unclaimed body in the state morgue.

Right now, though, the best she can do is to peer through the windshield and make sure she doesn't miss that sharp left, finding herself, to her astonishment, back in it because the story—the lines and the chalk, the upturned faces, the river that cupped them all—had already begun to miss her.

Acknowledgments

I will be forever grateful to Jill McCorkle for her extraordinary generosity along the way, and especially for helping make this a wiser book. Heartfelt thanks go to Leigh Feldman for her boundless enthusiasm, wit, and sagacity, and Carrie Feron for her astute, respectful editing and bedrock belief in Florence's story. I appreciate Tessa Woodward's ability to make the production process seem effortless.

I am very much indebted to Grace Bauer, Susan Dever, Julie Mars, Margaret Randall, and Sharon Warner for reading the Whole Thing and offering a wealth of insight. Micaela Seidel and John Randall offered early support. Ellis Anderson provided a room, a desk, and a magnificent live oak. Mary Alice Kirkpatrick did detective work. Bill Andrews told about encyclopedia sales.

I thank family members for loving support: Carol and Shaun Leverton, Lynn Holland Brasfield, Shannon Grannon, Linda Jane Barnette, and Nicolle Salvaggio. For sage counsel and support, I'm grateful to Marianne Gingher, Lawrence Naumoff, Beverly

Taylor, and Linda Wagner-Martin. And thanks to the cheering section: Barbara Bennett and Fred Hobson, Angela Boone and Mary Bess Whidden, Karen Booth and Elyse Crystall, Barbara Ewell and Jerry Speir, Rebecka and Ed Fisher, Harolyn Cumlet and Patrice Waldrop, Rebecca Mark, Donnie McMahand, and Kevin Murphy, Sylvia Rodriguez, Judith Sensibar, and Marta Weigle.

I'm grateful for the opportunity to have read from early versions at Purdue University and the Taos Summer Writers' Conference. For their perceptive commentary, I thank members of the Global South group at the University of North Carolina at Chapel Hill. And I appreciate funding from UNC and the Kenan research fund for travel related to the book.

My greatest debt is to Ruth Salvaggio, who offered a skeptical eye and an open heart—the best of all combinations in a reader.

Millwood, Mississippi, and the characters of this book are fictitious. I have made every effort to be accurate about actual places and historical events. Sources that have been helpful and, in some cases essential, include the following:

Chafe, William H. et al, ed. *Remembering Jim Crow: African Americans Tell About Life in the South*. New York: The New Press, 2001.

Cobbs, Elizabeth H./Petric Smith. *Long Time Coming: An Insider's Story of the Birmingham Church Bombing That Rocked the World*. Birmingham: Crane, 1994.

Dennis, Jana. *Palmyra Street*. New Orleans: Neighborhood Story Project, 2005.

Dittmer, John. *Local People: The Struggle for Civil Rights in Mississippi*. Urbana: University of Illinois Press, 1994.

Ezekiel, Raphael S. *The Racist Mind: Portraits of American Neo-Nazis and Klansmen*. New York: Penguin, 1995.

Garis, Howard. *Uncle Wiggily's Travels*. New York: Platt & Munk, 1939.

Gates, Henry Louis. *Colored People: A Memoir*. New York: Vintage, 1995.

Harris, Trudier. *Summer Snow: Reflections from a Black Daughter of the South*. Boston: Beacon, 2003.

Hendrickson, Paul. *Sons of Mississippi: A Story of Race and Its Legacy*. New York: Vintage, 2004.

Hudson, Winson and Constance Curry. *Mississippi Harmony: Memoirs of a Freedom Fighter*. New York: Palgrave Macmillan, 2002.

The Clarion-Ledger; Jackson Daily News, June–August, 1963.

Kennedy, Stetson. *Jim Crow Guide: The Way It Was*. Boca Raton: Florida Atlantic Univ. Press, 1990.

——————. *The Klan Unmasked*. 1954. Boca Raton: Florida Atlantic Univ. Press, 1990.

King, Larry L. *Confessions of a White Racist*. New York: Viking, 1969.

Massengill, Reed. *Portrait of a Racist: The Man Who Killed Medgar Evers*. New York: St. Martin's, 1994.

McDowell, Deborah E. *Leaving Pipe Shop: Memories of Kin*. New York: W. W. Norton, 1996.

McIlhany, William H. II. *Klandestine: The Untold Story of Delmar Dennis and His Role in the FBI's War Against the Ku Klux Klan*. New Rochelle, NY: Arlington House, 1975.

Moody, Anne. *Coming of Age in Mississippi*. New York: Laurel Books, 1968.

Neilsen, Melany. *Even Mississippi*. Tuscaloosa: University of Alabama Press, 1989.

Rockwood, Roy. *Bomba the Jungle Boy: The Swamp of Death*. New York: McLoughlin, 1929.

Salter, John R. Jr. *Jackson, Mississippi: An American Chronicle of Struggle and Schism*. Hicksville, NY: Exposition, 1979.

Sims, Patsy. *The Klan*. Lexington: Univ. Press of Kentucky, 1996.

Taulbert, Clifton L. *Once Upon a Time When We Were Colored*. Tulsa: Council Oak Books, 1989.

Vollers, Maryanne. *Ghosts of Mississippi*. Boston: Little, Brown, 1995.

Insights,
Interviews
& More ...

Meet Minrose Gwin

Steve Exum Photography

MINROSE GWIN has been a writer all of her working life, starting out as a newspaper and wire service reporter covering politics, human interest stories, and the overnight police beat. *Wishing for Snow*, a memoir about the convergence of poetry and psychosis in her mother's life, was published in 2004 and hailed by *Booklist* as "eloquent" and "lyrical"— "a real life story we all need to hear." Minrose has published creative nonfiction and poetry in the *Women's Review of Books*, *IKON*, and several book collections, and has taught creative writing workshops at universities and the University of New Mexico Taos Writers' Conference. Wearing her other hat as a literary critic, she has written three scholarly books (one a CHOICE book of the year) and is a coeditor of *The Literature of the American South*, published by W.W. Norton, and the *Southern Literary Journal*. She currently teaches contemporary fiction at the University of North Carolina and lives in Chapel Hill. Like her character Florence, Minrose grew up in Small-town Mississippi. This is her first novel. ∾

On Writing
The Queen of Palmyra

The Queen of Palmyra *plunges deeply into the psyches of some riveting characters; it also tackles the big issue of racially motivated violence. How did you go about juggling those two balls?*

Very gingerly. Win Forrest is a particularly risky character. He's so despicable that he could easily drop to the level of a stereotype. We have to understand why he does the things he does, that terrible father of his who drives him every day of his life to uphold "purity." On the opposite end of the spectrum, Eva can't be just a saintly victim; she has to have her quirks, she has to be feisty and vulnerable, generous and selfish, fiercely intelligent and naive. That's why Eva's voice erupts in the next to last chapter; she can't be a mute victim.

This book is fiction but is based in the 1960s South. Did you personally live any of this history when you grew up in Mississippi?

I lived the white side of this history and observed the black side. My babysitter, Eva Lee Miller, to whom the book is dedicated, was African American, and I'd be dropped off at her house on the black side of town and spend hours there "helping" her sew and cook and clean, though I doubt I was of much help. Like Zenie Johnson, she was a witty, brilliant woman who fended off the burial insurance man with queenly aplomb. She had a wicked sense of humor where white people were concerned, and she let me know from the get-go that she didn't trust any of us. She and her husband, Hiram Miller, worked several different jobs to make ends meet. I visited her in her home until she died, and we wrote letters back and forth when I went off to college. Over the years, I became deeply attached to her and admired her enormously. She worked hard and she never gave up; she was a model for me. In my own family, my mother was rather progressive for the times, though not openly so, and my stepfather treated African Americans respectfully. But from an early age, I had the feeling that something was very wrong. I think of my generation of Southerners as the bridge between the Jim Crow days of this novel and the present, when things are far from perfect, but greatly improved. Would Medgar Evers or Eva or anyone fighting for the right to vote in the early sixties have expected the election of a black president by 2008? Even Myrlie Evers-Williams, Medgar Evers's widow, has said she didn't think it would happen this soon.

Uncle Wiggily, Br'er Rabbit, Nancy Drew, Bomba the Swamp Boy—this book is so much about stories.

Yes, how they mold us, how we depend so desperately on them, how they can ▸

make us whole or tear us into a million pieces. We tell ourselves stories that make our lives bearable. These stories shape us and show us how to make sharp turns and put one foot in front of the other— they can trip us up or take us by the hand and lead us home. The stories Florence hears and reads help her empathize with others. Because of that empathy, she casts aside the Bomba story, though it sinks into her unconscious in an insidious way. For her own survival, she must take to heart Uncle Wiggily's optimism and Nancy Drew's intrepidness. She must be tricky and scheming like Br'er Rabbit in order not to get stuck in the briar patch.

***Like Eva and Flo, you're a teacher. Do you see teaching as a major element of* The Queen of Palmyra?**

Teachers can change lives and open spaces in the world where there were none, in large ways and small. Eva does this for Florence; she arms her with "the sentence" so that she can make it through the fifth grade and move on with her life. Eva teaches Ray and other African Americans how to pry open the white-controlled world by using language as a lever. In her turn, Florence teaches semicolons and diagramming to her inner-city students in New Orleans to help them map out an incoherent world. That's why Florence takes that sharp left turn back into her story—it's the act of teaching that calls her back, it's Eva who calls her back.

What does* The Queen of Palmyra *say about the scales of justice?

That they're very wobbly at best and heavily weighted toward the powerful. Several white women, men, and children who witnessed horrendous crimes during the Civil Rights years have come forward in the past couple of decades to testify about these crimes. In most cases, these belated witnesses felt enormously threatened during the sixties when these acts of violence were committed and so just recently have felt they could speak. Some of them had actually forgotten the events and then remembered them in adulthood. Many of the perpetrators of these crimes were old and sometimes on the brink of death when their cases were reopened, so the question of justice, of how one can close one's eyes when fear is involved, of how people turn away from the most terrible things and the dire necessity that prods them to do so—all of these tragic stories drove me to create Florence Forrest. One thing Florence has to face in her adulthood is that her silence, her blindness, has precluded any chance at justice for Eva's murder. This seems to have been an unconscious choice—we're never quite sure—but it's a choice and, as the years pass, it can't be undone.

What would have happened if Florence had spoken up that summer?

If you look at the historical evidence, Win Forrest probably would have been ▶

acquitted. Southern juries back then were all white and all male; white murderers of African Americans got a free ride. Examples from that period abound. The murderers of Emmett Till went free. The trial of Byron De La Beckwith, who killed NAACP Field Secretary Medgar Evers, twice resulted in a hung jury; finally, in 1994, Beckwith was convicted, but by then he was an old man and had lived out most of his natural life. The two hung juries in the Beckwith case were considered a victory by the prosecution back in the sixties.

Did you have to do extensive research for the novel?

My research into the Civil Rights Movement in central Mississippi in the early sixties has been pretty thorough because I'm also working on a book about Evers. His death took place in Jackson, Mississippi, the summer of 1963, the summer of the novel. His murder and what it meant to black Mississippians figure in Florence's and Eva's side-by-side stories.

You're a scholar of Southern literature as well as a writer. What makes Southern literature Southern?

The rich variety of writing over the last couple of decades makes that a hard question to answer, but there's a sense of location that's peculiar to Southern literature—it can manifest in a character's voice, maybe a particular inflection, a resonance; in a groundedness in place or a sense of loss of home; in a painful awareness of what's been called "the burden of Southern history," the long shadow of slavery and Jim Crow and their present-day ramifications. Location, Eudora Welty says, is both "the crossroads of circumstance" and "the heart's field." Southern literature pivots around both, in ways that are mysteriously both specific and universal.

So, do you see yourself as a Southern writer consumed with your own cultural past?

I'm interested in the *idea* of being consumed by the past, how the ghosts of the past continue to haunt us despite our best efforts to erase them on the blackboards of our minds. For me as a writer, the Southern past is a teacher. It helps me understand the human willingness to avert the eyes from what we don't want to see, or deafen the ears to stories we don't want to hear. It's a human failing—this ability to blind ourselves to the terrible things that don't directly affect us. This is how the Holocaust happened—and it's something I think we need to question constantly in ourselves. Eva will always haunt Florence. Florence will always walk that levee and think about her. ∼

Praise for
Wishing for Snow

"*Wishing for Snow* sits on the short
shelf of books that I will never part
with. Minrose Gwin writes with a poet's
lyricism, a historian's scrupulousness, a
maverick's ingenuity, and a daughter's
immense love. A wholly original and
transcendent memoir."
—Sandra Scofield,
author of *Occasions of Sin: A Memoir*

"Astonishingly honest, tender, and brave,
Minrose Gwin's luminous memoir of her
mother's troubled life should be required
reading for anyone struggling to forgive
a difficult parent. *Wishing for Snow* is a
marvel of empathy and insight. With
lyrical intelligence and clarity, Gwin
distinguishes her mother as a vulnerable,
sensitive, and gifted human being apart
from a daughter's crushed expectations."
—Marianne Gingher,
author of *Adventures in Pen Land:
One Writer's Journey from Inklings to Ink*

"The mother-daughter tie is perhaps
the most intimate any of us will ever
experience. Stories of rage and laughter,
the songs of survival and destruction are
passed through the birth cord and from
the mother's milk. *Wishing for Snow* is a
testament to a difficult and disturbing
relationship between a mother and
daughter, both poets attempting to
sing in a difficult age. This gift of a
book made me question: how do any

of us become poets? Here is one very particular and moving answer."

—Joy Harjo, author of
How We Became Human: Collected Poems

"An eloquent memoir of a daughter seeking a clear view of her complicated, crazy mother and coming to grips with her. . . . Gwin's mother is very much alive in this lyrical book. She haunts the pages with her own words, shakes webs from Gwin's closeted memory, and stirs up the dust of a life lived intensely, madly, and often painfully. . . . This is definitely a real-life story we all need to hear."

—*Booklist*

"*Wishing for Snow* addresses the complicated nuances of love without ever descending to sugarcoated sentimentalism—and without allowing anyone (herself included) to be free from guilt, implication, or accountability. Gwin's memoir brings her . . . into conversation with authors from Eudora Welty and Flannery O'Connor to Doris Betts, Gail Godwin, Janisse Ray, and Dorothy Allison. Her book is one that demands to be read."

—*Southern Scribe*

"Gwin describes [anger] with honesty, conveying the complexity of simultaneously loving and being furious at the mother whose mental illness presented her with so many seemingly insoluble dilemmas. . . . The mother is marvelously present throughout the book."

—*Women's Review of Books*

Praise for *Wishing for Snow* (continued)

"Gwin's effort to reconcile her own identity with her mother's life and death is tender and haunting—a compelling and satisfying read."   —*Gulf Coast*

"At turns, Gwin's memoir is sad, hilarious, frightening, rambling, and positively operatic . . . suffused with both Gwin's wish to understand her mother and the knowledge that fulfilling such a wish is likely as impossible as snow that sticks in Mississippi at Christmas."
                          —*Mississippi Magazine*

Excerpt from
Wishing for Snow

THERE IS SUCH A THING as crazy-mother
bonding. This can occur unexpectedly
any time two women who have crazy
mothers are having a conversation. It
happens when one realizes the other also
has had a crazy mother, and it is both
painful and pleasurable. There are more
crazy mothers than you might think. You
can be having a professional lunch at a
conference or with colleagues in another
department and one of you will mention,
perhaps without even intending to, that
she has a crazy mother. Oh, she will say
to you or you will say to her, your mother
was, uh, mentally ill? Yes, she was crazy,
you will say. *Really crazy?* she will ask.
(Many people will claim that their
mothers are crazy when they do not
know what they are talking about.)
Yes, you will say, *really* crazy. Attempted
suicide, anorexia, paranoia, violent, the
whole bit. I had to commit her twice.
A flash of recognition across the table,
a sigh. So was mine. Yes, mine was too.

What follows is a conversation that
no one else can possibly follow. It is made
up of codes, silences, sighs, pauses. The
first question: Is she dead (yet); code, are
you still going through this? The second
question: What about the rest of the
family? Gone you say. My brother and
I have not seen each other since the
funeral. My sister calls when it snows
at home; she is unaccountably excited
by snow. Ah yes, my friend will say. Yes,
I know (silence). What about you, ▶

she says, how are you; code, do you sometimes feel crazy too, are you scared like me of becoming your mother? I'm okay now, you say. I kind of lost it—went over the edge and couldn't stop crying—after I committed her the second time. Therapy, anti-anxiety drugs, anti-depressants, anti-everything. None of it helped. It's only time that helps, don't you think. Now I'm okay. Yes, I'm okay now I think. Oh yes, she says, me too but I'm still on the Prozac. Hope to get off soon. Sometimes it seems impossible to think about it all. Sometimes it is too much to believe.

Sometimes, though, such conversations give me pause. They make me think my mother wasn't so bad. She was just always wishing for snow and usually it didn't come. And when it came, it didn't stick.

One friend was adopted. In my opinion, she had a perfectly good mother and father. Why trouble the waters? They were crusaders for civil rights during the fifties and sixties. Their lives were threatened and crosses were burned on their property. They were parents to be proud of. I wished they were mine. When my friend got older, she wanted to find her birth mother. Her adopted parents, being the good people they were, gave her the information she needed and she found her mother and her sister. Both were schizophrenic. Now I know why I've felt so crazy all my life, she says; it's kind of a relief.

A colleague tells me that, when she was four, her mother, who was an alcoholic, almost killed her two-year-old sister by starving her to death. My friend remembers the doctor storming into the apartment and yelling at her mother: "You've got to feed this baby or I'm going to take her away. You've got to *feed* this baby!"

Another friend believes that she was tortured by her father and some other people in secret ceremonies associated with their church in a small western town. When she was little she would be awakened in the middle of the night and taken from her bed to a room with bright lights. Her mother, she remembers, was always watching. Now my friend is afraid of electrical wiring. She remembers something about fur and feathers.

On the Death of a Bluejay

He was a jaunty fellow,
a bright and talky fellow.
He did me no harm.
A few berries here and there,
acorns snitched from squirrels
(who sometimes shared his fate)
and nuts stashed away in the eaves.
For the love of pecans
he was shot down in midflight
and lies festering beneath the tree.
I think of Icarus
gutstrung between earth and heaven
like a speck of red dust itching the
   eyeball
of the universe. ▶

Excerpt from *Wishing for Snow* (continued)

Gold-singer, dream-squawker
with a yen for nuts and bolts.
Tinkerer, tailor, candlestick-maker
with hot wax shrouding his wings.

Sun-streaker, moon-tamer
prancing on a pinhead,
breaching the walls of heaven.

Erin Clayton Pitner

Dear Erin the poet, Dear Mama, I tell you
if I had had to choose a crazy mother it
would have been you. ❦